The Desert Prince
JENNIFER LEWIS

First published in Great Britain 2011
Large Print edition 2011
Harlequin Mills & Boon Limited,
Eton House, 18-24 Paradise Road,
Richmond, Surrey TW9 1SR

© Jennifer Lewis 2010

ISBN: 978 0 263 21694 3

Harlequin Mills & Boon policy is to use papers that
are natural, renewable and recyclable products and
made from wood grown in sustainable forests. The
logging and manufacturing process conform to the legal
environmental regulations of the country of origin.

Printed and bound in Great Britain
by CPI Antony Rowe, Chippenham, Wiltshire

JENNIFER LEWIS

has been dreaming up stories for as long as she can remember and is thrilled to be able to share them with readers. She has lived on both sides of the Atlantic and worked in media and the arts before she grew bold enough to put pen to paper. Happily settled in England with her family, she would love to hear from readers at jen@jenlewis.com. Visit her website at www.jenlewis.com.

For my sister Caroline,
whose adventurous spirit and creativity
are an inspiration.

One

Did he know?

Celia Davidson took a deep breath and tried to stop her hands from shaking.

The Arabian Sea glittered outside the window of the elegant hotel offices, lapping against a ribbon of pure white sand.

The beach had probably been trucked in, along with the palm trees and the elegant hotel villas that lined its shores. With enough money you could remake anything.

Make it look as though the past had never happened.

The elaborately carved door in front of her opened and her stomach clenched in response.

"Mr. Al Mansur will see you now." His well-coiffed assistant smiled politely.

Celia brushed at her jacket, rumpled by the long journey from New York to Oman, and tucked a flyaway strand of mousy blond hair behind her ear.

Silly. He hadn't brought her here to rekindle their on-again, off-again romance.

Or had he?

That certainly wasn't going to happen. She wouldn't give him another chance to crush her heart beneath his heel.

And there was a lot more at stake now.

A rustling of papers from inside the office made her heart stutter, but she bravely took a step inside. Crisp white walls framed a high domed ceiling and two arched windows laid a spectacular view of the sea-lined horizon at her feet.

An antique desk filled the center of the room, its shiny surface devoid of clutter. Behind it, facing the windows, the broad back of a leather armchair concealed its occupant.

Her anxiety ratcheted up a notch as the chair swung to face her. Dark eyes locked onto hers. Black hair swept back from the aristocratic face and his wide, arrogant mouth sat in a hard line.

Unfortunately, he was every bit as handsome as when she'd last seen him, almost four years ago.

"Celia." He rose from the chair and strode toward her.

Blood rushed to Celia's head and she struggled to keep her feet steady on the thick carpet.

"Hello," she stammered. She extended her fingers and slid them into his large hand. A jolt of energy startled her, though it shouldn't since he'd always had that effect on her.

Her heart still ached from the last time he'd brushed her off and slammed the doors of his life against her—again.

Was that why she'd come? He'd finally invited her into the inner sanctum and she couldn't resist a chance to walk the glittering floors and fondle the treasures he'd never shown her before.

His eyes were expressionless as his palm pressed against hers, the formal gesture a stark contrast to the intimacy they once shared.

She pulled her hand back, skin humming.

Salim's stern good looks had always intimidated her as much as they'd attracted her. His tailored suit barely concealed the muscled body she remembered far too well.

"Thank you for coming." He smiled and gestured for her to take a seat. "As you've been told, I'm planning a land reclamation project. I understand that you specialize in sensitive treatment of ecologically challenging sites."

Celia blinked. Apparently he intended to gloss over the fact that they'd slept together the last time they met.

Focus. "I've worked on a number of desert projects, including an oil field in West Texas that I restored to native short grass prairie. I'm experienced with the issues involved and I—"

"Yes. I read your online portfolio." He turned and strode away from her. His broad shoulders tapered to his slim waist, accentuated by the well-cut suit.

He hadn't bothered to attend her presentation at the conference where they'd had their steamy tryst. No doubt he had more important things to do.

Silenced by his brusque comment, she scanned her surroundings. Pictureless walls and ornament-free shelves. The only decoration was a gold-sheathed dagger that hung on the wall.

Probably used to pierce his business rivals.

She knew he was capable of utter ruthlessness. He'd cut her adrift without a backward glance.

Twice.

Though, really, she had only herself to blame for letting it happen again. Their college relationship was long over, but she'd fallen back into his bed at the first opportunity like a lemming running for the cliff edge.

"The site is out in the desert." His deep voice jerked her back to the present.

He walked to the window and stood silhouetted against the bright view of the manicured bay. "My mother's people owned the land and it was explored and drilled in the 1970s. By the end of the decade it lay exhausted and abandoned and has remained in that condition ever since."

She steeled herself to ask the question landowners hated most. "Is the land polluted?"

"Probably." His eyes met hers, cool and dark, devoid of emotion.

Which was fine, because she felt enough for both of them. Sheer terror raced along her nerves at what still hung unspoken between them.

You don't have to tell him.

Her friends thought she was crazy to come here. They'd begged her to keep her distance and her secret.

Those sharp black eyes fixed on hers again. "I'll need to take you out to the site."

"Of course." She pulled her PDA out of her

pocket, trying not to think about being all alone with him, way out in the middle of nowhere. "That would be great. When would you like to go? I'm an early riser and I…"

"Right now." He rose from the chair as if ready to head for his car.

Not a question. A statement of fact. Apparently Salim Al Mansur was used to issuing orders and he expected her to jump.

"But it's afternoon. Won't the desert be awfully hot right now?" Couldn't she at least unpack and change? She was tired and disoriented. She'd come right here from the airport without even stopping to drop her bags off in her room at the hotel.

Though technically she was in the hotel right now. Salim owned it, part of his string of luxury resorts in the Gulf region. This office was his on-site throne room.

His eyes narrowed as he stared at her. For the first time the slightest flicker of humor seemed to glimmer in their lightless depths. "The desert is hot. It is in its nature."

She gulped. "You're right, of course." She forced a thin smile. "Might as well face things head-on."

She blanched.

The elephant in the room lumbered silently.

Had he summoned her here because he'd somehow learned the truth?

Salim strode toward his car. The desire to move—anywhere—surged through his limbs on a wave of thoughts and sensations.

He'd hoped that memories had deceived him, but unfortunately Celia Davidson was even more beautiful than he remembered. Although she'd come straight off a long flight, her skin glowed and her eyes shone blue as the Bahr al-Arab in the afternoon sun.

He dismissed the driver and pulled open the passenger door for Celia. His eyes strayed as she climbed in, and her boxy beige suit couldn't hide the lithe and shapely body he'd held in his arms.

Some memories were a curse that haunted you through all eternity.

"Buckle your seat belt." He started the ignition and pulled out of the hotel parking lot, leaving the sparkling oasis he'd created for the grittier and dustier world outside.

Celia belonged to that world, and he'd do well to remember it.

Funny how she still wore her golden hair pulled back in a tight ponytail, like the college student he remembered. She'd never been one to fuss over her appearance and he'd admired that at the time. Now it irked him that she glowed more than women who spent all day preening.

"Is it a long drive?" She stared straight ahead. Avoiding his glance, perhaps.

"That depends on what you're used to. Here in Oman almost everywhere is a long drive. Have you been to our country before?"

"No, never."

"You always said you wanted to come."

He watched as she turned, startled. She hadn't expected him to bring up the past.

"And I meant it." Her steady blue gaze stabbed him with accusation. Reminding him she'd expected so much more of him than he'd been able to give. She tore her eyes away with visible effort. "But that was a long time ago."

"I wasn't sure you'd be interested in this job." He shot a sideways glance. "I think I expected you to refuse."

He watched her neck lengthen. "Because of our history together?"

A moment of weakness had led him to her bed again after all those years apart. He'd been shocked at seeing her in the unfamiliar circumstances of a hoteliers' conference looking just as she had when they were in college together.

They'd been so young and innocent.

So foolish.

Celia had been deadly silent when he'd made it clear their renewed liaison had no future. She was a woman of reason. Surely she wouldn't expect a man in his position to continue an affair that could never end in marriage?

He glanced sideways at her, taking in the

unchanged elegance of her profile. "I expected you to refuse because of the challenging nature of the project. I imagine most sensible landscape architects would laugh in my face."

Their encounter four years earlier was at a Manhattan conference on hotel design, so he knew she was in the landscape field. Still, he'd been surprised when his assistant had brought him her portfolio to consider as the landscape architect for this project.

The odd coincidence had presented an opportunity to face the past head-on—and push it from his mind forever.

"I enjoy taking on challenging projects." She sounded defensive, but he wasn't sure why. "And the location is a new one for me."

"You must travel a lot." He guided the car out of the hotel's palm-lined drive and onto the road.

"Yes. Manhattan is my home base work-wise. I live nearby in Connecticut, but I'm on the road two weeks out of most months."

Curiosity clawed at Salim. Or was it jealousy?

"Your boyfriend doesn't mind you being away so much?"

She blinked. "I don't have a boyfriend." She tucked a strand of escaped blond hair nervously behind her ear.

"I'm sorry." Relief crept through his chest.

"Why should you be sorry? My life is very full." She stared straight ahead, jaw stiff as she uttered the words.

Why had he offered a condolence? She'd told him four years ago that she'd never married. Perhaps he felt guilty that he'd ruined her for all other men?

No doubt he gave himself too much credit.

But he'd never forgotten her. In fact, he blamed her for the demise of his first marriage, though she'd been at least three thousand miles away the entire time.

Their whirlwind romance at the conference had only deepened her infuriating hold over him. How could he take a suitable wife and hope for a successful marriage if he was enthralled by another woman?

Banishing Celia Davidson from his heart and mind would obviously be a challenge, but it must be done. The future of the Al Mansur dynasty depended on it.

Salalah's neat rows of boxy buildings gave way to plantations of palm trees. Celia couldn't help staring. How did they water this emerald forest of lushness out here in the desert?

"Salalah is naturally fertile. We get more rainfall than the rest of the country." Salim's low voice penetrated her scattered thoughts.

"That must come in useful when you're landscaping your hotels. How many do you have?"

Phew. She'd managed to get the conversation back on a semiprofessional track.

"Twelve, at last count." He turned the steering wheel with a capable hand.

A big, leather-clad wheel, on what was obviously a very expensive car. Salim Al Mansur could probably buy and sell a few small nations with his pocket change.

"You must have bought quite a few palm trees."

The side of his mouth nearest her hitched slightly. A smile or a scowl, she couldn't be sure. "And I'll buy a few more if fate allows."

The palm trees receded behind them as the landscape opened up to the kind of bare, brown nothingness she'd expected. Some places were meant to be bare and brown, yet she could rarely persuade her clients of that. They'd rather install thousands of sprinkler heads in a quixotic attempt to create paradise in a place that was never meant to be one.

Celia squinted. Had the sun created a mirage, or was she staring straight ahead at a range of mountains?

"The Fog Mountains." His low voice interrupted her disbelief. Salim must have noticed her staring.

"Wow," was all she could manage.

A band of clouds hung low over the tree-cloaked crags, green as Vermont, like something out of a fairy tale.

She gulped.

She'd been so wrapped up in her personal angst about coming here that she'd totally neglected to research the region. Better keep quiet about that, too.

Salim had always told her his country was full of surprises. Once upon a time she'd assumed they'd discover them together, but not like this.

How odd to be sitting inches away from him after everything that had happened. His solid, masculine presence next to her was only too familiar.

His unique scent, warm and spicy, drew her back into the past. He shared her bed for two whole years. They'd grown from childhood to adulthood together, sharing intimacies and joys and…incredible sex.

Her face heated at the memory. She'd fully expected to spend the rest of her life with him.

Then he'd ended it all in the most horrible way imaginable.

They climbed the lush green heights in silence

and descended back to the rumpled beige floor of the desert. Relentless in its bleakness, it stretched to the heat-blurred horizon, broken only by the occasional isolated building.

As they drove, Celia found herself waiting for something marvelous to happen, like palm trees or mountains appearing out of the dusty haze.

Isn't that why she'd come here? Hoping for a miracle of some sort?

Salim turned off the main road and headed west on a dirt track to...nowhere.

After some minutes he pulled over, next to a dilapidated metal shed whose roof had fallen in, and climbed out in silence.

Confusion clouded Celia's mind as he opened her door and ushered her out onto the hot, sandy ground.

"This is the place?" Her incredulity showed in her voice.

Salim's face darkened. "It was beautiful, once."

Hard to believe. An abandoned jeep with no

seats or wheels lay tilted on its side just to the left of them. Strange wheel-topped objects hunkered here and there amongst the rocky sand.

"Those are wellheads. All capped. There's an old pipeline running to the coast. It can all be removed. The oil is exhausted."

Salim strode amongst the detritus, his elegant dark suit an almost humorous contrast to the shabby surroundings.

"You're planning to build a hotel here?" Was this some kind of elaborate joke?

Beads of sweat broke out along her upper lip and she tried to dab them away gracefully.

"Come this way." The land gathered here and there into little rubble-strewn rises. She followed him behind one, and around the rise, signs of activity surprised her. Piles of dirt indicated a fresh excavation. She peered past a mound into a wide, shallow hole. The chiseled edges of dressed stone stood in sharp contrast to the rocky sand around them. "Stone blocks? Where did those come from?"

"There's a complex of buildings under the sand here. Maybe even a whole city."

Salim's gruff voice couldn't hide his enthusiasm.

"The famous lost city of the desert?" A rush of excitement danced over Celia's skin. She glanced up and realized that similar excavations surrounded them. Low walls emerged from the dusty terrain, tracing the ancient contours of buildings.

Ancient roads revealed themselves in the sand around them, cobbles worn smooth by time and the passage of many feet.

"We're on the frankincense trade route from the coast. There were caravan routes throughout the area, leading north into the Empty Quarter, to Saudi Arabia and beyond. Cities sprang up around oases where the merchants would stop to water their camels."

"But there's no water here." She glanced around, searching for the clichéd shimmering lake surrounded by palm trees.

"There was once." He kicked at a clod of rocky

dirt with his black leather shoe. "It's still here, buried under the ground. The remains of an aquifer."

Celia stared at the arid soil. "There's enough water left to irrigate?"

"More than enough."

Something in his voice jerked her gaze to his. Was it her imagination or did triumph dance in his eyes? Anticipation, anyway.

It echoed like butterflies in her tummy.

"There's enough water to supply the hotel and staff housing. The excavations stretch over a five-hundred-foot area. I plan to reconstruct some of the buildings so visitors can see how people lived and worked back then."

"And perhaps you could leave some in a state of semi-excavation, so visitors could see how you found them. It's startling to see such perfectly made blocks emerging out of the sand."

He looked at her, thoughtful. "Yes. Let people see how the past lay hidden here for so many centuries."

His vision for this desolate wasteland animated his features and made his eyes shine. He looked heart-achingly handsome, the sun burnishing his tanned features.

He peeled off his jacket and threw it down on a half-buried wall. Celia tore her gaze from the sight of his broad back straining against his thin white shirt.

Her faithless eyes tracked him as he strode, bold and athletic, across the rugged terrain. "Come here."

Celia scrambled over the rocky ground in her one pair of "smart" shoes. She certainly wouldn't be dressed like this if she'd known they were coming to the site.

"This is where the excavation started." He pointed to a wide, shallow pit, where layers of dirt had been brushed away to reveal the remains of several wide walls. "I hired a student to collect data about our family history. He became fascinated with this land and told me satellite imagery suggested signs of an ancient crossroads here. I hired an archeological team to excavate, and his suspicion was proven correct."

"What a find. Are you sure a hotel is the best use for the site? Perhaps archaeologists would like to study it in greater detail."

Salim's brow clouded. "I wish to bring this place back to life, not preserve it as a mummified corpse to be picked over by vultures."

"Of course," she stammered, chastened. She knew virtually nothing about his background. His home and family was a tacitly off-limits subject when they were in college.

She had found out why.

"I wish for people to travel here with a sense of purpose and anticipation. I want to share the history of our country and its people with anyone who cares to visit, not a few rarified academics." His dark eyes shone. "I hope people will come from other countries to visit."

He frowned and shoved a hand through his hair. She tore her eyes from the sudden clenching of his thick biceps when he looked back at her. "Perhaps you know that Oman's oil supply is limited. In a decade or two it'll be gone. It's my goal—personal and professional—to develop tourism as a well of riches for our future."

His zeal rose in the hot desert air like the frankincense that must have once perfumed it. Celia's chest swelled.

For a split second she saw a glimpse of the warm and excitable boy she'd once been so in love with.

She nodded. "The Salalah coastline is spectacular. The ocean is such an intense shade of blue. And those mountains…I'd never have imagined something like that here in the desert."

"Exactly. For every person who knows and appreciates the beauty of our country, there are untold millions who know nothing about it—yet." A wicked grin spread across his face. "I intend to change that."

Celia wiped another bead of sweat off her lip. Salim's mischievous smile was having a very unsettling effect on her.

He's dangerous, and don't you forget it. He'd already broken her heart twice.

And now there was another heart at stake, far more precious than her own.

"What kind of hotel design are you planning?" She managed to sound calm.

"Low rise. Buildings designed to blend with their surroundings, but to offer all the comforts a traveler would desire. Some will be luxurious—others will accommodate those with simpler tastes or a more modest budget. We shall welcome everyone."

He spread his arms in a generous gesture that tugged at somewhere deep inside her. She'd been so unwelcome in his life.

She cleared her throat. "And the landscape. What did you have in mind?"

That wicked smile played about his lips. "I don't. That's why you're here."

"Native plants or lavishly watered opulence?"

"They each have their own beauty. I imagine them coexisting here." He glanced around the strange half-dug excavations. "This was a meeting place of people, cultures and ideas. A place where anything was possible." His dark gaze fixed on hers. "And that's what I want you to create."

Her stomach fluttered.

Could she do it? Take this job and work with Salim Al Mansur after everything that happened between them? With a secret as hot and volatile as the desert air hovering between them?

The work sounded fascinating. To watch an ancient watering hole come back to life as a modern day resort, and to have free rein to plant it any way she saw fit…. The challenge was irresistible—almost.

"What's the budget?"

Salim's eyes narrowed.

Her question was crass—but she was in business.

"This project comes from my heart." He pressed a palm to his chest, broad fingers silhouetted against his fine white shirt. "I don't intend to put a number on the cost to restore it." He held her gaze just long enough to make her heart thud like a drum. "Whatever it takes."

Celia blew out a breath as his low voice reverberated around her brain.

What would it take?

If she worked with him she'd have to tell him.

Hell, she wanted to tell him. The secret ate her up inside. Every day she ached to tell him.

You have a daughter.

But the consequences might be unthinkable.

Two

As Salim piloted the car back to Salalah, he got the distinct impression Celia was trying to back out.

"How do you feel about honoring the land's history of oil production?" She glanced sideways at him, blue eyes alive with intelligence. "That's surely part of the area's heritage, too."

"You mean, incorporate the wellheads and pipelines?"

"Exactly." She crossed her arms over her chest. "I don't take a project unless I can implement my vision."

Ah. An uncompromising artist. He'd expect no less of Celia. Wasn't that part of her irresistible charm?

Salim turned and called her bluff. "Sure."

She blinked and her lips parted.

"Not all of them," she stammered. "I think an area's industrial history can be part of its magic. I designed a park two years ago around an old coal mine in England. We preserved the pithead as part of the project because that mine was the reason the town grew there in the first place."

Salim nodded as his hand slid over the wheel. "I appreciate original thinking. Too many tourist destinations are carbon copies of the same island fantasy."

"Aren't they? Sometimes it's hard to tell if you're in Florida or Madagascar. I have a heck of a time with some of my clients though. They don't want to use native plants because they don't see them as 'upscale.' I guess familiarity breeds contempt."

"We business types need educating."

Celia raised a blond brow. "Sometimes it's

not worth the trouble. Many people aren't in-terested in being educated. They want business as usual."

Salim turned to stare out at the empty road ahead. She wanted him to be one of those un-imaginative suits, so she could turn down his project without a qualm of conscience.

But he couldn't let that happen. "I'll pay triple your usual fee."

Celia froze. "What?"

"It's a big project and will take a long time."

She bit her lip, obviously contemplating the dilemma of turning down more money than she'd probably ever made.

He heard her inhale. "I'll need to travel back to the states regularly."

"Come and go as you please. I'll pay all your expenses."

She wanted to refuse him, but he'd make it impossible.

Seeing her again had already fanned that unfortunate flame of desire she kindled in him. It had never truly gone out. This time he wouldn't be done with her until it was extinguished—permanently.

A simple signature committed Celia to the uneasy partnership. A meeting with the architect and general contractor established they were all on the same page, and all systems were go by the time Celia headed back to Manhattan with her first check burning a large hole in her pocket.

She could fly back to visit Kira whenever she wanted. When this job was over she'd have enough money for a down payment on a house in Weston, near her parents. She could set down roots and have a real home base to share with her daughter.

She had thoroughly convinced herself that taking the job was a good idea—until Sunday lunch at her parents' house in Connecticut.

"But Mom, you're the one who said it was time for Kira to meet her father." Celia heard her voice rising to a whine the way it used to when she was a teen and they wouldn't lend her the car.

"I know, dear. But you met with her father. Did you tell him about Kira?"

Kira was napping in the upstairs bedroom she slept in when Celia was traveling.

"You know I didn't."

"Why not?" Her mother's clear blue gaze had never seemed more like an inquisitor's stare.

"I don't know." She sighed. "The time never felt right. It's a big thing. I should have told him when I was pregnant. I'm beginning to wish I had, but everyone talked me out of it."

Her mother nodded. "They had good reason to. He'd already told you there was no future between you. You know sharia law grants a father full legal custody of his children. He could have taken Kira from you and denied you the right to see her. He still could."

Celia frowned. "I don't think he'd do that."

"You've got solid gut instincts. If you didn't tell him, there was good reason for it."

"Your mother's right, dear," said her father,

pushing a brussels sprout onto his fork. His soft voice rarely offered anything but support and encouragement, but she could see that he, too, was apprehensive about her taking this job. "He seemed like a nice boy when you two were back in college, but that was a long time ago. You don't know what he's capable of. He's rich and powerful."

Celia snorted. "All the money in the world doesn't turn him into a god. He was a little intimidating at first, but I was completely blunt about my ideas for the project and we came to an understanding."

"Except about the fact that you *bore his child*." Her mother stared intently at her white wineglass as she took a sip.

Celia bit her lip. "I do want to tell him."

"Just be careful. Once you tell him, there's no going back."

"I know, I know, believe me. Still, she's Salim's daughter. He has a right to know about her. It's cruel to both Salim and Kira to keep him in the dark about her existence. When the time is right, I'll tell him."

Fear curled in her stomach, along with the guilt that had been her constant companion since Kira's birth.

"*Salim,* huh? I see you're back on a first-name basis. Don't you fall in love with him again, either."

"I'd rather die."

Upstairs, she crouched beside Kira's "big girl bed." Her daughter's long, long lashes fluttered slightly, as dream images flashed across those huge brown eyes.

They looked so much like Salim's.

Celia bit her knuckle. So many things about Kira reminded her of Salim. Celia's own pale coloring had been shoved aside by genes demanding shiny dark hair and smooth olive skin. Kira had a throaty chuckle when something really amused her that sounded shockingly like Salim's laugh.

Already she was fascinated with numbers, and with money and business, and she certainly didn't get that from her mom. She'd even convinced her grandma to help her set up a lemonade—and lemon cupcake!—stand last summer, when she'd barely turned two. She'd fingered the shiny quarters with admiration and joy that made the family fall about, laughing.

Celia was sure Salim, who'd majored in business and run a consulting firm of sorts while still in college, would be amused and proud beyond words.

A soft, breathy sigh escaped from Kira's parted lips. Finely carved lips that were unmistakably an inheritance from one person.

It was wrong to deprive her daughter of her father. If it was awkward to tell him now, it would be much worse when Kira wanted to find him ten or fifteen years from now. It wasn't fair to keep them apart.

When Celia returned to Oman two weeks later, Salim was in Bahrain, opening a new hotel. Every day she expected his return with trembling anticipation, but the days stretched out into six weeks with no sign of him.

She could be offended by his neglect, but she decided to view it as a vote of confidence. Apparently, he trusted her completely and didn't even want detailed updates of her plans.

The archaeological team was hard at work re-assembling structures and artifacts at the site. She'd put together a team of landscape professionals and made herself an expert in the unique local flora and fauna.

Suddenly word came from on high that his majesty was due back in three days. The coffee grew stronger and meetings stretched late into the night. Admins and accountants scurried faster from office to office. Celia found herself pacing the luxurious landscape nurseries, examining everything from specimen palm trees to prostrate ground covers with an increasing sense of alarm.

She planned to tell him about Kira at the first possible opportunity. She couldn't work for him and take his money while concealing something so vital. His loyal employees made it clear that he was a man of honor. He'd be angry, yes, but...

"He's here!" His admin burst into the conference room where Celia was organizing a set of drawings. "He's on his way up and he asked me to find you. I'll tell him you're in here."

Sunlight shone brighter through the elegant arched windows, and the sea outside seemed to glitter with a sense of menace. Celia straightened her new pinstriped suit and patted her hair.

You can do this.

It was going to be awkward any time she told him. Disastrous, even, but she couldn't work for him under false pretenses. The longer she waited the worse it would be when the news finally came out.

He had to know. Now.

"Celia."

His deep voice resonated off the thick plaster walls and marble floors. Her breath stuck in her lungs as she turned to face him.

An unexpected smile lit his imperious features.

He strode toward her and took hold of both her hands, then raised them to his mouth and kissed them. Shock rippled through her as his lips brushed her skin and sparked a shiver of sensation.

"Uh, hi," she stammered. "I was just organizing the plans."

"Ahmad tells me your designs are ingenious."

She smiled. "No more so than his." The architect was younger than her, but already accomplished and now apparently generous with praise. She made a mental note to thank him.

She made another mental note to rip her gaze from Salim's broad shoulders. Unlike last time he wore the typical attire of pretty much every man on the Arabian Peninsula: a long white dishdasha that emphasized the elegance of his powerful physique.

She cleared her throat. "I have some sets of plans to go over with you before I order the plantings."

And there's another little something I'd like to mention…

How on earth was she going to do this?

No time like the present. She screwed her hands up into fists. Drew a deep breath down into her lungs. Lifted her shoulders.

"Salim, there's something I…"

But the words dried on her tongue as another man entered the room. Almost a carbon copy of Salim, but with a stockier build. And this man wore Western clothing—jeans in fact.

"Celia, meet my brother, Elan."

Salim studied her face as she shook hands with Elan. She seemed nervous about something. According to Ahmad's daily reports her plans were brilliant: creative, stylish and ideally suited to the difficult environment.

So why did she look so…apprehensive?

Her eyes darted from Elan to himself. Her cheeks were pink and her lips appeared to quiver with unspoken words. The pulse hammering at her delicate throat suggested a heart beating fast beneath her high, proud breasts.

He cursed the thought as Elan's words tugged

him out of his reverie. "I've heard so much about you."

"You have?" Celia's voice was almost a squeak.

"What do you mean?" asked Salim. Surely he'd never mentioned his long-ago American girlfriend to his brother. They hadn't even lived in the same country since Elan was sent away to boarding school at age eleven.

"Oh, yes. You were definitely the highlight of his college education," he teased. "I suspect you may have rose-tinted the entire college experience for him. He certainly enjoyed it a lot more than I did."

Salim's ears burned at hearing himself discussed so casually. "That's only because Elan is a man of action and not academics. I assure you my pleasure was entirely pedagogical." He shot a dark glance at his brother.

Elan's eyes twinkled with mischief. "Yeah, sure."

"Elan runs an oil services company in Nevada." Salim looked at Celia. "He's busy ripping up the landscape so that people like you can put it back together one day."

Elan shrugged. "The world still runs on oil, whether we like it or not. And as my brother knows, conserving the environment is a passion of mine."

Celia smiled. "That is refreshing."

Salim suppressed a snort of disgust. *A passion of mine?* He didn't remember his brother being such a flirtatious charmer. "Where are Sara and the children?"

"They're on the beach." Elan tucked his thumbs into his belt loops in another American gesture that made Salim realize how little he knew his own brother.

"Perhaps you should join them."

Salim glanced at Celia. Sun shone through the windows and illuminated her golden hair, picking out highlights of copper and bronze. He wanted to be alone with her.

To discuss the plans, naturally.

"I think we should all join them." Elan held out his arm, which Salim noticed with irritation was as thickly muscled as a dockworker's. "Celia, come meet my wife. She's never left the U.S. before so I think she'd be glad to hear a familiar accent."

Salim studied Celia's face as she absorbed the fact that his brother had married an American girl. A perfectly ordinary girl without an ounce of aristocratic blood. Elan bragged cheerfully about her impoverished background. A stark contrast to the type of woman tradition had expected him to marry.

But Elan was not the eldest son.

Celia pushed a hand through her silky hair. "Sure, I'd love to come to the beach." She glanced nervously at Salim. "Unless you had other plans for me."

An alternate plan formed in his mind. It involved unbuttoning her officious pinstriped suit and liberating her lithe, elegant body.

He drew in a breath and banished the image before it could heat his blood. "None whatsoever."

She glanced down at her suit. "I'd better run to my room and change."

"Good idea." Elan smiled. "They're camped out near the snack bar. We'll meet you down there."

Salim bridled at the reference to his elegant beach café as a "snack bar," but he kept his mouth shut.

Elan was his guest and he'd resolved to end the long estrangement between the surviving members of their once-great family.

He may have failed in his mission to produce the son and heir his father demanded, but at least he could draw his scattered brothers back to their roots in Oman.

They were all he had left.

"Salim, I'm not leaving you here," said Elan. "You'll start working and that'll be the last we see of you until dinner."

Salim stiffened as his brother threaded his arm through his. Elan always had been affectionate. It was one of the reasons his father had sent him away to a spartan boarding school in England—to toughen him up.

It had worked, as he remembered from their guarded encounters afterward. And it had backfired badly. Salim recalled the forthright strength Elan had shown in refusing the bride their father had chosen and claiming he'd never set foot on their land again. A promise he'd kept until their father's death.

Apparently, Sara had un-toughened him again.

Salim snuck a sideways glance at his brother. Same strong nose, determined jaw, flinty black eyes. Even their close-cropped hair was similar.

But Elan's jeans and shirt were a striking contrast to Salim's traditional dress. A difference that spoke of the chasm opened between them.

Salim traveled regularly, but could not imagine living abroad.

Or marrying an American girl.

Even one as desirable as Celia.

Three

Celia couldn't stop laughing. A bright-eyed toddler was attempting to bury her feet in the sand, and the combination of sun and splashing seawater made her feel downright giddy.

Sailboats scudded on the sapphire horizon and, behind her, the elegant white buildings of the hotel reflected the magical afternoon sun.

Salim sat on the fine sand a few feet from her, his long white garment crisp and elegant in stark contrast to everyone else's swimsuits.

He showered lavish praise on his young nephew Ben's elaborate sand castle, and smiled indulgently when nine-month-old Hannah tugged at the hem of his robe and sprinkled sand on his feet.

Unlike his brother Elan, he showed no inclination to run in the surf with them under his arm.

Elan's wife, Sara, was athletic, outspoken and almost as blond as Celia herself.

Hah. So much for the Al Mansur men being pledged from birth to marry a handpicked local bride. She couldn't help gloating a little, under the circumstances.

How different things might have been if Salim hadn't broken off their long-ago romance to marry the bride his father chose.

"I hear you're one of the top landscape architects in the world today." Sara's comment pulled Celia out of her reflection.

"Oh, I wouldn't say that. I've just had the

good fortune to be offered some interesting projects."

"She's too modest," Salim cut in. "Her innovative approach has earned her an excellent reputation. I wouldn't have hired her otherwise."

"I'm impressed that you hired a woman," said Sara, looking straight at Salim. "Elan's told me the country is very traditional. I wasn't sure I'd see women in positions of influence."

"I wouldn't cheat my business of the skills and talents of half the population." Salim shifted position. "I've raised some eyebrows with my hiring practices over the years, but no one's laughing at the results."

"That's good to hear." Sara smiled. "Though I've noticed that even a man who believes in equality in the boardroom can be quite the knuckle-dragger when it comes to his private life." She shot a mischievous look at her husband. "Elan took a while to catch onto the idea of the emancipated woman."

"Really?" Celia couldn't disguise her fascination.

"It's true," said Elan ruefully. "I was all in favor of women in the workplace, until it came to my own wife."

"And this after I'd already worked with him for several months. Somehow, once the ring was on my finger I was expected to lie around eating bonbons all day."

Elan shrugged. "I guess I still had all those old-fashioned traditions etched somewhere in my brain, even though I'd rejected them a long time ago. Almost losing Sara made me wake up."

"Lucky thing he came to his senses. I'd have missed him." Sara winked. "And we wouldn't have Hannah." She looked fondly at the baby, who sat on Elan's knee sucking on a sandy finger.

Elan stretched. "We Al Mansur men come with some baggage, but trust me, we're worth the trouble." He shot a glance at his brother.

Celia's eyes darted from one man to the next. Had his comment been intended for her?

Surely Salim hadn't told his brother about

their long-ago relationship? With his hints about the past, he seemed to be trying to start something.

Salim sat, straight backed on the sand, brows lowered. Obviously the whole discussion made him uncomfortable.

As well it might.

Her breathing grew shallow. Elan had no idea of the bombshell she was about to lob at Salim.

"Salim," Elan flicked a bug from his baby daughter's arm. "Did I tell you Sara and I are eating out with one of my clients tonight? I hope you weren't counting on us for dinner."

Salim frowned. "I thought you wanted to eat that giant fish you caught this morning in the harbor. You should enjoy it while it's still fresh."

"Oh, yeah. I forgot all about Old Yellow." He glanced up at Celia, a twinkle in his eye. "It's a yellowfin tuna. Maybe you two could share it?"

Celia gulped.

What was Salim's brother up to?

A cautious glance at Salim revealed his brow lowered in distaste.

"Goodness, I wouldn't dream of imposing," she blurted, anxious to dispel the tension. "I'm sure Salim is busy since he's been away so long. A lot has happened at the site."

"Yes, I need to visit it this afternoon." Salim's face was expressionless. "Perhaps you could accompany me and fill me in on the details."

"Absolutely. I'd be glad to." She met his poker face with one of her own.

Was that a grin of triumph spreading across Elan's rather arrogant features?

He'd be grinning out of the other side of his mouth if he knew the truth about her. He had no idea he was trying to set his brother up with a woman who kept his own child a secret from him.

She bit her lip as dread crept through her.

The excursion would present a perfect opportunity to tell Salim about Kira.

Now that they were working together, every

day she didn't tell him made the secret weigh heavier. It was time to bite the proverbial bullet—or dagger, in this case—and face the consequences.

Salim chose a chauffeured car to drive Celia and himself to the site so there could be no suspicion of impropriety. His brother's bizarre hints made it sound as if he actually expected him to form a relationship with Celia.

Where would he get such an idea?

His unfortunate reunion liaison with Celia was entirely secret. He hadn't told a soul, and never would. He had no intentions toward her now, except to extinguish all thoughts of her from his heart and mind.

Celia stepped out of the car, her faded jeans giving away far too much information about her shapely legs. He glanced at his driver, but the man had tactfully averted his eyes.

"Guide me through the site as if it were built," he commanded. He cleared his throat as she walked past, determined not to be distracted by the tasteless and provocative way her pale pink T-shirt draped over her rather pert breasts.

Really, a mature woman should dress more modestly in a business situation.

It was entirely her fault that images of her snuck into his dreams and hung around his brain, ready to spear him with unexpected and unwelcome sensations.

It was annoying that his body responded so predictably to such simple and obvious stimuli.

She wore construction boots, too. Was there no limit to her desire to flaunt the expectations of feminine dress?

The boots were practical though, he couldn't argue with that. They picked their way across the rocky site until they reached an area where carved stone and mud-brick walls rose out of the soil.

"This will be the main entrance." Celia spread her arms, which had acquired a slight tan. "The road will be paved with stones to match those found at the site, and the drive lined with native plants like *simr* that need little water and provide nectar for honeybees. The original site appears to have been fortified, so the design incorporates a low wall and a wide, wooden gate, which will remain open."

"Unless invaders attack."

She glanced at him, surprised. A smile flickered across her shell-pink lips. "Always best to be prepared."

She strode ahead, long limbs covering the uneven ground with ease. "This open space will be the reception area of the hotel, and we've conceived it as the "marketplace." The various desks will be arranged like luxurious market stalls, and will in fact have handcrafted, traditional objects available for purchase."

The vision she conjured formed in Salim's mind. "A marketplace. I like it. We must have food available here, too. Coffee and dates."

"Date palms, bananas and coconut palms will be planted throughout the property. Of course they're not native, and will require irrigation, but it's likely they would have been grown here."

"Has the aquifer been tapped yet?"

"Come this way." Her mysterious smile intrigued him. He quickened his pace to keep up with her enthusiastic stride.

She paused at a circular section of wall, partially excavated from the surrounding ground. "The old well. And look inside."

Salim leaned over the edge of the wall. He inhaled deeply as the unmistakable, indescribable scent of pure, fresh water tickled his nostrils. It glittered below, just visible in the shadowed depths of the well. "Beautiful."

"Isn't it?" Excitement sparkled in her eyes. "I can imagine people sitting around this well a thousand years ago."

"People probably sat around this well three thousand years ago. Maybe even ten thousand years."

"Your ancestors." She peered into the depths.

Salim stiffened. The ancestors he'd let down by failing to sire an heir. But once he purged Celia from his mind he'd take a new wife and accomplish that, too.

"Perhaps they're all around us right now,

invisible." Her soft voice drifted in the warm air.

"Ghosts?" His skin prickled.

"Or something like that. Can't you feel all the energy here?" She lifted her shoulders as if sensation trickled down her spine. The movement brought her pink T-shirt tight over her round breasts and drew his eye to where the nipple peaked beneath the soft fabric.

Heat flashed through him and a long-lost memory surfaced: Celia naked in his bed, sleepy-eyed and smiling.

Salim cursed the tricks of his brain. What would his ancestors think of that little vision? "The guest quarters?"

"This way." She walked on, aglow with confidence she'd enjoyed even back in college. "They're arranged along the patterns of the ancient streets. They were thoroughly excavated and all artifacts removed for study. As you can see, we've started rebuilding using the existing remains as the foundation where possible. It's moving to see the lost city rise from the sands again."

Salim nodded. Maybe that was why his flesh tingled with unfamiliar sensation. Whole lives had unfolded here, only to disappear again into the dust.

"I've chosen plants that were indigenous at the time, or that could have been brought here by traders. Nothing from the Americas."

"Except yourself."

"Luckily I won't be a permanent feature." She kept her face turned from him.

"I'm sure you'd be a delightful addition, should you decide to install yourself." The words seemed to slip from his tongue. They both knew he didn't mean them.

Didn't they?

He saw her shoulders tighten. "I don't think I'd match the décor."

"I imagine that a desert oasis of this kind attracted travelers and merchants from all over the world. Perhaps even tall, blonde princesses from afar."

"I don't think anyone would accuse me of being a princess."

"If I recall correctly, you can be a little headstrong and demanding." He'd loved her effortless self-assurance and the way she always expected the world to come to its senses and see things her way.

"Oh, I still am." She flashed a smile. "That's how I get things done, especially with a crew of fifty to supervise. I'm impressed with the workers, by the way. They really are a diverse group. I have men from India, Africa, Saudi Arabia. They all have different skills and talents. You weren't kidding about this place attracting people from everywhere."

He shrugged. "People go where the work is."

Like her. He'd made it impossible for her to refuse this job. Not because he couldn't stand the thought of being rejected by her. Because she was the best person for the job.

And because he had unfinished business with her.

Celia marched forward, her construction boots striking the soil with determination. "Each guest will have their own house, arranged along the original streets and built in the traditional style. Each guest house will have a courtyard with a recirculating fountain."

"Perfect."

"I admit I'm nervous about how quickly we're forging ahead." She shoved a lock of hair off her face. "I know the archaeologists have been thorough, but there could well be more stuff down there."

"Then let it remain. This oasis probably has several layers of civilizations, each built on top of its predecessor. I wish for the tradition to continue, not for a lost way of life to be preserved in amber."

She smiled. "I think it's exciting that you're not afraid to embrace change and bring the oasis back to life. As you can see we're reusing a lot of the original building materials." She beckoned with her fingers. "The pool area is this way."

Salim let his gaze follow her for a moment

before he started to walk. Her graceful stride revealed the power contained within her slim body. He knew all too well the energy and affectionate enthusiasm she was capable of.

Not that he'd fully appreciated it at the time. Perhaps he'd thought all women were such bewitching creatures in the intimacy of a bedroom.

Their regrettable meeting four years ago only reminded him too vividly of all he'd missed in the intervening years.

"An open body of water would have been pretty unlikely in the old settlement, so we racked our brains about whether to go for a natural free-form shape, or a more traditional rectangular form like a courtyard fountain. Right now we're thinking that a perfectly round pool would be an interesting combination of the two. Formal in its geometry, yet soft and natural in its outline so people can gather around it like a natural lake."

She marched briskly around its imagined shores. "It will be zero entry on one side so that small children can splash in the shallow water and the other side will have a gentle waterfall to circulate the water and provide filtration."

The setting sun made the rocky sand glow like candlelit amber. The workers had vanished for the day, leaving their excavator baking in the sun, and the oasis hung suspended in time. Celia stood on the shores of her imaginary lake, golden hair burnished by the rich light.

Salim cursed the ripple of thick sensation that surged through his body.

He was in control here.

It irked him that Celia could be so cool and businesslike.

He'd brought her here in the first place to remind him that she was just an ordinary woman, not the goddess of his fevered imagination.

Unfortunately, spending time with her had further unearthed the past he hoped to bury. Surely he wasn't the only one suddenly pricked by shards of memory?

"We must leave before it gets dark." His gruff

tone seemed to startle her out of deep reverie. "You will have dinner with me."

Celia hovered in front of the mirror for a second.

Yes, it was her. She still had that little freckle next to her nose. Otherwise she might not have been so sure.

Her hair lay coiled about her neck in shimmering gold ringlets, arranged in her room by one of the hotel's hairdressers.

Her usual T-shirt had been replaced by a fitted tunic of peacock-blue silk, shot through with emerald-green.

She looked quite silly, but she hadn't wanted to be rude. She was now fit to be seen in the hotel's most exclusive dining room—at least according to the friendly staff member who'd bedecked her. Apparently, she and Salim were going to eat Elan's yellowfin tuna there, under the prying eyes of the hotel's wealthiest and snootiest guests.

Fun.

Especially since she *still* hadn't told Salim about Kira.

It seemed wrong to interrupt their work at the lost city with the news. The driver had invaded their privacy all the way back to the hotel. Now she had to smile and fake her way through a formal dinner, with the secret throbbing inside her like Edgar Allan Poe's telltale heart.

Her shoulders shook a little under the peacock silk covering. The dress was modest, Omani style, with embroidered gold trim at the neckline and cuffs, and matching pants underneath. The thick bangles on her wrists looked disturbingly like pure twenty-four-carat gold.

Naturally, she'd return them right after dinner.

She jumped when the phone on the bedside table beeped. She shuffled across the floor in her gold-and-blue slippers and snatched up the receiver.

"I'm on my way to your room." Salim's bold tones sent a surge of adrenaline to her embroidered toes.

"Great. I'm all ready."

She plastered on her best fake smile.

Maybe tonight would present the perfect time to tell him.

Kira was the center of her universe. She spoke to her every day on the phone, sometimes several times. Twice now Kira had wondered aloud where her "Dada" was. She'd noticed that other kids in day care had one, and she didn't.

Celia was painfully reminded that two people who were father and daughter weren't even aware of each other's existence. The entire future of their relationship, possibly the whole direction of the rest of their lives, lay on her shoulders.

The door flung open and Salim stood framed in the soft glow from the hallway. His strong features had an expression of strange intensity, which deepened as he stared at her.

"Where did you get those clothes?"

"Aliyah brought them for me. From the gift shop. She said you'd…"

"I told her to find you whatever you needed. I didn't tell her to dress you up like an Omani."

He himself had changed into Western clothes. A white shirt open at the collar and crisp dark pants.

Celia laughed, mostly out of nerves. "Kind of funny, isn't it? I look Omani and you look American."

Salim's gaze swept over her, heating her skin under the elaborate dress. A frown furrowed his forehead.

He hated it.

Her bangles jangled as she reached up to brush an imagined hair from her rapidly heating face. "If you think I should change I'm sure I can find something in my closet."

"No. You're fine. Let's eat."

He hesitated in the doorway then thrust his arm out for her to take.

Her stomach leaped as she slipped her arm in his. His thick muscle held rigid, unyielding, like he was steeling himself against something.

Celia drew a deep breath down into her lungs and tried not to trip over her embroidered slippers.

"Your work at the site," said Salim gruffly. "I'm very pleased with it."

"I'm amazed at how well it's coming together. Your team are magicians. I tell them what I want and they wave their magic wands overnight and make it happen."

"I've built and opened a lot of hotels."

She struggled to keep up as he strode along the hotel corridor, polished marble shimmering under their feet and lights glimmering in arched alcoves along the walls.

"Do you have a favorite, or is each new one the best and brightest?"

Salim frowned and his stride hesitated. "They're like children to me. I value each one for different reasons."

Celia faltered, tripping over her own feet as terror froze her blood at the word *children*.

"What's the matter?"

"I'm not used to wearing such a long dress," she stammered. "I spend too much time in jeans."

"You look different dressed up." His dark gaze

flickered over her face and body, leaving a trail of heat like a comet's tail.

Celia swallowed. "I guess almost anything is an improvement." She tried to walk gracefully, as the blue silk swished about her calves.

"I suppose that depends on the eye of the beholder."

Heat snapped between them, heating her arm where it lay inside his. Her skin tingled and she could feel her face, flushed like a schoolgirl on her first date.

It's not a date.

Why did it feel like one?

The hallway led into the hotel's main lobby, a well-lit atrium framed on all sides by the curved white arches characteristic of Omani architecture. Inlaid floor tiles glittered at their feet and hotel staff moved silently about, working their magic.

Celia's arm tingled inside Salim's as he guided her toward the restaurant. Her hand rested on his wrist, which she noticed was dusted with fine black hairs. His hand was broad and strong, more so than she remembered, but no surprise given all those hands had accomplished in the last decade.

She kept expecting him to withdraw his arm and push her politely away as they entered the restaurant, but he kept a firm hold as he nodded to his maitre d' and led her to the table.

Of course he probably behaved this way with business partners all the time. He was simply being polite. Nothing to get worked up about.

He pulled back her chair and she lowered herself into her seat as gracefully as possible. Glances darted to her from around the room, and she hoped it wasn't because she looked foolish in her getup. At least Aliyah hadn't suggested she wear a traditional gold headdress.

Salim frowned again. "You look beautiful."

His unexpected compliment left her speechless. It seemed at odds with his harsh demeanor. Almost like he was mad at her for looking nice.

"Thanks, I think." She grasped her water glass

and took a sip. "You're not so hard on the eyes, yourself."

She wasn't sure whether Salim looked more breathtaking in Western clothes or in the traditional dishdasha. The truth was, it didn't matter what he wore. His strong features and proud bearing made any getup look downright majestic.

His stern expression only enhanced the handsome lines of his face. But he wasn't the boy she'd once loved. Something was different, changed forever.

What was it? A playfulness she remembered. The mischievous sparkle in his eyes.

Every now and then she thought she saw a shadow of it, but maybe she was just imagining things.

Something had died in her, too, the day he'd told her their relationship was over—because he'd married another woman. Just like that, over Christmas break, while she was sitting at home penning dreamy letters and looking forward to seeing him again.

"How come you never married again?" The question formed in her mind and emerged from her mouth at the same time.

She regretted it instantly, and waited for his brow to lower. But it didn't.

He picked up his glass and held it, clear liquid sparkling in the candlelight for a moment. "I never met anyone…"

"As wonderful as me?" She spoke it on a laugh, sure he'd respond with a jab.

But now he frowned. Stared at her with those impenetrable onyx eyes. "We did have something, you and I."

Her belly contracted. "I thought so, at the time." Her voice had gone strangely quiet, like the life force had been sucked out of her.

"The marriage wasn't my idea, you know." He put down his glass and wove his fingers together. "My father sprang the whole thing on me without warning."

"You could have said no."

He shook his head. "I couldn't." That odd look in his eyes again. A flash of…something. "Not

then, anyway. I was still the eldest son, the dutiful one, my father's heir."

"So you had to do what he said, regardless
of what you wanted." She frowned as a strange
thought occurred to her. "Perhaps your marriage
was doomed from the start because of the abrupt
way you were forced into it."

"You mean, because I hadn't gotten over
you?" Again, a gleam in those normally lightless depths.

What was she thinking? She'd never seen
anyone so totally over her as the man who'd told
her there would be no further contact between
them—*ever.*

She waved her hand, dismissive. "Oh, I'm just
rambling. As you said, you always knew your
father would pick your bride, so it wasn't a surprise to you."

"You're right, though." His voice had an edge
to it, almost as if his own thoughts took him
by surprise. "I wasn't over you. I had to end
our…relationship…" The word seemed to stick
in his throat. "The way one snaps the shoot off

a growing plant. Maybe it stunted the way I grew after that. I couldn't be the husband my wife needed."

He leaned forward, frowning as he stared into her eyes with breath-stealing intensity. "Because I couldn't forget you."

Four

Celia almost fell off her chair. Except she couldn't move at all, because the blood drained from her body, leaving her brain empty, sputtering.

"I've shocked you." Salim sat back in his chair. "With the wisdom of hindsight I can now admit I couldn't love my wife. Maybe we could have grown into it slowly, as many people do, but she couldn't stand that I wasn't… romantic."

He inhaled deeply, chest rising beneath his

shirt. "How could I be, when my heart still belonged to someone else?"

Two steaming plates of grilled yellowfin tuna materialized in front of them. Celia blinked at hers.

"Come on, eat. The past is the past and there's nothing we can do about it." Salim picked up a fork and speared his fish.

Celia managed to pick up her knife and fork and slice a piece of the tender flesh. She struggled for a way to turn his stunning revelation back into a normal conversation. "Does that happen a lot here, where arranged marriages are common? You know, people having romantic relationships with someone they can't marry, then having to go marry someone else?"

"Sure." Salim nodded and chewed. "All the time. But it's usually restricted to a quiet flirtation at a coffee shop, or in the poetry section of a bookstore, not the full-on, sleeping together kind of arrangement we had. That's simply not possible here."

"Do you think that's better?" She kept her eyes carefully on her plate.

"It certainly would have been in my case. I might have been a happily married father of four by now."

"You could still marry again." She spoke casually, as if to reassure him that she didn't care one way or the other.

"I intend to."

Celia's eyes widened. Salim simply took a bite of fish.

Why had he invited her to dinner and brought up the past? Her breathing was shallow. What did he want from her?

"The thing is—" he lifted his glass "—I'm honor-bound to continue the family name. I don't have a choice but to marry again."

"You'd marry just to have a child?" Celia worked hard to keep her voice even.

He nodded, his dark gaze unwavering.

You already have a child.

If there was a perfect moment to tell him, this was it. She glanced around. Several tables were within easy earshot, and Salim's staff hovered all around.

No way could she drop a bomb like that here. She had no idea how he'd react.

"You think me old-fashioned." He rubbed a hand over his mouth. "But the failure of my marriage is my one big regret. I spend my days building a hotel empire, but if I died tomorrow, there'd be no one to hand it to."

"Hardly a big worry." She concentrated on her food, afraid to show him the panic in her eyes. "I'm sure you have a long life ahead of you. You'll have the heir you hope for."

She frowned. Would he consider a girl—illegitimate and American born—to be his heir? Probably not.

"Your confidence in me is inspiring. But then it always was." His soft gaze made her belly shiver. "Shame I didn't live up to it."

The confession—his admittance of guilt—touched her deeply. She had a sudden, typically feminine urge to smooth any ruffled feathers and reassure him. "What nonsense. You're one of the most successful men on the planet."

"You did say I'd succeed in business. I wasn't at all sure. I didn't speak English nearly as well as my brothers since I was educated at home while they went to school abroad. I wasn't comfortable around strangers." He rested his elbows on the table and studied her face. "But I grew very comfortable with you."

His voice lowered with what might be mistaken for a hint of suggestion.

She racked her brain for something to diffuse the tension thickening in the air. "I'll take some of the credit for improving your English. We used to stay up half the night talking."

"We had a lot to talk about." A hint of suggestion flickered across his striking features.

"True. I'd never met someone who read the entire *New York Times* from cover to cover every day. That's a lot of material."

"And you showed me that there's more to life than what you can read in the papers." A smile lit his eyes. "Do you remember the time you took me to the circus?"

She laughed. "How could I forget? You said the camels reminded you of home."

Salim's eyes narrowed. "They did. And when I was with you I forgot my home. I didn't think about where I came from. I was busy discovering new worlds and exploring them with you."

Celia blushed. "We were both virgins. Funny, isn't it?"

"Not really. I don't suppose that was as outrageous as we were led to believe. It did mean the first time was special for both of us."

His soft voice and tender words pulled at old chords of emotion. "Very special. And funny, too, considering that we'd approached it like explorers, armed with an illustrated Kama Sutra and a list of suitable positions."

Salim chuckled. "We did have a tendency to over intellectualize everything."

"We thought we were so darn smart, and that we could understand everything if we just thought about it and talked about it long enough."

"So true!" A smile tugged at his bold, sensual mouth. "No topic was off-limits."

"Well, except that you were going to take off and marry someone else."

The words fell from her lips, the accusation she'd never been bold enough to make. She was so shocked and hurt, at first. When they met again she was so surprised and delighted by their renewed connection that she didn't want to bring up the painful past.

Salim frowned. "You're right. I did avoid the subject of my future. I didn't like to think about it myself." His gaze drifted over her face, to her neck, which flushed under his attention. "And why would I, when it meant losing you?"

They hadn't talked much about his family at all. She'd assumed he didn't want to be reminded of the home that was so far away he only saw it once or twice a year.

He'd spent several weekends at her mom and dad's house and stayed with them once over spring break. Her parents had thought him sweet and funny. Being professors they were used to international students, many of whom stayed and settled in the States. They didn't think anything of her boyfriend being from another country.

It hadn't occurred to any of them that he had an entirely different life mapped out for him, thousands of miles away.

One that didn't, and never would, include Celia.

Salim's penetrating gaze locked onto hers. The flush rose over her face, and she let out a quick breath. "It might have been easier if I was prepared."

"How do you prepare to end a relationship?" He frowned. "I couldn't prepare for it myself."

"At least you knew it was coming."

Salim closed his eyes for a split second. When he opened them they were dark as a starless night. "It wasn't easy for me."

He leaned forward, holding her attention with laser intensity. "That was, and remains, the worst day of my entire life."

"Mine, too." The words rushed from her mouth before she could stop them.

He'd seemed so cold and distant, like he didn't care. Like he'd changed into a different person overnight. One who'd never cared for her at all, let alone loved her.

She wasn't sure she'd ever recover from such a brutal rejection of all her affections. Such a firm and thorough crushing of all her hopes and dreams.

Maybe she hadn't recovered? She'd dated again, but never for long. She'd never married.

Now, suddenly everything was different.

He'd missed her.

He'd never forgotten her.

Memories of her, and their relationship, had ruined his marriage.

Shock—and something else—unfurled deep inside her.

Was this why he cut off their renewed affair four years ago? Because it had meant more to him than he was willing to admit?

Questions raced around Celia's mind.

Questions about a Salim who'd been hidden from her.

A Salim who'd missed her and who still loved her and who might…

"Let's go." Salim swept up from the table without waiting for her reaction.

Celia rose, accidentally clattering her knife against her plate and almost knocking over her chair. Her heart pounded beneath her elegant silk dress and her pulse skittered beneath her bangles as she took his arm and swept out of the room on a tide of fierce and unexpected emotion.

Guests glanced up at them, curious, but she couldn't summon even a polite smile to greet them. She couldn't do anything except manage—just barely—to put one foot in front of the other.

They flew across the sparkling atrium and out through a dark arch toward the beach. Salim marched with such speed and concentration that no one even dared approach him, let alone speak. It was all Celia could do to keep up in her rustling dress and delicate slippers.

They stepped through the archway and walked down some steps to the sand. Warm evening air brushed her face like a breath. They hadn't even left the pool of light flooding from the atrium when Salim turned, wrapped his arms around her and kissed her with furious passion.

Celia melted into his kiss, rushed into it, her whole body cleaving to his, pressing against him from head to toe. Her hands fisted into his shirt and her nipples hardened against his powerful chest.

Salim's urgent fingers roamed into her elaborate hairstyle as he pulled her face to his and kissed her with breathless abandon.

"Oh, Celia," he murmured, when their lips finally parted for a second. "I tried to push you out of my mind." His words rang with pain, and tailed off as he crushed his mouth over hers again, a groan of relief shuddering through him.

Tears sprang to Celia's eyes. Fierce emotion

threatened to overwhelm her. "Me, too," she breathed into his ear, while he layered hot kisses along her neck.

She'd fallen so easily into his arms four years ago, despite how he'd hurt her. She couldn't help it. The connection between them was too strong to resist.

He grabbed her hand. "Come with me." He led her down to the beach, where she pulled off her hard-to-run-in slippers and let the cool sand welcome her toes. "My private apartment." He gestured to a small peninsula jutting out into the ocean's gentle waves. An elegant white building with typical Omani crenelations along the roofline—like a medieval castle in miniature—perched just over the rippling surf. Light illuminated a narrow arched window.

He ran so fast she could barely keep up.

Celia didn't protest. She couldn't even think, let alone talk.

He pushed open a carved door and ushered her inside. A lamp glowed in a corner, illuminating a simple, masculine space with bare white walls and a smooth stone floor. An ornate silver coffeepot glowed on a shelf, the only decoration besides the high arched windows shaded by carved wood screens.

Celia drank in the details, maybe because she'd been starved of information about Salim for so long. She'd wondered where he lived, and how, without her all this time.

He led her through a polished door in the far wall into what was obviously his bedroom.

A large white bed filled the center of the octagonal room. Tall windows punctuated each wall, providing slivers of ocean view where the moon danced over shimmering black water. Otherwise the space was ascetic as a monk's cell.

The space of a man who lived alone, with no woman in his life.

Salim closed the door behind her and slid his arms around her, muscles shuddering with urgency. His fingers roved over her back through the thin silk of her dress. He kissed her again and again, until her fingers plucked at his shirt buttons in thoughtless desperation.

"I missed you," his breath was hot on her neck. "Seeing you again four years ago only made it worse. I've craved you, wished for you."

Salim's blood hummed with tension so thick he felt he might explode.

He never forgot her. Not for want of trying. He'd done everything he could think of to expunge her from his body and soul.

He'd poured himself into his work, spent his time building an empire and filling it with people as passionate as himself.

But he never forgot Celia.

He'd had to try all over again after their fateful meeting in Manhattan. The very last person he'd thought to see there, she almost knocked him flat with her beauty and poise. He'd been helpless in the glow of her smile, and the warm greeting she'd offered, letting him know the past was gone and forgotten.

And he'd been forced to start over from scratch, trying to forget her again.

"It feels like heaven being here with you."

His words echoed off the walls, painfully true, as he touched her. She was so perfect, so precious, so totally unchanged, like time had captured her in amber and saved her for him, despite all his mistakes.

He lifted her diaphanous dress over her head in a swift movement and groaned at the sight of her breasts in their simple white bra.

Celia's hands gripped his upper arms with force as he lowered his mouth to her breasts, giving in to whatever primal forces drove him. He didn't fight the instincts he'd tried so hard to crush out of existence.

His lips brushed the cotton, tasting the shape of her thickened nipples through the soft fabric. Sensation kicked through him, firing his muscles and making his heart pound.

He unhooked her bra and slid her panties down her slender, muscled legs.

Celia laughed, a magical sound that filled his ears and echoed in his chest.

Laughter had been missing from his life for far too long. He'd tried so hard to do the right thing, to be the dutiful son and the upstanding businessman, when what he really wanted was…Celia.

Her hands tugged at his shirt and he realized that she'd undone all the buttons and was trying to remove it. Laughing again, he helped her, shrugging out of it and struggling with the fly of his pants.

Her face glowed in the soft moonlight, eyes closed and an expression of joy lighting her lovely features.

"You're perfect."

He said the words aloud right as he felt them, holding nothing back. Freed of his clothes, he pressed his skin to hers, enjoying the sweet, soft warmth of her in his arms.

His arousal was intense, agonizing, and if they didn't make love right now, he wasn't sure what would happen. He did still have the presence of mind to don a condom. The last thing he wanted was for her to get pregnant.

He lowered her gently onto the bed, where a shaft of moonlight danced over the sheets and her soft skin.

Celia let out a little cry as he entered her. He opened his eyes, worried that he'd hurt her. Her face soothed his fears. A smile lit her features and her golden lashes fluttered as she writhed under him, clutching him closer.

Salim moved gingerly inside her—easing into a rhythm, then pulling back—wringing every second of sweet pleasure from the closeness he'd craved for so long. He ran his hands over her skin, pressed his fingers into her back and through the silk of her hair.

Years ago he might have rushed, eager to take his pleasure like a child with a bowl of candy. Back then, there was always more candy, maybe even sweeter, waiting for him tomorrow.

Now he was wiser and knew that life's sweetest moments must be savored, for that single perfect moment would never come again.

Her cheek, hot against his, felt so familiar. Her body, moving under him in quickening rhythm, was different and more delicious than ever. Her breasts seemed fuller and her belly softer. Her hips had more of a curve to them, as they lifted to meet his. Celia's slim, girlish body had ripened and filled out into delightful feminine perfection. He could swear her body had changed even since he'd last seen her.

"Your curves are fuller," he breathed.

Her breath caught for a second.

"It's a compliment," he reassured her. He'd forgotten Americans praised slimness above all else. "You become more lovely with each passing year."

"Or your sight gets dimmer with each year," she teased.

He released a ragged sigh as her long fingers dragged a trail of passion along his back.

"I'm not using my sight." He caressed her soft and seductive backside with his fingers. Pleasure rippled through him. "Even if I was blind, my other senses wouldn't lie to me."

He opened his eyes as if to reassure himself that the madness of his desire for Celia hadn't deprived him of his senses. In the dim light of the lamp he saw her delicate features, glowing gold, her lips parted in breathy moans.

He slowed the rhythm, layering kisses along her collarbone until her eyes opened. In the semidarkness they were blue as the night-dark sea outside.

A smile tilted her sensual mouth. "You've filled out, too. All muscle." She squeezed his bicep between her long fingers. "It seems cruel that you should get even more handsome as you get older."

"I could say the same for you, but I'd rather enjoy your beauty." He kissed her cheeks and her mouth, slow and gentle, relishing each brush of their skin. Her scent was intoxicating, like wild honey discovered just where you least expect it, filling the senses to the point of madness.

Madness. This must be madness. Wasn't he trying to cure himself of Celia?

Their tryst was having the very opposite effect.

A flare of anger—mixed inexorably with pure lust—flashed through him.

How did this woman have so much power over him?

Almost as if she heard his unspoken question, Celia angled one of her long legs over his, and deftly flipped their positions until she was on top.

Triumph flared in her eyes as she took him deep.

Salim moaned as pleasure cascaded through him. He'd always adored her sexual confidence—which they'd found and nurtured together—and the way she loved to take charge.

Her nipples hovered over him in the dim light, darker and fuller than he remembered, tempting his thumbs to strum their peaks. Celia sighed as he stroked her breasts, and she moved in a hypnotic rhythm, like a belly dancer, drawing him deeper and deeper.

She was taking him into a world where none

of his senses functioned properly. A strange yet familiar place where his nerves were alive and tingling with pleasure so intense it felt like pain.

Celia bent and kissed him on the mouth, bold and beautiful, claiming him.

He kissed back, unable to stop himself. Lust and mischief soon had them clawing and nipping at each other. He was tempted to suck hard enough to brand her with the mark of his desire.

But he didn't. He was a gentleman, even in this moment of unbearable and delicious torture.

With a movement faster than her own, he grabbed hold of her thighs and maneuvered them both into a sitting position. Legs wrapped around each other, they sat face to face, with him still buried deep—and active—inside her.

She laughed. He'd picked one of the familiar positions from ancient India they'd studied and enjoyed all those years ago.

"It's a classic," he murmured, enjoying the face-to-face contact the position allowed.

He kissed her on the mouth hard, then pulled back.

"It always slows things right down, doesn't it?" She looked at him through narrowed eyes. Her tongue flicked over her lips, tantalizing.

"Sometimes it's good to slow things down."

"When you're about to lose control?"

"I never lose control," he growled.

"Now that's an outright lie." Celia leaned forward, and brushed his chest with the aroused tips of her nipples.

"Okay," he rasped. "Only sometimes."

"Like when you're with me." She brushed her thumb over the curve of his mouth, daring him to argue.

"When I'm with you," he echoed. He seized her, flipping them again until he was on top, and sinking deeper into her hot and enticing depths.

Celia let out a long, shivering sigh and clutched him close.

Her muscles contracted around him when

her climax seized her. In an instant he lost control.

He let out a tortured groan and clutched her to him while sensation rocked him like an earthquake. Colors and patterns burst in front of his eyes, and he clung to Celia as his whole world shook and shuddered and threatened to crumble.

He didn't want to let Celia go.

And that in itself was a big problem.

If Celia could stay right here, in Salim's warm, strong arms, she'd be fine. She was sure of it.

She could hear the sea outside the window, waves lapping against the soft white sand. The tide going in, or out, whichever it was, just as it did every day and night since the beginning of time.

If only she could stop the clock and hold them both here in this magical place where nothing else mattered but that they were together. But already, prying fingers of light crept around the blinds, ready to tug her back into real life.

She sat up with a start. Was it seven o'clock yet? She'd pledged to call Kira every day at 7:00 a.m. Salalah time, which was four in the afternoon in Connecticut, soon after Kira got home from daycare.

Salim stirred and his eyes opened a crack. His dark gaze sent a lightning bolt of guilt to her core.

She still hadn't told him.

And now she'd slept with him.

"I've got to go." She slid to the side of the bed, afraid he'd stretch out a muscled arm and pull her back into his embrace.

Salim lay sprawled on the pillows, broad chest bared, his seductive trail of black hair leading beneath the white sheet that barely covered his hips. "So soon? I think you should sleep in today. I'll talk to the boss." His mouth tilted into a sly smile.

A curl of fresh, hot desire unfolded in Celia's stomach. Which only deepened her sense of guilt. How could she do this to Kira, let alone Salim? Did she have no self-control at all?

Apparently not, at least as far as Salim was concerned.

She tugged her gaze from his dark, sleepy eyes and tousled hair and cleared her throat. "I wish I could, but I have a meeting at the job site. I don't want to mess up other people's plans."

"You're very devoted to your work." His low, seductive voice seemed to suggest that was a bad thing. He shifted onto his side, giving her an eyeful of his sculpted chest and hard biceps.

"Isn't that why you hired me?"

Something glittered in his dark eyes. "Not really."

Celia's belly tightened. Had he truly brought her here because he wanted…her?

He wouldn't have done that if he knew she'd concealed his own daughter from him.

Adrenaline propelled her from the bed. "I've got to get moving." She bit her lip at the sight of her crumpled blue finery. "I'm going to look pretty silly sprinting across the hotel complex in this."

"I'll call and have some of your clothes brought

here." Salim stretched again, bronzed muscle pressing against the soft mattress.

"Are you crazy? Then everyone will know."

He shrugged. Maybe he did this sort of thing all the time.

Celia drew in a long, fortifying breath. "No thanks, I'll take my chances. It's still early. I'll sneak around past the tennis courts."

Salim laughed. "You have no need to 'sneak.' You're not married, and neither am I. We have nothing to be ashamed of."

She gulped. "I'm sure that's true in an ideal world, but in this one I still need to be able to give instructions to the landscapers without them all falling around laughing because they're picturing me in bed with the boss."

He tilted his head back and surveyed her through narrowed eyes. "It's a pretty picture."

Her nipples stung with unwelcome arousal. In fact, her whole body still hummed with the memory of his touch. She needed to get out of here…now.

She shrugged into the blue dress and stepped into the sequined slippers.

"Come, kiss me before you go." He lay stretched on the bed like a sultan, sheets wound around his sturdy thighs. Celia's stomach flip-flopped.

She climbed onto the bed and leaned down to brush her lips to his. Salim captured her in his arms and claimed her mouth with a forceful kiss.

Desire surged through Celia, powerful and invincible. Her skin heated and her limbs trembled with arousal as she kissed him back. A low groan rose from Salim's chest, calling to a dark, sensual part of her that only he'd ever awakened.

Then the thought of Kira—possibly waiting by the phone—cracked in her mind like a whip.

She pulled her mouth from his with considerable effort. "I have to go."

"Shame." He lolled back into the fine sheets, propping muscled arms behind his head. "Since the project's going so smoothly I'm afraid I may lose you before we have time to become properly reacquainted. I find myself wanting to hinder your progress."

His words were a splash of icy water on Celia's lust heated skin. He spoke so easily of "losing her." No doubt if she didn't get lost by herself, he'd give her a neat shove out of his life again.

She stumbled for the door and pushed out into the sunlight, raking a hand through her long, tangled hair.

Why did she let this happen?

She came here to participate in an interesting project, earn good money…and tell him about Kira.

She certainly hadn't come here to sleep with him at the first opportunity.

Common sense deserted her entirely when Salim was around. She knew that. So why had she let herself be tempted into his bed?

Salim clearly saw this as an opportunity to enjoy her body and revel in the warm light of old memories, before he left her behind—yet again—and got on with his own life. Which, as she knew from long, painful experience, did not include her.

Or Kira.

How could she do anything so stupid? Had she thought that suddenly everything was different and he loved her?

A hard blast of air escaped her lungs. What an idiot she was!

She hurried along a neat brick walkway under a row of lush palms, keeping her eyes down so as not to make contact with any of the gardeners pulling dead fronds from the trees and sweeping the paths.

And what was her excuse now for not telling him about his daughter? They'd been alone all night in bed and she could have blurted the truth at any moment.

But the moment never seemed right.

Dammit, the moment would *never* be right.

She lowered her eyes as two hotel managers passed her on the path, with a hushed glance at her rumpled finery. Shadows slashed like knives across the path, as sun crept through the palms.

Oh, how he'd hate her if he knew the magnitude of the secret she still kept hidden while she lay naked in his arms.

How in the world would she ever tell him now?

Five

Salim's chest filled with pride as they approached the gates of the lost city. He was driving the new seven-seater SUV he'd bought to accommodate his newly expanded family, and the children played cheerfully in the rear-facing backseat, while Elan and Sara exclaimed over their first sight of the new complex.

"It's amazing the way it just rises up out of the sand," Sara said as she leaned forward. "I love the crisp whiteness of the buildings here. Maybe we should paint our house white?" She turned to Elan. "I think you painted it the exact same color as the land around it so that no one could find you."

Elan chuckled. "You're probably right. I didn't want anyone to find me, until you came along."

Salim smiled. His brother was obviously very happy, despite his unconventional marriage. He hoped he'd soon feel as settled and content himself.

"How come Celia isn't with us?" Sara's question deflated his momentary joy.

Guilt pricked him.

Sleeping with Celia last night was wrong on so many levels.

"She's here already. At least that's what my assistant told me. She came to supervise a delivery of plants. I'm sure we'll run into her." Would he even be able to look her in the eye in front of his family?

He'd taken advantage of her, knowing full well that their relationship—as always—had no future.

Sometimes he cursed the fact that he was the eldest son. That the burden of tradition and the future of the Al Mansur family rested with him.

But it did. Simple as that.

He pulled up inside the open gates and helped everyone out.

"It's loud." Little Ben covered his ears with his hands. Salim didn't usually notice such things, but there were quite a few pieces of machinery in motion.

"That's the sound of progress," Salim said as he bent down to pick him up. "You can't make things beautiful without some noise. Haven't you been to your dad's work sites?"

"No!" Sara laughed. "He's too young. And so far he's looking more like an artist than an oilman."

"You like to draw?" Salim peered into Ben's bright eyes.

The child nodded. "And paint. And I like to make up stories, but I don't know how to write them down yet."

"He's a genius," proclaimed Elan proudly.

Salim nodded. "He'll be the next Leonardo da Vinci." He stroked the boy's soft cheek. "You'll put the Al Mansur name on the map, won't you?"

"I think you're doing a pretty good job of that yourself," said Elan.

Salim snorted. "A few hotels, nothing more. I hope to make this area a popular tourist destination. It's good for our economy and provides work for the people."

"It's a lot more than that," Sara gushed as she walked forward, wide-eyed. "This is incredible. It's a whole city out in the middle of the desert."

Warmth surged inside him. "I can't take all the credit. The city was always here—we just found it and dusted it off again."

"It's breathtaking. Look at the artistry." A ribbon of painted frieze ran along the wall of a building next to them, and turned the corner onto another crisp, cobbled street.

"My architect hired talented craftsmen. It's

been a joy to bring so much talent together in one place."

"Speaking of which, there's Celia. Goodness, look at those beautiful trees. What kind of bush is that?"

"I have no idea. Celia knows far more about Omani plants than I do at this point." Her knowledge and expertise floored him. And the pleasure she took in her work made it a joy to behold.

Salim's heart ached with trepidation as they approached. What a night they'd spent together. A taste of heaven in the one pair of arms he could never resist.

He cursed his own weakness.

His torment was worsened by the sight of those faded jeans she wore. They hugged her long, strong legs and cupped her firm backside. She was reaching up to prune a branch as they approached, and her pale yellow T-shirt lifted to reveal a sliver of slim waist.

Arousal flashed through him, heating his blood and bruising his ego.

Had he no self-control around this woman?

"Hello, Celia." He managed the gruff greeting with a poker face. "Hard at work, as usual."

He didn't want the others to know about their tryst last night. Elan might tease him mercilessly, or worse, try to make more of it than it was.

She turned. Her face glowed with exertion, and he could swear her cheeks grew pinker at the sight of him. "What are you doing here?"

Her blue eyes glowed with excitement that only fanned his desire.

"What kind of question is that?" He tried to act casual. "It's my newest resort, not to mention the home of my ancestors." He attempted a smile. "This is where I *should* be."

He tried to keep his eyes on her face, to ignore the way her thin cotton T-shirt draped over her chest.

She pushed a strand of damp hair off her face, and dusted off her jeans as the others approached, apparently self-conscious. "What do you think of the lost city?"

"I'm thinking it's very happy to have been found again," Sara said with a grin. She held little Hannah in her arms, and the baby reached out for a dangling branch. "It's so beautiful. And rather mystical, too. If I rub on that pot over there, will a genie pop out?" She gestured to a tall reproduction oil jar beside a nearby doorway.

"No, but I'm hoping the vine I planted in it yesterday will pop out soon if it gets watered often enough."

"It's hot, Mommy," whined Ben. "Can we go inside?"

"Won't help, I'm afraid," said Celia. "They're not turning on the air-conditioning until next week."

"Ben, you must learn to enjoy the heat." Salim set him down and ruffled his hair. "We Omanis don't need artificially cooled air to live our lives." He'd make sure his own son didn't grow up too dependent on modern conveniences. There was a lot to be said for living according to tradition. He'd worn a long, white dishdasha today, perhaps to remind himself of his place in the world.

He averted his eyes as Celia leaned forward to offer Ben a cool Thermos, revealing a flash of cleavage. If she had on traditional Omani attire, such mutually embarrassing moments would be avoided.

Then again, she was wearing traditional Omani attire last night, and look what happened.

Apparently there was no helping him.

"I love the heat," Sara exclaimed. "It took me a while to get used to it when I moved to Nevada to work for Elan, but now I can't imagine living somewhere that never gets hot."

"Maybe I'll convince the two of you to move back to Oman." Salim let slip the words that had danced in his mind ever since they arrived.

"That would take a lot of convincing. I'm not sure my employees would be too thrilled." Elan chuckled. "But I can see Celia's taken to the place already. I heard her speaking flawless Arabic yesterday."

Salim frowned. Was Elan trying to paint Celia

as his perfect mate again? Couldn't he see that only did more harm than good?

"My Arabic is hardly flawless." Celia flushed a shade darker. She snuck a glance at Salim, who pretended not to notice. "I know just enough to make myself understood."

"Yours is probably better than mine," Elan said with a smile. "I've lived in the U.S. so long I've forgotten a lot."

"It's coming back, though," said Sara. "You did a fantastic job haggling over that rug for the dining room yesterday."

"Raw instinct. I'm sure you'd have gotten it for even less if you tried." Elan looked at Celia. "Sara's a demon negotiator. I think that's how she really won my heart. We Al Mansur men like our women made of pretty stern stuff."

Elan looked approvingly at Celia's work attire. Salim felt a twinge of annoyance—surely not jealousy?

Salim realized his brow had furrowed into a frown. He cleared his throat. Celia fidgeted, no doubt uncomfortable with this discussion of what kind of woman Al Mansur men needed.

"Would you like me to show you the plantings?" Celia's voice was a little squeaky. "The shrubs are *sarh*. They're native to the region and can go long periods between watering." She darted forward to stop Ben from plucking one of the berries. "They're not poisonous, but they might have been sprayed with something at the nursery." She looked at Sara. "I always check that plantings are nontoxic if they're in an area where children may find them."

"That's very thoughtful." Sara made a silly face at Ben, who grinned in response, then glanced up at Celia. "I'd almost suspect you of being a mother yourself."

Celia stood openmouthed. Salim could swear her skin turned pale. When she finally spoke, her voice was low and breathless. "Just being practical. My clients hate lawsuits."

She didn't glance up at him, the client. "She's right. I hate lawsuits. Such a time waster and so…unfriendly." He smiled. "I'm about to give

Elan and Sara and the kids a tour of our found-again lost city. Will you join us?"

"Uh, sure." Celia glanced around, as if looking for an excuse not to.

He couldn't blame her. It was awkward trying to act normal after the night of heady passion they'd shared.

If he could turn back the clock and undo their sweaty, embarrassingly emotional tryst, he would.

What kind of idiot thought that sleeping with a woman he craved would help him get over her?

He'd plunged the arrow of longing even deeper into his flesh. He doubted even a knife could cut it free now.

He couldn't begin to imagine how Celia felt. Didn't dare even let his mind wander in that direction.

"This way, everyone," he called, aiming for cheerful confidence. "Celia could tell you how the city rose up out of the desert, stone by stone. She's seen a lot more of the process than I have."

"It's been truly amazing." Celia marched boldly ahead. "I was nervous that a lot of construction would destroy the site, but Salim's crew really know what they're doing. They were so careful to preserve the past."

"Salim's very big on the past." Elan shot a narrow-eyed glance at his brother.

"Speaking of which…" Salim said as he paused in front of a two-story building of white stucco, shaded with native date palms.

Elan turned and frowned. He blinked up at the pale walls, ornamented with a strip of painted diamonds. "It looks like…our house. Where we grew up."

"It is." Salim paused, watching his brother's face. "Come inside."

He led them through the shady arched doorway, into the cool interior. "I know you don't have the happiest of memories from here, but that house is gone now, and for some reason I wanted to recreate it here."

Elan's mouth hung open as he surveyed the stone floor, the smooth stuccoed walls, all exactly like the home they'd shared long ago. "Wow," Elan said softly as he blew out a breath and ran a hand through his hair. "This takes me back."

"We were happy in that house once."

Elan frowned. "When we were all together. Before father sent me and Quasar as far away as possible and screwed up all our lives."

Salim swallowed. Their father's action had abruptly ended their happy childhoods. With his fun-loving and energetic brothers banished to distant boarding schools, Salim lived a lonely and cloistered existence. His mother had died soon after, leaving him alone with the harsh father who never had a kind word for him.

So what? He'd survived. And prospered.

Elan cocked his head. "You've recreated our home, and now you've brought me back to it." His eyes twinkled. "If Quasar was here, we'd be a family again. Of sorts."

"We are a family." Salim spoke gruffly. He

was determined the Al Mansurs would face the future together. "Quasar will come one day." Their wild younger brother was hard to keep up with. One day he'd settle down.

Or at least Salim hoped so.

Sara gazed up at the high ceilings, ringed with a simple painted frieze. "It's beautiful. Simple and elegant. I'm sure you'll recreate a happier version of the past here."

"I'm not nearly that ambitious." Salim crossed his arms, trying to ignore the rush of emotion in his chest. "It was a typical Omani building that seemed suitable for the site."

"Sometimes you have to confront the past in order to move forward," Elan said slowly, glancing around the familiar—yet unfamiliar—space. Salim's stomach clenched at his words. "I avoided the past like a dog that hunted me. I just ran faster to get away from it. Put as much distance between me and…home…as I could. I locked all that hurt and disappointment away, and vowed to never feel anything like it again."

Sara leaned forward. "Until one night in the desert, I pried open the lockbox of his emotions."

"And I've been a changed—and far happier—man ever since." Elan slid his arm around Sara's waist.

Salim swallowed. "I'm very happy for you. Naturally, since I've been here in Oman all the time, I've been surrounded by the past and have had no need or desire to run away from it."

He looked sideways at Celia. She stood rigid as a statue. No doubt she felt herself an unfortunate intruder in this family tableau. He quickly glanced out the window.

"Sometimes you can run from something without even knowing it." Elan's low voice penetrated the fog of his thoughts. "It's even harder to find your way back, in that case."

Salim frowned. "You speak in riddles, brother. I'm simply glad you're here and I intend to keep you here as long as possible."

"I'll tell you, it feels really good to be back.

We'll have to make a habit of it." Elan smiled at Sara.

She nodded. "I'd love Hannah and Ben to grow up knowing their Omani family, and being aware of their heritage." Her eyes shone. "We should visit as often as possible."

Salim watched his little niece, now crawling across the stone floor with impressive speed. His heart filled with joy, and a sense of purpose fulfilled. "You're welcome here every single day, literally. Nothing could mean more to me than to bring our family together again."

A sudden fit of coughing took Celia by surprise, and she struggled to get it under control. "Sorry! I don't know what happened," she stammered, when she finally managed to stop and take a sip from the shared Thermos.

"The dry air," said Elan, reassuring, as usual. "Can you believe that a family of five and at least five servants lived in this house?"

Celia's eyes widened. "Are there more rooms?"

"There'd better be." Elan chuckled. "Can't have

men and women in the same room. Anything might happen." He winked.

Salim narrowed his eyes. Some traditions had rather fallen by the wayside, at least in the bustling coastal cities. Still, better for Celia to see how different life was here than in the States.

Salim held a curtain aside so they could walk through the doorway into the next room. "Our room," Elan said as he stared, then glanced up at Sara. "Though Salim forgot the bed. We brothers shared one. We used to make up crazy stories in here, while the grown-ups were still sitting out in the courtyard. Wow, that was a long time ago. Probably the happiest time of my life, until I met Sara."

Sara glanced at Celia, who still stood there as if she'd seen a ghost. "He was far too busy working to be happy, until I sorted him out."

"Look who's talking, Miss Workaholic." Elan prodded her with his fingertips.

"That's Mrs. Workaholic, to you." Sara gave him a playful shove. "It's true, though. We both helped each other mellow out. I think when you enjoy your work it's good to marry someone else who's career-oriented. Then no one's left moping at home. What do you think, Celia?"

Celia's elegant throat contracted as she swallowed. "I suppose so." Her voice was scratchy. "I've never been married."

"It's not easy to meet the right person," mused Sara. "And sometimes they take some time to realize it themselves."

Salim frowned. Were they trying to cook up mischief again? Couldn't they see that Celia would rather be anywhere but here? No doubt all this talk of family and Omani traditions made her want to run for cover.

He frowned. "Let's go."

Salim and his family had left Celia at the site to finish her work. She'd almost died during all the talk of family and togetherness.

How would they feel about her if they knew she was hiding a member of their own family from them?

It hurt that she was depriving Kira of her own

family and heritage. Not to mention depriving Salim of the family he so openly craved.

She'd decided to tell him about Kira tonight. Whatever happened between them had happened, and she couldn't do anything about that now. All she could do was try to make the future brighter for all of them.

She was sure he'd come see her.

But he didn't.

Probably busy with work. She knew he had business dinners several nights a week. And he did have family visiting. Maybe they needed some time to themselves.

At least that's how she tried to reassure herself.

After a fitful night of broken sleep, she decided to go for a quick run on the beach to shake off stress. Exercise made almost anything easier to cope with.

Sensitive to Oman's conservative sensibilities, she dressed in light cotton pants and a shirt rather than her usual jogging bra and shorts. It was actually cooler to keep herself covered, she'd discovered. Which no doubt explained why most people in this region didn't expose their bare skin to the punishing sun.

No one paid attention to thermometers here. There were only two temperatures: hot, and very, very hot. Compared to the misery of the Connecticut winter she was missing, she wasn't complaining.

Once dressed, she picked up the phone for her daily call to Kira. Her daughter's garbled hello greeted her. This was Celia's usual time to call, so her grandparents allowed Kira to answer the phone. "Hi, sweetie."

"Mama come home."

"Mama will be home soon, sweetie. Two weeks. That's not long, is it?"

It felt like an eternity.

"Mama come home *today*." Tears thickened the words.

"I wish I could, lovie, but Mama has to work."

"Kira come, too, and help you work." Her little voice brightened and Celia could picture those dark eyes filled with excitement at her new idea.

Celia's chest constricted. "I wish you could, my baby. I wish you could." Tears threatened and she sucked in a deep breath.

"Why can't I?" Her brave voice sounded suddenly so grown-up.

Why couldn't she? She was too young to *need* to attend school. There was truly no reason why she couldn't "help" while Celia arranged potted portacula plants and studied the fall of shade over garden walls.

Except that this was her father's home.

And he didn't know she existed.

"I...I..." Celia's voice shook. She needed to get control of herself quickly and reassure Kira there was nothing wrong. "One day you'll be big enough to help me."

"When?" Again, the forceful clarity of a child far older than three.

"Soon," she lied. What was one more lie? Except that each one seemed to eat another hole in her soul. "Do you want me to sing you a song?"

"Okay Mama." Her reply didn't conceal her disappointment. "You sing 'Rock-a-bye Baby.'"

Celia gulped and inhaled. The song was so familiar she usually didn't pay attention to the words, but today they rang with threatening pre-science, echoing from one side of the world to another. "...When the bough breaks, the cradle will fall, down will come baby, cradle and all." Her voice wavered and she tried to turn it into a laugh.

She was so afraid of breaking that bough. Of rocking the safe world she'd tried to create for Kira thousands of miles away in Connecticut. But she was learning that sooner or later it had to break, and she'd just have to do her best to catch her.

Brushing away tears, she hung up the phone with promises that she'd send more pictures from her cell phone and tell Kira exactly what she ate for breakfast.

Running shoes laced, she pushed out into the invigorating morning warmth. Her shoes sank into the sand as she ran, and her calves enjoyed the extra work as she filled her lungs with fragrant sea air.

A high rock outcropping marked the end of the hotel property. She ran to it, then stretched in the shade on the far side for a few minutes. She was about to turn and run back, when she heard familiar voices.

"Celia's more beautiful than I thought she'd be." It was Elan's jovial voice.

The object of their conversation blanched and ducked behind the craggy rock. A fissure near eye level allowed her to see the beach beyond, stretching to the hotel complex. She shifted until a sliver of visibility revealed Salim and Elan.

"You thought I'd spend years pining over an ugly woman?" Salim sounded in good humor. Again he wore a long, white dishdasha, this time with the traditional ornamental *khanjar* dagger at the waist. Morning sun reflected off the hard planes of his handsome face.

He'd spent years pining? Well, he'd admitted as much to her at their dinner together.

Celia bit her lip and listened.

"I'm glad you're finally coming to your senses where she's concerned." Elan wore jeans and a white towel wrapped around his neck. Sweat shimmered on the thick muscle of his back.

"What do you mean?" She couldn't see Salim's face, but she could picture his thoughtful frown.

"You know, getting back together with her. I know the two of you spent the evening together the night before last. How come Celia wasn't with us at dinner last night?"

"She had something to do."

Celia bit her lip.

"Make sure you don't let her get away a second time."

"A third time, actually." Salim sounded somewhat embarrassed.

"What?"

"I didn't tell you we had a little…reunion…four years ago at the Ritz Carlton in Manhattan."

"And what happened after that?"

"I flew back here. She has her own career, her own life. It was obvious there was no future between us."

"She told you that?"

"No, but it was understood."

"You told her that." It wasn't a question. Apparently Elan understood his brother, despite their years apart.

"I don't like confusion."

"Brother of mine, you have a talent for screwing up your love life. I'm going to personally see to it that you don't mess things up this time."

Salim laughed. "Don't worry, I've got it all under control."

Celia's ears burned. What on earth did he mean?

She gulped. He'd be horrified if he knew she was listening in on their private conversation.

"How, exactly, do you have it under control?" Elan's voice grew closer.

Celia shrank against the rock, its rough surface digging into her palms and knees.

"Isn't it obvious? She'll go back to the States, and I'll stay here."

"How does that solve anything?"

"It's a clean break."

"Yeah, except that's not what you need. She's the one, Salim. You know it, don't try to tell me different."

Salim laughed, but it wasn't a genuine laugh, more of a forced guffaw. "No, Elan. Your romantic American notions are touching, but Celia is not the one. I intend to marry Nabilah Al Sabah."

Celia's jaw dropped as her ribcage tightened around her painfully swollen heart.

"Who's Nabilah Al Sabah?" Elan's skepticism showed in his tone.

"She's the daughter of Sheikh Mohammad Al Sabah."

"The guy who owns that big shopping mall in Dubai."

"Among other things. He has a large retail empire."

"So this proposed marriage is something of a

business arrangement?'" Elan didn't try to hide his distaste.

"Not at all." Salim had the decency to sound offended. "I've chosen her because I think she will be an ideal wife and will make a good mother for our children."

"How many children do you two have together?"

Celia gulped.

"Don't be ridiculous. I've never even kissed her."

Elan laughed. "Then how do you know she'll be a suitable wife?"

"She comes from excellent stock."

Elan let out a long dismissive snort. "Brother of mine, you know I have a strong appreciation for excellent stock. I pay close attention to it—when selecting my stallions and mares. With women and marriage it's entirely different, let me assure you."

"I've been married before."

"Not successfully."

Celia's breathing was in danger of becoming

audible, as she crouched painfully against the rock, a few feet from the brothers. Sweat trickled down her face.

She heard some movement in the sand, and when they spoke again they were farther away.

"I was young then, and unprepared for the responsibilities of marriage and family. I tried to fulfill them as best I could, but only disappointed a wife who wanted an affectionate husband, as well as a reliable head of household."

"Because you were still crazy about Celia and didn't want to make love to another woman."

The long silence made Celia aware of the pounding of her own heart, louder than the surf hitting the sand a few yards away.

"At the time, yes."

"And what makes you think that will be different now?"

"Because I'm older and wiser. I've accepted that I cannot marry Celia and I must choose a suitable wife and do everything in my power to make the relationship work."

"Do you have any idea how insane that sounds?" Elan's incredulity rang across the sand.

Probably his own brother was the only person to express an honest opinion to a man as powerful and revered as Salim Al Mansur.

"Why can't you marry her?" Elan demanded.

"She's American, free-spirited, she doesn't care about tradition."

"I can tell you from personal experience that such women make very fine wives and mothers." She could almost hear Elan's grin.

"It's different with you and Sara. You live in America. Celia would never live here in Oman."

"How do you know? Have you asked her?"

"Of course not. Besides, she wouldn't fit in. You've seen how she dresses. She'd never go along with all the arcane social rules and regulations we have here."

"You certainly don't. At least from what I've observed so far. I've seen you drinking wine, for a start."

"I may not always agree with traditions, but as head of the family I have a duty to uphold the best of them. I'm proud of the customs and mores of our country, and I want my children to be raised accordingly."

"Brother." She heard a rustling sound, like Elan taking hold of Salim. "If you plan to marry another woman, then why are you playing around with Celia? Why did you bring her here?"

"To purge her from my system." He had the decency to sound sheepish.

Tears sprang to Celia's eyes.

He hadn't hired her because he wanted to revive their relationship, nor even because he wanted her landscape design expertise.

He'd hired her because he wanted to develop immunity to her.

"And how's that working for you?" Elan's snide tone gave Celia a moment of satisfaction.

"Fine."

Elan blew out a snort. "Yeah. Right."

They moved along the beach, and she had to

struggle to catch their words above the sound of the waves.

Still, she heard Salim's final words: "In two weeks she'll be gone. I promise, on my honor, that I'll never see her again."

Celia peeled herself back from the hard surface of the rock and for the first time let an audible whimper escape her mouth. Her skin stung where she'd pressed it against the uneven surface. Her whole body ached, sickened by a destructive cocktail of rage and pain.

How could she have let herself imagine—even for a moment—that there could be anything between them but steamy sex and temporary intimacy followed by heartbreak?

She'd fooled herself into thinking that she'd come here to tell Salim about Kira, and she hadn't accomplished even that.

I'm proud of the customs and mores of our country, and I want my children to be raised accordingly.

Wasn't that the reason she'd kept Kira secret? She knew Salim was a man of tradition—it was why he'd dumped her in the first place. She'd always suspected he'd insist his child be raised in Oman by him.

Without her.

Her heart forcefully rejected the notion.

Kira deserved to be raised by someone who cared about her, not a bunch of centuries-old customs.

Maybe she wouldn't tell him. She'd finish the job—she had a contract and she wouldn't break it—and then she'd leave.

Her chest filled with anger and hurt.

And then I promise, on my honor, I'll never see him again.

Six

Celia managed to avoid Salim and his family for the rest of the day. She spent time driving to nurseries, looking for the last few elusive plants she needed, and going over paperwork in her room. When the phone rang, she didn't answer it.

She ordered dinner in her room, and by 9:00 p.m. she was fairly confident of being left in peace for the rest of the night.

A knock on the door made her start.

She frowned. If it were Salim she'd say she

had a headache and send him packing. She certainly wasn't going to give him another chance to *purge her from his system.*

"Who is it?" she said in a forced whisper.

"It's Sara. Can I come in?"

Celia bit her lip. What did Sara want?

She couldn't think of a good reason to turn her away. "Sure." She unlocked the door with fumbling hands. "Come in. It's kind of messy. I've been catching up on some spreadsheets."

She had a printer hooked up to her laptop, and the results were spread unartistically over the large bed and part of the tiled floor.

Sara wore a simple silver-gray dress that accentuated her pretty roses-and-gold coloring. Her dark blond hair was pulled back into a ponytail. She smiled warmly at Celia. "We missed you at dinner. I was hoping to pick your brain about landscaping our house in Nevada. We have a heck of a time getting anything to grow because it's flaming hot in the summer and under several feet of snow in the winter."

Celia laughed, glad for the familiar subject

matter. "I always advise my clients to start with native plants. At least you know they'll grow."

"Yeah, but you can get tired of sagebrush. It's pretty much all there is and we have plenty of it already."

"How about a nice sculpture?" She lifted a brow.

"Elan's horses are the most beautiful sculptures. We've got plenty of those. I guess you're right and I should focus on what works. Who's this?"

Celia's heart almost stopped as Sara leaned forward and picked up a photo from the cluttered bedcover.

A picture of Kira that she'd been mooning over earlier that afternoon, reminding herself to count her blessings.

"Uh…Kira." Her brain had frozen, and it was all she could come out with.

Sara peered at the picture. "She's adorable." She glanced up at Celia, expectant.

"Yes," managed Celia. She turned to stack

some scattered papers, as fear stung her fingertips.

"She looks a lot like Ben." Sara tilted her head, holding the picture at arm's length. "He's a boy, of course, and I can tell from the dress that this is a girl, despite the short hair, but there's a striking similarity about their eyes and the shape of their mouth."

"Oh." Celia pretended to busy herself shoving papers into a manila folder, while her pulse drummed at her temples.

The long silence finally made her turn to look at Sara.

Who stared right at her.

"She's your daughter, isn't she?"

"Yes." The simple word exploded from her mouth.

What mother could deny her own child?

Sara blurred as tears sprang to Celia's eyes.

"I knew it immediately." Sara pressed a hand to her mouth for a moment, staring at the picture. "She looks so like Salim. She is Salim's, isn't she?"

Celia nodded mutely.

"She looks like you, too. You can tell she'll have your lovely bone structure. And what a sweet smile. I think that's yours, too."

She handed the picture back to Celia, who accepted it with shaking fingers.

"Salim doesn't know about her, does he?" Sara's voice dropped, serious.

"He doesn't. I wanted to tell him. I was going to…but…."

"How old is she? She looks about two in that picture."

"She just turned three. She's started nursery school. She's living with my parents in Connecticut while I'm here."

The useless facts did nothing to cover over the bald reality that she'd kept her daughter's existence from the girl's own father.

"You have to tell him." Sara's intense stare— her eyes were an unusual pale green color—did not brook contradiction.

"I'm not so sure." Celia tucked the photo into her shirt pocket, and wiped her perspiring hands on the back of her jeans. "Sometimes it seems like a good idea, then something happens and..." She trailed off.

Heat rose to her cheeks as she recalled the humiliating confidences overheard on the beach that morning.

"What are you afraid of?" Sara rose and put a cool hand on Celia's arm. "I haven't known him long, but Salim's obviously a good man."

"He could take her. It's the law here—in any Islamic country, I think. A child belongs to its father."

"He wouldn't do that. Besides, from what I know, even in cases of divorce the child lives with its mother until it's eight or so. One of our business partners from Saudi told me that."

"Would you be willing to give up Hannah when she turns eight?" Tears threatened and were audible in Celia's voice.

"God, no." The very thought seemed to make Sara shiver. "Still, to not tell him..." She looked up at Celia, still holding her arm. "It took me a while to pluck up the courage to tell Elan about

Ben. I was his assistant at the time and our liaison had been a total accident—just one night, with no prospect of any relationship. He was so horrified by his lapse of judgment that he left the country afterward for several days without even telling me. I was sure I'd lose my job and be left pregnant with no health insurance. It wasn't easy, that's for sure, but I told Elan the truth, and look how wonderfully things have turned out." She shone a warm gaze on Celia. "That could happen for you and Salim."

Celia swallowed. "I don't think so."

"Why not? I know Salim wants to get married. He's absolutely charmed by Ben and Hannah and has said several times that he can't wait to have children. And—" she squeezed Celia's arm "—anyone would have to be blind not to notice that he's madly in love with you."

Celia blew out. "He isn't, really. We can't keep our hands off each other, and then it ends in tears. Trust me, it's a been-there-done-that situation."

"I don't know what's happened between you

in the past, but I truly believe things will be different if you tell him about his daughter."

"So we can get married and be a happy family?" Celia's voice rose to something between a whine and laugh. "Never happen. He likes me between his sheets, but I'm not what he considers suitable wife material."

"Perhaps he needs to have some sense drummed into him. As Elan said on the beach that day, sometimes the Al Mansur men can be a tad slow on the uptake. But they need our help. They had a deprived childhood."

"All that money can buy and very little else."

"At least after their mother died. They had no family life, just a cruel father bossing them around. No one helped them grow up into decent family men. Salim's proud and stubborn, I can see that, but he's got a good heart beating under that long white robe he wears. I think you can dig past all the baggage and find your way into it. Especially once he knows you share a beautiful daughter."

"Oh, boy." Celia shoved a hank of hair off her face. "I do want to tell him, but…" The overheard conversation made doubts stretch out like shadows. "Maybe Salim would prefer not to know. He has a whole life planned out. One without me in it."

"You know what? It doesn't matter what he has planned. Seriously, it's not fair to keep something like that a secret. It's not fair to your daughter, either. Kira will want to know her father one day. Why not now, when there's still a bright future possible for all of you?"

Celia inhaled a shaky breath. Sarah's words struck a painful chord of truth inside her. Not that they could live happily ever after, but that she had to tell him, no matter what.

"I'm not optimistic about the bright future, but I swear I'll tell him tomorrow, come hell or high water."

Sara smiled. "I guess either is a possibility, given that we're in a burning desert and on a beach at the same time." She gave Celia's arm a supportive squeeze. "Elan and I will be here for you. Everything will turn out okay."

Doubt sent a cold shiver down Celia's spine. "I hope so."

Celia called Salim on his cell first thing in the morning. She didn't even say hello. She didn't want to lose her nerve. "Can we drive to the site together at nine?"

"Um, I have a meeting at ten and a... Perhaps Hanif can drive you."

"Can you meet me at the site?" Maybe that was better. Less chance of causing a major road accident.

"Sure, I can be there by four. I'll drive you home."

"Fine." She hung up, fingers trembling. No turning back now.

As four o'clock rolled around she began to regret not telling him back at the hotel. At least there it was cool and she didn't have grit under her fingernails and no place to wash it out. She shoved a lock of damp hair off her forehead.

Luckily there weren't many people around as she'd sent her staff home early. The construction crews had knocked off for the day. A few painters and electricians worked here and there in the complex of elegant white buildings.

The muffled purr of an expensive engine made her skin prickle.

I have something to tell you.

How did you come out and say it? Each time she tried to find the words, it sounded more dramatic and shocking, and she felt more ashamed that she'd kept the truth to herself for so long.

The engine stopped.

He's here. No turning back now.

She strode toward the parking area in front of the future "marketplace" with her head held high and her courage screwed down tight. "Hi!" She hoped her breezy wave hid the sheer terror throbbing in her veins.

Salim climbed from the car with a warm smile. "Hello, Celia. Things have been busy the last couple of days. I've missed you."

He wore khakis and a white shirt with

the sleeves rolled up, looking deceptively Westernized and infuriatingly handsome. His dark eyes flashed with pleasure, as if he was genuinely pleased to see her.

Which she knew he wasn't. He just wanted to flush her out of his system like a nasty virus.

Shame he was about to find it had lingering effects—like fatherhood.

"Salim, there's something I have to tell you." Her heart hammered against her ribs.

"Oh?" He cocked his head, his expression quizzical. He strode closer, the outline of his sturdy thighs visible inside the thin khakis. A smile tugged at his powerful mouth. "I'm all ears."

If only he was. Ears would be a lot easier to deal with than bronzed muscle and chiseled cheekbones. "Three years ago…" Her voice trailed off.

Come on, you can do it.

"Yes?"

"A little over three years ago, I had a baby."

His eyes narrowed. "What?"

"A baby. I gave birth." Why on earth was she explaining like an idiot? He knew what a baby was.

"I don't understand." His proud bearing had stiffened, as if he knew something was up, but he couldn't figure out what.

Celia swallowed hard. "After our…reunion at the Ritz Carlton, I learned I was pregnant."

His lips parted, but no words came out.

"We have a daughter. Her name is Kira."

"Impossible." The word shot from his mouth.

Celia felt like she'd been slapped. "It's not only possible, it happened."

"You never mentioned a child." He spoke slowly, as if trying to unravel a mystery.

"I didn't mention her at the time because you were too busy brushing me off like a piece of lint. I tried to tell you. I called your office twice, and all I got in return was a brusque message reminding me that our weekend fling was over, and we'd better get back to our normal lives.

So I did, except by then my normal life had a growing baby in it."

Salim blew out a long breath. "A baby?"

"Yes, the human kind, with two legs and two arms. And dark hair and eyes exactly like yours."

"It can't be mine."

Her spine stiffened. "She's not an it. She's a sweet and funny little girl."

His proud forehead creased. "We always used…protection."

"Apparently it wasn't effective." Her blood heated. How could he argue with her about this?

There was incontrovertible proof. She reached into the back pocket of her jeans and pulled out the photo Sara had seen in her room. She held it out, hand shaking.

Salim looked at the picture like a snake that might bite. Or perhaps a scorpion.

His chest rose as he took in the image. She watched him frown as he raised it to his eyes and stared for a full minute. "*Alhamdulillah.* She is mine."

He didn't take his eyes off the picture. Adrenaline and emotion made Celia so punchy she had to fight the urge to scold him for doubting her.

When he finally looked up, his eyes were wide, stunned. "You should have told me."

"I wanted to, but you didn't let me."

He raised a broad hand and wiped it over his face. "Three years old, and I never knew she existed. You should have found a way." He growled with indignation.

Which only fuelled her own.

"Why? So you could try to take her away from me? You'd made it abundantly clear that you had no interest in pursuing a relationship with me."

And she knew from the previous morning's conversation with Elan that nothing had changed on that score.

She drew in a shaky breath. "I wanted to protect her. To protect myself."

* * *

Salim's brain felt numb, stunned by this new and shocking revelation.

A daughter.

The picture was all the proof he needed. Unmistakably a member of the Al Mansur family, the toddler already bore the distinctive mouth they'd all inherited from their mother.

How could Celia keep his own daughter a secret?

She trembled, despite the heat. Anxiety tightened the lines of her lovely face and wound her hands together.

He fought the urge to reach out and reassure her. "You didn't trust me."

"How could I? You'd betrayed me once already, when you married another woman without even telling me. Then I got my hopes up again and…" She closed her mouth as if anxious to stop the flow of words that revealed too much.

"I had no idea. How could I?"

"You could have asked." Her bright gaze

blazed with accusation. "You didn't care how I was doing, if I was even alive, as long as I was out of your life."

The ugly truth made his skin prickle. Celia got under his skin and made him itch and burn late at night. She made him ache in a way no salves or cold compresses could cure.

And he'd been looking for that cure for years.

"I was just trying to be practical, sensible." He frowned. What was the sensible course of action now?

He could handle executive problem solving—troubleshooting and issuing orders—but this situation called for tact and delicacy beyond his command.

A daughter. His own child.

Something clawed at his heart, a sense of desperation. His own child was out there, somewhere, without even knowledge of her father.

His anger—mingled with the strong emotions Celia always roused in him—made him want to shout and accuse her, but he knew that was foolish and counterproductive.

Celia brushed a stray wisp of hair from her high forehead. "I was also trying to be practical. It seemed best for both of us. I raise Kira and support her, and you get back to the life you were so keen to keep me out of."

Salim blew out hard. "It's not that I *wanted* to keep you out of my life, it's that…"

That what?

A vision of his lovely Celia, holding his child—their child—in her arms, assaulted his brain. Unnameable feelings, powerful and hypnotic, stole all words from his mouth.

The sound of an engine made them both turn. A black Mercedes pulled up the curved brick road near them and stopped.

A rear door opened and a woman, dressed in yellow-and-black with a scarf revealing only a few inches of her glossy black hair, stepped out.

He stifled a curse. "A friend of mine. I told her to come here to look around sometime. I had no ıdea she'd come now. I suppose someone at the office told her I was here."

Surely the universe was playing some kind of joke on him. He'd been formally courting Nabilah Al Sabah for months and she'd shown no interest in visiting the site. Now that his careful plans for the future had been tossed to the desert wind, she appeared like an ill omen.

This situation was certainly beyond even his considerable competence. As Nabilah walked toward them, elegant silk billowing in the wind, he decided to leave it to the fates to sort things out.

He tucked the precious photo in his pocket and crossed his arms over his chest.

"Nabilah. I'm glad you were finally able to come see the results of all our hard work."

"I've been dying to come for ages. I should have asked for better directions. My driver got lost twice on the way!"

Nabilah had a smile fixed to her beautiful face like it was painted on. Salim had thought this a charming feature in a young lady—until Celia appeared with her ready and mischievous grin.

"Celia, this is my…friend, Nabilah Al Sabah."

Celia's whole body stiffened. Which was odd. He'd never so much as mentioned Nabilah or his future plans, to Celia.

"Nabilah, this is Celia Davidson. She's the landscape architect for the project and…an old and dear friend of mine." The unexpected need to affirm his relationship with Celia took him by surprise.

Both ladies looked appropriately alarmed as they shared a cautious handshake.

Salim experienced a sudden, intense urge to vanish into the hot desert air.

He decided to act on it.

"I must go. Celia, please give Nabilah a tour of the site." He shot her a meaningful glance.

He had no idea at all what it meant. Probably something like *I can't believe you just told me I have a daughter. Help.*

Not, perhaps, the most heroic approach, but

better than several alternatives that threatened the gathered trio.

Celia swallowed. "Sure." Her voice was hollow.

"Salim, I'd hoped you would give me a tour yourself." Nabilah's treacly voice sent a crawl of aversion down his spine. Why had he never noticed that arrogant tilt to her eyebrows before?

"Another time, perhaps. I'm afraid I must run. Celia, I'll send Hanif to pick you up."

"Don't worry, I brought my own car. I suspected I might need it." Her cool gaze told him to get lost.

And he was more than ready to do so.

Fighting the urge to literally run, he nodded to the two beautiful, frowning women and strode for his car.

A daughter.

Kira.

A fist of emotion clutched his heart. A little girl, with big brown eyes and a dimpled chin, who needed a father's love.

He'd always suspected there was something

real—magical and painful at the same time—but undeniable, between him and Celia.

And there was. Now he'd seen her with his own eyes.

He couldn't feel more disoriented if his world had literally turned upside down and he'd banged his head on the hot desert floor. The unrelenting sun beat down on him from the bright sky, just the way it always did, but suddenly everything had changed.

Everything.

His life would never be the same again. He was sure of it.

"Men." Celia shrugged. "Just when you really need them, they turn and run."

She glanced at Nabilah to gauge her reaction. The other woman was as tall as she was. Her traditional attire fluttered against a slender yet flawlessly female body.

Nabilah Al Sabah was breathtakingly beautiful. She laughed, a melodious tinkle of sound.

No doubt that was the appropriate reaction for a woman of taste.

Celia fought to control the adrenaline charging through her veins. This was the woman Salim had chosen instead of her. "Well, where shall we start?"

"Wherever you prefer." Nabilah's smooth, unlined face revealed nothing but pleasure.

"How about right here?" She swept her arm around, to encompass the space of the marketplace. "As you can see the buildings are up, but still need a few finishing touches. Nearly all of the plantings are in the ground at this point. We're working on getting them established so we can remove any stakes and other unsightly props before the hotel opens."

"Fascinating." Nabilah beamed with more distilled delight. "I've always been intrigued by desert horticulture."

Celia didn't believe a word of it. "Your English is very good."

"It should be. I had a private tutor in the language for six years. I also speak French, Spanish and Japanese. It's important to be well-versed in world languages, don't you think?"

"Oh, yes." Celia mustered a chilly smile. "I often wish I spoke Chinese. One of these days I must learn. What aspect of our project are you interested in?"

She'd been unable to resist the possessive "our." A catty female urge to lay claim to Salim crept through her and sharpened her claws.

Which was idiotic, since this was the woman he intended to marry.

"Oh, I'm interested in all of it." She shone Celia a syrupy smile. "A lost city in the sands. Rather a fairy tale, don't you think?"

"Not a fairy tale at all, I assure you. It's quite genuine. It looks brand-new with all the fresh stucco, but underneath the bright veneer the bones of the old city are still there."

"Along with the history of Salim's family. His mother's family, anyway. I believe his father moved here from Egypt."

Celia hid her surprise. She'd never heard any mention of Egypt in his past. But why would she? Salim told her nothing about his family history. He'd never intended for her to be part of it.

Her heart sank even lower in her chest.

"His mother's family is very ancient. They controlled most of this area at one time. Their lineage dates back thousands of years." Nabilah lifted her proud head to survey the landscape.

"I think everyone's lineage dates back thousands of years, to the beginning of mankind. We wouldn't be here if it didn't."

"You know what I mean." Nabilah adjusted her headscarf to display more of her luxuriant dark hair. "They were influential."

Like your darling daddy, no doubt. Celia struggled to keep her claws sheathed. "Are you from Salalah?"

"Oh, no." Nabilah's laugh dismissed this idea as ridiculous. "I grew up in Muscat, the capital. For the last few years we've been living in Dubai. Salalah's so sleepy by comparison."

"It's spectacularly beautiful, though, don't you think?"

Celia was beginning to wonder whether Salim had chosen his bride carefully. He openly adored Salalah.

"People do go on about the mountains, and they are unusual for the Arabian Peninsula, but nothing like Switzerland, let's face it. Have you been to Switzerland?"

She clearly expected Celia to say no, and busied herself with rearranging her black-and-yellow finery.

"Yes, I designed the grounds for a bank headquartered in Zurich. Would you like to see the pool area?" She shot a bright smile at Nabilah.

Her rival's eyes narrowed for a split second. "A pool out here in the middle of nowhere? How quaint. I suppose it is just a hotel, after all." She strode alongside Celia, elegant nose high. "Salim said you were old friends. How did you meet?"

Her breezy tone didn't fool Celia.

Who couldn't resist turning the knife.

"Oh, we've been friends for donkey's years. We met back in college."

"That is a long time ago." Her voice dripped with the first hint of deliberate malice.

Celia stifled a chuckle. "Yes, Salim and I are both ancient."

That tinkling laugh. "Oh, that's not what I meant at all! Though, I am rather younger." She cleared her throat. "And you've kept in touch all this time?"

Ah. Now she's getting down to business. "On and off. I guess that thread of connection has always been there."

Though most of the time I'd have liked to strangle him with it.

"I don't imagine you'll see each other again once the project is over." Nabilah stared straight ahead, at the dry concrete shell of the empty pool.

Celia's stomach clenched. "What makes you say that?" she blurted, before she could stop herself.

"As a married man he won't be gallivanting

all over the world consorting with all kinds of people." She said the last words with marked distaste.

But it was the words "a married man" that jolted Celia. Nabilah was laying claim to Salim, and warning her off.

"He didn't tell me he was getting married," she said, as calmly as possible. She walked around the curved pool, lined by lush palms, which would soon shade guests basking in lounge chairs.

Nabilah's laugh echoed off the bare concrete. "Oh, yes, everyone knows that Salim and I are getting married. It's a perfect match. A profitable union of two important families and two successful businesses."

She turned her elegant profile to survey the guest cottages around the pool. Her perfect nose wrinkled. "I don't imagine we'll be spending much time here, though. No matter how much you paint and plant it, it's still a howling wilderness."

Celia frowned. "Thousands of people have

lived and laughed and eaten and slept in this place. Soon, thousands more will come. Can't you feel the energy?"

Her skin prickled with it. It wrapped itself around her as soon as she came to the site. The buzz and hum of humanity lingered in the air even when the workers had left for the day. Even the hot desert sand whispered with the bustle of life.

Nabilah laughed again, a tinny sound that hurt Celia's ears. "I think the unaccustomed heat is affecting your brain."

"Salim loves this place." She said it slowly, watching Nabilah's striking features for a reaction.

Nabilah simply waved her hand in the air. "Men fall in love with whatever wanders in front of them. Sometimes they make quite ludicrous choices." She adjusted her headscarf. "Besides, we'll be living in Dubai. Daddy is building me a house on one of the palm frond islands. I doubt we'll spend much time in Oman."

Celia stared, unable to formulate a response.

She was pretty sure Salim had no idea of his future wife's plans.

Then again, there was the possibility that if he married Nabilah, he fully deserved to be miserable.

Something he might deserve anyway, just for leaving her alone here with this woman.

An uncomfortable knot formed in her stomach. He'd been so shocked by her news he hadn't been able to stay and act normal.

He'd just learned he had a daughter.

How would Nabilah Al Sabah react to that news?

Nabilah marched around the empty pool. "I think it will be good for Salim to get away from past associations and influences. The world of business can bring one into contact with all kinds of inappropriate people." She cast a dismissive glance at Celia's work attire.

"Like me, you mean?" She couldn't help herself.

Nabilah raised a sculpted brow. "I hardly

think that Salim's association with you is significant."

Celia's lips parted in astonishment as the rude comment stung her.

Except that we have a child together.

She had to marshal all her self-control to keep the words in her mouth. She wanted desperately to whip out the picture of Kira and watch Nabilah's reaction as the monkey wrench of reality clanked down into the perfectly oiled machinery of her future plans.

Then she recoiled at the very idea. Kira wasn't a pawn to be played in a jealous game of one-upmanship. She was a little girl who depended on Celia to protect her and keep her safe.

And Salim had taken the picture with him.

"You must excuse me, but I believe my insignificant presence is expected back in Salalah," Celia murmured. "I do hope you don't mind me cutting our tour short."

"Not in the least." Nabilah lifted her neat chin. "I've seen enough already." She brushed imaginary dust from her silk-clad arm with an expression of distaste. "I doubt you and I will see each other again."

"I certainly hope not." Celia flashed a bright smile.

As Nabilah turned, she regretted her rash rudeness. What if Salim did marry Nabilah? She'd be forced to endure that woman's smirk as she shared her own child with her.

She shivered with revulsion.

The truth was out and the wheels of fate were turning. She bit her knuckle hard, hoping and praying with every fiber of her body that she and Kira wouldn't be crushed under them.

Seven

Celia had barely pulled into the forecourt of the hotel when Salim appeared. Brows lowered, he approached the still-moving car.

She stopped in front of the valet and climbed out, trying to look normal while blood thundered through her veins.

"We must talk." Salim's low voice revealed nothing of his emotions.

"Of course," she replied, attempting to sound businesslike.

"Come with me." He turned and strode along

a walk toward the beach. Bright blue sea glittered beyond the white sand.

Paradise.

Except that it felt more like hell. "Are you still angry?" She kept her voice low, not wanting to cause a scene in front of the employees.

Or maybe she should cause a scene? She deserved one.

He'd used her again, with every intention of casting her aside.

He'd left her to entertain his future bride.

She certainly had every right to the anger that simmered in her belly.

"No, I'm not angry." He turned and shot a glance in her direction. His stern gaze did nothing to comfort her. "It was my fault that you didn't tell me. I can see that now."

He waited for her to catch up with him. For an instant his arm twitched, as if he planned to thread it through hers, but he didn't. "What happened and didn't happen is in the past. We must talk about the future."

Celia nodded. Her stomach tightened.

The future shimmered with frightening possibilities.

"I apologize for abandoning you with Nabilah." A wry glance softened his grim expression. "I suspect you two had a lot to talk about."

"Not really." Celia swallowed. "I didn't say anything about Kira, if that's what you mean. She did tell me you two are getting married." She lifted her chin and braced for his reaction.

He frowned. "Nothing is formally arranged."

His cool reply, so formal and unemotional, flipped the cap off her hurt feelings.

"It wasn't *formal* yet? You slept with me while you were promised to someone else!" Her rasped whisper shot through the air. "How could you do that?"

"I'm not promised to her or anyone else."

"She seemed to think you were." She wanted to mention the conversation she'd overheard on the beach, but that would reveal too much. "Did you know she expects you to move to Dubai and live on one of those dredged islands in the shape of a palm tree?"

The look of horror that flashed across Salim's face should have made her laugh. But she was in no mood for laughing.

He inhaled sharply. "What I did was wrong."

"You were wrong to sleep with me? Or wrong to leave me to entertain your intended bride?" The words shot from her tongue. She glanced around to see if anyone heard. They were almost out on the sand now, and few people were nearby.

"Both." Salim narrowed his eyes. "I apologize sincerely. Leaving you with Nabilah was terrible, but I didn't have the mental reserves to pretend everything was normal right then."

"Why pretend? What is normal, anyway?"

Salim stared at her. "Nothing is normal. Everything has changed." He shoved a hand through his dark hair. "I don't know where to start, or should I say, how to proceed, since everything between us started so long ago."

He looked out at the ocean. Its blue, endless depths shimmered in the blazing sun.

Then he turned back to her. "I must meet our daughter."

The pronouncement, swift and certain, deprived her of speech. His dark eyes shone with excitement. "I've missed so much time with her already, and I ache to meet her."

A throb of emotion echoed deep inside Celia. Excitement mingled with fear. "She's so lively and curious and affectionate. And she'll be so thrilled to meet you."

His brow furrowed. "What does she know about me?"

"Nothing, really." Celia's voice sounded thin. "She's been too young to understand until lately. Now she's noticed that her friends have daddies and that she doesn't, but I don't think she's figured out the right questions to ask."

"She'll be able to ask me any question she likes." His expression brightened. "I've had plenty of practice with little Ben. He has a very inquisitive mind." A smile tugged at the edges of his mouth. "Can I keep the picture of her?"

"Sure. You can have it. I'll print out another."

Salim pulled the now-crumpled image out of his pocket and held it gingerly, like something precious.

"She has your smile. And I think she has your infectious optimism."

"Me? I don't think I'd call myself that optimistic. If I had been, I'd have told you about her." She glanced up at him, wary.

He rubbed his other hand over his mouth, staring at the picture. "You wanted to protect her. I don't blame you. I hurt you and you didn't want her to experience that pain." He glanced up at her, eyes black with emotion. "I promise you I won't do anything to hurt her."

Or you.

She read the words in his gaze.

"Would you join me for dinner tonight? Somewhere private. We can talk and…figure things out."

"Or try to figure things out." Celia crossed her arms over her chest, which swelled with some relief that he was at least being honest and admitting the situation was tricky and the way forward unclear. The future was all any of them had, and it was her responsibility to make Kira's future as bright as possible, regardless of her own reservations. "Okay."

"I'll pick you up at your room."

Celia was scrubbing the last of the day's grit from under her fingernails with a nailbrush when she heard a knock on the door of her suite. Was he early? She hadn't finished getting ready. She strode toward the door. "Come in."

She heard someone struggling with the handle. The kids? She hurried to open the door and was greeted by a wall of flowers.

"Delivery for Miss Davidson," came a muffled voice behind the barrage of lilies and orchids. Celia's eyes fixed on a particularly rare speckled orchid just center left of the design. The delivery man staggered into the room and carefully lowered the enormous bouquet onto a polished table. "There's a card."

He handed it to her, bowed and vanished, before she thought to tip him.

They've got to be from Salim. She should be mad at him for having rare orchids yanked from their habitat just to mollify her, but oh, boy.... Lush leaves wound through stunning specimen blooms, creating a magical garden that rose like smoke from a hand-painted vase.

"Celia, I can't apologize enough for my behavior this afternoon. Please accept these flowers as an offering of contrition." Handwritten in a familiar black script.

She couldn't resist a smile. What an offering. And a detailed note from the florist explained that these were hand-raised blooms, not wild specimens. It also gave a detailed history of each unique flower—further investigation revealed that their roots were in water so they could be repotted and kept alive—that kept Celia riveted for a full fifteen minutes, almost causing her to forget about getting ready. How well he knew her!

Another knock on the door made her drop the

note card. "It's me, Sara," she heard through the heavy wood.

Celia tugged open the door to see Sara grinning. "You told him."

"I finally did. Thank you for pushing me."

"He admitted to Elan that he refused to believe you, then he abandoned you in the desert with Nabilah Al Sabah."

"All true." She tried not to smile as she gestured to the flowers. "This forest is his idea of an apology."

Sara raised a brow. "I'm glad it's big. It should be. Still, he's very excited."

"I know. It took a while for the idea to sink in, but I think he's really warming to the idea of being a father."

"He'll be an awesome dad," Sara said with a smile.

Celia's shoulders tightened. How would that work? Could one be an "awesome dad" on occasional visiting weekends, or even extended summer vacations?

"I'm having dinner with him tonight," Celia

said. "Hopefully we'll figure out some of the details. I know he wants to meet her as soon as possible." Her stomach contracted again. There was so much to worry about.

"Of course he does. And she'll have him wrapped around her plump pinky in seconds," Sara added.

"Speaking of seconds, he'll be arriving in a few and I'm still not ready. I'd better at least put some aloe on my sunburn."

"You look radiant."

"I suspect being on the verge of hysterics has that effect."

Sara chuckled. "You can't fool me. You're a tough customer who can handle whatever life lobs her way."

"Yeah, like a dozen rare orchids in a froth of lilies."

"Or an Al Mansur man."

Celia shot a doubtful glance at her. Just then, a knock sounded on the door.

"You look ravishing," whispered Sara. "Enjoy your evening."

"Hopefully I'll survive," murmured Celia with raised brows. She turned to face the door. "Come in!"

Sara smiled and waved as Salim entered. "Yes, there's a conspiracy in progress," she confessed.

"What nonsense!" protested Celia.

Salim looked unfortunately devastating in crisp, dark pants and a collarless linen shirt.

Celia drew in a silent breath. "I'm almost ready. I just keep getting interrupted." She shot a wry glance at Sara. "Will you excuse me a moment?"

Without waiting for a reply, she darted to the bathroom and slammed the door. The enormous mirror revealed a face that was indeed glowing, with either good health or total panic.

She slapped some mascara on her sun-bleached eyelashes and brightened her lips with gloss. There was no need for blush on her hot, pink cheeks, so she quickly twisted her hair up into a knot and stuck a couple of pins in it.

Ack. I look like I'm getting ready for a date.

This was not a date. This was dinner with a man who'd trampled on her heart and smashed it flat.

Again.

At least she was one hundred percent sure she wasn't going to sleep with him tonight.

She burst out of the bathroom, a cheery smile fixed to her face. Sara had gone. Salim stood alone, apparently relaxed and pleased to see her, in front of the elaborate arrangement of flowers.

"The flowers are lovely," she said.

"You know they're alive? I suspected you'd hate cut flowers."

"You're absolutely right. Plants are only beautiful when they're alive and growing."

That bouquet had probably cost as much as the GDP of several developing nations, but she managed not to comment on that. It was the gesture that counted. "Do you want to see more pictures of Kira?"

"I'd love to." His voice was gruff with enthusiasm.

She reached for the mini-album she took on trips. It was freshly updated with pictures from her last return home: Kira rolling in the snow; building a tower of blocks; playing a toddler game on the computer and—her favorite thing— talking on her pink cell phone. In each picture her eyes glowed with joy and interest.

"She's a busy girl. She makes the most of every moment. And have you noticed she has far more fashion sense than me?" She gestured to a picture of Kira in an outfit composed of four different kinds of stripes. "She likes to set a trend."

"She's perfect." Salim sounded almost breathless. "Anyone can see how happy she is. You've obviously given her a warm and nurturing family environment."

"You've met my parents. They're sweethearts. And they have a lot of energy for people in their sixties. Which is good since they need it to keep up with Kira. She loves the outdoors. She told me this morning that she's building a garden in the snow for me."

"She's thoughtful, too." A smile tugged at his mouth. He stared at each picture for a long time. He was enchanted. "She'll be great friends with Ben."

Celia frowned. How would Kira meet Ben? Would she have to bring Kira here? She wasn't sure such a long flight was a good idea—or even survivable—with a toddler. Though Sara and Elan had obviously managed. It was probably easier when there were two grown-ups.

Salim apparently noticed her hesitation. "Let's go to dinner."

Celia had never seen the roof garden. Available for rental by the day or hour, it was a popular spot for lavish weddings. As she left the elevator—which opened directly onto the roof—she could see why.

White marble glittered in the last rays of sun. Porticos of pointed arches ringed the wide terraces, framing a stunning view out toward the watery horizon, where colorful fishing dhows returned to port with the day's catch, or set out to cast nets under the moon.

An elegant white gazebo shaded a single table, set for two. A bottle of champagne sat open in a bucket of ice, and a brass pot brimmed with white lilies in the center of the gleaming linen tablecloth.

"I figured we'd have some privacy up here. I asked the chefs to leave us a buffet to pick from." Elegant dishes piled with tasty hors d'oeuvres sat on two small tables that flanked the main dining table. Marinated shrimp kebabs rested on a steaming bed of saffron rice.

"Kira loves shrimp." Celia picked up a plate and helped herself to the delicacies.

"Does she? That sounds very sophisticated."

"Of course she's sophisticated. She's your daughter." The words sounded strange—but wonderful—coming from her mouth, like they'd been bursting to be free this whole time.

"So she is. Tell me more. Does she sleep well, or does she wake up all the time, like Hannah?"

He glanced up, almost shyly, from spooning braised vegetables on his plate.

"Oh, she was a terror as a baby. She woke so many times during the night that finally I just let her sleep with me in my bed."

Salim laughed. "That's the norm in most countries."

"So my friends kept reassuring me. Anyway, around nine months I finally convinced her that her crib wasn't a prison cell by putting her there for naps. She loved a music box I hung on it that played 'Rock-a-bye Baby.' Pretty soon I got her sleeping in there at night, too, and soon she slept like a log, right until morning."

"That must have been a relief." He pulled her chair back and seated her at the table. His elbow brushed hers as she slid past him, and unwelcome heat shimmered over her skin.

"I didn't know what to do with myself. It was a couple of months before I actually grew bold enough to sleep through the night."

Salim filled her tall flute with champagne. His eyes sparkled more than the golden liquid. "And

I was enjoying uninterrupted nights of peace the whole time. I suppose I should thank you for that." He raised his glass. "To you, Celia, for bringing Kira into the world and taking good care of her."

Celia clinked her glass against his, a little nervous. She didn't hear any accusation in his voice, but surely it had to be there. By her deception, she'd deprived him of the first years of his daughter's life.

But Salim glowed with enthusiasm. "Does she go to school?"

"She's only three. School in the U.S. doesn't start until age five. She goes to a kind of nursery-school-day care now. She loves it there. She likes to be around people, in the center of the action."

"She'd love a hotel, then, wouldn't she?"

"Um, sure. I suspect she would." This was the next step. Where they'd meet. Somehow she hadn't dared to think that far ahead.

"Will you bring her here? Next week perhaps?" The hopeful look in his dark eyes tugged at something inside her.

"It's a long flight. It might be better if you came to Connecticut."

"But she must see her country. And she can meet Elan's family. They're staying until the end of the month. Think how much fun it would be for her to play with Hannah and Ben."

Celia bit her lip. "It would be nice for her to visit. Let me think about the logistics and come up with a plan."

They chatted about the hotel and the final changes to be made at the lost city site, as well as about Kira, and the air between them crackled with excitement. Candles glowed around them as the sun set behind the liquid horizon, and bright stars and a slim crescent moon decorated the dark canopy overhead.

They rose from the table to fetch coffee from an elaborate urn on one side of the roof garden, but Celia was arrested by the shimmering lights of Salalah down below. "It's strangely quiet up here. It almost feels like we're in a magic kingdom up in the clouds."

"We are." Salim shot her a sly glance. "Except this one's man-made. You worked the magic to bring the lost city to life. It was nothing but empty buildings and unnamed streets. Now leaves rustle in the wind and cast lively shadows on the paths. The scent of nectar fills the air and brings bees and birds out into the desert again. And with even more powerful magic, you've brought me a daughter."

Celia's eyes widened. "It's not really magic."

"Nature is magical, don't you think?" A look of enchantment replaced his usually stern demeanor. "You think you know what to expect, what the usual rhythms and seasons are, when it will rain and when it will be dry, then suddenly…" He fixed her with a dark gaze that stole her breath. "Everything changes."

Celia's skin tingled under his intense stare. Was it magic that crackled in the air between them? Or something altogether more predictable? Her fingertips vibrated with the urge to wind into his soft linen shirt.

"You've always brought magic into my life, Celia. I've just been too blind to see it. Or too busy looking for something else."

"Oh, I don't know, I…" Her brain couldn't pull together a sensible thought. Her body was too overwhelmingly aware of his nearness.

He took a step closer and she could smell his scent in the dark: a rich, masculine fragrance that tormented her senses.

"We weave a spell together, you and I." His expression was serious, confused even, like he was trying to figure out some mystery. "It's dangerous, because I have no power to resist."

Before her scattered thoughts could gather into words, their lips met in a swift, fierce kiss. The simple sensation of his skin on hers brought a low murmur of relief that met and mingled in their mouths. In an instant her hands were fisted into his shirt, and his long, strong fingers slid around her back, pulling her closer.

Don't do this, screamed every last grain of sense left in her.

But her body didn't listen. Salim's solid arms felt like the only safe place in this confusing world where everything shifted and altered from minute to minute, and where dreams and nightmares seemed interchangeable.

I can't help it.

Her lips trembled with passion under his kiss. His hard body crushed deliciously to her breasts and belly. Her fingers wove into his thick hair as she inhaled the intoxicating scent of his skin. He was her first love and she'd never felt the same about anyone else.

Not even close.

His face lit up while she talked about Kira, and she saw once again the bright-eyed boy she'd fallen so hard in love with. The young man who'd held her tight in the privacy of her off-campus apartment, and told her he loved her.

She'd told him she loved him, too, and meant

it. Everything that had happened between then and now didn't change that one simple fact.

Their kiss deepened and she shuddered with longing as he wrapped his arms tight around her. Her fingers roamed into the collar of his shirt, feeling the strong shoulders that carried so much weight each day. Her skin ached to touch his, to claim the passion he always roused in her.

Salim's thick arousal pressed against her tummy, quickening her desire into a tight coil of need. She writhed against him, fighting the urge to unbutton his shirt and reveal the hot skin beneath.

Could this be a new start between them?

Salim was clearly thrilled to be a father, once he got over the initial shock. Maybe Sara was right and they really could be…a family.

The word caused a fierce pull of emotion deep in her chest. How much she'd love that for Kira. She'd enjoyed the support of two loving parents, and she still relied on both of them more than she could say. Would Kira grow up with that gift, now that the truth was out?

Salim caressed her, their lips still locked in silent, sensual communication. So much less complicated than the kind with words. She could feel the beat of his heart and the pulse of the emotion that ran between them like a spark jumping between two electrodes.

For a second the buzz of arousal seemed so intense that Celia wondered if they'd started a chemical reaction. Then she realized Salim's phone was vibrating.

"I told them to make sure I wasn't disturbed." Confusion and irritation warred on his handsome face.

"It might be important." Celia smoothed the front of her rumpled blouse as they moved apart.

Salim pressed a button and put the phone to his ear with a barked, "What?" Celia looked around, head still spinning with desire and emotion. "Don't be ridiculous. Don't you have your own life to worry about? Yeah. Fine. Good night, Elan."

He pushed the phone back into his pocket. A wry expression crept across his sensual mouth. "He wanted to make sure we weren't getting carried away."

"Uh-oh. Guilty as charged."

"He thinks it will mess things up between us."

"It usually does." She blew on a strand of hair that had escaped from her bun. "I think we should call it a night."

Salim pushed a hand through his disheveled hair. The moonlight revealed his frown of frustration. "All my baser instincts tell me otherwise, but I suppose you're right. We do have a tendency to get out of control."

"All that magic." She couldn't help smiling. "As you said, it's dangerous."

"In the best possible way." A smile crept across his mouth, revealing a sliver of his perfect white teeth. "But we are both rather on edge right now. I suppose my brother is right."

"He seems a sensible man." She blew out a breath. The collar of her dress was all twisted and her belt had slipped sideways. She tugged at them and tried to straighten the seams. "More than I can say for some." She glanced up.

Salim's eyes sparkled with mischief. "I'm perfectly sensible most of the time. In fact, I'd go so far as to say I'm the very model of prudence—except when a certain Celia Davidson is in evidence."

She shrugged. "Sorry. You might want to fix your shirt." She pointed to where two buttons had somehow come undone.

"See? My clothes even fall off when you're around."

"Nothing I can do. It's the magic." She blew on her fingers as if to disperse any dangerous rays that might be lingering there.

"Let me escort you to your room."

"I suspect it would be safer if I escorted myself there. But I promise, tomorrow I'll make arrangements to bring Kira here."

Salim's expression grew serious. He nodded, and excitement brightened his eyes and warmed her heart. "I can't wait."

Eight

Celia woke up in a cold sweat. The fan above her bed slashed in slow circles, swiping her with a breeze that made goose bumps rise on her skin.

She'd promised to bring Kira to Oman. She'd dreamed of this moment and dreaded it. She knew that, one way or another, it would change their lives forever.

A knock on the door made her clutch the damp sheets to her chest. "Who is it?"

"Sara. Can I come in, just for a sec?"

Celia grabbed the yellow silk kimono she used as a dressing gown and slipped it on. She opened the door and ushered Sara in. Her new friend's green eyes sparkled. "I heard it went well last night. I can't wait to meet Kira. Salim's so excited, it's adorable."

"Yes, I promised to bring her as soon as possible. In the blistering light of day, though, I'm nervous. He *is* really excited and I know he'll adore Kira. What if he won't let me take her home?"

Sara chewed her lower lip for a second. "What makes you so sure you'll want to go home?"

"You're getting carried away with romantic visions again, aren't you?" Celia put her hands on her hips.

"Well, did Elan's call interrupt anything, or not?"

Celia let out a long sigh. "It did, which I should be totally ashamed of, since it seems crazy under the circumstances."

"It's not crazy. The two of you have an undeniable connection. You're nervous, and trust mc, I know how scary it is when there's another life on the line, as well as yours. It made me defensive and anxious when Elan and I were trying to figure things out, but having a child together really does mean a lot. I realized that in the end. That's what made me decide to put my doubts aside and take a chance on the love we shared. You're a family now, whether you admit it or not."

Celia raised a brow. "He hasn't made any promises to me. He has all kinds of grand ideas about a suitable marriage and the respectable heir he's so set on. Kira's a girl, so she's not going to carry on the Al Mansur dynasty. Maybe he'll decide to keep her and marry that horrible Nabilah anyway." Her voice grew thin.

"Oh, come on, you don't really think he's capable of that, do you?"

Celia swallowed. "He left me to marry another woman once already. I'd be crazy to think it couldn't happen again. I'm a survivor, so I'm not worried about me...."

A sudden image of her heart, patched and

nailed with bits of soldered metal, filled her mind. "But I'm truly nervous about Kira. I can't just ignore the sharia laws. If he wants to take her from me, he can."

Sara walked farther into the room and crossed her arms over her chest, staring out the window. "Well. We're both businesswomen, so perhaps that's the way to approach the situation. He has screwed you over before, so you have a perfectly legitimate reason for caution." She spun and looked right at Celia. "How about a contract?"

"What do you mean?"

"A document in which you spell out exactly what you require. You must have the right to take Kira home as you see fit. Salim must relinquish the right to keep her here against your will."

Celia's eyes widened. "That'll make him furious."

"Only if he intends to hurt you. If he plans to tread carefully—as he certainly should—it won't be a problem."

"You're very optimistic."

"Let's just say I became optimistic the hard way." She winked. "You know what? I'll arrange it all. You go about your business and book the flights, and I'll draw up the contract. I do that all day long at work so it'll be easy as pie. I'll show it to you when it's done, and if you're on board with the terms, I'll take it to Salim myself."

Celia stared at her. "You'd do all that for me?"

"Not just you." She smiled. "For Salim, for Elan, for Hannah and Ben and for me. For all of us."

Thick warmth rose in Celia's chest. Could she and Kira really find a place in this growing family? "Okay."

Salim stared at the black-and-white printed words until they blurred. His blood heated at the idea of signing a contract relinquishing rights to his own flesh and blood. Rights that had been kept from him for far too long already.

Sara stood very still on the other side of the large desk in his office.

"Why are you asking me to sign this?" He glanced up at Sara. "Where's Celia?"

"She's working. I convinced her to tell you about Kira with the assurance that nothing bad would happen. Now I'm just making sure nothing bad does happen." Her innocent smile did nothing to conceal the sharp mind he'd heard so much about.

"Does Celia know about this? Did she tell you to make me sign away my rights?"

"She knows about it." Sara was calm, her gray-green eyes rarely blinking. She tilted her head. "You must admit it's only prudent. You've let Celia down before."

Salim recoiled from the accusation. "That was different. There were no commitments between us."

"And are there commitments between you now?" Sara lifted a slim brow.

"No formal arrangements, no." He bristled. How could she pry into his personal life at a time when even he didn't know what would happen from minute to minute?

"Maybe you should make some." Sara's eyes narrowed. "Celia has feelings, you know."

"She told you this?" He leaned forward in his chair, fighting the urge to get up and pace around the room.

"No. That's my personal view. Celia expects nothing from you at all. And why would she, given what's happened between you in the past?"

Salim shifted in his chair. "I had no choice. I had family obligations to fulfill."

"And have you fulfilled them?"

Her rhetorical question poked him like the tip of a sharp knife. He had failed in his one duty to take a proper wife and provide the Al Mansur house with an heir.

"No." Now he did rise, swiftly, and planted his hands on his desk. "I've made mistakes, done things I regret." He narrowed his eyes. This small woman wasn't the slightest bit intimidated by him. She formed her own opinions and spoke her mind readily.

And she made his brother very happy.

Elan had taken charge of his own destiny. He'd chosen the mate who captured his heart and they were building a happy life together.

Both Elan and Sara obviously thought he and Celia were meant to be together.

And was that so crazy? According to tradition and convention, yes. But according to his own desires, the needs and hopes that still ached in his time-hardened heart…

Signing this contract went against everything he'd ever been told about how to conduct himself as a man. He was taught to seize control and hold it tight. To set the agenda and ignore or banish those who objected.

But now the stakes were far too high.

His own daughter, Kira, was out there, looking at something with those big brown eyes—or were they closed tight in dream-filled sleep? Her plump cheeks might be creased in a smile.

A smile he'd never seen—and might never see if he chose to stand his ground.

Everything was different now. He was different. And he couldn't wait to meet his little daughter.

"I'll sign."

The week spent fetching Kira was the longest of Celia's life. Salim hadn't wanted to speak to Kira on the phone—he said he wouldn't know what to say in such an awkward situation. He did want to meet her the moment she arrived at the airport.

The journey had taken almost twenty-four hours, on three planes, with lengthy stopovers in Dubai and Muscat. Kira had slept little. Instead, she'd played and listened to stories and eaten Goldfish crackers and stared at her fellow travelers and listened to songs on the iPod, and, finally, when Celia was too exhausted to stop her, she ran up and down the aisle, laughing.

Kira was now completely wiped out and—

naturally—fell into a deep sleep just as the wheels touched down on the tarmac.

"Wake up, sweetheart. Wake up!"

Eventually she abandoned efforts at stirring Kira and managed to hoist the toddler onto her shoulder while wrestling with her purse, her large carry-on bag and Kira's backpack filled with toys. As she stepped out of the arrival gate into the bright, gleaming airport, she had a momentary wish that she'd remembered to put on lipstick, but she shoved it to the back of her tired brain.

Kira woke up as they went through Passport Control, and was begging for milk by the time they got her bag and walked out to where the waiting drivers and relatives stood behind a rope.

Celia scanned the crowd, heart pounding. Salim had told her he'd meet them at the airport. Did he get cold feet? Kira's tiny hand clutched hers tightly.

Please don't let her down.

She'd told Kira they were coming to meet her

father. Kira had been astonished at first, then delighted. Now the little girl toddled bravely beside her, looking distinctly worried.

"Celia!" A low voice called from the rear of the crowd.

She saw Salim push through, tall and regal, dressed in a crisp white shirt and dark pants. His eyes immediately swiveled to Kira, and he stared at her unabashedly. Then he ducked under the rope and walked up to them.

They all stood there for a second, as Salim and Kira gazed at each other. He held out his hand. "You must be Kira. I'm pleased to meet you." He spoke slowly, like someone talking in an unfamiliar language.

Kira stared at his hand, alarm in her wide, dark eyes.

"I don't think she knows about shaking hands," Celia blurted. "They don't do that much at nursery school."

Salim withdrew his hand, and crouched down to Kira's level. "How silly of me. Still, I am pleased to meet you."

Kira peered at him, frowning slightly. "Are you my daddy?"

"Yes, I am."

"You're very tall."

His face creased into a smile. "And so will you be, one day."

Salim looked as if he wanted to pick Kira up, but Celia hoped he wouldn't try, because Kira's hot little hand gripped hers like a clamp.

"Maybe we should go get in the car," she stammered. "It's been a long flight."

"Good idea." Salim stood and took Celia's bag. "I drove here myself so we could be alone." He glanced down at Kira, an odd sparkle in his eyes. "Just the three of us."

Celia did her best not to hyperventilate on the way out to the car. The Omani heat enveloped her in a warm hug as they left the chill of the airport.

"It's hot, Mama!"

"Yes, sweetie. It's always hot here."

"I like it." A big smile spread across Kira's face. "Look, palm trees. Like in *Babar*."

"*Babar* is a kids' book series," explained Celia to Salim.

"I know." Salim smiled as he held the rear door open for them. "I read them in French. My tutor brought them from Paris. I was always a big fan of Zephyr the monkey."

Celia laughed.

"I like Zephyr, too," said Kira, quite serious. "Are we in Paris?"

"No, we're in Salalah, Oman."

"Salalalalah." Kira tried to wrap her tongue around the word.

"Climb in, sweetie." Celia prodded her gently. People swirled around them, and cars honked and weaved through the airport. Kira and Salim, however, felt no sense of urgency.

"That's right. Salalah. I know you're going to love it here."

Kira finally climbed in. No car seat. Of course Salim wouldn't have thought of it. Celia managed to buckled the lap belt over her and move the shoulder strap out of the way.

Salim climbed into the driver's seat and

started the engine. Kira watched intently out the window as they pulled away from the curb and out onto the streets of Salalah, with their crisp, whitewashed buildings. "Mama, are we going to live here now?"

"Oh, no. We're just visiting." The words flew out of her mouth as the breath rushed from her lungs. She glanced at Salim and saw his brows lower.

"But don't people usually live with their daddies?" Kira glanced up, a frown puckering her tiny forehead.

Her heart pounded like the jackhammer on a nearby street. "Some people do, and some people don't. Everyone's different." Celia prayed for a change of subject.

When they arrived at the hotel, Salim asked a porter to take their bags upstairs. Unbeknownst to Celia, who'd left her room a mess, he'd moved them into a vast penthouse suite with several bedrooms and a wraparound terrace with a panoramic view of the ocean.

Kira ran around, exclaiming. "It's a castle! I'm a princess!"

"Don't run so fast, sweetie!" called Celia. "The marble floor is slippery."

"She'll be fine." Salim beamed. "She's full of energy after her long flight."

"She might fall and bang her head."

"Nonsense. She's graceful as a gazelle."

Celia frowned. "Are we having our first parental argument?"

Salim let out a snort of laughter. "I think we are. And in that case, you win." He winked. "Kira, come here. I want to show you off to everyone. You can run around and frighten your mother later."

Kira took his offered hand. "Are you a king?"

He grinned. "No. But you're definitely a princess."

"I know. Mama calls me princess sometimes." She smiled and twirled in the new pink dress she'd chosen. "I like living here."

Celia's heart seized.

Salim looked up, an expression of quiet triumph on his face.

"This is Kira, my daughter." Salim said it over and over again, as they walked around the hotel and grounds. Everyone, from the maids to the head chef, exclaimed over her and complimented her dress or her smile and sometimes even her stuffed bear. Kira handled it like a true princess, with charming thanks and giggles.

Celia stumbled along, wondering what people were really thinking. They must be shocked that Salim had a daughter, yet no one gasped or started babbling nonsense. Had some informative memo been circulated?

Kira's hand, tight in her own, probably informed them of Celia's role in the drama. What did they imagine was the story of her relationship with Salim? What did they think would happen next?

She certainly had no idea.

She should be happy that Kira seemed to settle

in so well here. Instead, she felt a sense of foreboding. What if Kira didn't want to leave and
go back to their life in America? What if she
wanted to stay here with Salim?

Icy fear gnawed at her gut, but she hid it behind
a bright smile.

Salim strode around with the easy grace of
a king. If he felt the slightest bit flustered by
the odd circumstances, it was entirely invisible.
Pride and obvious joy lit his handsome features
and made him laugh readily.

Whenever Kira saw something new, like a
fountain, he'd stop and crouch down next to her,
patiently explaining all the details of what it
was and how it worked. He listened to her often
outlandish questions and answered them with
thoughtful consideration.

Celia's chest filled with happiness and anxiety
as she watched Kira blossom in the strange new
environment. Always talkative and friendly, her
daughter was delighted by her bustling new surroundings and legions of admirers.

She'd worried that Salim might want to keep

their relationship secret, that he'd be circum-spect about Kira's origins.

Quite the opposite was true. He claimed her at every available opportunity, and took pride in pointing out countless similarities between them, real or imaginary.

"Kira's naturally suited to running a hotel, look!" Salim beamed as Kira ran across a wide plaza near the beach, toward another toddler carrying a shovel and pail. "She's welcoming the guests."

"She's not shy, that's for sure." Celia sipped the cool drink they'd picked up at the bar. "It's really sweet of you to introduce her to everyone."

"It's my very great joy." He stared at Kira as he spoke. Emotion thickened his voice.

Guilt soaked through Celia. "I feel terrible that I waited so long."

Salim turned to her. "I feel terrible that you were forced to wait so long. The guilt doesn't lie with you." He waved a hand in the air. "But it's the past. Let's enjoy the glorious present."

And he strode across the plaza after Kira, who was now attempting to rip the shovel and pail from her new acquaintance's hands.

The present was one thing, but soon enough they'd have to talk about the future. They both seemed to be avoiding it, treading carefully around it. And with good reason.

That's when things would get messy.

Kira got on famously with Ben. Equally active, they ran up and down the beach and in and out of the shallow surf, with their mothers running after them, beseeching them to slow down and be careful.

Celia shot an exasperated glance at Sara. "I think we need a drink with an umbrella in it."

Sara laughed. "I'm terrified of Hannah learning to walk. I haven't figured out how to run in two different directions at the same time." She glanced back to where Hannah played on the beach under Elan's watchful gaze.

"At least I don't have that problem." Celia gasped and leaped forward to stop Kira diving under a wave.

"Not yet."

"Seriously. Not going to happen."

"So you say now." Sara's mouth twisted into a sly smile. "Time will tell."

"Thanks for the clichés."

"Don't look now, but he can't take his eyes off you."

Hairs prickled on the back of Celia's neck. "I'm sure he's just looking at Kira."

Kira squealed and splashed Ben again, totally ignoring the conversation.

"Maybe he's watching both of you."

Celia angled herself to the beach and peered behind the lenses of her sunglasses. Sure enough, there was Salim, standing a few feet from Elan. A tall, elegant figure, fully dressed among the reclining sunbathers.

He was too far away for her to see where he was looking, but she could feel his gaze on her. Suddenly self-conscious in her swimsuit, she crouched and lifted Kira up. Kira waved her legs in the air, splashing water everywhere, her excited squeal pealing across the water. "Mama! Lift me higher!"

"I can't, my arms aren't long enough." She lowered Kira down into the water.

"I bet my daddy could lift me higher." Kira stared at the beach. "Daddy!" She tugged on Celia's arm, dragging her through the shallow water toward the shore. "Daddy!"

Salim loped across the sand and into her outstretched arms. "Yes, my princess." He picked her up and twirled her around, while seawater soaked into his expensive shirt. "Are you sure you're not a mermaid?"

"I don't have a fishy tail." She pressed her chubby fingers to his cheeks. "But I like to swim."

Celia laughed. "She's not kidding. I'm turning into a prune from spending so much time in the water."

"You're the loveliest prune I've ever seen." Salim glowed with good humor. It heated Celia's wet skin like the warm sun. "And I'm hoping you'll join me for dinner tonight, after Kira goes to bed."

"I could come, too," chimed in Kira.

"You need some sleep." Salim pushed strands of wet hair off her flushed face. "You've been on the go nonstop all day."

"Will you read me a bedtime story?"

"Any story you like." Salim looked at her, his expression serious. "I'd be delighted." He turned to Celia. "What time?"

Somehow the idea of Salim reading Kira a story—a favorite part of their daily routine—struck fear into her heart. Kira was growing attached to Salim.

Too attached. Leaving him would be very hard for her, even now.

Every moment they spent together made their inevitable parting more ominous.

But he was her father.

Celia swallowed. "She usually goes down around seven o'clock. Of course with jet lag, anything could happen."

"I was actually inquiring what time I should

pick you up for dinner." His eyebrow lifted, a hint of flirtation.

Celia's stomach clenched. Why did she have to feel excited and apprehensive at the prospect of dinner with him? "Why don't you come at six-thirty for story time and we'll see what happens."

Nine

Kira was already asleep when Salim arrived. She'd passed out on the bed while watching cartoons, and Celia watched, smiling and biting her lip at the same time, while Salim gently lifted her and carried her into her room.

The nanny he'd arranged settled herself in an armchair and promised to phone them if she woke up.

"Where are we going?" whispered Celia, once they stepped out into the hall. "I had no idea what to wear." Aware of conservative Omani sensibilities, she'd put on a tiered skirt and a thin, long-sleeved blouse. She probably looked like a cartoon peasant.

"You look breathtaking, as always." Salim's admiring gaze made her skin shimmer.

He was infuriatingly gorgeous himself, dressed in black from head to toe, his hair swept back from his bold features.

"We're going out on my boat." He pressed the elevator button and the doors opened instantly. Probably someone downstairs at the controls made sure an elevator was always at his majesty's disposal. "I've arranged for dinner to be delivered."

"I didn't know you had a boat," Celia said and then frowned, looking down at her skirt and wondering if she should have worn pants.

"There's a lot you don't know about me." A mysterious smile lifted one corner of his mouth. "But little by little, I'm letting you in on my secrets."

Heat flickered in her belly. "Why do I have a feeling there are thousands of them?"

"You're a woman of mystery yourself. If you can keep a daughter secret, who knows what else you might be hiding." The gleam in his eye revealed no hint of hostility.

"I can't tell you how relieved I am not to be keeping that secret anymore. Secrets don't sit at all comfortably with me. And she's so enjoying her time here."

"I don't have words to express how I feel getting to know her." He glanced up at the mirrored elevator ceiling for a moment, as if searching his mind for the missing words. His chest heaved. "She's more wonderful than I could have imagined."

The doors opened, and Celia managed to govern her face into a blank expression as they strode through the glittering lobby. She didn't want to reveal any of the confusing mix of emotions that roiled in her chest: pride at how well her daughter had handled the strange new surroundings, admiration for Salim's complete and enthusiastic acceptance of his new role as a father...and anxiety about the future.

Smartly dressed patrons milled about, greeting their guests and friends and heading for the restaurant. Salim ushered her out onto one of the brick walks, heading toward the hotel dock.

"This day has been…astonishing. I could never have imagined what it would feel like to be a father. Kira has left me speechless."

His expression of fatherly delight brought a smile to her mouth. "You don't need much speech around Kira." She raised a brow. "You may have noticed she talks a lot."

"And runs a lot, and laughs a lot and smiles a lot."

"She's very bright." They walked along, side by side. "She knows the whole alphabet already."

"We'll have to teach her the Arabic alphabet."

Celia swallowed. How far would this go? Would he really want her to come visit regularly? Familiar fear clutched at her heart. Now he'd met Kira, could he stand to let her go?

At least she had the contract.

He'd signed it, and she had the copy locked in her file cabinet back home.

They'd never spoken about it.

Guilt tightened her muscles. "They do say it's good to learn a new language while you're still young. It wouldn't surprise me if Kira figures out Arabic pretty fast."

"Naturally she will. She's an Omani." Salim marched forward, proud chin lifted, a smile tilting his mouth.

Celia didn't contradict him. She didn't want to. He looked so…happy.

It couldn't last, of course. Sooner or later they'd have to confront the ugly, sticky details of child visitation rights and haggle over where Kira would spend spring break. But for now she wanted him to revel in the simple joy of being a father.

She'd deprived him of that for long enough.

Salim leaped onto the dock in a single, powerful move, then turned to offer Celia a hand. Heat flared in her palm as she took his fingers.

Why did she still have to be so attracted to him? It wasn't fair.

She stepped up onto the dock, avoiding his fierce gaze. Her own eyes were soon fixed on the gleaming white yacht floating before them. "That's quite a boat."

"She's capable of a long ocean voyage."

"Why do people call boats *she?*" Celia felt a twinge of jealousy. Which was way too silly. It's not like the boat was her rival for Salim's affections.

"Perhaps because they're beautiful, and they can take us to places we'd never discover by ourselves."

"That sounds rather exciting."

"Tonight we'll only go out a mile or so, but some other time I'll take you and Kira to Muscat or to Yemen. We Omanis have always been a seafaring people. It's obvious that Kira loves the ocean."

Celia nodded. "The ocean in Connecticut is freezing cold and gray. She always used to scream if it so much as touched her toes. Here I can barely get her out of the water to eat."

"Not many places in the world compare favorably with Salalah."

Salim's smile warmed her to her toes as he helped her aboard.

The deck was huge, at least thirty feet across, and lined with padded seats. Every inch of the ship was polished to a high shine. Brass railings gleamed in the sunset and colorful flags fluttered high above.

A smell of delicious cooking came from somewhere inside the mahogany paneled bowels of the boat. "Yusef is cooking our dinner. He'll steer the vessel, too. We can be frank in our conversation around him."

"He's discreet?" Celia wondered what Salim was telling his staff about her and Kira.

"Yes. And he speaks about eight words of English, most of them filthy." His infectious grin made her stomach quiver. "Let's go see what he's prepared for us."

Dinner was arranged on a lower deck,

inches above the rippling surface of the water. Moonlight danced across tiny waves on an evening breeze that blew away the day's heat and made Celia draw her silk shawl around her shoulders.

"Are you cold?" Salim shrugged off his suit jacket, "Here, put this on."

"Oh, no. I'm fine. Perfect." The last thing she needed was to be surrounded by his seductive masculine smell. It was bad enough sitting directly opposite him while he glowed with joy and enthusiasm about the daughter they shared. "I like the breeze."

Yusef, an older man in a dark dishdasha and a brown turban, served the meal with a smile.

Tender spiced fish on a bed of saffron rice made Celia's mouth water just to look at it. "Omani food is sensational. I don't know how I'll survive without it."

Salim frowned slightly, as if he wanted to say something.

But he didn't. He tore off a hunk of freshly baked flatbread and chewed it silently.

No doubt neither of them knew quite what to say. They were walking along a delicate bridge between the past and the future.

Salim had made no mention of Nabilah or his plans for the future. Celia didn't dare look beyond the end of the week.

Her landscaping project was nearly done. She'd return to the States soon, and take Kira with her.

Neither of them wanted to talk or think about that.

It was easier to exist here in this magical realm, suspended between realities, where anything seemed possible.

They sat at the table like…a couple.

But she didn't dare to imagine a possible future between her and Salim.

She glanced out over the silvery water, to where lights shone on the distant shore. "I can understand why you wanted to come back here. Life in Massachusetts must have been pretty grim compared to your existence here. You never told me you had people waiting on you hand and foot in your regular life."

Salim shrugged. "The experience did me good. I learned how to do things for myself, how to make my own decisions." Something flickered in his dark eyes. "Though I'm not sure I would have survived without your help."

"We had some really good times together." For years she'd suppressed the happy memories of their halcyon days in college. It hurt too much to remember how it all ended. "I guess everything good has to come to an end some time. That's just how life works."

"And sometimes an ending isn't really an ending, as proved by our tryst four years ago and its very delightful results."

Celia smiled. *Don't go getting your hopes up.* "We do have a colorful history, you and I."

Salim placed one broad, tanned hand on the white tablecloth. If she'd wanted to—or dared— she could have placed her own on top of it, to seal the connection between them.

But she didn't.

An ancient wood fishing dhow moved slowly through the water close to them. She could make out its curved outline in the moonlight. Fishermen on the lamp-lit deck called out and waved and Salim replied something in Arabic with a grin. "They're jealous."

Celia laughed. "Who wouldn't be? This boat is like a floating palace."

"It's not the boat they're jealous of." Mischief glimmered in his eyes. "They said I've caught a very beautiful fish."

Celia struggled not to squirm with pleasure under the idle flattery. "How silly. I'm sunburned like a fisherman myself. If it wasn't for the flattering candlelight I'm sure they'd be saying something quite else."

"You don't enjoy being beautiful, do you?" Salim cocked his head.

Celia stiffened. "If I actually was beautiful, maybe I'd have an opinion on that subject."

"Or perhaps you feel you won't be taken seriously if you look too feminine?"

"I prefer to let my work speak for itself. I'd

expect to be taken just as seriously in chandelier earrings. In fact, maybe I'll wear some tomorrow." She raised a brow.

"I'll be sure to take you seriously." His smile revealed his perfect white teeth.

She couldn't get a rise out of him tonight. Apparently he, too, was determined to enjoy their evening. "I wish Kira was here." She sighed. "It's so lovely."

"We'll bring her. We'll come out for a long sail along the coast. I do know how to sail her, you know."

"I believe you. I suspect that you could do just about anything you put your hand to." She glanced down at Salim's sturdy, capable hand, where it rested on the white linen.

Oh, how she'd like to put her hand in his and leave it there for a lifetime.

But that was another lifetime than this one.

And maybe now, while things were calm and cordial between them, and Kira was tucked up quietly in bed, was the best time to plan the future. "Kira and I can come visit regularly.

Whenever there's a school holiday, really. My schedule is usually pretty flexible, since I set it myself."

She wanted to make it clear that if Kira came, she would, too.

Salim's brows lowered. "I don't want to see Kira only two or three times a year."

"You could come to the States whenever you want. I'm sure you have business to do there. You'd be welcome to come visit anytime." Her cheerful invitation rang hollow in the sea-scented night air.

"I don't want to be 'welcome to visit' my daughter. I want to be a *father* to her. Those things are very different."

"I know, but the situation is complicated. We live on different continents. You're rooted here, and Kira and I have friends and family there."

"You have friends and family here." His voice was almost a growl.

Only you. And I've learned better than to depend on you for my happiness.

She kept her thoughts silent, not wanting to stir up more trouble.

"You can see how happy Kira is here. How well she fits in. We have excellent schools here in Salalah. She will grow up surrounded by people who care about her and want the best for her."

Panic flashed through Celia. And a flare of indignation. "She's already growing up surrounded by people who care about her. That's why she's so happy and outgoing." She straightened her shoulders and braced herself. Her hands were shaking and she hid them under the table. Things were about to get ugly. "And I told you, I'm taking her back home."

"Home. Isn't there an American saying, 'home is where the heart is?'"

"Maybe one's heart can be in more than one place, but I'm Kira's mother and she belongs with me." She couldn't hide the tremor in her voice.

"And that's why you had me sign that *contract*." Salim's eyes narrowed to dark slits.

"Yes." She lifted her chin. "I knew that sooner or later we'd have this discussion. I needed to protect my rights, as you can see."

"Why didn't you bring it to me yourself?"

Because I'm afraid of what a pushover I am where you're concerned. "I didn't want to get overemotional, or have us get into an argument."

"You mean, like we're doing now?" He raised a brow. "Surely you didn't think I could meet Kira, get to know her and then simply kiss her goodbye?"

Guilt and fear knotted in Celia's stomach. "I knew you wouldn't. That's why I was afraid. Why I am afraid."

Salim stood, scraping his chair on the deck. Water lapped against the side of the ship, punctuating the thick silence. "You must think about what's best for Kira."

He loomed over her. Moonlight picked out the hard lines of his jaw and cheekbones in silver.

"I am. There's no neat solution. There never has been."

Salim blew out a hard breath and stared out over the water. It shimmered in the bright streak of moonlight that lit its heaving surface.

He frowned, then extended a hand to her. "Come, let's walk on the deck."

Celia stared at his hand, broad palm and long, sturdy fingers, reaching out to her.

If she took it, was she somehow agreeing to his terms? Or would she get sucked into the vortex of madness that gave him such infuriating control over her mind and body?

She didn't want to make trouble. Really, she wanted this to go as smoothly as possible, so rejecting a friendly gesture didn't make sense.

She stood slowly and extended her hand to meet his.

Energy snapped between them and shot up her arm as her fingertips met his. He wrapped his fingers around hers, taking hold of her gently but firmly. "From the far side of the deck we can see the lights of Salalah."

She let him lead her across the polished wood deck with its brass railing. The flags fluttering overhead in the starry darkness echoed the rapid beat of her heart. They passed the stairs leading down to the galley and cabins, and the shore came into view. The city lay spread before them, flickering dots of golden light in the distance.

"It's beautiful," she admitted. "It looks like a floating city." The ocean shimmered and rippled like a flying carpet in the space between the yacht and the glowing shore.

"You can see why I had to come back here. Why staying in the States was never an option for me."

"Yes, of course. I understand everything now. You were always going to come back here. I was young and naive and it didn't occur to me that we weren't entirely in charge of our own destiny."

"Salalah could be your home, too." He spoke low, looking out into the far distance, rather than right at her.

A mix of terror and longing rose inside her. *Oh, stop it! He doesn't mean for you to all be a family. He'll probably set you up in a nice out-of-the way house somewhere and treat you like a maiden aunt, while he gets on with his "suitable marriage" to someone else.*

Did she imagine it, or did his fingers just tighten around hers? Her palm heated and a tingling sensation crept up her arm and rippled to her breasts and belly.

Maybe he did mean for them to be romantic?

She drew in a shaky breath.

"I never truly thought about the joys of being a father." Salim spoke, gazing out over the silver water. "I knew it was my duty, and that I would have children one day." He turned to look at her. His dark eyes held hers fixed on his. "I didn't realize she'd capture my heart and carry it with her every moment."

His words shot a bolt of fierce emotion to Celia's core. She knew exactly how he felt. And that was why everything they said, everything they did, was so important.

And so very difficult.

He turned to her and captured her other hand,

holding them both tight in his. "Thank you for bringing Kira into the world." He spoke with force. "Thank you for raising her to be the bright and happy child she is. You're a wonderful mother."

Celia gulped as a rush of feeling threatened to choke her. She'd felt his censure that she continued to work and travel and spend time away from Kira. His praise now warmed her more than she wanted to admit.

"Thanks," she managed.

"So you must realize that Kira needs both of us."

His statement hung in the night air for a moment as his gaze held hers.

"Yes." She knew he was right. But how could they make it happen?

His eyes drifted to her mouth, which twitched under his stare. Heat sizzled in the air between them, heating their clasped hands and stinging her taut nipples.

Uh-oh.

Their mouths moved inexorably closer. Her

lips tingled with awareness of his mouth, hov
ering close to hers in the darkness. His eyes
darkened as passion flared between them.

Then Salim dropped her hands and turned
abruptly away.

He strode across the deck, leaving Celia standing there by herself, lips parted in unkissed
astonishment.

Ten

The next morning, Celia guided Kira out of the sunlit breakfast room where they'd both had freshly made crepes with fruit. She planned to let Kira play on the beach for a while, then take her to the site so she could look over a few final details.

Her evening with Salim had ended abruptly after their almost-kiss. He'd gruffly suggested they should return to shore, and she'd agreed, glad the darkness hid her flush of humiliation.

Where had she thought that kiss would lead? Nowhere sensible, to be sure.

She should be glad Salim had put a stop to it.

Still, the rejection—on top of all the other rejections she still smarted from—hurt.

Kira stopped and cried out in distress. "We forgot my water wings!"

"You can't swim right after breakfast, sweetie. You could get a cramp."

Kira's lower lip stuck out, and she looked up with big, imploring eyes. "I won't go in deep."

"You're darn right you won't." Celia grinned. "We'll build a sand castle."

Kira was at stake. Kira's future happiness depended on both her parents coming to some kind of sensible arrangement. And breathless kisses were anything but sensible—at least between the two of them.

"Miss Davidson!" A female voice behind her made Celia turn around. She squinted in the morning sun as a woman with red hair rushed across the open courtyard toward her. "Mr. Al Mansur would like to see you in his office."

"Oh." She frowned.

Why didn't he just call her? She always had her phone with her.

"He asked me to take Kira to the Kids' Club. We're making clay sculptures this morning."

Celia frowned. What was he up to? She didn't know this particular hotel employee and she wasn't too delighted about handing Kira over to a total stranger.

"I'm Lucinda Bacon, director of the children's activities." She thrust out a hand. Celia shook it. "How silly of me not to introduce myself. I was a nanny for tots in England for eight years before I came here. I'll make sure Kira has a lovely time." Her bright smile and warm gaze gave Celia some reassurance.

Still…

"She might need a nap soon. She's had an exciting couple of days."

"Not a problem at all!" Lucinda squatted to Kira's height. "We've got a lovely nap room with the prettiest beds you could imagine." She looked right at Kira. "And we sing lullabies. Do you have a favorite bedtime song?"

"'Rock-a-bye Baby,'" said Kira.

"Oh, that's one of my favorites. And did you know, one of our beds rocks, just like a cradle?"

"Can I try it?" Kira looked up at her mom, eyes wide with excitement.

Celia's stomach tightened. "Um, sure, I guess so. Salim is in his office, you said?"

"Yes, he's waiting for you. He asked us to look after Kira until you're done. No rush at all, we're open until ten in the evening." She beamed, and took Kira's hand.

Celia wiped her empty palms on the back of her pants. "Okay." She wrote down her number for Lucinda and watched as she led Kira away.

A nasty feeling of foreboding crept over her.

Was this how it would start? Kira being pried from her and seduced into a new world of unimagined luxuries—things that she could never provide for her daughter, but Salim could produce with a snap of his powerful fingers.

She swallowed and lifted her chin. *He's waiting for you.*

Celia felt as if she'd been summoned to the principal's office.

The feeling only increased when she was ushered into his spacious office, and found him sitting behind the desk, attired in a crisp, dark suit.

Salim rose and nodded, a formal greeting. His grim expression deepened the churning in her stomach. "Please, take a seat."

He gestured to the richly upholstered chair beside her, and she managed to lower herself into it. Her knees were wobbly and she had a sudden urge to diffuse the tension in the air. "Kira was so excited to go to the Kids' Club. I didn't even know there was one here. Every time I turn around, I find something new at this hotel. It's really amazing."

The nonsensical babbling hung in the air as Salim simply stared at her, eyes narrowed.

Something in his gaze was more focused, more intense than usual.

Her stomach tightened.

Salim leaned forward in his chair, which magnified the sensation of being in a laser sight. "As you know, I consider family to be of great importance."

Uh-oh. Celia squirmed under his hard stare.

He frowned before continuing. "I originally broke off our relationship because I considered my responsibility to my family to be paramount. I was the eldest son, and therefore it is my duty to sustain the family into the next generation."

Celia straightened her back. *Here we go again.* All the reasons why she could never be a suitable wife and must thus be banished from his life, yada, yada.

She should be used to it by now. But apparently she wasn't.

Pain lanced through her and she swallowed hard. Had he summoned her here to reject her—yet again? She hadn't even suggested or hinted that she expected anything of him.

Rapid blinking shoved back any tears lurking behind her eyelids.

"I have always intended to fulfill my father's wishes and take an Omani bride of good family."

Didn't you try that once already?

His words stung, but she managed to keep her retort to herself. What good could come of bickering with him? He was still Kira's father, even if he was a heartless clod where she was concerned.

"But now I've decided that, once again, I must put my family first."

Celia's heart clenched. Did he mean to break the contract? It might not even be legally enforceable here. What did she or even confident and chipper Sara know about such things? She struggled to keep her breathing under control.

He hadn't arrived at his point yet.

"I have a daughter now. I believe it is important—in fact, I feel it is essential—that she is provided with a proper family. To that end I have decided that we must marry."

His words hung in the air above his polished desk.

All thoughts deserted Celia's brain. Had he just said what she thought he said?

And who exactly did he mean by *we?*

Salim's frown deepened. "As my wife you will no longer have the burden of supporting yourself and Kira. You will not need to travel, or to be away from her for long periods of time, as you are now. You can stay at home and take care of our daughter, which, I'm sure you will agree, is the most sensible course of action."

Celia stared at him, unable to form a coherent idea, let alone speak a sentence.

"Naturally we must be married as soon as possible. The wedding can take place here at the hotel. I have a full staff of wedding planners and caterers who can take care of all the arrangements. Is there any particular day you prefer?"

"No."

Salim frowned. Celia had been silent while he made his proposal. Not the reaction he'd expected. He was sure she'd be thrilled. "Do you mean, no, you don't have a particular day in mind?"

"No." She sat up straight in her chair, blue eyes flashing. "I mean no to all of it. No, I won't marry you."

Her response hit him like a punch to the gut and he found himself braced against his chair. "What?"

"How can you reduce our whole lives to a business arrangement?" Her hands shook as she gripped the arms of her chair. "You want to marry me entirely out of a sense of duty or some old-fashioned, wrongheaded idea of responsibility. You don't want to marry me. You're just offering because you feel you *have* to." Her voice rose to a high pitch and color flushed her neck. "I don't need to marry you. I can support myself and my daughter and I don't *want* to marry you."

Her words crashed over him, smashing his plans and his vision of their happy family life.

Adrenaline surged through him. "But why not? Surely you can see it's for the best?"

"Best for who? Best for Kira? Best for you? It surely isn't best for me."

"It could be. I know you'll have to leave friends behind to come live here, but you'll make new ones. You can see we have a busy, friendly environment with people from all over the world here at the hotel, and the new property will bring even more visitors."

"I don't want to be a hotel guest in your life." She tossed her head, and gold hair flew around her face. "Can't you see that? It's not enough for me."

Salim frowned. Why wouldn't she see sense? Panic crept over him. "We don't have to live at the hotel. We can build a house, together. You can design the grounds exactly how you like."

"Design the grounds?" Her voice rang with incredulity. "You don't understand me at all." Tears glistened in her eyes. "I don't want my life to be a project, organized according to deadlines and budgets, with all the limits carefully set out from the start. I don't want my marriage to be a carefully orchestrated contractual agreement." Her voice started to crack. "I can't live like that, and I won't have Kira live like that."

She rose from the chair, which screeched on the marble floor.

Salim stood, horror exploding in his chest.

How could she reject him? That would ruin everything. Didn't she see that all of their futures depended on this?

She was totally irrational. Was she reacting emotionally because he'd rejected her in the past? "I know I've hurt you. I wish I could turn back the clock and handle things differently—"

"How?" Celia cocked her head to one side, steel glinting in her blue eyes. "By never getting involved with me in the first place? That would have been the sensible thing to do. No mess, no fuss, no broken promises. No disappointed brides or illegitimate children." She crossed her arms over her chest. "Yes, that would have been much easier. You could have married your suitable bride and lived with her happily ever after."

I didn't want to marry a suitable bride. I wanted to marry you.

The truth of it crashed across his brain. But he didn't say the words.

He'd asked her to marry him—and she'd said no.

His pride smarted and stung. Maybe she took pleasure in causing him the pain he'd once given her.

Except this was far worse, because she had the power to keep his own daughter from him.

His heart ached, too full to express the hopes and fears now lying crushed inside it.

Celia turned and strode across the room. "And you think I should stop working and stay home. Where would I be if I'd done that when Kira was born?" She wheeled around and stared at him. "After I'd called you to tell you about her, and you brushed me off?"

"I didn't know about her or naturally I would have paid all your expenses."

"Oh, how gracious of you." Fury flashed in her eyes. "I do hope I would have been suitably grateful. Perhaps you could have paid to have us hidden away somewhere. Your secret second family. The one no one knows about, except you."

"That's ridiculous, and you know it. I'm not asking you to be a second wife." He paused and frowned. "Well, I suppose technically you would be my second wife, but I'm long divorced from the first. You would be my only wife."

"I don't think I could ever be *appropriate* enough for your needs." She lifted her chin. "I want my daughter to be raised seeing women support themselves and fulfill their ambitions. I want her to know that she can shape her own life however she pleases."

She shoved a stray lock of hair off her forehead. "My parents take excellent care of her when I travel. She's surrounded by friends and family at all times. As you've seen with your own eyes, she's happy and well-adjusted." Her eyes, still blazing like the sea in the noonday sun, defied him to argue.

"She should grow up knowing her father." His voice emerged as a low growl he hardly recognized. Words were so inadequate to express his feelings.

"I agree." She paused and frowned.

Hope unfurled in his chest.

Celia put her hands on her slim hips. "She should grow up knowing her father. And I'm sure we can come up with some mutually acceptable *contract*..." She spat the word. "To provide for that."

She inhaled and he watched her chest rise, cursing the lust that licked at him, even now. "But there is no need for either of us to commit to a loveless marriage that will diminish us both." Her voice rang, clear and resolute, across the wide space of his office.

She turned and walked to the door.

Salim sprang from his chair.

"Don't worry, I'll be discreet," she said, her expression stony. "I won't tell anyone that I turned down your *generous* proposal. I've all but fulfilled the terms of our original contract, the one that brought me here. There are just a few small details to take care of. Then Kira and I will return to the States, as planned."

Her golden hair flew out behind her as she swung the door open and stepped out. It closed behind her with a decisive slam.

Salim rushed for the door. Then stopped.

He couldn't *make* her stay. Which was an unfamiliar sensation, since there was so little in his life that he didn't have total control over.

He didn't have any control—or any influence at all—over Celia.

A mix of indignation and frustration pricked his muscles. Could she simply leave and take his daughter with her?

Of course she could. He'd signed that stupid contract agreeing to let her.

He wasn't sure what hurt more. The prospect of losing Kira, his bright-eyed and affectionate daughter who'd already crept into his heart.

Or the prospect of losing Celia—again.

No matter how hard he'd tried to shove her out of his mind, there she was, lingering somewhere in the dark nether regions of his consciousness, an eternal temptation.

He could never resist his attraction to her. It was gut level, visceral and raw in a way that pushed reason and sense aside.

All his carefully cultivated plans fell into disarray as soon as she walked into the room. He could never marry Nabilah now. Celia had ruined him for any other woman.

She was all wrong—foreign, outspoken, bold and driven. She didn't even seem to notice convention, let alone conform to it. She never had.

And the way she dressed…

She was all wrong for him.

But tradition be damned, he loved her. And she was the only wife he wanted.

Eleven

Celia jogged across the hotel complex, heart pounding and breath coming in unsteady gasps.

Salim had just asked her to marry him.

And she'd turned him down.

A proposal from Salim was something she'd once dreamed of and hoped for. But not one like this, a crude business arrangement to suit his idea of propriety.

A sob caught in her throat.

He didn't love her.

He didn't even care about her. Not if he thought she'd be happy to give up her career to sit quietly at his feet in some blond-haired, blue-eyed imitation of a "suitable wife."

The cruelty of the situation choked her with anger and sadness. The man she loved had asked her to be his wife—in a way that made it impossible for her to accept.

She had to get Kira. Who knew what orders Salim might issue to his staff. Here in the hotel compound he was surrounded by his friends and allies, his loyal family members. All of them might gang up against her and try to convince her to leave Kira here.

Even to force her, contract be damned.

Fear pricked her nerves as she hurried past the plate-glass windows of the beauty salon and the store selling local arts and crafts. She scanned the signs for the Kids' Club and was relieved to see it just past the massage parlor.

Breathless and sweating, she pushed open the door, her whole body pulsing with terror. She scanned the interior, decorated with elaborate fairy-tale murals and painted furniture.

Where was Kira?

She needed to leave now, today.

And she intended to keep Kira at her side until she did.

Kira burst through a door in the middle of a Little Bo Peep mural and ran to her. "Mama!"

Relief washed over her in a tidal wave. Kira's bright eyes sparkled. "It's so fun here!" Celia hugged her, and clutched her to her chest, careful to conceal her own trepidation.

"They read stories and I learned a new song."

"That's great, sweetie, but we have to go now." She wiped her palms on the back of her pants. "We'll grab some lunch and I'll take you out to the site. Remember how I told you about the old city?"

"With the castles and everything?"

"Exactly. We're going to see it right now." She needed to wrap up a few final details, and leave some last instructions for planting and maintenance with the crew. Then she'd fulfilled her obligations and could leave with a clear conscience.

At least as clear as it ever would be.

"Come on, sweetie."

Kira pouted. "Can't I stay for nap time? I didn't get to try the cradle."

"Another time, okay?"

Would there be another time? She couldn't keep Kira from Salim. She didn't want to, but maybe he wouldn't want a relationship on any terms other than his own. Sooner or later he'd take his "suitable" bride, who probably wouldn't want anything to do with the illegitimate child of a former liaison.

"Okay." Kira's glum face sent a stab of guilt to her chest. Was she doing the right thing for Kira?

On the other hand, she couldn't be a good mother to Kira if she was living a lie, married to a man who saw her as nothing but an obligation.

Celia helped Kira into her pink ballet flats and

picked her up. Her baby was obviously ready for a nap. "You can sleep in the car, so you'll be awake to see the ancient city."

"Okay, Mama."

Kira trusted her completely. In her innocence she still saw her mom as her protector and savior and someone who always did the right thing. Celia inhaled deeply, and wondered how long she'd inhabit that role in her daughter's imagination.

"I love you, sweetie," she whispered into Kira's dark hair.

She thanked the nursery staff and left the well-appointed facilities with mingled feelings of relief and sadness. What a lovely place for Kira to play and interact with other children.

If only her father hadn't issued his impossible demand.

She rushed to their hotel room and threw their few belongings into her duffel bag. She hurried down the outside staircase, anxious to avoid the staff. At first Kira protested, wanting to go to the beach, but perhaps something in her mom's tone, let her know that this was no time for play. She held Celia's hand as they hurried along the palm-shaded path to the car park, where Celia bundled her into the back of her rented Mercedes and strapped her into the car seat she'd borrowed from the rental agency.

"If you stay awake a little while, you'll see the Fog Mountains."

"Okay, Mama." Kira must be really sleepy. What had happened to the feisty terror who resisted her car seat with energy and persuasive arguments? Maybe all the action and events of the last few days had sucked the chutzpah out of her, too.

Too many ups and downs. Too many high hopes and foolish fantasies.

She started the engine and pulled out of the hotel complex. She'd miss the bright, white walls of Salalah, and the backdrop of blue sea shining in the background. She'd miss the tall, graceful palms and the friendly people.

She'd miss Salim.

But she'd missed him—and survived—most

of her adult life. She should be used to that by now.

Her heart ached with longing for everything that could never be.

She and Salim just weren't destined to be together. The gulf between them was wide and windswept as the Rub' Al Khali. That desert wilderness was once criss-crossed by caravans of brave and hopeful traders who visited the lost city on their journey. Now it was virtually impassible, and even the Bedouin no longer walked its sand-choked passes.

Things changed, and there was no going back.

The mystical environment of the Fog Mountains engulfed her like a hug as she drove through their now-familiar passes. Then the desert floor welcomed her again, with its austere mysteries and quiet beauty.

The lost city rose, majestic, through the haze of midday heat that shimmered over the sands. Bright walls enclosed the lush oasis that would soon welcome visitors back to its ancient streets.

Already she'd seen it come alive again as a crossroads of cultures and peoples. She rolled down the window as she pulled up alongside one of her crews, mulching freshly planted date palms. "Faisal, do you have a few minutes? I need to go over some final details. Turns out I have to leave...very soon." She gulped. The crew chief frowned and nodded.

She parked and spent a few minutes in her makeshift site office—soon to become a luxurious bedroom—going over maintenance details. Plants didn't survive long in rainless desert conditions without carefully planned care.

Celia kept her voice steady while she gave instructions for watering and fertilizing. Kira slept quietly on a soft pillow nearby. Would either of them see the majestic date palms in maturity, heavy with rich fruit?

Or would the rebuilt lost city live on only in her imagination? Suspended in time just the way it was when she last saw it.

Which might well be today. She intended to drive her rental car directly to the airport in Muscat and get on the next available flight to the States.

Her stomach clenched at the thought of leaving all this behind. Of tearing Kira from the new surroundings she'd grown to enjoy. But it was better to make the break now, so they could start rebuilding their lives.

She left Kira sleeping and took Faisal outside to go over instructions for fertilizing a new ground cover. As he typed the name of it into his PDA, a car engine roared into earshot.

"I can't get used to the way people drive around here," she exclaimed. "In the U.S. pedestrians have the right of way. Here they have the right to get out of the way—and fast."

She stepped back off the road as the car squealed around the corner.

Salim's sedan.

It screeched to a dramatic and noisy halt, sending a cloud of dust into the air around it.

"I've got to go." Instinct fired her veins with

adrenaline, and she turned to run toward the building where Kira slept.

She wouldn't let him talk her around. She wouldn't let herself fall for his fatal charms.

He'd caused her too much pain already.

"Celia." His voice rang out behind her as he leaped from the car. "Stop." His command boomed through the air.

She ignored it and kept marching. She was done being told what to do by Salim Al Mansur.

Footsteps on the path behind her made her heart pound harder.

"Celia, wait." His words stuck her like a knife and every muscle in her body yearned to respond.

How did he have such power over her?

Still, she kept walking, steeling herself against whatever appeal he might be ready to launch.

A hand grabbed her upper arm, jerking her to a halt.

"Let go!" She spun around.

"No." He grabbed her other arm and held her, facing him. Her first instinct was to fight—

Then their eyes met.

His were blacker than she'd ever seen them, piercing and intense. His gaze locked onto hers, fierce and pleading. "I won't let you go."

Breath fled her lungs.

"I love you." His eyes narrowed, their fierce stare penetrating to her core. "I *love* you and I need you." His voice cracked as raw emotion spilled out.

His words crashed over her, draining the strength from her muscles. She struggled to resist them. "You don't," she whispered.

Her skin burned under the heat of his palms. Already the forceful—and purely physical—attraction between them threatened to overwhelm her. "You don't love me," she managed. "You just want me."

She frowned, fighting the emotion—the sobs—that hovered just beneath the surface of her voice. "You want to make things right, and you think you can do that by capturing me and keeping me here. Me and Kira..." Fear flared in her heart as she thought of Kira sleeping, innocent and unsuspecting, just a few yards away. "You can't. You can't make yourself love me no matter how much you might want to, and you can't make me stay."

"Make myself love you?" The words exploded from his tongue, "I've been trying for over a decade to make myself *stop* loving you. I've always loved you and I always will love you."

A groan issued from somewhere deep inside him, and echoed off the white buildings around them. "I'll love you until my last breath."

Desperation—and passion—flashed in his dark eyes. "Can't you see that? Can't you see that I can't live without you?" He inhaled a shaky breath. "I don't want to live without you."

Celia stood, unable to move, held up only by the strong hands that kept her captive.

The force of his words had turned her blood to vapor. She felt weightless, breathless, helpless.

"But you… But you…"

"I've been a fool." He lifted his head to the sky and let out a curse. "I've been a stubborn idiot who wouldn't know paradise if he fell into it."

His eyes fixed on hers, this time wide with wonder and brimming with raw emotion. "I've lived an empty, soulless life since I lost you— since I threw you away out of my own cowardice and stupidity." He made a strange sound, somewhere between a howl and a growl, primal and piercing.

Then he drew in a sharp breath, frowning as if in agony. "I should have fought for you, claimed you, and told my father that *you* were the only bride I could take." His voice rose to a crescendo, echoing off the buildings.

Celia swallowed. His words wrapped around her like the warm desert air.

Like the siren call of madness.

Then he let go of her arms and fell to his knees at her feet. He took her hands in his. "Don't leave, Celia. Please don't leave." His words were muffled in her shirtfront. Breathless and rasped, they scratched at her skin and clawed inside her. "I crave you with my heart and I love you with all my body and soul. Stay with me."

His strong hands held her tight.

And she had no desire to push them away

He looked up, his handsome face taut with emotion. "Will you be my wife? Will you share my life and help me be the man I should have been all along? I can't do it without you."

Dark and shining, his eyes implored her.

"Oh, Salim." She fought the almost over-whelming urge to shout yes.

But she knew she couldn't. "I'm still the Celia you couldn't marry. The one who didn't fit and wouldn't work in your life." Her voice shook. "I'll always be that person."

She gestured to her work shirt and her dusty jeans. "I couldn't ever be the polished and proper bride you need. It's just not me. You may think you can change me, but you won't."

She narrowed her eyes and girded herself against his emotional appeal. "I don't want to change. I don't want to live a lie. That's not fair to me or the people around me."

"I know." Salim dropped her hands. Losing their warmth left her cold, even in the desert heat.

He sat back on his heels and looked up at her. "I know you won't change. That you can't change. That you don't want to be anyone but just you." She saw his Adam's apple move as he swallowed. "And it just makes me love you more."

His words, spoken so low as he stared up at her from the dusty pathway, gripped her guts like a clenched fist.

"I love you, Celia Davidson. I love your work and your passion…" Wearing a serious expression, he picked up one of her hands and pressed his lips to it. "And the grit under your fingernails."

Warmth swept through her.

"Everything about you is precious to me." A flicker of pain crossed his face, and he closed his eyes for a second. "When you turned me down and walked out of my office, I felt like my heart had been torn from my chest."

He clasped her hand in both of his. "I tried to tell myself—*you can live without a heart.*

You've gone this far without it. You don't need it." He frowned. "But I knew I couldn't."

He climbed to his feet, still holding her hands fast in his, eyes riveted to hers. "You've shown me that I do have a heart, and that I can't keep acting a role I've learned the lines for, but that I don't believe in."

He let out a long, shuddering breath. "I've tried to live my life for my family, for its honor and pride and for the future of our line.…" He shook his head, confusion sparkling in his eyes, then bursting into a laugh. "When all along, *you* were my real family. You, and now Kira. You're the people I should care about and love and cherish."

Celia's breath came in unsteady gasps. "We're family." She tested the words aloud as the truth of his passionate words echoed in her core.

"You were always meant to be my wife. That's why we fell in love and were so happy together. In my youthful stupidity, I had no idea what a mistake I was making to toss that away and go along with someone else's plan." He squeezed her hands. "You are my wife. You always have been and always will be, whether you like it or not."

Mischief—or was it sheer conviction—glinted in his eyes.

Celia bit her lip. "I ruined you for everyone else."

"You did. And I wouldn't have it any other way. We're husband and wife and we don't need any contracts or ceremonies or rings to prove it."

Eyes wide, she stared at him. "So you don't even want to marry me?"

He shook his head. "I'm already married to you. I don't need a piece of paper to make it real."

She stared at him. The hard lines of his regal face seemed softer than usual. He glowed with… hope.

But maybe they were getting carried away. "But what about the practicalities? We can't live together."

"Of course we can." He raised her hands to

his mouth and pressed his lips to her fingers. Her skin shivered in response. "We can live together here, and in New York, and in Muscat, and Bahrain and…wherever your work takes you. We'll be nomads, like my Bedouin ancestors." His eyes sparkled. "I think that will suit us very well."

"But what about Kira? Where will she go to school?"

"Life is school for the Bedouin." A smile tugged at his arrogant mouth. "And we'll hire a tutor. I had one, and I still got into the same college as you, with your genius-professor parents."

Celia smiled. "You do have a point there."

She racked her brain for more objections. All sensible thoughts seemed to have departed on the hot, blossom-scented wind. "So, this would be our home base, but we could travel to, say, New Zealand, if I had a job there?"

She peered at him, unable to believe this was really possible. It was just too perfect. With

Salim and a tutor she really could bring Kira with her when she worked.

"Of course. Wherever we travel to, we'll always be home because we'll have each other."

She stared at him, openmouthed. Why not? The genius—and beauty—of it swelled in her heart.

"Mama!" Her daughter's high-pitched voice rang through the air. Celia turned to see her standing at the door of the building where she'd left her. Tears streaked her face and her mouth was turned down in an expression of dismay.

Celia tugged her hands from Salim's and ran to her. "Sweetheart, what's the matter?"

"We're leaving, aren't we? That's why you packed my toys." A fat tear rolled over her plump cheek.

"Um, actually…" She couldn't seem to find words. Her mouth hadn't caught up with her brain.

"I don't want to leave." Kira blinked, eyes wide and brimming. "I'd miss my daddy too much."

Kira glanced behind her, and a rumble of emotion emerged from Salim's chest. "I'd miss you far too much, as well, my princess."

"So we're not leaving?" Kira's eyes brightened.

"No," Celia said firmly. "At least not unless we're all together."

"And Daddy could come with us to America?"

"Of course. He knows America well."

"My two favorite people in the world are from there." Salim smiled and brushed away a glittering tear with his thumb. "And we'll go to other countries, too. Now, when your mommy gets a new job, we'll go with her. And we'll all manage my hotels together, as well. I think you'd be a big help with that."

"Me, too." Kira's tears had vanished, replaced by her sparkling smile. "I'll help you get rich. I'm good at that."

Salim guffawed.

Celia smiled and hugged Kira close. "She's right. I told you about her lemonade stand. Watch out or she'll set one up by the pool."

"That sounds like an excellent idea."

"And you have to have a wedding so I can wear a flower girl dress. My friend Rachel wore one with little blue flowers." Kira frowned. "But I want pink flowers."

Celia's eyes met Salim's. His twinkled. "What do you say? Does she get to wear the flowers?"

Celia bit her lip, willing tears not to pour from her own eyes. "Yes. I'd like that very much."

Epilogue

"The guys are here!" Sara poked her head from behind the beaded curtain separating Celia from the prewedding festivities outside.

"What? I thought today was a no-guys-allowed thing." Celia glanced down at the fresh henna, drawn in swirling organic patterns on her arms and hands. She couldn't move until it dried. It was rather fun being propped up on cushions while everyone came behind the curtain to see her.

Everyone female, that is. Today's wedding

celebration was the party for women, and hundreds of them milled about in colorful finery, laughing and chatting and picking their way over the cobbled stones of the lost city in high heels.

"We're only sticking with the good traditions, remember? What fun would your wedding party be if your husband-to-be couldn't share it?"

"You're right." Celia giggled. "He does know he can't touch me, I hope."

"I'll fight him off with a stick." Sara cast her eyes around for a weapon. "Maybe one of those sticks they all carried in the men's ceremony yesterday. Look out, here they come."

Salim and Elan burst through the curtain. Salim swept forward, careless of her elaborate paint job, and pressed his lips to hers. Heat rushed through her, mingled with excitement and elation that the wedding was finally underway after all the weeks of planning.

With effort, she pulled her lips from his and drew in a shaky breath. "Farah spent nearly three hours on my arms. Don't smudge the henna!"

"It's nearly dry." He leaned forward, and his hot breath caressed her ear as he whispered, "And when it is I'm going to trace each precious line with my tongue."

"Salim." She glanced over his shoulder. "We're not alone."

"We'll be alone soon enough," he murmured. His eyes flashed with desire that echoed inside her.

She glanced behind him, as Sara walked in with the children. "I'm not so sure. There must be a thousand people staying here and in Salalah."

"As well there should be. It's the celebration of the century." Salim beamed proudly. He did have the decency to step back. He stood next to Elan, both of them tall and regal in long white dishdashas, with the traditional curved *khanjar* dagger tucked into a sash at the waist.

"Elan's not wearing jeans!" Celia exclaimed.

"I'm getting in touch with my heritage." He grinned. Ben tugged at the long robe and Elan turned to pick him up. "Next thing you know, I'll be riding a camel."

"Can we, Dad? Oh, please!" Kira ran into the curtained tent like a blast of air, her sequined dress sparkling.

"Of course you can." Salim picked her up and whirled her around. "Anything for my princess."

"Those camels are more dressed up than I am." Celia glanced ruefully at the embroidered silk dress she was trying not to get henna on. "I think I need a few more tassels to compete."

"I think the camels look adorable." Sara smiled. "Where on earth did you get them, Salim?"

"Faisal brought them from his village. His uncle owns them. They walked for five days to get here."

"The lost city welcomes camel trains once again." Celia grinned. "They look right at home here, too, nibbling on those native trees I picked out so carefully."

"Speaking of the lost city." Salim cocked his

head. His intense gaze made heat flash over Celia's skin. "It's been found again and it needs a real name."

"But the archaeologists couldn't seem to figure it out." Celia sighed. She'd put quite a bit of effort into tracking it down herself. "They kept calling it 'the city of the Ubarites' which is more a description than a name."

"I'd imagine the name changed over time," cut in Elan. "Depending on who was living here and running the place. They'd name it after whatever was important to them."

"And I intend to do the same." A sheepish smile tilted Salim's arrogant mouth. "We shall call it Sal-iyy-ah." He pronounced the syllables slowly.

Sara burst out with a laugh. "Ce-l-ia! I love it."

Celia gasped as surprise and embarrassment reddened her face. "You can't! I'm not even from here."

"No one is from here." Salim crossed his hands over his broad chest, eyes glittering. "It was abandoned. Empty, lying in ruins. You helped bring it back to life, and now we shall all enjoy it together." He lifted his chin, defying her to disagree.

"That's crazy…" Celia fanned herself, henna be damned.

"It's perfect." Elan hoisted Ben higher on his waist. "It's both Arab and Western at the same time. Just like our family."

"The city is our vision come to life, just as the rest of our lives will be." Salim kissed Kira's cheek, and she giggled. "And Kira likes the name."

"Well, if Kira likes it, who am I to argue?" She felt a goofy smile spread across her face.

This was all a bit too much, and the actual wedding wasn't even until tomorrow!

"Someone bring this woman a cocktail!" exclaimed Sara.

"No, please, I'm far too light-headed already. The frankincense is making me giddy." She gestured to the aromatic lump smoldering in an open brazier. "I know it's fabulously valuable and the entire city was built around its trade, but I'm starting to think it's possible to suffer overexposure."

"Maybe you're just delirious with happiness," Sara said as she winked.

"Yeah. That could be it." She grinned and leaned back in her cushions.

Salim could honestly say the wedding was the most spectacular event he'd ever attended, let alone hosted. Over a thousand people joined in the festivities, many of them from the States, including Celia's friends and relatives, Salim and Elan's younger brother, Quasar, and Sara's large troupe of brothers and sisters and their children. They danced and sang and feasted and shared a four-foot-high cake decorated with candied lilies and orchids, until the stars twinkled over Saliyah.

The noise of revelry still filled the air as Celia and Salim hurried, hand-in-hand, along a lamp-lit stone path toward their lavishly decorated honeymoon suite.

Once inside, Celia closed the door behind them and clicked the lock. "Alone at last." Her eyes shone. "It's past 3:00 a.m. They're never going to leave, are they?"

"Why would they? They're having the time of their lives." Salim's chest swelled with pride and happiness. "As am I. Especially now that I have you all to myself."

Kira was happily settled in a suite with Sara's children for the night.

Celia threw off the emerald silk shawl that covered her shoulders. "Why did we both have to wear green?" She stretched and her delicate gold dress clung to her curves.

Heat stirred inside him. "It's traditional." His words were a throaty growl. "For fertility."

Celia raised a slim brow as she strolled toward him, limbs lithe. "I'm not sure that's a problem for us."

"Not in the least." He slid his hands around her waist.

Mischief lit her eyes as she wrapped long, slender fingers around the hilt of his *khanjar*. "Is an

Omani wife allowed to grasp her husband's... dagger?"

"Only in the privacy of the bedchamber." Heat roared through him. "And only if she's looking for trouble."

Celia licked her lips. "Trouble is exactly what I have in mind. We haven't had nearly enough time for that lately." She tugged at his elaborate embroidered sash, pulling until it came loose and tumbled to the floor.

Salim's fingers plucked at the delicate shell buttons on her dress to reveal glowing, silky skin. He sighed at the rich, floral scent that filled his senses as he stripped off her elegant layers. "Gold underwear," he breathed, as the wickedly scant lace bra and panties revealed themselves.

"Got to match." Celia's cheeks glowed, and her breath came in unsteady gasps through parted lips. Together they removed his formal dishdasha with unsteady hands, until he stood naked, and very aroused, before her.

Celia wore nothing but her sensual gold satin

lingerie—and a single green silk garter just above her left knee.

Salim slid a finger inside the unfamiliar but strangely erotic accessory. "Why do women wear these?"

"To drive men crazy."

"It works." He frowned. His arousal thickened as he slid his hand up her thigh and cupped her soft backside in its delicate satin and lace shell.

"Good." Her eyes flashed. "About this fertility thing...." She cocked her head slightly. One henna-decorated hand strayed to her belly. "What if it works?"

"All the better." Emotion filled his chest. "Kira should have siblings, don't you think?"

"Absolutely. And this time you'll get to enjoy each glorious second of..." She slid a finger over the muscles of his chest, and down over his stomach. The muscles contracted as shivers of sensation shot to his groin. "My labor and delivery."

Her eyes flashed as she tossed her head, flicking her golden hair behind her shoulders.

"I'll put up with every word of abuse you hurl at me." He rubbed his palms over her nipples. She wriggled, enjoying the sensation. "I'll enjoy it."

"And when the baby cries at night…" She laid a line of kisses along his collarbone.

"I'll call for the nurse." He peered at her, hiding a smile.

She laughed. "You'll go get our baby for me."

"Unless she's lying between us."

"Which she probably will be." Celia's smile lit her lovely face. "Unless she's a he."

"Either one would bring me great joy." Warmth filled his body and the rich scroll of possibilities unfolded in his mind. "As long as we're all together."

Heat seared him as their lips met. His erection throbbed against Celia's soft belly, shoving all thoughts from his mind. In an instant they were on the bed, and her delicate undergarments fell to the floor. She shuddered when he entered her, and he let out a soft groan of sweet relief.

Could he really be lucky enough to have won the bride of his dreams?

The evidence lay in his arms.

Well, not exactly *lay*.

Before he knew what was happening she'd somehow reversed their positions and taken charge. Salim moaned aloud as she rode him hard, driving him to new heights of pleasure. Outside the window, traditional music mingled with a thumping dance beat, and revelers laughed and called to each other in many languages. He gripped Celia and moved with her, challenging her and flipping them into a third position, where each could guide their sensual dance in turn. Celia cried out as the first shocks of her orgasm crashed through her and drew them both into a realm of shuddering bliss.

"I wonder how long it's been since someone made love here?" she rasped as they lay panting on the sheets.

He couldn't take his eyes off her. Her golden

hair sprawled on the embroidered pillow and her skin glowed in the lamplight.

"A thousand years. Maybe more."

Her eyes sparkled. "Then we'd better get cracking. We've got a lot of lost time to make up for."

He wrapped his arm around her waist and leaned in until his lips brushed her ear. "There's no time like the present."

* * * * *

It only took ten minutes to walk to Skiddaw View. Ross walked Cat to her front door, waited till she had found her key and opened it.

'Goodnight, Ross,' she said. Then, before he could turn to go, she put her hands lightly on his arms, reached up and kissed him.

Cat had intended just a gentle kiss on the cheek—a thank-you kiss, a kiss recognising that two *friends* had just spent a pleasant evening together. That was the idea.

Perhaps he moved his head—but instead of kissing his cheek, her lips touched his. And then they lingered.

He drew her towards him so that not just their lips but their bodies were touching. Just touching. Whatever was between them, the feeling, the tentative understanding was fragile. A moment to enjoy with no thought of consequences.

Ross knew this had to end before things went too far. There was too much to think of, too many things holding them apart. Slowly, reluctantly, he released her, eased her away from him. His thoughts were whirling. What had happened between them had been an accident, a small mistake. There was no need to talk about it. Both understood the fact.

But he couldn't forget the kiss.

Gill Sanderson, aka Roger Sanderson, started writing as a husband-and-wife team. At first Gill created the storyline, characters and background, asking Roger to help with the actual writing. But her job became more and more time-consuming, and he took over all of the work. He loves it!

Roger has written many Medical™ Romance books for Harlequin Mills & Boon®. Ideas come from three of his children—Helen is a midwife, Adam a health visitor, Mark a consultant oncologist. Weekdays are for work; weekends find Roger walking in the Lake District or Wales.

Recent titles by the same author:

NURSE BRIDE, BAYSIDE WEDDING*
THEIR MIRACLE CHILD
A BABY OF THEIR OWN†
THE DOCTOR'S BABY SURPRISE†
A SURGEON, A MIDWIFE: A FAMILY†

*Brides of Penhally Bay
†Dell Owen Maternity

A MOTHER
FOR HIS SON

BY
GILL SANDERSON

MILLS & BOON®

Pure reading pleasure™

First published in Great Britain 2008
Large Print edition 2009
Harlequin Mills & Boon Limited,
Eton House, 18-24 Paradise Road,
Richmond, Surrey TW9 1SR

ISBN: 978 0 263 20499 5

Set in Times Roman 16½ on 20½ pt.
17-0309-52526

Printed and bound in Great Britain
by CPI Antony Rowe, Chippenham, Wiltshire

A MOTHER
FOR HIS SON

For the REAL Gill Sanderson's love and support.

CHAPTER ONE

SO THIS was going to be the new start to her life, Dr Cat Fraser thought. Working in a cottage hospital in the Lake District, miles from her beloved London. And in a rainstorm too. Well, the previous attempts at therapy hadn't worked. Perhaps this new start idea would work—though she doubted it.

She'd just had a quick tour of Rosewood Cottage Hospital, tiny in comparison with the great London hospital she had left. She had been invited to go to the doctors' lounge to make herself a coffee, but as she started up the polished wooden staircase she saw a movement through the glass of the entrance doors. A man walked into the sheltered porch, head hunched in his hooded jacket. He took off the jacket, shook it then walked through the swing doors into the centre of the foyer. He was limping—badly. As Cat watched he bent to rub the side of his leg. She wondered...old injury or new? Physiotherapy or A and E?

He looked around, finally fixed on her. Apparently unsure of where to go. Well, she had only been here an hour herself, but perhaps she could direct him. She went over to him, smiled. 'May I help?'

'Perhaps. Help is always good. And you are?'

Not the answer that she had expected. Still. 'I'm...I'm...Dr Fraser.' No need to explain that she wasn't a doctor on the staff. Well, not yet anyway.

Now she was closer to him she could see him better. Her first impression had been of a well-built man, with broad shoulders. She'd seen plenty of them in her time. But was this man different? A few droplets of silver rain had fallen from the jacket hood and they sparkled in his hair. He lifted his head to look at her and she felt a shock thrill through her as she saw his face. A weather-beaten face. Not a pretty face but a face that fitted this iron-boned land. It was tough, there were harsh lines round his mouth.

Long afterwards, she wondered if she had fallen in love with those eyes the minute she had seen them. But now she was confused—and irritated.

She shook herself, realised that she had been silent for too long, just looking at him. But he had been silent too. He stood there, impassive, those blue eyes fixed on her with a faint quizzical expression.

'Which department do you want?' She couldn't help it, her question sounded abrupt, irritated.

He didn't seem to mind. 'Well, Doctor, I'm going to the A and E department.'

Perhaps she could make up for her apparent rudeness. 'It's that way. Would you like me to go with you?'

'If you would be so kind.' His voice was low, musical, with a faint note of mockery, as if he found life a joke.

She said nothing more but took him down to A and E. 'You can sit here a moment,' she said, pointing to a bench. 'I'll get someone to come to see to you.'

But when she had pushed her way through the swing doors she found, to her annoyance, that he had followed her. 'Please, wait outside,' she said in her best clinical voice, 'We'll have someone with you as quickly as—'

Jenny Carson, an A and E nurse Cat had been introduced to a few minutes before, came into the room.

'Oh, Dr McCain...'

'It's Dr Fraser,' Cat said, assuming Jenny was addressing her. 'My name is Fraser.'

There was silence for a moment and she was aware of being looked at, of being misunderstood. The nurse looked baffled. When Cat glanced sideways she saw a slight smile on the man's face. And then she remembered. McCain! 'Dr McCain? You're not a patient, you're a partner in the practice I'm joining!'

'I am. And you thought I was a patient with an injured leg. Doctors shouldn't jump to conclusions, Dr Fraser. We get enough patients coming to find us, we don't need to go out and look for them.'

Cat saw the nurse smile, before she turned to rearrange the dressings on an already perfectly tidy trolley.

It hadn't been said unkindly but Dr McCain didn't intend to hide his amusement. The slight smile said it all. And what was worse, she knew that he was entirely correct. It cost her, but she said, 'You're quite right. Doctors shouldn't jump to conclusions. I'll do better next time.'

Her answer appeared to please him. He looked at her speculatively a moment, then said, 'I'm sure you will. Don't take it to heart, Dr Fraser, we all make mistakes sometimes. And yours was a tiny one. And motivated by kindness too.'

Dr McCain turned to the nurse and asked, 'So what have you got for me this afternoon, Jenny? Frank Lyle again?'

'Frank Lyle again.' The nurse's voice was resigned. 'I've got him resting now. I've given him glucose, got his blood sugar up again. I've put temporary dressings on his injuries but I'd like you to have a look at him rather than just bandage him up.'

'Fine. I'll go and get something dry on and then we'll see to Frank.' He turned to Cat. 'We weren't really expecting you till this evening, Dr Fraser. For a general introduction to the practice and so on.'

She felt uncomfortable again. 'I'll be there for the introduction, of course. It's just that…I arrived here in Benthwaite a bit early and…I saw the sign that said Rosewood Cottage Hospital. In his letter Dr Matthews said I'd be doing a lot of my work here…so I thought I might just drop in.'

Even as she said it, it sounded a bit weak, but Dr McCain didn't seem to see it that way. 'Good idea. Now, are you willing to help with this case? I might need an assistant.'

Cat blinked. This was the last thing she had expected. 'Of course I'd like to. But am I insured and so on? Officially I've not joined you yet.'

'You'll be insured. Harry Matthews and our practice manager are demons at paperwork. Now, Jenny here will take you to find you some scrubs and we'll meet here again in ten minutes.'

Compared to the steely efficiency she was used to, it all seemed a bit casual to Cat. 'Aren't you going to ask to look at my papers or something, see I am who I claim to be? I've got papers in the car and…'

He shrugged. 'I'll know if you're a doctor or not in five minutes.'

It was casual and Cat felt a bit uncomfortable. This would never happen in a London hospital.

'If you're talking about being a doctor,' Jenny put in, 'it strikes me that a doctor ought to know enough not to go out and get wet through. Give me that coat and I'll hang it in the drying room. Anyway, what were you doing out walking in this weather?'

'I needed the exercise,' he said. 'I was supposed to be off this afternoon.'

It was said lightly, but Cat caught an exchange of glances between the two and felt some undercurrent that she didn't quite understand. Why did he need the exercise? Still, it was none of her business.

Jenny took her to a changing room, found her

a set of scrubs and told her that she could scrub up in the A and E department. Cat wanted to know a little more before she went back to meet Dr McCain. She felt at a disadvantage, that things were moving too fast for comfort.

'I don't quite understand. If Dr McCain was supposed to be off this afternoon, why did you ask him to come in?'

'It's the way we work here. Technically, the hospital is independent of the practice. There's no doctor on duty in the hospital A and E department, it's supposed to be staffed by us nurses. The rule is, if we need help we make a formal request to the surgery. In fact, we just phone whoever we think is available and who will be most use. Harry Matthews is the senior partner, he'll turn out for anything. Finn Cavendish used to be a surgeon, we send for him when there's awkward suturing or anything like that to be done. Ross McCain is our star A and E man. And he's treated Frank Lyle before.'

'He seems very casual about it all.'

' "Seems" is the right word. Don't let his attitude fool you.'

'He was limping when he came in. I thought he was a patient, that he'd injured his leg.'

Jenny didn't answer straight away. Then she said, 'It's an old injury. Don't ask him about it, he'll tell you when he's ready.'

'Of course I won't ask him,' said Cat. It struck her that medicine here was going to be greatly different from that back in London. Things seemed far too informal and she wasn't sure if she liked it.

Jenny accompanied her back to the A and E department and she found herself scrubbing up next to Dr McCain. She noticed that the shapeless scrubs that he now wore hinted at a fit body beneath. His bare forearms were muscular, tapering to broad strong hands.

Why should she care what he looked like? She was still annoyed at him for not telling her he was a doctor. He could have told her! No one liked to be made to look a fool.

He spoke to her, still in the same light, casual tone. 'Dr Fraser, what is your first name? As I remember, it's Catherine. Do you go with all of that? Or are you Kate, or Cathy, or Katie?'

'Does it really matter?' She hadn't meant to be snappy, it just came out that way. It was the second time she'd been brusque with this man. She didn't know why because it wasn't like her. Perhaps she was tired.

He didn't appear to mind her shortness but answered thoughtfully. 'We're a team here, we tend to address each other by our first names. I'm Ross. We'll call you whatever you'd like to be called.' He smiled at her, his usual half-mocking smile. 'Even Dr Fraser, if you wish.'

'No, I don't wish,' she said after a while. 'In fact, I'm usually called Cat.'

'Cat?' He turned, looked at her carefully. 'Yes. You know, I think that's very suitable. Have you heard the theory that a people grow into their names? Call a boy George and he'll not be the same person he would have been if he'd been called Maurice.'

'I've heard the idea. But I don't feel like a cat.'

She didn't want to talk about her name or how

it affected her personality. She felt vulnerable. But the idea interested her. 'So you're a Ross. What is a Ross like?'

He thought a minute. 'Ross means from a peninsula. Surrounded by water on three sides.'

This was odd. 'Almost cut off, in fact? Are you almost cut off?'

'Possibly. All doctors have to be, to a certain extent. But I am connected to the mainland on one side.'

'Just as well. As you said, the name I was christened with was Catherine. It's Greek, it means pure.'

'Is that right?' he said easily, and she sighed with relief. There had been so many men in her life who had felt compelled to make some witty remark when she had told them that—but this man didn't. She liked him for it. And she liked him for the odd subject he'd picked to talk about. He seemed an interesting man.

She glanced at the clock on the wall. They seemed to have been talking for hours but it had only been two or three minutes.

'Time to work,' he said. 'We'll go and meet our friend Frank Lyle. But first...' he picked up a folder and handed it to her '...have a quick look through this. If it's possible I always like to look at a patient's case notes before I see him or her. But not in front of them. It makes them feel that you've taken some trouble, that you know what you're talking about.'

'It's a good idea.' But not a common one. In London she had seen far too many consultants arrive at the side of a bed, ignore the patient and just stand there, reading the notes. Of course, life was faster there.

She did as he'd suggested, had a quick flick through the notes. 'Tell me what you think,' he said after a while.

Common medical teaching practice. Ask a junior doctor to glance through notes, come up with a tentative diagnosis. Not a proper, serious diagnosis, of course, not one you could use to suggest treatment. But just to see that you could extract the most important facts from a thick sheaf of papers.

'Young man, Francis Lyle, aged twenty-five,' she said. 'Diagnosed as insulin-dependent diabetic, the usual treatment—insulin, diet control. Seems to respond well to treatment.' She flipped through the notes. 'But…treated here four times in the last three years for assorted accidents—three falls, one RTA.'

'Suggesting what, Cat?'

'If he does respond well to treatment, takes his insulin—well, it's just a guess. I'd need more proof, but I'd say that he gets over-confident, misses a meal or two, his blood sugar drops till he's hypoglycaemic and then he endangers himself. All these accidents look as if they were his fault.'

'So what do we do?'

'Check to make sure I'm right,' she said. 'Then…well, it's a social problem rather than a medical one. Persuade him to take his medication regularly and remind him that he has to eat regularly for it to work properly.'

'Too true. Now, let's go and look at the man in question.'

Frank Lyle was lying in a small side ward, temporary dressings on the side of his head and on his chest. He looked up at Ross, his expression plaintive.

Ross didn't speak at once, just looked at the figure on the bed. Then he shook his head and said, 'Frank, you know I'm wasting my time coming here. I've got better things to do. Why can't you carry on with your injections, keep an eye on your food? Everyone else I know manages it. And we've been through what you have to do often enough.'

'I'm sorry, Dr McCain. It's just that I...' The voice trailed away.

'It's just that you get a bit carried away. Forget about what you've got to do. Frank, it's not good enough! You know what could happen?'

'Well, yes. I suppose so.'

'Don't just suppose. Tell me.'

'I could go into a coma,' Frank muttered. 'And then I could...'

'You could die,' Ross said. 'And what would your mother think then?'

Rather to Cat's surprise, he didn't give Frank enough time to answer, but went on, 'Anyway, how's she doing in her new job?'

'She's enjoying it. Got fed up working in the shop. She likes it in the open air.'

'Good. Be a pity if she had to come back to the shop just so she could keep an eye on you, make sure you kept up with your injections. Wouldn't it be a pity?'

'Yes,' Frank said gloomily after a while. He realised he was being emotionally blackmailed but that there was nothing he could do about it.

'Well, think about it. Now I'm going to have a look at you and then I've got another doctor here who's going to stitch you up.'

Cat hadn't expected that. She was still reflecting on the rather unorthodox way Ross had treated his patient. Though she had to admit it seemed to work. Still…

She didn't have any of her own equipment handy so Ross had to perform the usual initial tests. But then Jenny pushed the trolley forward and it was time to suture. There was a slight initial apprehension, but then she thought that this was a job she had done many times before.

She had heard Frank explain how he had fallen off his quad bike while driving around the back yard of the builder's yard where he worked. After a quick inspection she realised that there were only two injuries. First, a cut to the head, which had bled a lot. But there were no signs of concussion. Then a long jagged wound from the right shoulder down across to the pectoral muscles. That would take quite some skill to suture—but she had that skill.

Jenny was the perfect A and E nurse, knowing in advance what Cat needed, making sure it was to hand. At first Cat was slightly nervous, aware of the silent figure of Ross watching her. But soon she became engrossed in her work. It took a while but then it was done. 'This is a slightly different suturing kit from the one I'm used to,' she said. 'I think it's a bit…old-fashioned. But I've done the best I can. Would you like to check?'

'Nothing to check. If you ever got tired of being a doctor, you could take up embroidery.'

He turned to her patient. 'Frank, we're keeping you in overnight, you've lost too much blood to send you home. But remember in future? Think of your mother?"

'Sure thing, Dr McCain. I will.'

'Good.' Ross turned and winked at Cat. 'Coffee time, I think,' he said.

She remembered that she had been about to go for a coffee before they'd met earlier on. A quick glance at her watch—that had been only three-quarters of an hour ago! Suddenly her life seemed to be moving quickly since Dr Ross McCain had entered it.

It was a pleasant, slightly untidy doctors' lounge. Ross poured them both a coffee, then opened a tin and looked gloomily into it. 'This place is dreadfully run,' he said. 'Look! No chocolate biscuits! How can I function without a chocolate digestive?'

Cat took a non-chocolate digestive from the offered tin. 'Chocolate is a comfort food,' she said reprovingly, thinking of her own recent vast consumption. 'Do you need comfort?'

'Everyone needs comfort at some time.'

They were having a light-hearted conversation, she was enjoying it. But Cat wondered if there had been just a touch of bitterness in Ross's last remark. Or perhaps she was imagining things.

He sat opposite her, drank from his coffee mug and smiled cheerfully at her. 'So how do you think you're going to like working here? Take your time, don't rush your answer.'

It had not been the kind of first day she had expected. She knew that it would be a shock, moving from a vast London hospital with an international reputation and a staff of hundreds. She had come to work in a rural general practice where there was the promise of some work in a cottage hospital with a staff of perhaps fifty. The shock, the change was to be part of her therapy. And Dr Ross McCain was not the kind of partner she had expected to be working with.

Over the telephone she had talked at length to the senior partner, Harry Matthews. She had formed an impression of a steady, professional, caring man, the kind of GP she wanted to become. Harry had mentioned the two other partners, Ross McCain and Finn Cavendish, had said he was sure she'd get on with them. Well, she was getting on with one. After a fashion.

Cautiously, she said, 'Things here are a bit different from what I'm used to. Not like London at all. A bit more…casual? I mean, I haven't even been through an induction programme yet. And was what I've just been through a test?'

'If it was a test then you've passed. And as for being casual—what do you think is the basic purpose of a GP? You've just spent nearly ten years of your life trying to become one. Why? Once again, take your time. No need to hurry.'

She drank her coffee, staring at him over the rim of the mug, trying to make him out. She had not expected that kind of question, not from a man so obviously relaxed, mug in hand, feet on the coffee-table. She would have liked a proper induction programme. Ross McCain was a bit of an enigma.

As it had been suggested to her, she would take her time. She remembered a lesson from one of her tutors that had been invaluable.

When seeing a patient for the first time, don't just start asking questions. Have a good look first. You can tell a lot about people just by their attitude. Are they scared, at ease, defensive, aggressive, uncaring? Look at their clothes, manner, jewellery; look at the way they walk, the way they look around. Listen to the sound of their words as well as the content. Feel for the person before you start to question.

So she looked closely at Ross, something she had not really done so far. Things had moved too quickly.

He was a few years older than her—perhaps six or eight years. Still young to be a full partner. She noted his muscular build, his apparently uncompromising face. But with those gorgeous blue eyes! Then it came to her almost as a shock. He was attractive! And he was even more attractive because he didn't seem to care about it or realise it. Most unlike many of the men she knew.

She hadn't recognised whether a man was attractive or not for quite a while.

That was his appearance. What about his character? He seemed friendly, as far as she could tell, got on well with staff and patients. His informal manner didn't hide his obvious medical competence. But she couldn't help feeling that there was something else to him, something hidden, a side he didn't want to show. The casual, friendly, outward appearance hid something darker. She wondered what it was.

He had asked her a question. What was the basic purpose of a GP? It was both a simple and a complex question, and she decided to give him a simple answer. 'A GP's job is to look after her patients' physical and mental health so that they have the chance to live a happy and productive life.'

He sighed. 'A good textbook answer—and I'm sure you really believe it. But it's not entirely correct. A GP's basic purpose is to work out if someone is really ill—and then send them on to the relevant consultant. Only one person in ten needs to see a doctor for treatment. A good nurse—like Jenny Carson downstairs—could do three-quarters of the average GP's work. No, more than three-quarters.'

Cat was shocked by that but tried not to show it. 'I think that's a bit cynical,' she said. 'I really feel that I want to, that I can do, more than that.'

'Just wait a few months until you've some idea of the average patient. You might change your mind. But, then, I don't want to spoil your illusions.'

He smiled, and when he smiled he was more attractive than ever. She wanted to get to know him better.

'Why were you limping when you came in?' she asked.

Instantly she knew it had been the wrong question. His face set in a mask of displeasure, even the temperature in the room seemed to drop. 'It was an old accident. It happened a long time ago, it seldom bothers me now.'

She knew she ought to leave things alone, he obviously did not want to talk further. But he had to know that she had a mind of her own. 'It does bother you,' she said. 'I saw you limping, saw you were in pain. The nurse saw it too, and she sympathised.'

'You observe quite a lot.' His words were cool and she saw anger flare in his eyes. Suddenly, she was a little afraid. This man was to be her tutor, she ought to…Then she realised that her fear had little to do with their professional relationship. He was a man and she was a woman and he felt that his pride had somehow been… 'Sorry,' she said. 'I shouldn't have been personal. It won't happen again.'

There was a pause. Then, with reluctant humour in his voice, he said, 'I doubt that. I suspect it will happen again. You've got one of those enquiring minds that won't let things go. You question and you want answers. A good thing in a young doctor.'

'But not in an older doctor?'

It was a while before he replied. Then he said, 'Perhaps older doctors know that to some questions there are no answers. And they learn not to let it worry them.'

He looked at his watch. When he spoke again

his voice had reverted to the light tone it had had before. He said, 'I'd like to stay and chat but time is passing, I have to go. We'll meet again in the surgery at six tonight. Look forward to seeing you then. Why not stay here and drink coffee? It's better than driving around in the rain.'

And he was gone. Cat thought that his limp was now less pronounced, wondered if he was making an effort for her benefit.

She poured herself another coffee then sat and thought. What was it going to be like, working here? She hadn't met him in person yet but she knew she was going to like working with Harry Matthews. They knew where they were with each other. But she hadn't even thought about the other two partners. What did she think of Ross McCain?

She couldn't work out her feelings. She wasn't quite sure that she liked his apparently casual attitude to life. And especially to medicine. But…she had always tried to be honest with herself. She had to face the facts. She was attracted to this man. She liked his sense of humour.

She liked the odd things he talked about—like the meanings of names. She loved the sound of his voice. And when he smiled and turned those blue eyes on her she felt her legs go weak.

This was ridiculous! She was off men. She'd had no great interest in them for a year now. She had parted from the one man she had been seeing because there hadn't seemed to be any pleasure or point in being with him. And she knew it had not been his fault. Her therapist had suggested that she try to avoid falling in love until she was completely healed. It seemed a good idea. But now she felt…different.

From outside there was a sudden outburst of childish chatter, young voices calling and shouting. Curious, she went to the window. She remembered she had been told there was a nursery downstairs. Obviously the day was at an end.

Now she knew why Ross McCain had had to leave in such a hurry. Below her there was a handful of people collecting children. Ross was one of them. He held the hand of a little boy, was smiling down at him. He was a little boy of about four. A sudden stab of memory pained her, she had to look away.

She sat again, feeling angry with herself. Never, never, never jump to conclusions. Ross had a little boy, he was a father. And so, obviously, he had a wife.

Cat was surprised at how upset that thought made her.

CHAPTER TWO

NOTHING was what it seemed in this topsy-turvy world. This morning, when she had set off from London, the sun had been shining. It had rained nearly all day after she had arrived in the Lake District. But now, in the evening, the sun was shining through her window and her room was warm.

She opened a window, let the air in. It was fresh, nothing like the smoke and fumes of London. She thought she liked it.

Her home, probably for the next year or so, was to be a cottage called Skiddaw View. And there was a view of Skiddaw from her living-room window. In fact, there was a view of a mountain or lake from nearly every window, Again, not like London. Her London home was quite a pleasant flat, but the only views it had were of other pleasant flats and a major road.

She had leased the cottage for six months with the option of extending the lease for another six months. At present the rent was quite expensive because it was the middle of the holiday season. Later it would be much cheaper. But altogether it was much less expensive than London. And she loved it already. It was like nothing she had ever lived in before. Things were changing!

There was a fireplace. Outside there were logs, delivered by the forestry commission. She'd never had an open fire of her own. She wanted the weather to change so she could light a fire.

The meeting at the surgery had been brief. She had talked to Harry, liked him as much in person as she had over the phone. She had seen Ross again, but had said little to him. The third partner, Finn Cavendish, was away on holiday with his wife Alanna and his daughter Eleanor.

'He's our mountain rescue expert,' Harry had said. 'Often called out. You might be asked to cover for him.'

She had felt apprehensive. 'Will I be asked to go out on rescues?'

Harry had shaken his head. 'Mountain rescue is a highly skilled business. We leave it to experts. But still…I wouldn't be surprised if, after a month or two, you wanted to go out to see what it's like.'

'Possibly,' Cat had agreed, thinking that it was possible but not likely.

The next day she was to be shown round the practice by the practice manager. There were people to meet, papers to sign. Then she would shadow Ross for a day or two.

'We'll all help but Ross will be your official mentor,' Harry had said. 'Is that OK?'

Cat had looked at Ross, unable to read his expression. 'Yes,' she had said.

And that had been her first official meeting. After the strict procedures she had been through in London, once again it had all seemed a bit casual. She had felt slightly uneasy. She would have to make up her own mind about things instead of referring to someone in authority.

There was a freedom here that she was not used to. She had realised it was time-saving and efficient but it was also a bit frightening.

Harry had brought her to Skiddaw View, there had been a short meeting with the landlord's agent and she had become the tenant. She had looked around the place, had fallen in love with it at once.

In the tiny kitchen, to her surprise she found enough food for an evening meal and breakfast. 'My wife Alice's idea,' Harry had explained. 'A small present to welcome you to the practice.' That had *never* happened before, not to anyone she knew.

And now she was sitting alone in her new home. There were her four cases on the living-room floor, the rest of her stuff would come up later. She made herself a cup of tea, checked her watch. It was only seven o'clock. So she sat on the couch and thought about her day. It had been eventful.

A weird feeling came over her, which she didn't recognise at first. A sort of longing, but she didn't know what for, a sense of loss. Then it struck her. She was lonely. For the first time in years she was not surrounded by friends or family, not in familiar surroundings. She was lonely. It was lovely here—but she was missing the roar, the bustle, even the smells of London. A single tear rolled down her cheek.

This was stupid! She was stronger than this! She realised it was not just loneliness but the usual sadness and guilt creeping up on her. The depression she had come here to escape, to put behind her. She had to get a grip. The cure was work.

She threw herself out of her chair, rushed around the little cottage, making the bed, unpacking her clothes, lining up her books on the bookshelf. Round the bed were the pictures of her family. Thoughts of them would be her company.

And as she worked she thought about the people she was to be working with. She had liked the staff she had met in the cottage hospital, liked the few she had met in the surgery. Harry Matthews had been everything she had suspected he would be, a striking white-haired figure who inspired confidence at once. She guessed the other partner, Finn Cavendish, would be just as good if Harry worked with him. Which left Ross.

Cat was not too sure of her feelings about him, he was not the kind of man she had met before. His casual attitude to medicine was contradicted by his obvious skill at it. One thing, though—she had to admit to herself that she found him physically very attractive. And he grew more attractive the more she thought about him.

Why was she doing this? She was here to work. And she was off men.

She looked in her larder. There was spaghetti, sauce, mince there. It would be easy to cook for herself. But she felt that restlessness that often came with being tired. She decided to walk outside, look around.

Quickly she changed into jeans and a T-shirt, threw a light jacket over her arm. Then she went out to survey Benthwaite.

It had a pleasant little shopping centre. There were many outdoor clothing shops—would she ever find herself buying that kind of kit? She thought not. Not her kind of thing.

Finally she went into a café, had a meal and afterwards found herself feeling considerably better. She should have known! Her blood sugar had been low, that was all.

It was still quite early, still light. Totally different weather from earlier. She thought that in future she'd need to take a coat with her everywhere. She decided to walk towards the lake.

There was a café, an ice-cream kiosk, two jetties where you could hire rowing boats. In a wired-off compound there were coloured dinghies lined up, a sign said 'Benthwaite Sailing Club'. The lake stretched silver across the bay to the mountains beyond, and a warm breeze caressed her bare arms.

'Lovely, isn't it?' a familiar voice said.

She turned in shock. There behind her was Ross. He was dressed differently now, in old blue jeans and a polo shirt. The shirt showed he had a flat stomach, muscles that had previously only been hinted at. There was that weather-beaten face, with the half-smile that she was coming to know. As if feelings were there but not to be recognised.

There was a lurch inside her, a sudden feeling that things now had changed. Quickly she decided that this was because meeting him had been unexpected. 'It is very nice,' she agreed after a moment. 'Strange, meeting you again.'

It was a pointless remark but he took it seriously. 'This is a small town, you're one of its doctors. Soon you'll be known to practically everyone. That is, everyone who lives here. Visitors come and go—but in time you hardly notice them.'

She looked at the crowds of holidaymakers. 'Perhaps,' she said.

He pointed to the dinghies inside the compound. 'You can always get away from the visitors. There's a breeze, the sun will last for another couple of hours. I'm going for a sail. Do you sail, Cat?'

She was surprised at the question. 'No. I've never been in a sailing boat in my life.'

'Can you swim?'

'What sort of a question is that? Of course I can swim.'

He looked at her thoughtfully. 'Then do you fancy an hour's sailing? A new experience.'

She hadn't expected that, was not sure how she felt about it. 'Sailing? With you?'

A small smile. 'Well, if you haven't even been out before, I wouldn't expect you to go out on your own.'

The next thing she said she regretted the moment she had said it. 'What about your wife? Won't she—?'

She saw his face freeze. 'I have no wife.'

'But I saw you with a little boy. I assumed he was your son. Wasn't he?'

'Yes. That was Stephen, my son. I have a son but no wife. There's just the two of us living together. My wife is dead.'

Dead. A leaden, final syllable. She shook with shock. 'I'm sorry,' she mumbled. 'I shouldn't jump to conclusions, that's the second time you've told me that.' In spite of herself, she felt a tear trickle down her face.

He looked at her curiously. 'Tears, Dr Fraser? Why should you feel so deeply about someone you have only just met? Surely a doctor gets used to death, the pain of other people? You have to learn to distance yourself in order to survive.'

'I know! And I can distance myself. It's just that…death and people I know. Just sometimes I… Don't worry, Dr McCain, I know how to distance myself. I won't embarrass you professionally.'

'I never thought you would.'

He stretched out his arm, rested it on her shoulder a moment. She thought she felt the warmth of his hand travel through her body. Apart from shaking hands, it was the first time they'd had any physical contact. She liked it. But she said nothing.

'It's still a lovely evening,' he went on, 'and there's no shortage of time. Stephen is having a wonderful time with his grandmother. She'll put him to bed. I like him to spend time with his family, though I love being with him myself. I have to make his life as normal as possible.'

'Stephen is with his grandmother? Is that…your mother or your wife's? Does she live with you?'

'My mother. And she doesn't live with me. She's a teacher, she has a flat and a life of her own. She loves Stephen but she's determined to remain independent. Still…it would have been hard to have coped without her and sometimes I wonder if I'm being fair to her.'

'If she's genuinely independent then it's her decision whether you're being fair to her or not.'

Ross looked at her thoughtfully. 'That's a very good point,' he said. 'So why not come for a sail for an hour?'

'Why not indeed?' she asked.

Of course, there was a reason why she should not be so close to this man. She was not sure of her feelings towards him. There was that undeniable attraction—just physical, of course! That was all it was. And she knew the foolishness of getting too close to someone you were working with. But…

'It'll be something quite new,' she said. 'I came up here for a different life, a new life. This can be part of it.'

'Good. And you'll be dealing with nature, not people. Nature is simpler than people. It's honest, but unforgiving when crossed. And I like that. I like knowing where I stand.'

He led her into the compound, walked towards what looked like a very small sailing boat. It was painted dark blue with its name in gold—*Naiad*.

'Naiad?' she questioned.

'The Greek nymph of fresh water. A source of inspiration for poets and those enraptured.'

'Enraptured? Do you get enraptured in it?'

'Not in it, in her,' he corrected her. 'Boats, ships are feminine. And I don't get enraptured in her. Take time out to get enraptured in a dinghy and you tend to get wet as well. Sailing takes concentration. Now, let's go for a couple of life jackets.'

She wasn't convinced with his answer, she thought there was rapture in him. Or, at least, the capacity for it. Still, it was no concern of hers.

It was exciting, it was fascinating, she loved it. The first time the little boat heeled to a sudden gust of wind, she screamed—just a bit. And they seemed to be going so fast. But they weren't.

He held the tiller, sat towards the back of the boat. She sat more or less in the middle. She had thought that he was taking her for a kind of cruise, that she could sit in comfort and watch the passing scenery. Nothing could have been further from the truth. When a particularly strong gust of wind hit the sail, she had to sit on the side of the boat and lean backwards towards the water, her feet caught under what he called a kicking strap. The wind was erratic. Sudden little squalls raced across the water so she was constantly changing her position.

She ought to have been nervous, but she wasn't. Ross inspired confidence. He didn't say much, and what he did say she wasn't sure she understood. 'If the wind gets too strong then you just put your helm down and the air spills from the sails—see?'

She wasn't sure that she did see, but she shouted 'Yes' anyway.

She was excited. It wasn't just the movement of the boat, or the glimpses she got of the passing countryside. She liked watching Ross. He moved deftly about the little boat, as if it was an extension of himself. And as they sailed he seemed to grow—well, easier. The barrier she had felt between them slipped away.

Eventually they crossed the lake, drew into quieter waters. 'I could see you enjoying that,' she said. 'I enjoyed it too, but not the way you did. I just enjoyed the ride. You enjoyed it because you were in control—like fighting something and winning.'

'Perhaps,' he said. 'I told you before, nature is simpler than people. The rules are there but they're obvious.'

'You sail a lot here?

'And canoe sometimes. I like watersports and this is the place for them.'

'So you're not a walker and a climber, like everyone else?' Then she remembered his limp, the obvious pain that walking had given him, and realised what she had just said. 'Oh, heck,' she mumbled. 'That was really insensitive of me and I'm truly sorry.'

She saw the wry grin she had come to know so

well. A recognition that the world was an imperfect place—but what could you do?

'Dr Fraser, you must learn not to upset patients with careless remarks. Especially when those remarks are true.'

She blushed. 'It won't happen again.'

'No matter. An easy mistake to make.' There was another quite friendly pause and then he went on, 'I used to walk a lot. I loved it.'

'I'm not going to ask you what happened,' she said. 'I think I've made enough mistakes already.'

'Good. Don't ask.' His voice was brusque. But it changed. 'Now, slide over here. Don't try to stand!'

She had half risen to her feet.

When she swiftly sat down again, he said, more calmly, 'You never stand up in a dinghy. If you stand, you can fall. Now, just try to slide over here to where I am and I'll take your place. It's quieter here so I'll give you a sailing lesson.'

'But I've never done this before!' She was still a bit unsure, a bit frightened.

'You were enjoying yourself, I could tell. I

could see by your face and the way your body moved. You'll be a good sailor.'

He'd noticed that much? She hadn't realised he'd been paying so much attention to her.

There was a gentler breeze here, in the shadow of a great hillside. He put her hand on the tiller and then covered it with his own. Again, the apparently casual touch thrilled her. She felt a tremor, wondered if he felt the same way. She looked at the two hands clasped, and then at him. A tiniest flicker of recognition suggested that he had felt the same. But then his face relapsed into the half-smile that hid all feelings.

'A boat is a living thing,' he said. 'You must become part of her, just as you must become part of a horse when you ride. If you know what she's feeling, she will respond to you.'

She couldn't resist. 'Like a lover?' she asked.

She might have guessed his answer. It was sardonic. 'A boat will never betray you without cause. It will treat you as you deserve. Take liberties—and you will be punished. But a lover...' He left the sentence unfinished.

She decided that this was something that she didn't want to pursue. At least for the moment. But later perhaps…

'Tell me more about sailing, 'she said. 'How do I get the sails to fill with wind? They're just flapping now.'

For perhaps half an hour he taught her and she became more and more entranced. He was right—you had to feel the boat, recognise the little signs that came from the stiffness of the tiller or the hesitation when the wind spilled from the sails. And that lovely gurgle of bubbles when the boat surged forward!

'I'm going to do this again,' she told him. 'Could I join the club?'

'Probably. But don't forget it's not always like this. You haven't capsized yet.'

'A treat to come,' she said.

He glanced at the sky. 'It's getting dark. Time to get back. Fancy a quick drink in the club-house?'

Things were moving fast, Cat thought. But, then, this wasn't a date or anything like that—

it was just two colleagues enjoying themselves. 'I'd love one,' she said.

She liked the clubhouse. It was really only a wooden hut, vastly different from the sophisticated bars she sometimes went to in London. But it was well decorated and cheerful, and she felt at home at once. She asked for a glass of white wine.

Ross was popular. As he made his way to the bar a good dozen people said hello to him. He could have stayed at the bar longer to chat, but instead he came back to her, sitting at a little table that looked over the now darkening lake. He had a glass of white wine for her, a beer for himself.

She was interested in Ross, needed to know more about him. So she asked him about his son, a subject she'd usually avoid as too painful.

'Ross, what's it like, bringing up a child as a single parent?'

He shrugged. 'There are plenty of unmarried mothers. Why not an unmarried father? And don't forget, I may not have a wife but Stephen's grandmother helps out a lot. She and Stephen get on well. One thing I like about this town and this practice is that we can make arrangements among ourselves. In fact, until recently another practice member was in the same situation. The partner you haven't yet met, Finn Cavendish, was bringing up a daughter on his own. But now he's got a wife and Eleanor, the little girl, now has a mother as well as a father. Everyone is happy. Theirs is rather an interesting story but I'll let him tell you.'

In fact, Cat was curious about Finn. But she was more curious about Ross. 'So Eleanor now has a mother and everyone is happy. Don't you want Stephen to be happy the same way? Doesn't he need a mother?'

'Perhaps.'

The brusque, single-word answer should have warned her but she pressed on anyway. 'And that would mean that you got a wife.'

'That I do not want.' A flat, definite answer.

He stood, indicated her empty glass. 'I'll fetch you another drink.'

Cat was going to offer to get him one but decided that this time it wasn't a good idea. Ross appeared to have had enough of women asking awkward questions. And she didn't want to fall out with him.

Ross stood at the bar, waiting for the steward to open another bottle of white wine. He thought he was quite enjoying his evening—more so than he had thought he would. And he wondered if he ought to be enjoying himself.

Cat Fraser was not at all what he had expected. Certainly he knew that the practice needed a junior doctor to ease the pressure. They were always overworked. He also knew it was a good idea for the practice to have a female doctor on the staff—though in general he would have preferred a male. They were often easier to get on with.

And if he had to have a female doctor, perhaps ideally he'd have preferred one just a little less attractive than Cat. He'd noticed the admiring eyes as he'd walked into the club bar with her. Unusually, she didn't appear to have noticed. Now, why would that be?

She was attractive. Tall for a woman—which meant tall enough for him. No! He shouldn't be thinking that way! Her body was slim but didn't have that haggard look that too much exercise and slimming could produce in a woman. Dark brown hair, cut short in a style that looked careless but he suspected had cost quite a bit. Brown eyes that could smile but too often seemed thoughtful, downcast. Her face was beautiful, classically beautiful in the way that no particular feature seemed outstanding but the whole was perfect.

But there was something wrong. She seemed to be holding something back. Something had worried her, had hurt her. Something made her feel guilty.

And why had she come here from London? He had noticed her lack of ease at the informal way the practice was run, knew she wanted the certainties of a large hospital. Something must have brought her up here.

He was intrigued by Cat. He told himself that his interest was purely professional. Then he grinned. He had never lied to himself. He was still a young, virile man. Of course his interest wasn't all professional. But he knew that the professional interest must outweigh the personal.

He carried the drinks back to their table. Time perhaps to dig a bit deeper into Cat's character. After all, she had asked some quite personal questions of him. Then he paused and thought. He had answered her questions—well, some of them—quite openly. Unusual for him.

He sat opposite her, sipped from his drink and attacked at once. 'You seemed a bit in doubt when asking me about Stephen,' he said, 'almost as if you had to force yourself to ask about him. Why?'

He saw that he had shaken her. To avoid replying at once, she lifted her glass to her lips, but he saw her hand shaking. But then she recovered. 'You're imagining things,' she said with a weak smile. 'It's just that I don't…I don't…I haven't had much to do with young children, especially lately.'

'Dr Fraser, as a GP you'll have to learn—not exactly how to lie to patients but how to dissemble. There are things they ask about—but they don't need or really want to know. You have to be able to recognise that. And your skills at dissembling are poor.'

'Are you saying that I'm lying to you!' Her anger was obvious.

'Not at all,' he said calmly. 'Tell me that I'm wrong and I'll believe you. We're colleagues, we'll probably end up as friends. Friends trust each other.'

She thought about this for a moment, and then said, 'Will you accept that there's something that I just don't want to talk about? Something that's too personal?'

'Of course. I know exactly how you feel.' He couldn't help himself, there was more sincerity in his voice than he had intended. He saw that she had noted this. She looked at him, her brown eyes showing an intensity that hadn't been there before. For a moment they stared at each other, a communion that was deeper because it wasn't expressed in words. Then both decided to back away. At least for now. 'So you'd like to go sailing again?' he asked.

It was getting late, and after they'd finished their second drink they decided to leave. When he told her that he'd walk her home she didn't protest that it might be out of his way. Good, he thought. She should know that there were things he would expect to do as a matter of course. And the walk through the warm night was pleasant. They chatted about medical problems, about odd patients each had had in the past. It was an amiable, safe conversation.

It only took ten minutes to walk to Skiddaw View. He walked her to her front door, waited till she had found her key and opened it. 'Goodnight, Ross,' she said. 'I've enjoyed this evening no end.' Then, before he could turn to go, she put her hands lightly on his arms, reached up and kissed him.

She had intended just a gentle kiss on the cheek, a thank-you kiss, a kiss recognising that two friends had just spent a pleasant evening together. That had been the idea.

Perhaps he moved his head for, instead of kissing his cheek, her lips touched his. And then they lingered.

She was just a dark shadow in front of him, he had no idea of her expression. But he could feel the warmth of her breath, feel the warmth of her body.

He put his hands on her hips, drew her towards him so that not just their lips but their bodies were touching. Just touching. Whatever was between them, the feeling, the tentative understanding was fragile. For a while both were happy. A moment, minutes, to enjoy with no thought of what they were doing, no thought of consequences.

But it could not go on. He took his hands from her hips, made as if to move away from her. But her grip on his arms tightened. She didn't want him to go.

His arms slid round her waist just as she reached up and pulled his head down to hers. Now their bodies were tightly together. He could feel the softness of her body, so wonderful against his own tight-muscled frame. And the kiss! Her mouth opened, she took him willingly, taking and giving at the same time.

But he knew this had to end before things went

too far. There was too much to think of, too many things holding them apart. Slowly, reluctantly he released her, eased her away from him. She sighed. He could feel her sadness, her disappointment.

Now they were apart. The distance between them was inches but it could have been miles.

'Well, thank you…thank you for the evening, Ross,' she said. Her voice was unnaturally high. 'I have enjoyed myself. But it's been a full day and I didn't realise just how tired I was. I really don't know what I've been doing.'

'Nor me,' he said. 'I'm looking forward to working with you tomorrow, Cat. Goodnight.' He turned to stride away. Behind him he heard the door click shut.

His thoughts were whirling but he guessed that they had parted on the right note. What had happened between them had been an accident, a small mistake. There was no need to talk about it, both understood the fact. They would be all right working together the next day.

But he couldn't forget the kiss.

It took him fifteen minutes to walk to his own

home and he was still slightly dazed when he got there. His mother smiled and said that she'd had a great time with Stephen and he'd gone to bed happily. But she wouldn't stay for a late-night drink. Then she left.

Ross was restless. He crept into his son's bedroom, for ten minutes stared at the sleeping face. Children's faces were like blank sheets of paper, he thought. Smooth, unspoiled. Life had not yet had time to write on them, produce the lines that showed misery—or, for that matter, happiness.

He went to his own bedroom and for another ten minutes stared at a photograph of his wife. His son was growing to resemble her, he realised. Would that cause him more pain in the future?

That was enough gloom!

He moved decisively, prepared clothes for Stephen and himself for the morning, set out the breakfast things. He liked order. He had always been like this, especially in the bush. Besides, for him memories were always strongest in the morning. Good to have everything ready. Then there was no time to mope, no time to get angry.

Bedtime. He slept in a small, single bed, which got rather lost on the large master bedroom. He wouldn't sleep in a double bed, it brought back memories. And in a double bed, if you were half-asleep, there was always the chance that you'd reach out your arm for someone—and there'd be no one there.

To bed. Usually he went straight to sleep. At one time he'd thought he'd never sleep again, but he'd learned a technique that helped him. Take a powerful scene out of your past. A scene of peace, serenity, happiness. Then associate those feelings with your present life.

He thought of his son, his wife, himself. Sitting together in the warm African night, tired but happy. They had been good times.

But tonight the technique didn't work. And more and more he found himself thinking of Cat. He realised he had been avoiding thinking of her. Why? He wondered why he had offered to take her out sailing, he was usually most happy on his own. But this time he had enjoyed being with her.

He turned over in bed yet one more time and

frowned. Cat wasn't for him. She was young, inexperienced. He was seven years older than her—and felt very jaded.

CHAPTER THREE

CAT slept well. After Ross had left the night before she had gone straight to bed, exhausted, both physically and mentally. Too much had happened, too much to think about. She had found refuge in the deepest sleep she'd had for weeks.

She was woken up quite early, not by the customary roar of traffic but by birdsong. Now, this was a change! She felt refreshed, discovered she was quite looking forward to the new day. But for a while she would lie in bed and think about the day before. A lot new had happened.

Medicine here was different. It was more… hands on. It was more personal. If she were honest, it seemed a bit old-fashioned, well away from the cutting edge she was accustomed to. It was new to her now, but she thought perhaps she'd get to like it.

Sailing! She'd really enjoyed it, it was like nothing she had ever done before. She wanted to go again. She'd ask Ross again if there was any chance of joining the club.

So, now to the memory—the problem?—that had been underlying the other two thoughts. Ross McCain. And that kiss. She had intended it to mean so little. Just a sign of wary affection between two new friends. In London, if she wanted, she'd kiss a new acquaintance without thinking twice about it. But this wasn't London. And the kiss had ended up meaning so much more.

Or had it? She thought of her last boyfriend, Richard. Kissing him ought to have been pleasant but ultimately it had degenerated into something that they just did. The listlessness that seemed to have taken over her personal life had spread to her love life too. But kissing Ross had been different. It had surprised her, the reaction she had felt. As if there was something new stirring inside her.

This was wrong! Her therapist had told her not to think of falling in love until she was fully well. That she'd known it when the time came. And then a sour taste came to her mouth. Ross had a four-year-old son, he wasn't for her. In fact, no man was for her. Not for a while. And so now it was time to get out of bed.

A quick shower, a quick breakfast. She reminded herself that she had to buy food and also some flowers for Harry's wife. She dressed in a rather plain blue dress and checked the contents of her doctor's briefcase. And then she discovered that there was still an hour before she was due at the surgery. There must be something in the air here!

So she would walk to work. She left her cottage and headed for the centre of not-yet-awake Benthwaite. The day was fine, the sun promised heat later. There was mist on the lake—real mist, not traffic fumes. There was the green-grey mass of Skiddaw in the distance. This was magic!

Today she was to shadow Ross at the surgery,

watch him work, see what she could learn from him. She was looking forward to it. He was a different kind of doctor from the ones she knew best. All her friends were go-getters. They were competent, dedicated, determined to get on in their profession. People like she had been—no, still was. She shook her head, she had to remember why she was here. This year was a year out, a rest period. At the end of it she would return to London and to her previous high-flying life. And she'd enjoy it.

But Ross seemed very competent. He seemed happy where he was—almost in a backwater. She wondered about his background. Twice when she had asked she had been rebuffed. Perhaps she should ask again.

'We've got the patient's consent for you to observe a consultation,' Ross said cheerfully. 'I'll introduce you as Dr Fraser. For this morning, you just watch. Or perhaps I'll ask you to join in. We'll talk afterwards about what we've seen and done.'

When she had seen him first thing that morning he had smiled at her, asked her if she had slept well. She had smiled back, saying she had, thank you. Just two new colleagues about to work together. But she thought there had been a hint of speculation in his eyes, perhaps even some relief. Obviously the kiss was to be forgotten. Which was probably a good thing.

Their first patient was Andy Green, a white-faced young man of twenty-one. There was a rather dirty white bandage wrapped round his right hand and he was obviously in pain. 'So what have you got for me today, Andy?' Ross asked.

Cat still couldn't get used to the informality Ross used with his patients. It was quite different from her own experience. Still, most of her previous patients she had seen only occasionally. Ross obviously had his regulars.

'Tripped and fell against the kitchen stove last night,' Andy mumbled. 'Burned my hand.'

Let's have a look at it, then.' Ross snipped off the bandage, peered at the hand. 'You say you fell against the stove? Last night?'

'That's right! I'd had a bit too much to drink. I did put some stuff on myself, but it still hurts so I came here.'

'A good thing you did. Dr Fraser, what do you think of this injury?'

So she was going to be involved. She didn't mind, felt quite confident. She'd had quite a long rotation in a burns unit. She inspected the burned hand, even bent over it to smell it. Yes, she was certain. But what was she to do now? She was going to flatly contradict Andy's statement.

She looked at Ross, who looked back at her with his noncommittal half-smile. She remembered the way he had dealt with Frank Lyle yesterday. She'd do the same.

'This burn wasn't done last night, it's at least two days old. And it wasn't done on a kitchen stove. I'd guess it was a petrol burn.'

'I tell you I fell against the kitchen stove!' Andy was angry.

'Are you sure?' Ross asked politely. 'It looks like a petrol burn to me too. But if we treat it as a stove burn rather than a petrol burn, well, there's a difference in treatment. Your hand could be permanently damaged. Which would be a pity, as I know you're a car mechanic. You need to use your hands.'

There was silence in the room for a minute. Cat looked at the two men—Ross with that half-smile, Andy obviously torn, not knowing what to say. But eventually Andy said, 'Perhaps there was some petrol,' he said.

'Right. Now we know the proper treatment. I should send you to the nurse for dressing, but I think I'll do it myself this time.'

Cat was intrigued. Nurses' and doctors' jobs were usually well defined, separated. And it was always nurses who did the dressings. But Ross was dressing the hand with tremendous skill. Obviously he'd done this kind of thing before.

As he worked he said to Andy, 'I heard there was an old car burned out in the quarry near your house a couple of night ago. Apparently stolen first. From a friend of yours.'

'Nothing to do with me!'

'Of course not. But if the police see you with

this burned hand, if the park wardens find out—especially if your boss finds out—they might suspect that you had something to do with a burning car. Might think it had been burned as an insurance swindle.'

Cat listened to these apparently casual remarks with mounting horror. Did Ross know nothing about patient/doctor confidentiality? This was entirely unethical. She had to say something.

'Dr McCain, I wonder if we should—'

'Thank you, Dr Fraser. This is my patient. Please let me deal with him.'

She was shocked at the coldness of the reprimand. But there was nothing she could do about it, there was no way could they have an argument in front of a patient. But afterwards it would be different.

Ross went on, as casually as if she had never spoken. 'It's not my business and I'm going to say nothing. What would be a good thing would be for you to sort things out with the police. If there's no insurance claim, I doubt there'll be too much trouble.'

He finished the bandaging. 'That's better. Make an appointment to see me in three or four days. We'll see how the hand is getting on. And it would be nice to see the problem with the car sorted out.'

'Thanks, Doctor.' Andy slunk out.

Ross turned to her, raised his eyebrows. 'You have a comment, Dr Fraser?'

'I have several, *Dr* McCain. You threatened that man. In effect you said you would report him to the police. You interfered. That's not the kind of medicine I want to practise. My job is to heal the sick, not to send them to prison. What about your Hippocratic oath?'

Her comments didn't appear to anger him—which annoyed her more. He merely smiled and said, 'I was practising community medicine as best I could. Trying to do the best for everyone. Don't forget, this is a community here. It's not London, where people wander in and out of doctors' surgeries at will.'

'At least in London we treat our patients professionally!' Then she winced. Had she really said that?

But Ross didn't seem to mind. He glanced at his watch. 'We've got a couple of minutes, let me tell you about a problem I had last year. You tell me how you'd have dealt with it.'

'All right,' said Cat.

'I had a patient last year. Born locally, wandered a bit but always came back to stay with his father. Usually, I suspect, when he'd made a mess of his life elsewhere. This is a small community, I knew all about him. He was a petty thief, fighting in the pub, father of at least two babies—to whom he contributed nothing. He had a certain flashy charm. Still, he was a patient so I treated him as best I could. And I found he was HIV positive.'

'We're not allowed to pick and choose when it comes to patients,' Cat said. 'We're doctors.'

'Quite so. I had another patient, a young girl who came to me for a prescription for the contraceptive pill. I was in doubt. She wasn't very bright—in fact, she was just out of a special needs class at school. But she was over eighteen and she was entitled to have the Pill. And then I learned she was seeing rather a lot of my patient with HIV. Soon I was going to have two patients with HIV. What should I do?'

'Not break the Hippocratic oath! You have a duty of silence to your patient.'

'Which patient?'

'You can't interfere! It's not your business.'

'Is it interfering if you push a drunk out of the way of a car that's about to run him down?'

Cat sighed. 'I know it's a criminal offence to deliberately infect someone with HIV.'

'Which is a great consolation to the person who has been infected.'

She had to ask. 'So what did you do?'

'Nothing,' he replied urbanely. 'The word just got round about him being HIV positive—and he was warned off by someone. Wasn't me. He probably talked about it in the pub.'

Cat shook her head. 'It all sounds a bit suspicious to me. A bit vigilante.'

'Perhaps so. Or perhaps it's the community looking after its own.' He looked at her thoughtfully. 'Cat, we're disagreeing about something that obviously concerns you deeply. Like you said, this isn't London. We tend to do things in a more old-fashioned way here. Do you want to have another mentor? I can easily arrange for you to have Harry or Finn.'

'No! I want you!' Perhaps it came out a bit more forcibly than she had intended. So she added, 'I think you're a good doctor and I can learn from you. Perhaps I'll take some of your ideas back with me when I go.' She went on, 'And I was very impressed by the way you did that bandaging. Not many doctors can do it so well. Where did you learn that?'

'Just something I picked up,' he muttered. Not a convincing answer and there was a blankness to his face that showed her that he didn't want more questions. More for her to ponder about later.

It was a typical GP's morning surgery. A visitor who had been diving in the lake and was now deaf. 'I bought this stuff from the chemist and put it in my ear,' he explained, 'but it hasn't made things much better. Could I have my ears syringed, please?'

Ross invited her to look in the ear. 'No wax,' she reported, 'but a definite infection.'

The man was prescribed drops. 'If you've any doubts at all,' Ross told him, 'come and see us. It's what we're here for.'

When the patient had gone Ross smiled at her and said, 'Did you learn anything from that?'

'Not many London GPs would encourage a casual visitor so happily,' she told him.

'This isn't London. We're a community here. We look after each other.'

That word, 'community'. She heard it a lot. 'Community medicine' was one of the latest concepts in medicine. Here it really seemed to mean something.

Next, an old lady, in, she said, for her regular check-up. Ross introduced her as Miss Jayson. Miss Jayson shook Cat's hand and said she was very pleased to meet her. There was a few minutes' polite chat and then Ross asked Cat if she'd give Miss Jayson a quick physical examination. But he didn't move from his position in front of the computer. Cat looked at him. She needed to be in his seat to access Miss Jayson's notes. He smiled at her.

Cat understood. Another small test.

Miss Jayson's blood pressure was high but not excessively so. Cat took her pulse, frowned and then asked if she could listen to Miss Jayson's heart. Yes, what she had suspected was there. She looked at Ross, feeling that, as the doctor in charge, he ought to be the one to give the news. But there was no need.

'You've detected my arrhythmia,' Miss Jayson said cheerfully. 'It's atrial fibrillation, you know.'

'Three doctors and no patient in one consulting room is too many,' Ross told her with a smile. 'Dr Fraser, what treatment do you suggest?'

'A statin to lower the levels of lipoproteins in the blood,' Cat answered, 'and perhaps warfarin to thin it. For the arrhythmia, an ACE inhibitor to widen the arteries and a beta-blocker to stimulate the heart.'

'Sounds like just what I'm taking,' Miss Jayson trilled. 'Very good, Dr Fraser.'

This seemed to be a two person test that Cat

was taking, so she decided to try to push her marks up even higher. 'I would have thought that you might have tried a cardioversion but, of course, that is not always successful.'

Cat had watched quite a few cardioversions—they had to be performed by a consultant. Under a general anaesthetic, an electric charge was applied to the walls of the chest. Sometimes the shock cured an irregular or too speedy heartbeat. Sometimes it did not.

'Excellent! Just what happened!' Miss Jayson was enjoying herself. 'But it didn't work for long.'

Ross tipped the screen of the computer towards Cat. She read what was there but frowned. Her diagnosis and treatment was almost exactly the same as Ross's. But instead of the beta-blocker she had suggested, he had prescribed digoxin. A reasonable choice, she thought. But she would have… She'd question him about it later.

The medical bit was over. Now was the time for the chat. 'You're watching your diet, exercising regularly but not overdoing it?' Ross questioned.

Yes, Miss Jayson was doing exactly as she had been told.

'And how is Maria doing with the baby? How do you like being a great-aunt?'

Miss Jayston compressed her lips a little. 'I'm sure she's doing very well. I don't see as much of little Oliver as I'd like.'

'New mothers are often overprotective,' said Ross.

'So what did we learn from that visit?' Ross asked, when an obviously satisfied Miss Jayson had left.

'We learned that you like to gossip.'

He grinned. 'Read correctly, gossip is often more accurate than a medical diagnosis. People here are interested in each other, care for each other. I read a case in the paper last week. An old man living alone in a tower block had died and lay dead in his flat for ten days before someone noticed. That wouldn't happen here. Someone at least would knock. It might be nosiness—but there'd be care there too. Now, what did you learn about Miss Jayson—apart from diagnosing her perfectly?'

'She used to be a teacher?' Cat guessed. 'Liked it when the class got things right?'

'Very good. She taught at the local primary school for over forty years. What else?'

'She wants to see more of Oliver, presumably her sister or brother's first grandchild.'

'True. Her sister is dead. Miss Jayson brought Maria's husband up—and did it very well. I'll have a word with Maria when she comes in, and mention things to the midwife. Miss Jayson could be a great help to her sister's daughter-in-law.'

'Ross, that isn't medicine! You're a doctor, not a social worker.'

'A doctor has to be part social worker. Remember, you don't treat a complaint. You treat a person.'

'Right,' said Cat. It was an interesting idea.

But now there was something else she had to ask about. 'Ross, to regularise the heartbeat, I suggested a beta-blocker for Miss Jayson. You've prescribed digoxin.'

'An old but still efficient drug. Once a herbal

remedy. Where would we be without the purple foxglove?'

Cat felt she had to step carefully here. It wasn't her place to correct a man as obviously experienced as Ross. But... 'There's been some research in the past three or four years that suggests that digoxin is usually fine, but if the patient is physically or emotionally distressed, it doesn't work as well. A beta-blocker is better.'

He was silent for a moment. 'I didn't know that. Do you mind if I check it out?'

'Of course not. In fact, I might be wrong.'

'Now, that I doubt.'

Cat looked up, feeling relieved. Ross was smiling.

It was an interesting morning. There were other cases, most not very serious. Ross always found time to exchange a few friendly words and Cat came to realise that people liked coming to see him. At the end of their session she realised that this apparently casual country doctor was actually much more skilled than her slicker colleagues in London.

There was one thing more. At lunchtime she was having her sandwich and coffee in the staff lounge when Ross came into the room. He was late and he was carrying a sheaf of papers—obviously printouts from the computer. He came to sit next to her.

'You were right and I was wrong,' he said. 'Beta-blockers before digoxin. I've just checked the web for details and then I phoned a consultant heart man I know. I'll change Miss Jayson's next prescription. Cat, I'm learning from you.'

'Not half as much as I'm learning from you,' she said.

'And there's another thing. I've been wondering about your point of view about patient confidentiality. If we believe that a patient's actions may result in serious injury to another person then we are entitled to break that confidence. But only if it is absolutely necessary.'

'I've been wondering about that too. In A and E in a large London hospital patients come and often you never see them again. They drop out of your life. But in a community…I can see that it might be different.'

'You're learning,' he said, 'and I suppose so am I.'

The afternoon was different. Harry had said that he wanted her to understand the working of all parts of the surgery so she was to observe the district nurse, the practice nurse and the midwife. That afternoon she was to go on the rounds with Paula Kirk, one of the midwives.

Some of the calls were local, but more than a few were in outlying farms and villages. It was a new world for Cat, driving up and down narrow tracks, seeing vistas stretch out for ever. Mostly it was simple calls to check up on the progress of pregnancies.

The last stop was at a large farm perched high on the shoulder of the fell. Cat knew nothing about farming, but she thought the farmyard looked well organised, the flower-beds round the house now in full bloom.

'Patient's name is Anna Summers,' Paula

said. 'Baby's due any day now—almost any minute. I've been called out once but it was a false alarm.'

'She didn't send for an ambulance?'

'She's having the baby at home,' said Paula.

They were greeted by a smiling Anna, her hands clasped lovingly round her bump. This time they did accept the offer of a cup of tea. Practically every home offered them hospitality of some sort.

'Just wait till Christmas,' Paula had warned her with a grin. 'It's not tea then, it's alcohol. You make a call, they say just have a little one—a glass of sherry or some home-made wine—and if you accepted each time, you'd be roaring drunk before you'd completed half your round.'

'I'll remember that.'

After a couple of minutes' chat Anna led them into a room on the ground floor that had obviously been set up as the place where the baby would be born. There Paula carried out the usual inspection and then told Anna that all was well—it could happen at any time.

'I'm ready,' said Anna. 'I'm looking forward to it.'

Paula sat at a table to write up her notes and it was left to Cat to chat to Anna. 'Why do you want to have your baby at home?' she asked. 'I'm sure nothing will go wrong but you know you're a long way from emergency help. And it's not as if the cottage hospital is a vast, impersonal place. You'd find yourself among friends.'

Anna smiled. 'Look out of the window,' she said.

Cat did—and sighed. There was a view that stretched for miles, over the hills, crags and forests, as far as the glint of the sea in the distance.

'I want my baby to be born to that view,' Anna said. 'After he's seen me, seen his father, then I want him to be held up to see the fells. They're his birthright. I know that babies so young can't really see—but somehow he will feel them.'

'This is something new to me,' said Cat. 'Mothers-to-be in London don't feel this way.'

'John, my husband, was born in this room. His father was born in it too, his grandfather was born in it. It's a tradition I want to carry on.'

'I think that's wonderful,' said Cat. 'But if there's any problem...'

'I'll be in Rosewood like a shot.' Anna grinned.

'So how are you finding Benthwaite so far?' Paula asked as they drove slowly away from the farm. 'Bit of a change from London?'

'A big change,' Cat said honestly. 'It's a whole new way of life and I'm not sure what I think of it yet. I like it but it's different. It even smells different here. I never thought it possible to miss petrol fumes, but there are times when I think I do.'

Paula laughed, waved her hand at a field of cows they were passing. 'We have our own smells,' she said. 'You'll get used to them. Even get to appreciate them.'

'In time,' Cat said doubtfully. Farmyards could get a bit...strong. Still, she'd see. 'Are you from round here, Paula? Your accent seems a bit different from everyone else's.'

'I'm originally from Manchester. I came here on holiday, met a local man, and after a fortnight he asked me if I really had to go back. By then

I'd fallen in love with him and I'd fallen in love with Benthwaite. I did go back—but just to pick up my belongings. Been here thirty years now, got to know everybody, and I love it.'

'Right,' said Cat. 'I'm just getting to know people. Dr McCain is my mentor. I'm hoping to learn from him.'

'You will. He's a great doctor because he won't stand any nonsense. He says what he thinks. You know where you stand with him.'

'Sounds good,' said Cat.

'He's not been here very long,' Paula said, obviously settling herself in for a comfortable gossip. 'He came to the practice three years ago.'

'But I thought he was a local! He seems to know everybody.'

'So he does. And he is from around here but not a lot of people know him. Really know him, I mean. He'll say hello, stop for a chat, ask after your family, but he doesn't say a lot about himself.'

'I gather his wife is dead,' Cat said, trying desperately to sound only vaguely interested. 'That's tragic.'

Paula looked at Cat with an assessing eye and Cat realised that her attempt to sound casual had not been very successful. Was her interest too obvious? But that was the way Ross worked. Find out what you know by gossip. So she went on, 'He seems devoted to that son of his.'

'He is,' Paula agreed. 'And he's a nice boy.'

She was silent for a moment as she tried to squeeze the car past a couple of sheep who just did not have the sense to stand still. Then she went on, 'Quite a few women around here have set their cap at him. But none lasted long. He was willing to be a friend but that was all. He might find the right woman in time. But I suppose he's still in love with his dead wife.'

In a choked voice Cat said, 'If there's an unexpected death in the family, it can take a long time. Not to forget, you never do that. But to…to be at ease with yourself.'

Paula obviously found this interesting and said, 'That's very true. You've experienced it yourself?'

'We all have problems,' Cat muttered, and decided she had to change the subject. 'I've not got used to the shopping here yet,' she said. 'Where's the best place to buy locally grown stuff? And is there a supermarket?'

Paula obviously thought that talking about shopping was a poor second to gossiping about Ross. But, still, this was one woman talking to another. 'Well, it's a bit expensive but I get all my meat from Trent's,' she said. 'As I say, it can cost but it's worth…'

Cat scribbled down notes.

'Hi, Cat. Look, the countryside suits you. You've got that colour that comes from being out in the open air.'

It happened in the entrance hall of Rosewood. She had finished work with Paula and was about to walk home. It was the surprise, the unexpectedness that did it. She'd been so wrapped up in her work in the maternity section that it never crossed her mind that Ross might be there. But here he was. Appearing from a corridor. And she had blushed but she knew it wasn't the country air.

It was him. She hadn't had time to prepare her professional exterior.

'How did your afternoon go?' he asked.

Just a friendly question from one colleague to another. There should be no difficulty in answering. 'It went fine, I enjoyed it,' she said. 'Though I never realised that a doctor's kit included wellington boots.'

He laughed. 'Just wait till winter. In some farmyards you'll need waders. Now, I've brought someone to see you.'

He turned, and from behind him appeared a small boy, the one she had seen yesterday. Ross's son.

'Say hello to my new friend Stephen. Her name is Cat.'

Cat froze. What should she do now? She looked at the little boy, who was staring at her shyly. He was dressed in dark shorts and a dark T-shirt with a dragon on the front. He clutched a lunchbox. He reminded her of…

There was a little of Ross in his face—the large blue eyes. But there was no hardness. He must have his mother's features. One thing was certain—when he grew older he'd be gorgeous-looking.

'Why are you called Cat?' he asked. 'You don't look like a cat.'

She knew what she ought to do. She should kneel, get down to his level, say hello and treat him as a friend. If she was given a chance she would say something about always having wanted to be a cat, even try and say miaow. She had made friends with dozens of children that way.

But she just couldn't do it. She was aware of Ross watching her but she just couldn't do it. Instead, she said hello, and held out her hand. After some hesitation he took it. Then she muttered that her real name was Catherine and asked some stupid question about what he had done at school that day.

Stephen was obviously confused, and mumbled something inaudible back.

She knew she was being stiff, awkward, but she just couldn't help it. Then the tears sprang to her eyes. This was madness!

Ross seemed to sense the situation. He said,

'We're just passing through, Cat, I called to pick up Stephen.'

He gave a bunch of keys to his son and said, 'Let yourself into the car and get into your seat. I'll be with you in a minute.' Stephen scampered away.

'So, it was an interesting afternoon?' Ross's tone was casual. 'You enjoyed looking around?'

'Very much so. Paula is a good midwife. I learned a lot from her.'

'Good. Well, see you tomorrow. Hope you're settling in.' And he was gone. Cat sighed. That was one social encounter in which she had been utterly hopeless. Would things ever come right? Just one tiny moment, just enough time to turn her head—and her life was wrecked. For five minutes she sat in one of the chairs in the entrance hall. She stared at the pictures on the panelled walls and thought hard about nothing. Then she was calmer and it was time to go home.

She got as far as the front steps. A car raced up the drive, braked hard outside the steps, scattering pebbles onto the flower-beds. An agitated woman jumped out of the driving seat, rushed round to the passenger door. She looked up, saw Cat. 'Please, I need help,' she cried.

Cat walked quickly to the car and looked inside as the woman wrenched open the door. Sitting there was a white-faced teenage girl, clutching one arm to her chest The arm was wrapped in what seemed to be a towel and the towel was sodden with blood.

'It's my daughter. The wind blew the glass door shut and she put her hand out to stop it,' sobbed the woman. 'And she's bleeding to death and—'

'She's not bleeding to death,' Cat said firmly. 'Not in this hospital. Now, help me get her to A and E. What's your name, sweetheart?'

'Annie,' mumbled the girl. 'My arm hurts and I'm cold.'

'We can see to that. Now, out of the car and we'll hold you till you can lie down. Don't worry, we'll get you fixed up and it's all going to be all right.'

Reassurance was always necessary in A and E, both for the injured parties and for any lookers-on.

The matron came out of her office as the two women helped Annie into the hall and down towards A and E. Obviously the sound of the car arriving had disturbed her.

'Looks like a straightforward suturing job, Stella,' Cat told her. 'I'm sure I can cope but if there's any problem I'll ring you.'

'There's a nurse on duty there. I'll come and see you in a moment. Do you need to get changed into scrubs?'

Cat looked down at her now blood-stained dress and sighed. 'It's a bit late for that but I will,' she said.

After that it was pretty straightforward. Jenny Carson, the nurse who had been on duty before, was in the A and E department. Cat quickly checked that no artery had been cut and then let Jenny take over while she went to change. Jenny was to treat the girl for shock, put a temporary pad on the wound, help Annie undress and calm the mother as best she could. When Cat had changed and scrubbed up she went to examine the arm in more detail.

First, a quick check. Were there any other injuries at all? No. Just one wound, a long gash down the arm, quite deep but fortunately missing the artery. Quite a lot of blood loss. Jenny had already set up a drip in readiness. And Annie was calmer. Jenny's treatment for shock had been quite successful.

Cat spent a couple of minutes talking to her patient, reassuring her, and then sent the mother out to where someone would find her a cup of tea. This was one of those cases in which a friend or family member only made matters worse.

It was not a difficult job. Cat injected a local anaesthetic. When the arm was numb she carefully cleaned the wound, taking out a couple of glass shards. Then there was the suturing. She knew she was good at this—she had had plenty of practice. But had this hospital never heard of glue to seal a wound? She would ask Ross.

When she was happy with her work she went to arrange with Annie's mother for Annie to stay in overnight. 'There's absolutely no need to worry, Mrs Chalmers. This is merely an extra precaution. She'll be able to come home tomorrow.'

'What'll my husband say?' asked Mrs

Chalmers. Fortunately, just at that moment her husband turned up. He was concerned, but a much calmer person than his wife. He listened to Cat's account, went to kiss his already sedated daughter's forehead. Then he told his wife, 'She's in good hands here. Doctor says we can sit by her bed for an hour. Then we'll go home.'

Cat glanced at her watch. An hour and a half since she had first set off for home. Well, she wasn't ready for a walk now, she was tired and she needed coffee.

She was in the entrance hall and this time she saw Ross coming. His big car drew up outside, he stepped out and walked slowly to the door.

'Ross? What are you doing back here?'

'Stella phoned me and told me Annie Chalmers had been brought in with a cut arm.'

Cat felt annoyed. 'She was and I've dealt with it. It wasn't too serious, there was no need for you to come and check up on me.'

'I'm not checking up on you. I've confidence in your ability. But Martin Chalmers is a friend. I wanted to be a bit supportive.'

She sighed. 'Sorry. You go and see him. I'm going to make myself a really strong coffee.' She waited a minute and then said, tentatively, 'Shall I get you one too?'

'Marvellous. I'll be right with you.'

First she went to change out of her scrubs. And then she discovered just how bloody her dress was. Well, she had nothing else to change into. But she couldn't walk home looking like this. She sighed. Perhaps she could borrow a coat from someone.

She made enough coffee for two and five minutes later Ross walked into the room. She'd known he was coming, but still there was that little thrill of excitement.

He limped over to the coffee-machine, poured himself a drink. 'Confession time,' he said. 'I did look at your suturing and I was very impressed.'

'Thank you. It wasn't really too hard a job.' In fact, she was rather pleased with the compliment. So pleased that she felt confident enough to raise another matter. 'Ross, have you thought of using glue instead of suturing? There's some new stuff coming from Switzerland—it's expensive but it makes the work easier and quicker. I've used it myself and I like it.'

He raised his eyebrows. 'Changing things already?'

Perhaps it hadn't been a good idea to bring the matter up. 'Sorry. Just a suggestion. I know I'm new here, and here to learn and…'

'We can all do with learning. Write out the details and we'll talk about it to Harry.'

He sat opposite her. 'Your first real day as a member of the team. Settling in well?'

'Very well. Everybody's so…so friendly.'

'We try.'

He had taken a deep draught of his coffee, now he put the mug on the table and reached down to rub his leg. She noticed that his face looked a bit drawn. He was obviously in pain. Then she realised that he had seen her concern. There was that half-smile again.

'I was going to ask about your leg,' she told him. 'Normally I would. But I know you don't want me to so I won't.'

He nodded. 'Very bright of you, Dr Fraser. A good doctor knows when to ask and when not to ask. Now, we've established that you're settling in and that you're finding people here very friendly. In a day or two I'd like you to come over and have tea with me and Stephen. Some time this weekend perhaps?'

She panicked. This was the last thing she had expected. The last thing she wanted. Tea with Ross that would be fine. Well, it would be interesting—perhaps dangerous. But tea with Stephen...

'I don't think this weekend,' she gabbled. 'I'm not settled in yet. Got things to do. Perhaps in a week or two, when I've got things sorted...'

She knew she was being rude but he didn't seem to mind. He looked at her in silence for a minute and then in an almost meditative voice he said, 'You don't want to come to tea with Stephen and me. Fair enough. You're entitled to your choice. I'm not angry.'

'It's just that—' she started.

But he held up his hand and said, 'Let me finish. You seemed happy enough with my company last night. And I really enjoyed your company. So it's not me. Not us. Perhaps it's best for us not to get too close but I think we can get along together as friends. So what have you against a four-year-old boy who you've never met before? It can't be just him, it must be all four-year-old boys. Do you feel the same way about four-year-old girls?'

The question was unexpected so she answered it. 'No. Nothing against little girls. I mean, I think you've got things wrong.'

He had a soft voice, she was only just realising how persuasive it could be. 'You don't have to tell me, Cat. But you can if you want. It helps to talk. I know that sounds corny but it's true.'

She drank her coffee without tasting it, clutched the mug in both hands. She didn't want to look at him. Instead, she stared through the window at the tree tops in the garden.

'I don't want to tell you here,' she said. 'Someone might come in.'

'Right. In my car, then. And I was going to take you home anyway. You can't walk through the streets of Benthwaite covered in blood stains. Might get a bad name.'

She looked down at the drying stain on her skirt. She had forgotten about the blood. 'Seems a good idea.'

'We'll not go straight to your home. I'll take you somewhere quiet for a while. You can sit and look at the view. Not for long, though. If we're seen, it'll be all over town.'

She laughed nervously. 'Where is Stephen now?'

'At a friend's birthday party.'

He didn't know that had been the wrong thing to say. The tears came and she just could not stop them.

CHAPTER FOUR

SOMEHOW he managed to hustle her out of the hospital without anyone seeing them. He slid into his car, then drove out of town, up a quiet, lonely road that eventually led to the brow of a hill. He turned off, bumped down a path for fifty yards and eventually parked in a clearing. Below them the ground fell away and there was Benthwaite and the lake below them. It was beautiful.

'We can't stay here too long,' he said, with humour in his voice. 'This is the local lovers' lane—or lovers' clearing. But it doesn't get busy until it gets dark. Then it can get quite crowded. Or so I am told.'

'Not experienced it yourself, then?' She didn't know where she had found the strength to tease him.

'Not yet. But an old man can dream.'

Her hands were clenched in her lap. For a moment he reached out, placed his hand over hers. Then he moved it. 'You were going to tell me something,' he said.

'It'll take a while.'

'We've got plenty of time. And I want to know. I want to know about you.'

She took a deep shuddering breath. Where was she to start? And how much would it hurt to go over things yet one more time? Still, now she wanted him to know.

'My older brother Tom is a doctor and he's married to another doctor called Anita. The three of us were—are—very close. We all worked in the same hospital, went out together. I had a flat of my own but I also had a bedroom in their house and I spent most of my spare time there.'

She had to pause. 'No hurry,' he said gently. 'Take your time.'

But she had to go on while she could. 'They had a little boy called Kim. I was his godmother and I loved him as if he were my own. He was a little tearaway, he'd never walk if he could run. I spent an awful lot of my time babysitting him. I suppose I was a godsend to Anita and Tom, but I loved it.'

The tears were coursing down her cheeks now but she had to carry on with her story. 'About a year ago I took him for a picnic in the park. Just the two of us. It was a lovely day, like today. It was three days before his fourth birthday. We were having a party, had sent out the invitations, ordered a cake with four candles.

'I sat down on a blanket and turned to unpack my basket. Ross, I only turned my head for a minute! And when I turned back he was running. I shouted at him and he turned his head. I can still see that mischievous face. Anyway, he ran into the road, into the path of a car. He was killed instantly.'

She was reliving the moment, but she still had to add the last heart-breaking detail. 'Then I had to go back to my brother and sister-in-law and tell them.'

Her sight was blurred with tears but she still

turned to look at him. His hands were clutching the steering-wheel, the knuckles tight. His face looked set in stone.

For a while he said nothing, then he said, 'There's no comfort I can offer, is there?'

'None.'

'I won't try, then. And I'm not going to say I'm sorry—you know that already.'

'Aren't you going to tell me that it will all pass in time?'

'No. Some things never pass but you get used to the pain. And in time the pain might ease. Do you see Kim every time you see a little boy?'

'Something like that. At work I can detach myself, treat them as cases rather than as children. Though I know that is wrong.'

'And is your godson's death the reason you came up here?'

'Yes. I needed a complete change. I got so de-pressed people thought I was headed for a nervous breakdown. I had a boyfriend, you know, the casual sort of relationship you get into when you're both working very hard but working together. I liked him and I thought that perhaps we had a future. He was a nice man and I think he deserved better than he got from me.'

Cat broke off, stared out of the window. She was glad that Ross didn't ask her to carry on. She would finish her story in her own time. And a distant part of her brain told her that she wanted to tell him her story. Why? She usually tried to keep it secret.

She turned to face him. His expression was alert, compassionate. She went on, 'But after the accident...I just couldn't get interested in him. There was nothing he could offer me, though he tried. I couldn't get interested in anything but my work. It was as if I was emotionally frozen. So we drifted apart. And then I felt guilty because I'd let him down.'

'Did you get any...any professional help?'

'Yes. My brother saw the state I was in, insisted that I see a therapist. Her name was Jeannie Carr, she was very good. It was her idea that I come up here, take a complete break from the life I was leading. My boss at the hospital was an old friend of Harry Matthews. He suggested I do my first year as a GP up here instead of in a practice in London. Try to get my head clear before I started work again at the hospital.'

Ross nodded. 'And your brother and sister-in-law?'

'Anita and Tom? They never blamed me, and in some ways that made things worse. But the three of us clung together. They're both getting away—they've got temporary jobs in America. They invited me but I just couldn't face it. So I came here. A complete change of scenery, a completely different life. Not a place where everything reminded me of what had happened.'

'Does anyone else here know?'

'Only Harry.'

Ross grinned. 'And he told you he sympathised but he wanted a doctor, not a patient?'

She had to smile back. 'More or less that. And he'll get a doctor.'

'I'm sure he will.' He handed her a large white handkerchief. 'Now, if you were Stephen I'd say blow—but I'd like you just to dab. I can't have our new lady doctor climbing out of my car with tears on her face.'

She took the handkerchief and did as he'd said. Mysteriously, she felt a little better. 'Aren't you going to offer me any advice?' she asked.

He shrugged. 'I'm sure you've had lots of advice already and all of it good. I won't push Stephen in your face and I hope we two can still be friends.'

'I hope so too. In fact, I'm sure we can.'

'There was a pause and then he said, 'And I want to be friends with you.'

Cat thought that they were simple words but perhaps they held more meaning than they appeared to.

They set off then. And as they drove back to Benthwaite she thought about what she had just told him. She seemed to have a new clarity of thought, things were more obvious now. Talking did help. After a while she said, 'You're playing the cool, calm, collected doctor. I like that. But it's not how you feel. When I was telling you, I saw your hands on the steering-wheel. If you'd been squeezing it any harder, it would have broken. And you can't make that stone face of your completely emotionless, no matter how hard you try. You felt for me. No, more than that, you felt with me. What I've been through— you've been through too.'

There was silence for a while and she wondered if she'd gone too far. She didn't want that to happen. Whatever her connection was with this enigmatic man, she wanted to keep it.

After a moment he said, 'You know, I seem to spend all my time with you telling you what a good doctor you are or will be. You see under— or through—what's on the surface.'

'I'll take that as a compliment,' she said.

Then neither of them spoke.

He pulled up outside her cottage. 'I must go and pick up Stephen from his party,' he said.

'So you haven't time to come in for a minute. Fair enough. But there's another thing. I've just got to say this. We only met yesterday afternoon and last night you kissed me.' She frowned. 'No, that's not exact. If anything, I kissed you and then things just sort of…went on a bit. Ross, I just don't do that sort of thing. Not so soon anyway.'

'Neither do I,' he said. 'I think I was as shocked as you.'

'This morning I just couldn't believe it had happened. What must you have thought of me?'

'Nothing that was not good.' There was that half-smile again. 'To be honest, I worried about myself more.'

'And since then things have been different between us.'

'They must be. But we have to remember who we are. We're two doctors working together. I'm your mentor. You're only here for a while, I'm settled, with a four-year-old son who must come first in my life. And we've both got…I believe the term is emotional baggage.'

'So what are we going to do?'

'Nothing,' he said flatly. 'There's nothing we can do. Just wait and see.'

'Right,' she said, and smiled at him. 'That seems good to me.'

Then she was out of the car and gone.

The birthday party was just ending when Ross arrived. There was the usual little cluster of people—mostly mothers—waiting and gossiping at the gate. They greeted him happily.

He knew most of them, either as patients or fellow parents. He was even accepted as an honorary mother because everyone knew that he was a single father. It was appreciated that he did as much for his child as he could.

Two mothers gave him especially warm smiles. He knew them both—one was separated, one divorced. Both had made it obvious that they would like to see more of him. No way! That could only cause trouble for the practice, for Stephen, for him. He smiled back at both but then joined a larger group of parents.

Then the children came spilling out of the front door. There was Stephen, as ever a great smile on his face when he saw his father. Ross loved it when his son smiled but there was always a flash of pain, a feeling of loss. Perhaps not so often now—every feeling had to pass. But why did his son have to look so much like his dead wife?

He strapped Stephen into his seat, drove them home. As he drove he thought of Cat. She had suffered loss too and like him had a feeling of guilt. He wanted to help her...help her! He needed help himself.

He remembered the conclusion he had reached the night before. That they were poles apart in age and experience. He wasn't quite so sure now. Perhaps now he knew her story he could empathise with her more. But, still, she was not for him. This year for her was a rite of passage, and at the end of it she would return to the city. She had made that very clear. And although it was a year before she would go, he felt sorry. He liked her company.

Cat hardly saw Ross the next day but it was still a full one. Harry had arranged for her to spend the morning with the practice nurse. But as she ate her breakfast, he phoned her to tell her that Anna Summers had gone into labour and Paula, the midwife, was already there. There were no apparent problems but would Cat like to go and help? And as an afterthought, of course, she'd have to drive herself there.

'I'm on my way,' said Cat. She suspected that part of the reason for sending her was to see if she was entirely happy in taking her little car over the rough tracks and up the steep and narrow roads that led to the farm. Well, she was.

It was a hard ride but the sun was out and she enjoyed it. She parked in the farmyard, and when she knocked on the door she was invited in by a smiling older lady who introduced herself as John's mother. Cat was directed to a bathroom where she could change into scrubs and then she went into the room where Anna was to give birth. She smiled at the panting Anna and the man who held her hand.

Then she looked at Paula. As the midwife, this was her domain, and she was in charge until she asked specifically for the doctor's help.

'Stage one,' Paula reported. 'So far everything is going fine.'

'Nothing you want me to do?'

'Not yet. But it's good to have you here.'

So Cat went to say hello to Anna, shook hands with John and talked to them both for a while.

'Have you thought of a name yet?'

'He's going to be called Alan James Summers,' said John. 'We'll call him Alan but he has to have James as a name. I was born in this room, I'm John James. And my father was born in this room and called James, and so was his father and his father before him.'

'Right,' said Cat.

Things progressed as they should. From the kitchen next door Cat heard the occasional rumble of voices. John's mother looked in regularly to tell them that someone had called, that they were hoping for news and had left good wishes.

After that it was a textbook birth. Paula the midwife, Cat on take. They delivered a big baby with a high Apgar score. After being on his mother's breast for a while Alan James Summers was carried by his father to the window. There he was shown the lands that one day would be his.

I've never seen anything like this in a London hospital, Cat thought. I like it. Soon after that it was time for her to leave.

* * *

The practice nurse was working at the cottage hospital that afternoon, and Cat went there to shadow her. It was interesting work, and she didn't notice how the time was passing.

But through the ward window she saw Ross's car arrive—he had come to pick up Stephen. So somehow she managed to be in the corridor just when Ross walked out of the nursery, holding his son's hand. Cat stayed in the shadows, not wanting to be seen. Ross and Stephen passed through the entrance hall and she stared after them.

She just couldn't analyse her feelings. They were mixed, part hope, part fear, part doubt. She wasn't sure whether it had been a good idea, coming up here. Was the sheer abrasive novelty of things causing her to have feelings, make decisions that were wrong? She just didn't know. But she remained still in the corridor until long after they had gone. She had a plan—of sorts.

On her way home that night she stopped to buy some flowers and took them round to Harry's house. They were for his wife, to thank her for the food she had left in the cottage. Alice invited her in, took her into the back garden to have a cool drink and to play with a little girl.

'This is Eleanor,' Alice said. 'She's the daughter of Alanna and Finn Cavendish. They've been on holiday but you'll be working with them shortly.'

It was odd, Cat could cope with little girls. In fact, she liked them. So she played with the doll's house on the grass and listened to Eleanor telling her how she was learning to swim.

'Eleanor's had an odd life,' Alice told her when they had a moment together. 'Something terrible happened—and then by chance it all came right. It's not my story, I'll let Alanna tell you. But it shows you that no matter how bad you think things are, they can get better.'

'Sometimes,' Cat said.

She left shortly after that, went back to her cottage. It was a beautiful evening so after tea she decided to walk down to the edge of the lake. She was not hoping to see Ross, she just wanted to enjoy the peace. So she sat on a bench and watched the sun go down over the fells.

When it was dusk she walked home, decided

to have an early night. She was tired, but calmer than she might have expected to be.

It struck her that she was enjoying her new life, much more than she had expected. She had come here as therapy—but it was turning out to be much more than that. She was enjoying making new friends. And not just Ross.

'You have your own list of patients today,' Ross told her next morning. 'I'll be right next door so if you've any queries, don't hesitate to ring me. But you're going to be OK.'

'But, Ross, I don't yet have your skills in interpreting gossip.'

He looked at her mournfully. 'You're running down skills I've taken years to develop. Interpreting gossip only comes with age and experience. You'll just have to work at it.'

'I'll do the best I can.'

She liked talking to him. Whether they were making fun of each other, arguing or confessing, she liked being with him. She went into her consulting room with a light heart.

There were no cases she felt she had to refer to him. She dealt mostly with the simple things that came into any GP's room. One case she had to refer to a consultant—a middle-aged lady who had high blood pressure and had developed a small blurred patch in her vision. Definitely a case for specialist advice.

When lunchtime came she felt satisfied with her morning's work. She had even enjoyed herself. She joined Ross, Harry and a couple of other staff in the lounge. Tea, coffee and juice were available and she had brought a sandwich with her. She felt like a real doctor. More than that, she felt like a member of a tightly knit group. And that was something new to her. Of course, there wasn't the rush, the sense of excitement that she felt in London. She missed that. And some of the medical ways were downright old-fashioned. But she was enjoying herself.

It took her a week to get to know all that the practice did, and to meet most of its members. There were the three partners. There were two practice nurses. There was a dispensary, with a full staff. There were the midwives. Overseeing all of this was an administrative team.

What made Cat wonder most was how apparently relaxed the connections were with the cottage hospital, the district nurses, health visitors, physiotherapists and the consultants who ran clinics at Rosewood. It shouldn't have worked. It wouldn't have worked in London, where there were strict rules about who worked where and when. Cat missed that certainty. But she had to admit that this system worked well.

Although he was still her mentor, she didn't see so much of Ross. There were occasional meetings but they were all purely professional. She thought that he was giving her a breathing space, letting her settle into her new job. He must know how busy she was.

But she thought about him. In one sense he was unfinished business. She needed to be certain just what kind of personal relationship she had with him.

Each evening she went back to her cottage

and picked up her mail. All doctors were sent vast amounts of unsolicited mail. Often it contained freebies, which made her smile. Would the gift of a pen really influence her to choose one drug rather than another? The pen and the accompanying letter usually went into the bin together. But then she received a package, opened it and found that it interested her. She put it to one side.

Something much more important. There was a card from her brother and sister-in-law in California. They wrote at least once a week. Sometimes there was a little parcel, sometimes a card. They were enjoying themselves, they were missing her. *But you can't run from memories for ever. We'll be back in London when we are ready, picking up our old life. Which we know will include you.*

As ever, when she thought of the two of them, she thought of their strength. How they had never blamed her. Which only meant that she blamed herself more. Well, she had come here to try to get over things so she would do so. This therapy had to work and then she would go back and join them in London.

She went back to the package that had interested her, thought for a while. Then she made a decision—and tried to nerve herself for the ordeal to come.

She was booked in to do a ward round at the cottage hospital the next day. Nothing exciting, just to check up on the patients, make sure their medication was working. She suspected that the most beneficial thing she did was the few minutes' talk she had with them.

She had timed her visit carefully. That afternoon she watched out for Ross's car, waited until he had come to collect Stephen, then went into the entrance hall. This was going to be hard! But she had to do it.

Ross came into the hall, Stephen holding his hand. He looked at her with some surprise. 'I didn't expect to see you here, Cat.'

'I haven't come here to see you. I've been waiting to see Stephen.'

Stephen looked confused.

Cat knelt in front of him, took the package from under her arm. 'I got this through the post yesterday and I thought you might like it.'

She showed him what it was—a small wipe-clean board and a set of coloured markers. 'You can draw a picture first, and then when you are ready you can wipe it off and draw another one.'

Quickly, she drew a picture of a house on the board, then wiped it clean. She offered the markers to him, held up the board. 'Would you like to draw something yourself?'

A moment's hesitation, then Stephen began to draw. After a moment he seemed quite intrigued. He changed markers, wiped away a bit of his picture and started again.

'Do you like your present, Stephen?' Ross's gentle voice asked.

'Yes.' Stephen was at the age when he didn't want to use unnecessary words.

'Well, say thank you, then.'

'Thank you,' Stephen said. Then he leaned forward and kissed her, on the cheek.

She had not been expecting it. There was the warmth of his cheek against hers, the feel of his breath, the little-boy smell. The shock was almost too much, this had not been part of her plan. Memories rushed back, of another little boy who had sometimes kissed her on the cheek. 'That's all right, darling,' she managed in muffled voice. 'Now I have to go. Bye, Ross.' She turned and half ran down the corridor.

She had thought it might hurt, she had not known how much. It all came back—the games she used to play with Kim, his smile, the odd things he sometimes said, his excitement with just being alive. And he wasn't alive any more. But she had taken a step.

For a quarter of an hour she hid in the ladies' cloakroom. Then she drove home. It was warm, she changed out of her work clothes and put on shorts and an old short-sleeved shirt. Then she made herself a salad and looked out of the window.

The cottage had a tiny back garden with an equally tiny shed at the bottom of it. She had explored, there was some plastic garden furniture there, a table and set of chairs. She fetched out the table and one of the chairs. Then she took out a tray with her salad and orange juice on it and sat in her back garden. It was something she had never done before. There had been no garden for her to sit in in London.

When she had finished she took in her tray. She made a pot of coffee and carried it out again. Then she sat in the sun and slowly felt at peace.

Her doorbell rang. Odd, she'd never had a visitor call before. She went to answer it—and there on the doorstep was Ross.

Her first thought was that the clothes she was wearing were a little revealing. Not to mention being a bit old. She hadn't expected a visitor. She felt the urge to fasten the top button of her shirt, but thought that it would only call attention to where it wasn't needed.

What could he possibly want? But still they were colleagues, friends. 'Come in,' she said.

'I'm sitting in the garden, having a coffee. Would you like one?'

'I'm not intruding, am I? Is this a bad time? Because if it is, please, tell me.'

'Not at all. You're very welcome.'

The exchange of polite small talk seemed unreal to her and she thought it seemed unreal to him too. She went on, 'Have you had your tea?'

'I had tea with Stephen. I like sitting with him.'

This was more real. She saw him looking at her as he mentioned his son, knew that he saw her flinch slightly. But he said nothing.

She fetched an extra chair and coffee-cup, found a packet of unopened biscuits. Then they sat opposite each other. He too was in casual clothes—a dark blue T-shirt to go with his fawn chinos. And as ever, he looked fit, muscular. A real man.

He sipped his coffee and said, 'That was a brave thing you did this afternoon. Why did you do it?'

'What brave thing did I do?' She needed to pretend that she didn't know what he was talking about.

'Giving that present to Stephen. Incidentally, he's delighted with it. It was very thoughtful on your part. But it hurt, didn't it?'

'Just something that I got in a…' she started. Then she shrugged. She may as well be honest. 'Yes, it did hurt,' she said.

'So why did you do it?'

'It's something I've got to face. Kim's death was an accident, I know. Intellectually, I know it was not my fault. But I feel that it was.'

'So you have to keep going over and over it. Did talking to Stephen make it any easier?'

She thought back on the meeting, knew she had to be honest again. She found it easy to be honest with this man. 'A little bit,' she said at last. 'It was easier than I had expected.'

He nodded. 'So I won't be inviting you to tea with him yet. But I wanted to tell you that I thought it showed courage on your part and I didn't want to say it at the hospital. Not in a place where we both have to be professional.'

He finished his coffee, glanced at his watch. 'I'd better be going. I only wanted to have a quick word with you. I mustn't take up your time.'

She didn't want him to go. She had been happy just sitting alone in the sun, she would be more happy to sit in the sun with him and chat. Just like a couple of friends, of course.

'You're not taking up my time. I'm doing nothing very much. If you like, you could stay for a while. I've no beer but you could have a glass of white wine.'

The invitation had to be casual. She didn't want him to know how much pleasure it would give her if he did stay. Then she wondered why it would give her so much pleasure.

However, he stood—and she stood too. Apparently carelessly he said, 'I'd like to stay but I've got to call at the sailing club. I'm not going sailing—there's just a few details to be sorted out.' Then, as casual as she had been, he went on, 'You could walk down there with me if you liked.'

Equally casually—why were all their remarks so casual?—she said, 'I'd like to come. Let me change out of these clothes into something a bit less revealing. I'll only be five minutes.'

'I like your outfit as it is.' But he said nothing more.

Five minutes, she thought as she rushed upstairs. What can I find to wear in five minutes? And it mustn't look as if I've made an effort. Be relaxed, low-key, casual. She remembered her brother once saying of an acquaintance that he was so laid-back that when he stood he was horizontal. Well, right now that's what she needed to be.

Just inside her promised five minutes she managed to find white jeans, matching high-heeled sandals and a rather fetching red silk blouse. She added a touch of lipstick and mascara, a comb through her hair and a light jacket to carry over her arm.

'Very nice,' said Ross. It wasn't much of a compliment. But she could tell by his eyes that it was meant.

They walked down to the lake, into the clubhouse. Her arm burned when he touched her, she shivered when he put his arm behind her to guide her through a doorway. All this reaction to what was probably just a friendly—or an accidental—touch. It wasn't usual.

Ross led her into the clubroom again. Someone approached them. 'This is our club commodore—Commander Hugh Langley,' Ross said. 'Hugh, Dr Cat Fraser.'

Cat smiled. The commander looked so much the part that he wasn't quite real. He had a neat white beard, wore a blue blazer and a tie in the club colours, carried himself as if he were still in the navy.

'So pleased to meet you, Dr Fraser.' Hugh beamed. 'Now, what will you have to drink?'

Hugh left an order at the bar and the three of them sat at a table by the window again. As ever, Ross went straight to the point. 'You left a message saying you need a doctor, Hugh?'

'I need one desperately. Well, the club does. Ah, the drinks.'

Her white wine, beer for Ross and a drink that smelt like gin and tonic for Hugh. Together, they all sipped and smiled with pleasure.

'You know we offered to host a party of handicapped children next Sunday. We wanted to offer them the experience of sailing.' He looked angry. 'All we wanted was to take them out on the lake for a couple of hours. Perhaps more if the weather was good. Less or not at all if the weather was bad. You know how safety conscious we are here—I've arranged extra safety boats, got the best members to take people out. And I've had to fill in no end of forms. The world's gone mad!'

'Do you know we had to have our members vetted? Make sure they weren't on the sex offenders' list? Because they'll be in one-to-one situations. Who could abuse someone in the middle of a lake in a tiny dinghy with other dinghies all around and every pair of binoculars in sight trained on them?'

'Health and safety rules,' Ross said gloomily. 'Hugh, we live in a different world from when you were a lad.'

'Don't I know it. Ross, what I want to ask you. They need a doctor on standby. They were bringing their own but he's dropped out. We haven't enough money to pay for one and it's not part of a GP's job. So if we pay for someone to look after Stephen, will you give up the day for no pay? I know you like to spend your time with your lad, but we could do with you.'

Cat saw Ross think a moment. Eventually he said, 'I'll see to Stephen and there's no need to talk about payment. I'll do it.'

She saw Hugh sigh with relief. 'Ross, that's so good of you. Now I don't have to cancel it all.'

'I'll come as well if all you need is a GP,' Cat said. 'I've had a lot of experience in A and E.'

She wasn't quite sure why she volunteered. But why not?

Hugh looked at her in surprise, replied quickly in case she changed her mind. 'We'd be really grateful,' he said. 'But I have to tell you, there'll be a lot of just hanging round.'

'I can deal with that. I'll just look at the view. I'm looking forward to it already.'

She had to admit that she was hoping to spend time with Ross.

They stayed a while longer, chatting about sailing. She told Hugh that she was interested in joining the club, he said that they were always pleased to have a doctor handy. Perhaps he could arrange for her to act as crew for a while. And then it was time to go back home. Ross walked her back.

It was dark now. They talked casually as they strolled back to her cottage. Ross asked her how she was fitting in, she said she was finding it interesting but different. It was nothing like London. Then they were at her front door and he waited until she had fumbled her key out of her handbag and unlocked the door. 'Well, goodnight,' she said. 'Thanks for the evening. I've enjoyed it.'

It was meant to be nothing special. Of course, she remembered the last time they had kissed. Perhaps this was some attempt to show him—and herself—that the last kiss had been just an accident.

She took him lightly by the elbows, reached up to kiss him on the cheek, as she might any number of male friends. Completely sexless. A kiss like you might give your mother, or a baby.

That was her intention.

She found herself pressed against a muscular chest, her thighs against his. There was the smell, part maleness, part aftershave. She could feel the slight stubble on his cheek, he certainly was a man. But a friendly kiss was all that either of them intended it to be.

And he did nothing but bend his head a little. For nothing but a friendly kiss.

In fact, her lips had not yet brushed his cheek. They just stood there, their bodies touching, waiting for her to give him a friendly kiss. That was all.

Why was she waiting so long?

But she just leaned against him. It was warm and pleasant and he didn't seem to mind and who knew what might happen, and he didn't seem to mind and…

He moved. His arms slid round her back, pulled her closer to him. After a tiny hesitation she did the same to him. As if she hadn't known her own mind. But she really had intended this to be just a friendly kiss.

She looked up. His face was a dark oval against the star-speckled sky. She couldn't see his expression, could only guess what he was feeling. But now she knew with devastating certainty what she was feeling herself.

She wanted to be kissed. Not a delicate peck or a rubbing together of cheeks. She wanted to be kissed properly, truly, by a man who she... She sighed. Perhaps the sound of her sigh, the movement of her body told him how she felt.

He kissed her and the relief in her was only matched by the excitement. He was kissing her because he wanted to and because he knew that she wanted him to. She knew that there was still something that she was holding back. So was he. She was still unsure where this would lead. Then she decided it didn't have to lead anywhere. Her feelings were now!

His lips touched hers, softly. His hold on her was still light, she could pull away easily if she wished. She didn't wish to. Instead, she leaned towards him, wondering if he could detect the heat rushing through her veins, if he could feel her hardening nipples against his chest.

Perhaps so. The kiss increased in intensity, their hold on each other tightened until she felt that they were one body, sharing every experience, every feeling. He kissed her lips, her cheeks, her closed eyes, and when she leaned back he kissed her throat. And each tiny kiss brought more bliss.

His mouth sought her lips again. She opened them, willing him to penetrate, to be more and more a part of her. They stood there—what?— a minute, an hour, she did not know. And she whimpered when he eased her away from him, took his lips from hers, parted their bodies.

'Cat, this is wonderful but I don't think it's a very good idea.' His voice was hoarse.

She had to disagree. What was wrong with the man? 'It is a good idea! You're happy, aren't you? You seem to be.'

'Of course I'm happy! Happier than…' His voice trailed away.

'Happier than what?' she demanded. He tried to step back from her but she held onto him. It didn't take much of her strength to prevent him from moving.

But now his voice was getting stronger, there was determination in it. 'This could lead to something and it has to stop now. We've just met, I'm your tutor and we have a professional relationship. We have to make sure that—'

'Rubbish! I'm not a child and I'm a qualified doctor. I've had boyfriends before. You are not taking advantage of a poor, stupid, inexperienced girl. You know, I'm really quite bright.'

'I know all of those things!' Now he did pull himself away from her. But he kept hold of her hands. And he surprised her by leaning forward to kiss her softly on the forehead. He went on, 'I also know that you're vulnerable. You're hurting and you're turning to me for comfort.'

Now she was angry. 'I'm turning to anyone who will offer me comfort? You don't think much of yourself, do you, Ross? You're just the most convenient man? Let's get one thing straight. You kissed me—presumably because you wanted to. I kissed you because I wanted to. Now you seem to have decided that it was a bad thing. So shall we forget it?'

To her surprise she discovered that he was still holding her hands. Now he dropped them and even through her anger she felt a touch of sadness.

He remained calm. 'I think that forgetting it is best. We both lost our heads a little.'

'So tomorrow we carry on as if nothing happened? OK, that's fine.'

He stepped back away from her, looked at her for a moment in silence. He said, 'But one final thing, Cat. I did enjoy it.' And then he was gone.

Cat entered her cottage. Now this is a fine start to my new life, she thought. She knew she ought to think about things, work out what she felt. At the moment she felt angry with Ross. They had just had an argument, though it had been an argument largely over nothing.

She swept into the kitchen made herself a bedtime drink. And as she sat on her couch, mug clasped between her hands, the realisation came, so suddenly, so shockingly, that she could hardly deal with it. Ross. Her feelings for him were more than recognition of his physical attraction. She liked Ross the man. And growing inside her there was an emotion that she hadn't enjoyed in months. It was as if something icy in her heart had suddenly melted. She could feel again. Feel what, she wasn't sure. There was potential for pain as well as for joy. But something had returned, and Ross had brought it back. The months of depression were slipping away. She was becoming a whole woman again.

She smiled to herself contentedly, finished her drink. Then she decided to go to bed. Once there she slept at once. Going to sleep so quickly was something she hadn't experienced for a long time.

CHAPTER FIVE

BUT things were different in the morning. True, she woke up with a smile on her face, felt content with life as she hovered in that half-conscious state between sleep and waking. But then she did wake up properly and things were different.

She had been sent here by her therapist, told that she needed a break, needed to get away from the London life that she had once loved so much. For a while she needed to change her life, to try to lose the feelings of guilt. In fact, to heal herself. She was to take things easy, to avoid excessive emotional entanglements. New friends would be fine. But a new lover…? Her therapist had shaken her head doubtfully when bringing up the idea. 'There is a danger. You must not run to the first person who apparently offers you peace. Until you are healed, that would be unfair on both him and you.'

Cat sighed as she remembered how angry she had been the night before with Ross when he had said that she was turning to him for comfort. Just what her therapist had said. Well, she hadn't just turned to him for comfort! She had kissed him because…well, she'd have to think about it.

Anyway, she didn't want any kind of relationship that might result in her having children. The idea of having a child—a child that could die—was just too much. How could she risk losing a child of her own? She knew that this fear was irrational, brought on by the horror of Kim's death. It might be irrational—but it was still real. Whatever there was between Ross and her, she had to keep it within bounds.

It was a thoughtful Cat who walked into work that morning.

Her induction period was now nearly over. There was just one more person she had to work with—the district nurse, Alanna Cavendish. She knew that Alanna was married to Finn Cavendish, the third partner in the practice. Finn and Alanna had been away on a holiday with their daughter Eleanor, had returned early to do a week's decorating. Cat hoped that she'd get on as well with them as she had with the rest of the staff.

The minute she met them she knew there'd be no need to worry. Finn was a tall, lean, smiling man and Alanna fizzed with energy. She liked them both at once.

'Can't wait to see my regulars, make sure they haven't been up to mischief while I've been away,' Alanna said briskly. 'Do you know your way about yet, Cat?'

'I think I know a lot of the town—but the country round about is still a bit new.'

'We'll sort that out. Take you walking with us one day. Now, first we'll drive round to see Mrs Lennox, see how her arthritis is.'

Cat enjoyed her morning. Alanna obviously felt that an important part of her job was to cheer up her housebound patients, to let them know what was happening, make sure that they were as happy as they could be in their lives. Cat had never quite realised that gossip could be therapeutic. But it was.

There was the usual district nurse's work. There were injections to be given, dressings to be changed, the odd old lady who needed help in washing. Cat was introduced, sat and joined in the chat. This was real community medicine.

Their last call was far out in the countryside, to a cottage where eighty-eight-year-old bachelor Barney Troop lived. A couple of weeks ago he had fallen and broken his arm. Alanna checked the dressing and then asked Cat to give him an examination. Cat decided he was in pretty good shape.

'So, Barney, we can't persuade you to come and live in Benthwaite?' Alanna asked him afterwards. 'Stay in Cadell House? There's one or two of your old friends there.'

Barney sniffed. 'Last I heard there were three women to every man there. That's not the kind of company I want. I've been a bachelor all my life, I'm not going to change now.'

'You don't have to be married to get in there!

Besides, who'd want to marry a grumpy old man like you?'

'Lots of them,' Barney said with evident self-satisfaction. 'But I'm not giving them the chance.'

So Cat enjoyed her morning.

'Everyone seems to know everyone else here,' she said to Alanna as they drove away from Barney's cottage. 'I don't know if that's a good thing or a bad thing.'

'It takes some getting used to. It's impossible to keep a secret for long. For example—have you heard about Finn and me?'

'Well…odd things here and there. Nothing definite.' Cat was being cautious.

Alanna giggled. 'I'll get my version of the story in first. Finn and I are from around here, we were childhood sweethearts. Eventually finished up married. I had a baby, I thought it died in childbirth.'

'*Thought* it died? What do you mean?'

'I was told in hospital that my baby had died. Finn and I couldn't take it, we parted, I went wandering the world. After a couple of years the hospital got in touch with Finn. There had been a mix-up in the delivery suite, and it wasn't my baby that had died but another woman's. And now she had died and the hospital found out the mistake and my baby was still alive. Finn took the baby and tried to get in touch with me. He didn't succeed. I came back two years after that to find that I had a four-year-old child.'

Cat was appalled. 'That's the most terrible story I've ever heard! How did you feel?'

Alanna shook her head. 'Emotions you just can't imagine. It felt as if my baby had come back from the dead. And now Eleanor, Finn and I are deliriously happy.'

'It must be wonderful,' said Cat. 'I'm really pleased for you.' She tried, she really tried. But she just couldn't get the right feeling in her voice.

Alanna glanced at her but said nothing for a while. Then she pulled off the road, stared straight ahead at a set of great grey-green peaks. 'One of the reasons I love living here,' she said, 'is that there's always a view to comfort you. Do you want to tell me, Cat?'

'Tell you what?

'When I told you how happy Finn and I were, you were a bit upset. I didn't mean to hurt you but I know I did and I'm sorry. But could you tell me why?'

This has happened before, Cat thought. Ross had noticed her misery too. Was she going to disturb everyone? Couldn't she keep her troubles to herself? But she knew that Alanna felt for her and so she told her about Kim's death and how it had affected her.

Alanna reached over and hugged her. 'There's nothing I can say, is there?' she said. 'But I can sympathise.'

'I think,' Cat said hesitantly after a while, 'that things might be changing. I've only been here a few days but life isn't as dark as it was. I can see light.'

'A change of scenery. New work, new country-side…meeting new people?'

'Something like that.' Cat thought of the night before. Could a couple of kisses change things so much?

The two were silent for a moment, and then

Alanna drove on. 'How are you getting on with Ross?' she asked after a while.

'Very well. He's a good mentor.'

'You've met his son Stephen? He comes to play with Eleanor sometimes.'

'I've met him. It was a bit difficult but we can rub along.'

'We all like Ross and the way he dotes on the boy. 'Do you know about his wife?'

'I know that she's dead,' Cat said, 'but not why or how. Is there anything I should know?'

Alanna frowned. 'It's his story. I'm sure he'll tell you in time. Now, shall I drop you off back at Rosewood?'

Cat had work of a different kind that afternoon. Two new patients, both in their seventies, had been moved into Rosewood from the hospital in Carlisle. They were too ill to be sent home but it was felt that they could convalesce a while in the village hospital. Cat introduced herself to them, gave them both a quick examination to make sure they were settled after the journey by ambulance. There seemed to be no likely trouble. Then she had time to have a talk to them both. It would settle them, make them feel they were getting some kind of personal care. And she would call to see them again the next day.

She was thinking about a mid-afternoon coffee as she walked away from the little ward. And there was Ross, walking along the corridor ahead of her. He didn't see her at first, he was talking to the matron.

He was limping, perhaps a bit more than normal. She wished he didn't have to limp, she suspected that it angered him. But she knew he'd never acknowledge it. She looked at the outlines of his shoulders, his arms, his waist. His figure was nearly perfect for a... This was silly!

Perhaps he had heard her coming because he turned his head. His face was stern but she remembered that when his guard was down, when he relaxed, he looked like an entirely different man.

'OK, Stella, I'll see to that and get back to you this afternoon.'

Stella smiled at him and walked rapidly along the corridor. Just the two of us talking, Cat thought. What I wanted.

She braced herself. She had worked on this speech, had got it just right, knew exactly what she wanted to say to him. And she knew she needed to say it.

She tried not to react when she saw the expression on his face. It was only a flash but she thought she saw caution there—even anxiety. She had to stop that! Somehow she managed to keep her amiable smile.

'Hi, Ross. I'm just going to make fresh coffee. Are you busy or do you want one?'

She fancied she saw relief in his face. 'I'm never too busy to turn down fresh coffee. I'll be with you in a minute.'

'It'll be waiting.' She gave him her amiable smile again. The kind of smile you gave colleagues or friends, not the intimate smile of a lover.

As she had expected, the staff lounge was empty. She made the coffee and he came in a minute later. She passed him his drink and then offered him a plate of biscuits. 'Special chocolate biscuits that I bought this morning,' she told him. 'It's sort of in place of an apology. Last night I was a bit...overexcited and perhaps said things I shouldn't have. But I've only just arrived in Benthwaite and I'm just getting used to things.'

'I see.' He looked at her thoughtfully.

He's not being much help, Cat thought. Can't he see I'm struggling? She diverged from her carefully worked-out script.

'Ross, it was just a kiss, nothing more. I liked it, I think you did, but that was all. We'll forget it. See, nothing to it.'

Then she made a mistake. She hadn't planned it but it suddenly seemed like a good idea. She stepped up to him, put her arms lightly round him and kissed him.

It was meant to be a quick kiss—but on the lips. As it had started the night before. But somehow she lingered a bit. The was the feel, the smell, the closeness of him. And when she stepped back she was breathless.

He had stayed motionless.

She had hoped to set things right, to convince him that there was no need to worry. Perhaps she had also hoped to convince herself that there was no real attraction between them. It hadn't worked. Whatever she felt, it was as strong as ever—and it was growing. And Ross knew it.

'Nothing to it?' he said eventually. 'Do you mean that?'

'I've got to mean it. I've come here to…to get away from feelings and emotions. I've come here to heal myself.' And then, her voice forlorn, she added, 'Do you feel that there's nothing to it? What do you feel for me?'

'I'm not entitled to feel anything for you,' he said. 'Yes, I'm attracted to you, you're a very very attractive woman. But I can't give you anything but friendship. I've been in love once, I'm not going through that again. Now my life is centred on my son. Cat, I'm sorry.'

'There's nothing to be sorry about. We'll stick to what I just said. We kissed and that was all.'

'I'll ask you again. Would you like me to find you another mentor?'

'No! I'll get nowhere running from a problem. Besides, I'm learning a lot from you.'

For a moment they stood in silence, facing each other. Then Cat smiled at him, a seemingly broad, confident smile. 'Don't worry,' she said. 'I've just realised that everything is going to be all right.'

He looked a little surprised at that. Then he nodded and left the room.

Cat poured herself another coffee, forced herself to sit and be calm. She had a few minutes free, she could forget medicine for a while, think about herself. And the weird thing that had just happened to her. It had happened so suddenly, for no apparent reason. Except that she had been with Ross.

She thought about what she had just said. *I'll get nowhere running from a problem.* And she realised that for the past year she had been running from life—but now she was strong enough to stop running. Now she could stand still, be mistress of her own destiny.

She didn't know what had brought about this change. Perhaps it was just that the time was right, perhaps it was moving from London. Perhaps it was kissing—and being kissed by—Ross. Now, there was a thought.

So what about Ross? One thing was certain. She would not now just sit and accept what life apparently offered her. There were things that she wanted, and now she felt she could fight for them. And fight she would.

Then, just as quickly as her new-found confidence had appeared, it evaporated. Was this what her therapist had warned her about? Was she turning for comfort to the first man who offered it? She didn't know.

But now it was time for work. She opened her briefcase and took out a wad of papers.

Harry had asked her to check over some drug allocations. It was just what she needed, intellectually demanding but ultimately soulless work. She worked steadily. No time to think of what to do next, or even what she really wanted. She had to work and to concentrate. A mistake could be very embarrassing. She became engrossed.

There was a knock on the door. Unusual. Most people came straight in. She went to open it and blinked. It was Stephen.

Stephen looked apprehensive. He lifted the board he had been clutching and showed her. 'I did this picture on the board you gave me and Daddy said it was very good and I should show you.'

'It's lovely! Come in and show me properly.' Cat took his hand, led him into the room. Then she knelt in front of him for a better look. 'This is a boat and this is the lake! I recognise them.'

Stephen relaxed a little. 'It's Daddy's boat. I like drawing and I like the blue marker the best.'

'That's good because there's plenty of water for you to draw. Now, I think you need a reward. Would you like a chocolate biscuit?'

'Yes, please,' said Stephen. 'And I think I'll draw another boat on the lake.'

Cat fetched him a biscuit and when she turned Ross was there. He said, 'Stephen was pleased with the picture and I suggested that he show it to you.'

Cat smiled then whispered, 'As some sort of

test? Some kind of therapy perhaps? See if I can get over my stupid and irrational feelings about small boys?'

He shook his head. 'They're not stupid or irrational feelings. Believe me, I know that. But I'd like to help you deal with them.'

'Ross, I know Stephen is a nice little boy. And whatever feelings I used to have about little boys, they're altering.'

'Good,' he said. 'Why the change?'

'Because I can see where I was wrong, can see more of what life has to offer. You helped me and for that I'm grateful.'

'If I've made you happier, I'm very pleased,' he said.

As he drove home he felt pleased that Cat was so much more relaxed in Stephen's company. He felt that to a certain extent he had helped her. And it was good to help a colleague—and a friend.

Then he realised that part of his pleasure was for himself. He had—just vaguely, of course— thought of Cat and himself as a couple. Just as friends. But any such relationship couldn't progress very far because of Stephen. Anyone who took on him had to take on Stephen too. But now that was possible. It could be not just Cat and Ross—but Cat and Ross and Stephen. Just as friends, of course.

Stephen doted on his grandmother. But there was only so much she could do, she couldn't be a mother. A mother would be someone nearer…Cat's age.

Ross shrugged irritably. These were foolish thoughts! He had decided. He had been in love, been married, had lost what seemed like everything. The pain was too great to try again.

Next morning was a typical surgery and she enjoyed it. It was a life that she wanted. But she was certainly ready for a short break.

'How did you get on?' Harry asked when she joined the group in the doctors' lounge. 'Anything exciting?'

Cat collapsed into an armchair, accepted the cup of coffee offered to her. 'I still find it so different working in the city,' she said. 'Do we know an old gentleman called Arthur Harris?'

'Slade End Farm,' said Harry. 'Got some fine sheep there. I bet he came in for a check-up. Arthur is careful that way.'

'True,' said Cat. 'I thought he might have been overdoing things a bit, but when I listened to his heart, took his pulse and BP, he was fine. And while he was being examined Arthur talked. I learned more about the relationship between temperature, altitude, rainfall and the best pasture for sheep than I really need to know. The only thing I've ever grown is a few herbs in a window-box.'

Her colleagues laughed. Cat felt she was becoming part of the group and she liked it.

Ross came over to sit by her. 'Stephen is going to spend Sunday with Alanna, Finn and Eleanor,' he said. 'Do you still want to join us at the sailing club?'

'Will I be any use?' She wanted him to say yes.

'I'd like you to be there. But I hope you won't be needed at all. I love the idea of anyone getting the chance to sail. But I can't get away from the fact that these are handicapped children and that the water can be dangerous. So the more helpers we have, the better. If there is any trouble, it's likely to be sudden and dangerous.'

Then he smiled and said, 'And apart from all that, I'd just like you to be there.'

'I'm looking forward to it.'

He'd just like her to be there. Was that some kind of a declaration on his part? And how should she react to it?

The rest of the day was busy but enjoyable, and she didn't have a chance to think about anything but medicine until she got home that night. But then she thought about Ross. Why was she arranging to spend so much time with him? It was no use pretending that she had volunteered to help at the sailing club out of charity. She wanted to help, of course—but mostly she wanted to be with Ross.

Exactly why did she want to be with him? She was growing to realise that he was one of the most attractive men she had ever met. He had a sense of humour, was a good doctor, was kind and gentle. He didn't want to climb ahead in his profession on the backs of his colleagues. Too many of her acquaintances were like that. And now she was realising that she wanted him as more than a friend.

She had kissed him twice—perhaps three times if you counted the kiss at Rosewood. Each time she had intended it to be friendly, casual. She had intended! But those kisses had started something that she could hardly believe. An intensity of passion that she had never felt before. Now she knew she was coming out of her previous depression. And there were things she desperately wanted.

She had never been someone who wanted to indulge in casual affairs. And she doubted if Ross would want that either. Besides, Ross would come as a package. It wouldn't be Ross, it would be Ross and Stephen. That would be fine. She liked the little boy. Now she felt that she had put the shadow of the tragic death of Kim behind her. She was a new Cat.

Then she frowned. Her therapist had warned her against sudden alterations in attitude. *You may suddenly feel that you are healed, Cat. And perhaps you will be. But there could be...shall we call them false starts? You must be careful. Feelings, emotions can be treacherous things.*

Was she betraying herself? Priming herself for another descent into depression? She thought, hard. She didn't think so.

But was she wasting her time anyway? Ross had stopped the kisses, not her. He was tempted, she knew—but he was strong enough to resist the temptation. He was still in love with his dead wife. Could she compete with that? Well, she could try. If she thought it was wise.

Sunday was sunny and looked as if it would stay that way. Cat was looking forward to spending the day with Ross. She wanted to be near him even though she might be harbouring false hopes. She would live for the day and see what it brought.

She had been told to wear clothes that she wouldn't mind getting wet. Something lightweight but which could keep her warm. And to carry a complete change of clothes in a waterproof bag. That sounded more like an expedition than a day out with a man that she fancied. But she was looking forward to it.

She thought the water's edge looked glorious. Dinghies were pulled half on shore, their sails adding bright splashes of colour. The children and their carers had already arrived, were chattering and shouting to each other. Everyone was excited and Cat felt the excitement too.

She saw Ross talking to the commodore and a few other volunteers so she went over to join them. 'Dr Fraser!' the commodore boomed. 'Good to see you here. I hope you won't be needed in any way. But whatever—enjoy the day.'

'I expect to,' she said.

She was more excited when Ross took her by the arm, turned her round. 'Look! the pirate ships are about to fly their flags.'

Cat looked, then laughed and cheered with the rest of the crowd. Every dinghy flew a tiny flag at the top of its mast. Ross had told her that it was called a burgee, that its purpose was to show the direction of the wind. But the pastel-coloured burgees had been taken down and in their place were sets of black skulls and crossbones.

'I'm afraid we're not going to be together,' he said as they strolled down towards the dinghies. 'We've got two motor launches to act as safety boats and it seems best if there's a doctor in each. We sail in formation down the lake to a pub on the far bank, where there a picnic lunch has been arranged. There's a very good first-aid kit in each launch and every child that might need special medicine is carrying an emergency kit in a waterproof bag. Every child has been certified fit for this trip by their own doctor. But there's one or two we have to keep a special eye on. You've got your mobile phone with you, I'm sure, so we can keep in touch that way. Now, ready?'

'Looking forward to it,' she said.

She was in a motor launch with the commodore and a couple of other helpers. They stood away from the flotilla of dinghies and watched them start their colourful way down the lake.

Then the two launches took up position behind and to each side of the dinghies, like a couple of sheepdogs and a herd of sheep.

'Nothing quite like messing about with boats, is there?' the commodore said after a while. 'Especially on a day like this.'

'It's wonderful. I'd like a boat myself. There are marinas in London but I don't know of anywhere like this.'

'The answer is simple. Stay here.'

It was a simple answer and for the first time she thought about it. Her life had been in London, she was a big-city girl. After a year she was going back to her career and… But then she thought again. She was enjoying herself here more than she had in ages. This was silly! Of course she was going back. But that would mean leaving Ross. And there was no future for her with him anyway, he had made that clear. This was a problem to which there was no answer. Or was there? For the first time in over a year she felt she had options, choices she could make.

After a couple of hours they reached the hotel.

The dinghies were beached, the children helped out and led to where tables had been set out for them in the shade. She saw Ross helping the carers to get everyone seated. And after a while he came over to speak to her. 'That's our job finished for a while. The carers can manage perfectly well on their own and I think they'd prefer it. So shall we go and get a sandwich and a drink at the pub?'

'I'd like that. And I'd like to stay outside if possible.'

'Agreed. Find a table on the terrace and I'll join you in a minute.'

She felt perfectly happy. She was sitting in the sun with a man she liked and the view was great and the sandwiches and tea were just what she needed. What more could a woman ask for? She thought she would tell him how she felt. 'I feel happy,' she said. 'How about you?'

'I feel a bit ashamed of myself. We're here with these children who have a variety of conditions that stop them from leading the life that we lead. And yet they're happy. And I feel sorry for myself because I've got an injured leg. I can't run and can't walk as well as I used to, but things could be so much worse.'

He grinned at her. 'I'm baring my soul to you, Dr Fraser. I hope I'm covered by patient-doctor confidentiality.'

'You are indeed. But I feel you're holding something back, aren't you? Will you tell me in time?'

'Possibly, possibly. If there's anything to tell. But for the moment let's just enjoy the day.' He closed his eyes, lifted his face to the sun.

Sometimes I think I'm getting close to him, she thought. But then he slides away. Will he always do that? What will there be in our future—in fact, do we have one? But she had decided. She wasn't just going to let things happen, she was going to fight. They would have a future.

It happened in the worst possible place. They had set off back, were about halfway home, in the middle of the lake, when there was a scream from a dinghy quite close to Cat's motor launch.

Shortly afterwards there was a shout and a desperate wave from a carer on the dinghy.

The commodore piloted the launch so it was just downwind of the dinghy. The dinghy helmsman spilled wind from the sails and the two boats bumped gently together.

The carer, a young woman, shouted, 'It's Meg! I tried to brush it away but I couldn't. She's been stung by a wasp.'

'That doesn't sound too dangerous,' the commodore commented, but Cat had already guessed what was wrong and shook with horror.

'Is she allergic to stings?' she called back. 'Is this anaphylactic shock? Do we need to get adrenaline in her?'

'It's happened before. Her throat closed up and she nearly died. But she's got these special syringes with her with the adrenaline already in. They're called Epipens, she's got some in her bag. But I'm not her usual carer and I don't know how to use them.'

'Sounds serious,' the commodore said. 'Can't mess about trying to treat someone in a dinghy.

We'd better get the girl over here. Cat, you hang onto the dinghy's bow rope, make sure we don't drift apart.' He looked at the dinghy helmsman. 'Micky, lean over and hang onto our rail. We'll be tight together then. Now, you, the carer, what's your name?'

'Helen, sir.'

'You're doing a good job, Helen. Now we're going to lean over and pick Meg out of the dinghy. You just sit tight and cradle Meg's head so it doesn't bump against anything. OK?'

'I've got that.'

'Well, we're going to— Might have guessed you'd want to be involved.'

Cat had been vaguely aware of a buzzing noise behind her and a slight bump that shook the launch. She looked over her shoulder and there was Ross, stepping from his own launch onto hers.

'Thought I might lend a hand,' he said. Then he glanced down at Cat and added, 'Though I know Cat here could cope easily.'

She liked him for that. 'Meg here has been stung by a wasp. I suspect she has gone into anaphylactic shock. She's got adrenaline syringes with her.'

'That's good news. We've none in our medical kit. OK, let's lift her aboard.'

Cat hung onto the dinghy bow rope as the Commodore, Ross and a crewman leaned over and carefully lifted the nearly unconscious Meg into the launch.

'There's her medical kit here,' Helen shouted. 'The stuff you want is inside.' She threw the bag across to the launch. But at just that moment the dinghy rocked. The bag bounced off the side of the launch—and splashed into the lake. Cat made a frantic grab for it but was too late. With horror she watched the bag disappearing into the dark green waters.

'Cat! Look after your patient. And phone for an ambulance to be waiting for us when we dock.'

Bewildered, Cat looked up at Ross. He stood, kicked off his canvas shoes. There was another, much bigger splash as he dived into the water.

For a moment Cat stared at the water, saw the bubbles rising. Ross was trying to dive down to the bag. But how deep was the water? He couldn't possibly...

The commodore's voice was curt. 'Cat! You have a patient. Leave Ross to look after himself. He can do that.'

It was hard but she knew she had to do it. Meg was now unconscious. Cat put her into the recovery position, took her pulse, listened to her breathing. Her heartbeat was erratic and she was wheezing, and Cat knew without taking it that her blood pressure would be dropping. Gently, she felt Meg's throat, detected the swelling. If the swelling stopped Meg's breathing completely, it might be necessary to perform an emergency tracheostomy. Cat hoped not. If only Ross could recover Meg's emergency medicines!

How was Ross? He seemed to have been underwater an awfully long time. Fearfully, she looked up at the commodore. 'Do you think he's all right? How deep is the water here?'

'It's about thirty feet deep.'

'He can't dive that deep!'

'He can if he's determined, and I know he's a very strong swimmer.'

Could she detect tension in the commodore's voice?

Behind them there was another splash and both turned to see Ross's head break the water, heard him pant for breath. 'I can see the bag,' he gasped. 'I'll get it this time.' And he was gone again.

All Cat could do for Meg now was watch, wait and hope. She dialled 999, arranged to have an ambulance waiting. Then she looked over the side of the launch. Ross seemed to have been underwater an awfully long time again. Just how long could a fit man hold his breath?

She saw his head break the surface. One hand grabbed the launch rail, another passed a wet bag to her. 'Take this and inject her at once. You know what to do?'

'I've dealt with anaphylactic shock before. I know what to do.' Cat turned, placed the bag carefully on the deck and opened it to reveal Epipens.

She eased Meg's shorts up, took the cap off a pen and pushed the spring-loaded needle into her thigh. After ten seconds she withdrew it. It might be necessary to inject Meg a second time...

She had been aware of splashing behind her. Ross was being helped back into the launch. Then there was a crash and a grunt of pain. Alarmed, she looked round. A soaking-wet Ross was lying on the deck, clutching his leg. As Cat looked she saw a dark stain of blood appear from between his fingers.

He had slipped on the wet deck and gashed his leg on the corner of a steel strut.

Horrified, Cat stood, made to move towards him. He waved her back. 'Look after your patient. I can see to myself. It's just a cut, I can put a dressing on it myself.'

'But you're bleeding.'

'All I need is a pad and some tape to hold it on. Now, have you asked for the ambulance?'

'It'll be waiting for us.'

'Good. Commodore, I suggest you take Cat and the patient straight back to shore. I'll put a quick dressing on this and the others can carry on with the trip with just one safety boat and doctor.'

'Right. Just one thing. Dr Fraser here takes a look at your leg before we go and decides if you're fit to be left on your own. I want no heroics here.'

'Anyone would think you were back in charge of your destroyer,' Ross said sourly. 'But she can have a quick look.'

Cat pulled up his trouser leg and winced at what she saw. But Ross was right. In no way was it life-threatening, though it was obviously painful. It took her only a minute to grab the medical bag, put a sterile dressing on the wound and bind it up tightly. 'That's just first aid,' she told him. 'I'll see to it properly later.'

She reached into the medical bag and took out a space blanket. 'And wrap this round you. You're cold, you're liable to go into shock.'

He looked at her a moment, then did as she'd told him. 'Let's go,' he said.

It was obvious he was in pain but somehow he managed to climb back into his own launch, the silver blanket clutched round his shoulders. The other dinghies had been circling the two launches.

Now the commodore waved to them and they set off for home again. The commodore's launch set off at full speed for the shore. 'We're having an exciting day,' he said placidly.

Meg's eyes were now half-open and her breathing was much easier. Cat took another space blanket from the kit and wrapped it round her patient. She felt a lot more confident about her. What could have been a really nasty incident had been averted. She thought she'd suggest to Ross that in future their medical kit included adrenaline.

And how was Ross? The golden rule in A and E was simple. Don't panic. You are a doctor, you distance yourself from your feelings so that your patients can have the full benefit of your professional skills. She'd tried to distance herself, or her feelings, from Ross. He was a patient. But she had worried so much about his diving and then she had seen the pain in his eyes. That cut must hurt!

Right now she didn't want to think about what her feelings were for Ross. There were other things she had to do.

The ambulance was waiting by the jetty, two paramedics standing by with a stretcher. Cat was happy to hand Meg over to them. She made her report to them. and the three of them decided that Meg should not go to Rosewood but to the larger hospital in Carlisle. Then Cat stood back and watched the commodore take over. He was impressive. He would make sure that everyone necessary was informed; he would ensure that someone came to the hospital to look after Meg; he would make sure that official statements were taken. If there was any problem, they must ring him on his mobile.

The ambulance drove off. The commodore turned to Cat and said, 'Now I think we have time for a cup of tea in the clubhouse.'

She looked at him in amazement. 'But what about Ross and the others?'

'It'll be an hour or so before they get here. When they do there'll be lots to do, lots of running about, no time to stop. I learned that in the navy. If you're busy and there's a chance of a break—you take it. There might not be another chance.'

'Right,' said Cat.

They went to the clubhouse and had their tea, but she noticed that the commodore sat them by the window and kept looking to see how the little fleet was progressing. Eventually it neared the shore.

'Let's go down and welcome them,' said the commodore. 'But before we do that, on behalf of the club and the young people who've been on this trip, thank you. Now, the minute we get Ross on shore we can cope. I want you to take Ross and look at that leg of his. He was hurting more than he wanted us to know.'

'So why didn't you leave me to act as doctor and bring him ashore?'

The commodore chuckled. 'Because he's Ross McCain,' he said.

There didn't seem to be an answer to that, but she knew what the commodore meant. Together they went down to greet the arriving launch and dinghies. The commodore took charge again.

'Ross, many thanks. Now you've done your bit, you're to stand down. Cat here will drive you to the hospital and you can get that leg seen to. Any questions or problems we can deal with later.'

'I'm OK. It's just a small—'

'You're not OK. Now, just for once in your awkward life, do as you're told.'

Cat looked at Ross. He had taken off the space blanket and his clothes had largely dried on him. He looked bedraggled. She also thought he looked gorgeous. 'The commodore is right, you know,' she said. 'If someone came into A and E with a cut like that, you'd insist on them taking things easy.'

Ross looked from the commodore to Cat. 'I appear to be outnumbered,' he said. 'OK, I'll go. But if I'm—'

'It's all under control! Now, off, the pair of you. I've got work to do.'

Cat led Ross to her car.

'I don't want to go to Rosewood,' he said. 'The less made of this, the better. It's nothing but a scratch. If Harry and the others find out then they'll—'

'So I'll take you home,' she said. 'But I come in to treat the cut.'

'Right.'

She knew the cut on his leg wasn't too serious, although it did need attention. Attention she could easily give. But she was going to his home—something new. She wondered why her heart was beating so quickly, if this was going to be a new stage in their relationship. She hoped so.

CHAPTER SIX

IT WAS not the kind of house Cat would have expected Ross to live in. It was detached, modern, obviously built in the last three or four years, in a small close. It was pleasant enough but it didn't have the character of her own little cottage.

He saw her looking around, guessed what she was thinking. 'You were expecting that I'd live somewhere more interesting? Not a dull modern house?'

'Something like that,' she had to agree.

'When I came here I wanted a complete change. I'd spent a lot of my life in "interesting" houses and I was tired of it. I wanted something brand-new, with no history.'

'Starting a brand-new life for yourself?' When he didn't answer she added, 'Trying to forget?'

'Some things you can't ever forget, Cat. Now, come inside.'

The inside of the house was much like the outside. There was a living room with an open-plan kitchen leading from it. 'I like to talk to Stephen while I'm cooking,' Ross explained. 'So he reads or draws or watches the occasional bit of television, and I potter around in here.'

'Sounds a good plan. Now, why don't you go and have a shower and then come down, and I'll take a look at that leg.' She saw that he was about to argue, so she held up her hand and said, 'It's either me or back to Rosewood. That cut might need stitching.'

'I suppose you're right.'

Then it struck her. 'The cut is on your injured leg, isn't it? The one that makes you limp. And you don't like people looking at it or talking about it.'

'True,' he said after a moment.

'Ross, I'm a doctor, like you. Whatever is wrong with you, I suspect I've seen worse. Now, shower!'

'Have I got to leave the bathroom door open, Matron?' he asked with a grin.

Good. He could joke. 'I'll promise not to look,' she said.

He came down fifteen minutes later in a dressing-gown. 'Do your ministering-angel act and then I'll get dressed, he said. 'And here's my medical bag. I've washed the cut out as best I can.' He sat in an armchair, put his leg up on a stool.

She crouched over the leg, took off the temporary dressing he had put on to stop the bleeding. 'I don't need to ask, do I? Your tetanus jabs are up to date?'

'They are.'

'Good. Well, you seem to have done a good job but I'll clean the cut up a bit more. I don't think this needs suturing, we can manage with butterfly stitches. But it's deep, you know it's going to hurt for a few days.'

'Nothing new there. I can live with it.'

Of course. Although he always tried to hide it, she had seen how his leg sometimes pained him. That made her look at the scar tissue further down his leg.

He saw her head move, knew what she was

looking at. 'A bullet through the ankle,' he told her. 'Then inadequate medical attention, though I got the best there was.'

'Want to tell me about it?'

'It's not important. It's done and that's it.'

'I won't push you. But you're the one who told me that it was good to talk. And I did feel better afterwards.'

He was silent as she finished dressing his leg. When she had finished she said, 'Are there likely to be any ill effects from your dive? I don't know much about it.'

He shrugged. 'Not really. There was a build-up of pressure in my ears when I was at the deepest part, but it's easy to compensate. You just hold your nose and blow.'

'I see.' But she could feel that something was troubling him. 'What's wrong, Ross? I'll fetch you some analgesics.'

'I try to keep off painkillers. You can get too fond of them. There's no pain now, just throbbing. No it's not that, it's just that I remembered how close we are to accidents. That trip this afternoon was perfectly organised by the commodore. But one little thing—the medical kit dropped into the water—and that girl could have died.'

'Ross, life's like that! Accidents happen. They're nobody's fault and you have to put up with them.'

'Like you put up with the death of Kim?'

She was shaken when he said that. So perhaps what she replied was a little foolish. 'It's different when it's someone you love.'

'Isn't it just. It makes you wonder…was loving so much a good idea in the first place? Since you always run the risk of being hurt.' Then he frowned. 'What rubbish am I talking? That cut must have affected my brain as much as my leg.'

Cat braced herself. She knew she was trespassing where it was dangerous. 'It wasn't rubbish. It was you, for once being honest about your feelings. And I liked it. Tell me more about you being hurt.'

She watched him think. After a while there was that quiet half-smile and she knew he had retreated back into his self-contained little shell. 'Someday I might,' he said. 'But not now.'

So they might as well get back to normal. 'When is Stephen coming back?'

'Not for quite a while yet. Would you like to stay for tea? I've got stuff in the fridge'

Did she want to stay for tea? Yes, she did. Any previous thoughts about keeping distance between them had already vanished. 'I'd love to stay. But you should rest that leg for a while. Either we send for a take-away or I cook. And I like messing about in other people's kitchens. It's like looking at their bookcases. You get to know them that way.'

'I can't invite you round for a meal and then expect you to cook it!'

'You didn't ask me. I volunteered. Now, what were you going to have?'

'I've got all the makings of a curry.'

'At curry making I am a queen.'

'Then cook away. One thing more. I know you've got a bag of spare clothing and you've been out in the sun all day. Would you like a shower and then get changed?'

Yes, she would, she decided. It was thoughtful

of him to think of it. But then another random thought crossed her mind. She was sitting in a man's living room, about to cook in his kitchen, about to shower in his bathroom. The only important room she hadn't been in was his bedroom. She blushed at the thought. Why had she thought that?

He might have been reading her mind. 'If you don't mind, you could use my en suite,' he said. 'It's through the bedroom, the first door on the right upstairs. You could use the main bathroom but it's in a bit of a mess.'

'Right. I'll go now, then.' But when she went upstairs she saw the bathroom door was open and she peered inside. There wasn't too much of a mess. But scattered around were Stephen's things. There were toys. There was a wall chart measuring his height and his weight. There were special Stephen towels. She realised that he had directed her to his en suite so that she wouldn't be upset by the obvious presence of a little boy. Well, that was thoughtful of him but it wasn't so important now. The memory of

Kim would never disappear—but the pain had receded more recently.

She felt odd, going into Ross's bedroom. It was very much a masculine room, simple, even stark. There were blinds, not curtains, built-in dark wood fittings, a plain duvet on the tiny bed. Why was the bed so narrow? Was he afraid that someone might want to share it with him? There were no pictures on the walls, just two photographs on the bedside cabinet. One was of Stephen. The other was of three people—a baby, presumably Stephen, a younger, happier-looking Ross and a woman. Presumably the woman was Ross's wife and she was beautiful.

Cat stared for a moment. Then she decided that she was intruding and went to shower, dressing quickly afterwards.

While Ross went back upstairs to get dressed, Cat looked around his kitchen. She was impressed. It wasn't just a simple bachelor's kitchen—there were spices, herbs, a variety of fresh vegetables and fruit. Ross and Stephen ate well. She collected what she needed and started to make a curry.

When he came down she waved him to an easy chair. 'Just sit and rest,' she said. 'I'm fine.' The next time she glanced across at him he was asleep. There was a throw on the couch, gently she laid it across him. And as she did so she wondered exactly what she was doing.

Of course, she was enjoying herself, she did enjoy cooking. But since she had come to Benthwaite she had cooked very little. There was no point in cooking a fancy meal for one. When she had been with her brother and sister-in-law she had often made them a… But that had been in another life. She had to put it behind her.

What was she doing here with Ross? She knew she wasn't really needed, she was fooling herself if she thought he needed her help. Ross could cope. He could always cope, he needed no one. She was here because she wanted to spend time with him. It did her good to admit it to herself.

After fifteen minutes or so a voice said, 'That smells really good.'

'I thought you were asleep.'

'Sorry about that. Diving was a bit of a shock,

and your core temperature can go down when you've been in cold water. It makes you sleepy. Will that curry be ready soon?'

'Very soon. You really did have all the ingredients ready, didn't you?'

'I like to be prepared.' He shook off the throw, swung his feet to the floor.

'Don't you dare get up. I'm doing fine here! Why don't you just rest?'

He shook his head. 'I've just got to do something. I hate being treated as an invalid. Call it male pride. How about if I fetch some wine, lay the table?'

'Just stay there, doctor's orders. I can fetch wine, lay the table. You know very well that rest is the best thing for that leg now.'

'Very well, Doctor,' he said with a grin. 'I'll do as you say. There's a bottle of excellent Sancerre in that cupboard.'

They ate at the kitchen table and she thought she had done well. 'Food always tastes better if someone else cooks it,' he said, 'and you are a really good cook.'

It was only a small polite compliment but his praise pleased her more than it should have done. 'I do my best,' she said lightly. 'Medicine isn't my only interest.' She sipped the wine. 'Now, this is seriously good!'

'Aim for what is seriously good and sometimes you get it,' he said.

He was looking at her with his customary half-smile that gave so little away. She wondered if there was a message hidden in his words, but if so she could not decipher it. 'Have some more curry,' she said.

When they had finished the meal with fruit, she made him go back to the couch while she cleared the dishes into the dishwasher and made coffee. Then she went to sit beside him on the couch. 'When will Stephen be back?' she asked.

'Not for a while. He's having his tea at my mother's. She usually brings him home in time for bed. Sit here, drink your coffee and relax.'

So she did. She felt warm, comfortable, even a little sleepy. 'I'm tired,' she said. 'It's been a full day.'

'Spending the day on the water and in the sun is always tiring. And we've had our bit of excitement. Why not close your eyes for a moment?'

So she did. And soon she was in that lovely state of being half asleep, half awake. She didn't want to wake fully. Waking might bring problems, questions to be answered, and she didn't want that. Vaguely she realised that there was an arm round her and her head was resting against something warm. Warm and moving slightly. And there was a smell, a fresh soapy smell. She recognised it—she had used it in his bathroom. But underneath there was another smell. Very faint. Something...something masculine?

She realised she was half leaning, half lying against Ross's chest. And she was so comfortable there. Cautiously, she opened her eyes then quickly shut them again. Ross was looking at her, gazing at her with an expression she couldn't make out. Sadness? But mixed with something else.

'You were falling asleep,' he said. 'You leaned against me.'

He tried to move his arm but she pulled it back round her. 'I'm comfortable,' she mumbled. 'Leave your arm there.' Then, suddenly anxious, she added, 'I'm not hurting you, am I?'

There was a pause. Then a soft answer. 'No. I like holding you.'

She wanted to remain half asleep. But she realised that one of her arms was round his waist, her head was on his shoulder and her breast was pressed against his chest. She liked that too. And as slowly she came to full consciousness she realised that they were holding each other like two lovers. And she loved it.

She loved the closeness between them. Her desire for him intensified.

Needing him closer, she slipped her arms round his neck, pulled his head down towards hers. He resisted at first, then he bent his head as she wanted him to.

She rubbed her cheek against his, there was a roughness to his skin. Well, it had been a while since he had shaved. Anyway, she liked it. She turned her head, her lips met his. Of course, she had kissed him before. It had led to nothing—though it could have done.

She felt him hesitate. But then he accepted the invitation she had so freely given. And this kiss was something different. His arms round her tightened, his head pressed hers back into the cushions of the couch as he touched open her lips with his tongue, tasted the sweetness there.

The blood was racing though her veins, she felt her heart beating so rapidly, felt the breath sweeping in and out of her lungs. She wanted him! Whatever he was doing she wanted more! Her arms wrapped more tightly round him, eased him even closer.

With a gasp of excitement she felt his hand close on her breast, caress it, excite it so she felt her nipples stiff and taut with longing. Now he was pressed against her, she could feel the need in his body. She leaned backwards so that he was above her. She felt his lips move from her face to her neck, gentle, feather-like kisses. One of his hands felt for the buttons of her blouse and she eased herself downwards so that they would undo more easily.

She wondered what would happen next. Whatever it was, she didn't care, it would be something she wanted. Perhaps he would...

'Daddy?' a small voice called. She wondered whose voice it was, cross that someone should interrupt when she— But as she wondered she felt Ross jerk away from her and quickly stand. He bent for a moment, gave her a lightning kiss on the lips and then he was out of the door.

'Stephen, where are you? I've got a friend with me. Remember Cat?'

Stephen here? Horrified, Cat sat upright, pulled her blouse together, tried to smooth her hair with her hands. She realised that if Stephen was here, there must be someone with him. What did she look like? Could anyone tell what she had been doing just by looking at her? Well, she would just sit here and wait until called for.

Trembling hands took up the newspaper from the coffee-table in front of her. It made no sense at all. She stared at it a moment and then realised it was upside down.

Thirty seconds ago she had been in ecstasy. Now she had to act like a friend and a colleague—and it was hard. Hadn't Ross said that Stephen wouldn't be back for quite a while?

She heard a murmur of voices at the door. Ross's loud voice said, 'Thank you so much, Mum.' And then the door closed. She was glad that his mother didn't want to come in. There was the rattle of small feet running upstairs and then Ross came back into the room.

He stooped, took her hands in his then kissed her. 'I'm so sorry,' he said. 'I thought we had more time.'

'It doesn't matter. Now, look, it must be near his bedtime and you'll want to spend the rest of the evening with him. I'd better go.'

He looked upset. 'You could stay. Afterwards, when he's asleep, we could talk some more and—'

She had to laugh. 'Talk? We weren't talking then, Ross. We were doing something very different.'

She stood too. They were facing each other, holding hands, each trying to work out what the other was thinking. Cat was at a loss. They seemed to have reached some kind of understanding, which was stronger because it hadn't been put into words. Their bodies had spoken to each other and the message had been unmistakable. But where did they go from here?

There was the rattle of feet again and they released each other just before Stephen came into the room. ''Lo, Cat,' he said, and held out a book to Ross. 'I can read a bit more,' he said. 'Can Cat stay and listen to me read as well?'

Cay recognised the book, it was one of the adventures of the snail and the whale. An evil coincidence. She'd often read it to Kim. Memories rushed back and her emotions were in turmoil. Stephen and Kim were so alike! But...it didn't matter as it had before. She had attained some kind of serenity.

She felt Ross glance at her and then he said to Stephen, 'You sit on the couch and read for a while and I'll talk to Cat. I won't be a minute.' Stephen obediently did as he was told and Ross went on, 'Fancy another coffee, Cat? There's more in the kitchen.'

The coffee would be cold, and she worked out that he had suggested that as a way to speak to her on her own. 'I certainly would,' she said, and followed him into the kitchen.

'I'm sorry about this,' he said in a low voice once they were in the kitchen. 'I wasn't expecting him back for quite a while yet. And I think we both got a bit carried away. But there's no reason why you can't stay a while longer.'

She shook her head. 'I don't think that's a good idea. I think I know what I want—but I'm not sure that you want the same thing as me.'

'Some part of me wants it, I know. The thing that happened to you just now, it happened to me as well. I could feel it.'

She looked at him, knew he was telling the truth. 'Then what are we going to do?'

For perhaps the first time since she had met him she saw that he was at a loss. He shook his head, as if trying to think clearly. 'I don't know. But there can't be any hurry. Tomorrow I'm off on a course for a week in Leeds.'

'I remember Harry telling me about it. So we

won't meet for a week. That might be a good thing. But will you phone me?'·

'No. Not a good idea. We both need a week to get our thoughts sorted out.'

This was a shock and a disappointment. She wanted him to need to phone her, she certainly needed to talk to him. Just to hear his voice, to know what he was doing. Why didn't he feel the same about her?

But perhaps this was neither the time or place to discuss it. 'I'd better go,' she said. 'But there's just one thing. I want to talk to Stephen for a minute. On my own.'

'Why? Are you trying to prove something to me?'

'No. I'm trying to prove something to myself.'

'Do you still see Kim every time you see Stephen?'

'Yes. But it doesn't hurt now. You've helped me that way, Ross. You and Stephen.'

Before he could reply she walked back into the living room, smiled as confidently as she could at Stephen and said, 'I think Daddy's making you a sandwich so will you read to me for a while?'

'Yes, please. I like this story. Shall I sit on your knee to read? I sit on Daddy's knee.'

'That's a lovely idea.' Surprisingly, it wasn't too hard when he did. The warm little body, the happy questions, they brought back so many memories. But the memories were happy.

Eventually Ross came in with a milk drink and a sandwich. 'I'd better go now,' Cat gabbled. 'I've enjoyed today but I'm tired and I've a lot to think about.'

'I feel the same way,' he said. 'Cat, this will be a day I'll remember.'

She didn't dare ask him why.

Back in her cottage she prepared for the next day, laid out everything she might need. Then she went to bed early to think. Her feelings were in a state of utter confusion.

She had come to Benthwaite to escape. She had intended to meet new people, live a different kind of life for a while and then, after a year, go back to London and take up her career again. She had wanted not to forget Kim but to get over the horror of the memory.

In a remarkably short time her escape had worked. She was happier than she had been in months. She was enjoying more than her work, she was enjoying her life. And now she thought more often of the happiness she had had with Kim. Not his death.

One thing she had not done had been to come looking for love. In the past she had had a small succession of lovers, but none of them had been too serious. She had never felt that great blast of passion that she felt was needed—and that she had seen in other people. Like her brother and sister-in-law. Now she realised she was starting to feel that way about Ross.

She made herself say it out loud. 'I think I love Ross McCain.' Even to herself, her voice sounded strained. And it wasn't much of a declaration, was it? So she tried again. 'I love Ross McCain!' Better. More confident. It was a revelation.

So now to think about him. Whatever he felt

for her, he seemed to be fighting against it and what encouragement he was giving her seemed reluctant, even grudging. Certainly he was attracted to her. Perhaps that attraction could deepen into love, she just didn't know. But she was hopeful. Once again her therapist's warning came back to her—she was not to fall for the first person to offer her comfort. Well, she thought she had done so. And she was not too worried.

She was loving her work as a GP. She was also enjoying the fact that there always seemed to be a bit of extra time to do the job properly. And the population of the little town seemed to be interdependent. It was surprising too how many people talked about her other patients—sometimes with an embarrassing knowledge of their ailments. Cat remembered Ross telling her how useful gossip could be.

Of course, many of her cases didn't really need the attention of a GP. An experienced nurse would have done quite as well—in some cases, probably better. All that was necessary was a friendly word or some reassurance. But there was the odd case…

She had an interesting case with her now, a burly lorry driver called Peter Frith. His wife had come in three days before, asking for sleeping pills because her husband's snoring kept her awake.

'Sleep in another room?' Mrs Frith's face had been shocked when she had considered Cat's tentative suggestion. 'Oh, I couldn't do that. We are married, you know.'

'Of course.'

'And it's not just his snoring that upsets me,' Mrs Firth had carried on. 'It's when he stops snoring. He stops everything—even breathing. And then he wakes up with a great jerk.'

Cat had become concerned now. 'How often does this happen?'

Mrs Frith had shrugged. 'Could be a dozen times in a night.'

'Right. Well, will you ask him to come and see me? I'd like to have a chat. And I'd like you to manage without sleeping pills if you can, Mrs Frith. They are a last resort.'

'I think you might be suffering from sleep apnoea,' she was now telling Mr Frith. 'That is when the muscles in your throat relax when you are asleep, and you can't get enough oxygen into your system. You suddenly wake up because your body tells you to try to grab air as quickly as possible. And overall you just don't get enough sleep.'

She knew he was a lorry driver, so the next question had to be handled delicately. 'Do you ever feel very sleepy during the day? So tired that you might fall asleep while you're working? While you're driving perhaps?'

'No!' Mr Frith said. 'Of course not!'

But Cat had seen the fear in his eyes. 'I'm going to refer you to a respiratory consultant. They'll give you tests and find out if you are suffering from sleep apnoea. Don't worry, there is a cure. It might be a case of just losing a bit of weight. There used to be an operation but mostly these days your consultant suggests that you wear a CPAP mask at night. That's a continuous positive airway pressure machine. With that you'll feel far less tired in the day because you'll be getting enough sleep.'

'That would be a good thing,' said Mr Frith. 'And the wife will be happy too.'

'Our aim is to please,' said Cat.

Mr Frith had been the last case on her list but just as she was about to go for a coffee Cat had a call from Harry. 'Just had a walk-in case, Cat. I could deal with it myself. I can guess what's needed but I'd prefer you to deal with it. Have you got time?'

'I've got time Harry, but why me? Any special reason?'

'You're young and female. I think that's what's needed. I'll bring the girl round now.'

Tracy Brett was a holidaymaker, young, red-faced and tearful. 'I want the morning-after pill in case I get pregnant.' She burst into more tears. 'It was the first time and I didn't even really like it.'

'I'd better examine you first,' Cat said, 'then we'll take things from there. You say this was this first time? Who was the boy?'

'It was my boyfriend, Vince. We've been going out together for a couple of months now and we thought we'd wait but…'

'So Vince didn't force you in any way?'

Even through her tears Tracy was indignant. ''Course not. We love each other. Mind you, we'd both had a bit to drink.'

'And you'll be how old next birthday?'

'Eighteen.' The tone was defiant. Cat said nothing but looked at her patient. After a while Tracy sighed and said, 'Well, I'm nearly seventeen.'

'And Vince is?'

'Same as me. Six months older, in fact.'

'Right, then. Come over here and get on this couch.'

The examination was soon over. Tracy seemed to be telling the truth, she was over the age of consent, she had not been forced so no crime had been committed. Unless stupidity was a crime. Cat sighed.

'I'll give you the morning-after pill,' she said when Tracy had dressed again. 'But what you've got to understand is that this is for an emergency. It can't be used regularly, it gives your system too much of a shock. If you're going to do this again then you need to think ahead and have some reliable means of contraception. Are you going to do it again?'

'I suppose so, now we've started,' Tracy said, without much evident enthusiasm. 'But I didn't think much of it.'

'Well, it's up to you to decide. Don't always rely on Vince. You could always carry condoms with you.'

'I could what? What if me mam found them?'

'She'd rather find them than have you pregnant,' said Cat.

She talked to Tracy for a few minutes more, fetched her the pill and then sent her on her way. She wondered just how good a job she had done. Telling someone how to organise their love life? She wasn't sure she was entitled to. How well was she organising her own love life? Well, at least she was trying. And she certainly knew what she wanted.

As she walked down for her coffee she realised how much she was missing Ross. Well, she'd expected to do that. Then, slightly to her surprise, she found she was missing Stephen too. She wanted to be part of Ross's life—and she would need to be part of Stephen's life too. The two of them went together. That made her think. She would never get over losing Kim but…life could go on.

She found herself making quite a friend of Alanna Cavendish. Alanna was often in and out of both the surgery and Rosewood, and Cat found they worked well together. Alanna was forward-looking and energetic. And the story of how she had found her lost child was almost a fairy-tale. Perhaps there was good in the world.

On Wednesday Alanna came up to her, took a card from a large pile and said, 'Wedding invitation. I do hope you can come. I'm sorry it's such short notice but did you know there's a waiting list to get married at St Mary's?'

Cat was surprised. 'But I thought you were already married?'

'We are. A registry office job, and it suited us very well at the time. But Finn always wanted a big white wedding and we wanted to celebrate finding Eleanor so…we're getting married again. Only properly this time.'

'I see,' Cat said with a grin.

'So you'll come? Great, then there's a favour I have to ask you. Will you come up to Carlisle with me to help me look for a wedding dress? I always think that two opinions are better than one.'

'I haven't been on a big shopping expedition in months. I'd love to come,' said Cat. 'When were you thinking of going?'

'Some time this week. I'll have a word with Harry, he'll be happy to arrange for us both to get off for an afternoon. If not—no invitation for him.'

They went on Friday afternoon and Cat looked forward to spending some girly time with Alanna. Alanna had a clear idea of what she wanted and had a list of the best shops to visit. They found something that seemed ideal practically at once—but, of course, it was necessary to check all the other shops. But after wandering around them all, they stopped for a coffee and a well-earned cream cake. And it was a joint decision. The first dress Alanna had tried on. It was in white silk, high-necked, long-sleeved, with a tight fitted bodice.

'It's lovely on you but not every woman could get away with wearing it,' Cat said.

Alanna grinned. 'Good thing that the wedding's so soon, then. The figure will disappear shortly.'

'You're not!'

'It's time Eleanor had a little brother or sister,' Alanna said. 'And then perhaps another one after that.'

'Congratulations!' Cat said.

They drove back to Benthwaite, Alanna obviously delighted with her purchase, Cat a bit confused about her own feelings. She was happy for her friend, of course. But there were memories of five years ago, helping the friend who was now her sister-in-law to buy her wedding dress. She remembered the fun. She remembered wondering when it might be her turn to pick a dress. Not yet, she had thought then, but some time.

'You're looking serious,' Alanna said. 'What's the problem?'

For once Cat decided to be honest. 'I'm jealous and broody,' she said. 'I want to get married.' Then she grinned to show that it had been a joke.

But Alanna knew that it wasn't entirely a joke. 'Any particular man in mind?' she asked.

A long silence. 'Not really,' said Cat. 'Well, possibly. It's all a bit difficult.'

She looked at her friend, realised that Alanna knew who she was talking about.

'Things turn up, things change when you're just not expecting them,' Alanna said. 'I should know. Perhaps they will for you.'

'Perhaps,' said Cat.

CHAPTER SEVEN

Ross had only been away for a week but it seemed much longer. And when he returned Cat was amazed at the strength of her feelings. It was early Monday morning and she was at Rosewood when she saw him through a window. He was bringing Stephen into the nursery.

She was excited, she could feel her heart beating faster. It had only been a week but he seemed different. Or the way she thought about him seemed different. She had thought about him every day. And every night as well.

Once or twice she had considered phoning him. They'd agreed not to phone—but she'd considered changing her mind. Then she had realised that she didn't know what she had to say to him, her feelings were in turmoil. After all that they had shared. A kiss? Well, several kisses, in fact. And how they had affected her. Had they affected him in the same way?

But now he was back and he seemed so much more real than he had in her dreams. Still, when he came into the foyer her greeting had to be casual. 'Hi, Ross, good to see you back. How was the course?'

'The course was good. It was on the "golden hour". There's a few things we might put into practice. I'll print off a set of notes and we'll talk about it some time.'

Then he reached forward, took her arms in his hands. 'But how did you get on without me?'

'I missed you a lot,' Cat said with more than necessary honesty. Then she tried to retreat a little from what she had said. No need to alarm him by showing too much passion. 'I need my daily dose of realism. In your absence I was in danger of turning into a bright-eyed enthusiast.'

He laughed. 'I love you for being an enthusiast,' he said. 'Now, let's get to work. Who have we got in?'

They bustled towards the wards and she wondered why her heart was tripping extra hard. Then she realised. He had said he loved her. Just as a joke, of course, for being something that he really didn't care about. But she had felt more than small pleasure that he could say that he loved her for anything.

When they had coffee together at mid-morning she said, 'I've been invited to a wedding. Finn and Alanna's.'

He nodded. 'I knew, but I wanted Alanna to have the pleasure of inviting you in person. Finn has asked me to be his best man. I'm not sure I'm a good choice. I'm not that comfortable at weddings and I'm not convinced that being best man is the kind of thing I want to do—but, of course, I accepted. Will you come with me? As my partner?'

Her heart was now beating faster than ever, but she couldn't let him know that. Casually, she said, 'Of course I'll go with you. Apart from anything else, it'll give me the excuse to buy a new hat. What about Stephen when you're on the top table, giving your speech?'

'Well, I gather there's going to be a children's table. He'll be happy there. I'll arrange for someone to—'

'I'd like him to sit with me.'

She felt uncomfortable as he looked at her. 'It's not a test any more, is it?' he asked. 'You're not seeing if you've got over Kim?'

'I'll never entirely get over losing Kim but I don't feel guilty now. No, I want to sit by him because I like him. He's a nice little boy. I enjoy his company.' She didn't dare tell him that being with Stephen would bring her closer to him. So she asked, 'Why do you say you're not sure you like weddings?'

He shrugged. 'I like all the people involved. But I'm not really a party man. There's to be a dance at the reception. I suppose we'll have to turn up but I won't dance if you don't mind. I'll slip away early and leave you to—'

'Ross McCain! I *do* mind. I'm not going to have you as a miserable old kill-joy. You'll turn up and be my escort to the end. I'll be pleased and proud to be with you. So you'll stay!'

'Right, then,' he said after a moment. 'Interesting to see that you can make a point when you want to.'

Cat had to say that it was a perfect wedding. Unusually for the Lake District, the weather did them proud. It was a sunny late September day. There was the full wedding service except for the signing of the register because legally the couple were married already. A beaming vicar gave a short address about the importance of never giving up hope. There was a wonderful choir. Harry gave the bride away, Finn and Ross both looked elegant in morning suits. Eleanor as the single brides-maid was glowing with importance, obviously thinking that this had all been arranged just for her.

And Alanna, the bride, was radiant.

The reception was held in the grounds of the Elton Hotel, an elegant Victorian greystone building on the outskirts of the little town.

Cat looked after Stephen but saw very little of Ross as he had the best man's duties. But when they did have a moment together she told him he looked both dignified and debonair in his morning suit. He scowled. 'I feel like a mannequin in a shop window.' Then he looked at her. 'But, Cat, you look really something. That dress is stunning. '

'Thank you, kind sir,' she said with a demure little curtsy.

In fact, she felt really something. She had gone back to Carlisle on her own and treated herself to a dress she had noticed when shopping with Alanna. It was made of a light blue silk. The bodice was tight and just low enough to show the swell of her breasts, the skirt was flared and swirled dramatically if she turned quickly. She had also bought new, matching underwear and a ludicrously expensive pair of shoes. She felt good!

She had once heard that the speeches ruined more weddings that anything else. This wedding was made by them. Conventionally, there were the speeches and toasts by the groom, the best man, the bride's father—in this case Harry. But Alanna was not to be bound by convention and made a speech herself. 'I told Finn that I would be happy to have the original wedding service, in which I promised to love, honour…and obey. The only thing I asked was that he promised the same. He obeyed.' It was that kind of wedding.

Cat was curious, even a little apprehensive, about Ross's best man's speech. She knew he wasn't a man who found it easy to talk about feelings. But she had a shock. 'I know of no happier way of living than the union of a child—or children—a woman and a man. And if putting the child first seems odd—then let me say I did it on purpose.'

Then a smile, a change of tone. 'It is traditional that at a wedding no one looks more beautiful than the bride. I understand that some brides have gone to considerable lengths to ensure this. Not Alanna. Today she is the most beautiful among us. But following her closely there is the beautiful Eleanor. Ladies and gentlemen, I give you the bridesmaid.'

Yes, it was a wonderful wedding. Cat noticed that Ross took his duties seriously—any small problem was dealt with quickly and effectively. He was his usual calm, efficient self.

After the meal was over she managed to have a word with him. 'I'm running home to take Stephen to stay with his grandmother and to get out of this outfit,' he said. 'But I'll be back quite quickly.'

'I like you in that. You look distinguished.'

'I feel extinguished. If I'm going to enjoy myself then I need to be in something lighter. I'll be right back.'

'You'd better be. Remember, you're going to enjoy yourself.'

She had wondered if she dared bring it up. Now she decided that she could. Nerving herself, she said, 'I liked your speech. I noticed that you said that you knew of no happier way of living than a child, a woman and a man. You meant yourself, didn't you?'

'Yes,' he said after a moment.

'You were thinking of your own life, your life as it was before. You were happy then.'

'I was.'

She must have been excited by the occasion or perhaps the two glasses of champagne she had drunk. 'You know, you could be that happy again,' she told him. 'And for the same reason.'

* * *

Ross came back wearing a lightweight suit and joined Cat, Harry and his wife and one or two other staff at a table by the dance floor. It was a warm evening, the French windows were open and people were wandering in and out of the garden. Cat felt happy. Perhaps it was the occasion. Perhaps it was the champagne. It could even have been the prospect of spending time with Ross. But she was happy. The night seemed full of possibilities.

The dancing started. Bride and groom first, of course, then Harry and his wife and after a few moments other couples. Cat looked at Ross. 'I know how you feel about dancing,' she said, 'but we'll just get on the floor, you can put your arms round me and we'll just rock backwards and forwards.'

'Right. I can do that. Just so long as you don't demand that I wriggle around the floor like these young people are going to do.'

'You're a young person! Now, come and dance with me.'

She had expected just to sway with him, as she

had said, but to her surprise he could do much more than that. 'Why didn't you say? You're a very good dancer!'

He shrugged. 'I used to like dancing. But I've not done any for years.'

'Do you miss it?'

Another shrug. 'Not as much as I miss walking. But, yes, I do miss it. And when I'm dancing with you…'

'Yes?' she demanded as his voice trailed away.

'I miss it even more.'

This was supposed to be a night that the bride and groom would never forget. She added herself to that list.

They did dance again—but only the slower dances. Other men came over and asked her to dance and she enjoyed that too. The bride and groom came to their table, it was good to see how happy they were.

After a while Ross asked her if she would like a walk round the garden, and she said yes. It was an old garden, well kept, with trees, shrubs, odd beds of flowers and little unexpected corners.

She felt entitled to take his arm. It was dusk, the evening was beautiful.

They stopped at a corner where they couldn't be seen and he kissed her. It was a gentle kiss, they stood there, their arms loosely round each other, their bodies just touching.

'I think this is a magic night,' she told him. 'For now we can forget the past, forget problems and troubles and the future. For now there is only tonight. I want you to feel as I do. We will live just for tonight.'

His voice was hoarse. 'Do you know what you are saying? Do you mean it?'

'Oh, yes. I know what I am saying. I promise you that. Now, shall we go back to the dance?'

She felt calm as they walked back but she knew that things were different. She had made a decision and she was happy with it.

They danced once or twice more then Alanna, Finn and Eleanor left and the rest of the party started to drift away.

'I want you to come back to my home,' she told him. 'It's nearest and we can easily walk there.'

'As you wish.'

So they walked to her home, holding hands and saying nothing. They were perfectly happy. All that was necessary had already been said. But as they neared her front door her heart started to beat faster. She fumbled in her bag for her key and he said, 'Cat, you can still change—'

She turned her head, pressed a kiss against his lips. 'Don't say any more. Just come in.'

In her little living room she said, 'It's been a lovely night but it's not over yet. You're to take off your jacket and tie and I'm going to get out of this dress. What would you like to drink? I've got wine and brandy—perhaps even a beer.'

'I haven't drunk much but I think I've drunk enough. I'd like tea please.'

'Tea it shall be.'

She filled the kettle and then went upstairs to change. The blue dress was carefully hung up—but she decided to keep on her new underwear and slipped a light gown over it. Then she went back downstairs, made two mugs of tea and went to sit next to him on the couch.

'I can feel two things fighting in you,' she told him. I suspect you feel for me what I feel for you—we won't say what it is. But you're also holding back. You're scared. And I think things will be easier for you if you tell me about your past. I've told you my secret, about Kim, so can't you tell me your secret?'

He looked uneasy. 'I don't like talking about the past.'

She took his hand. 'Just start when you are ready,' she said. 'I know it's hard but you might feel better when it's over.'

She watched him, saw his body tense and then slowly relax. She knew he had made his decision.

'First, I don't want you to say anything,' he said. 'I don't want sympathy. And above all I don't want any tears. This has been a happy day, I want to keep it that way. OK?'

'OK,' she said. But now that she had got what she wanted, she was feeling apprehensive.

'I'm not going to give details, you'll have to imagine them.'

His voice took on a curt tone, as if he was giving an emotionless report to a set of strangers. 'I met Judy at medical school, we were married in our last year there. And we were happy together. Ultimately we wanted to be country GPs but first we decided to see a bit of the world, perhaps help people who needed it. We took a job in Africa. We enjoyed life out there, although sometimes it was hard—there was never enough money for the work we had to do. And we had a baby—Stephen. He was wanted and he was loved.'

He paused a moment, took a breath. 'And suddenly we were in the middle of a civil war. I still don't know why. But where previously we had dealt with diseases and gynae and paediatric work, now we were dealing with bullet wounds and machete cuts. The charity we worked for said things were getting dangerous, they wanted us to pull out. I said that they could take Stephen and Judy, I would stay. Stephen was taken to some nuns a hundred miles away but Judy refused to leave me.'

His voice got even more toneless, even more emotionless. 'I drove out to an emergency call some fifteen miles away—a Caesarean. When I got back I could see our little hospital and our bungalow on fire. All my patients killed, Judy killed trying to protect them. I was shot through the leg. An hour later government soldiers came and carried me away. My leg was patched up as best the staff could, but it's never been right since. Possibly my foot will have to be amputated in time. I decided I'd done my bit for suffering humanity, so I picked up Stephen and came back here.'

Cat had promised no tears but no way could she stop them. She sat in silence, feeling them run down her cheeks.

'I loved Judy so much that coping with the pain of her death was almost more than I could bear. But I had Stephen to think of. So I came here, took on this job and decided that never again would I let myself love as I had done. I would never again get involved with a woman in that way.'

'So you don't want to get involved with me?'

'I daren't! Perhaps I would like to but I daren't!'
He stood. 'I think perhaps I'd better go now.'

'Don't you even think about it! Sit down.
We've got things to decide.'

He sat, and looked at her curiously. 'Things
to decide?'

'Have you been in any kind of relationship
with a woman since that time?'

He shrugged. 'Just a couple of brief liaisons.
But I made it very clear that they were in no way
permanent.'

For something to do, she picked up the two
empty mugs from the table and took them into
the kitchen. She thought that this represented a
turning point in their relationship and she was
afraid of what might come next. The easiest thing
to do would be to back away, to stay friends, to
agree with him that it might be better if he went
now. But that was not what she wanted. They had
just been to the most wonderful of weddings,
had glimpsed the happiness that two people—or
three, for that matter—could have together.

It was a gamble. But perhaps she could bring him to see that he could be as happy again as he had been with Judy. He—and Stephen—could be happy with her.

She walked back into the living room, looked down at his troubled face. Her voice trembling, she said, 'You said you'd had a couple of brief liaisons. So, right. Then you can have that kind of liaison with me. Perhaps just once.'

'But, Cat, we—'

'Are we going to talk about it all night?' she asked. 'Isn't the time for talking now over?'

The longest of pauses. Then he said, 'I think it is.'

He stood, put his arm round her, drew her towards him. He kissed her, almost a chaste kiss, only their lips touching. He had kissed her like this before. But then they had stopped. And with a mixture of joy and slight fear she realised that this time they would not stop.

She felt his hands on her face, his fingertips tracing a line from her forehead down across her cheeks. His thumbs circled her ears, a caress that was surprisingly exciting. Then his fingers slid downwards, touching her neck, her throat, and into the V of her gown. He eased the gown aside and stroked the swell of her breasts as they rose from her half-cup bra.

Surely he could feel the beating of her heart? Her whole body was reacting to him, she felt her nipples suddenly become tight with excitement, felt the warmth in her chest, bringing a flush to her cheeks. No man had ever made her feel like this before! This was Ross, the man she loved. And they had tonight.

She felt his arms tighten round her and knew what was likely to happen next. She leaned back a little, looked at his face. This was a new Ross. His eyes were dark with desire, the air of casual humour behind which he usually hid—it had gone. The was the true Ross, letting his feelings for her show, and she revelled in it.

When she spoke her voice seemed strange, remote. 'Not here, Ross. Come to my bedroom.' She stood, offered him her hand. He said nothing in reply, just took her hand and let her lead him.

She had left the bedroom as she wanted it. It was half in shadow, only two Tiffany-style lamps spilled coloured light onto the bed, the dressing-table. For a moment they stood facing each other. Then he stepped forward, undid the belt of her gown and eased it back from her shoulders. The gown fell to the floor, a puddle of white silk around her feet. She heard his gasp of excitement.

He reached for her, pulled her to him, kissed her, a full-tongued kiss of desperation. She realised that this would be no long drawn-out gentle seduction, his need for her was too great. For that matter, her need for him was the same. Somehow her bra was undone, fell to the floor. Fingertips slid inside the elastic of her briefs and eased them downwards. And the returning hand brushed against her in that most exciting of places.

He took her in his arms for another kiss that seemed to drag at her very soul. Then he lifted her, placed her on the bed. 'You're wearing too many clothes,' she muttered. And she closed her eyes.

There was the rustle of fabric. Then the bed dipped as he climbed onto it. She didn't open her eyes but she knew he was looking at her. She could tell by the catch in his breathing.

She lay there, happy in anticipation. For a while all decisions would be up to him. A half-sensed movement and she felt a kiss, gentler than before, on her lips. But before she could wrap her arms round him, he had moved.

A moment of happy apprehension. Then she called out in joy as his lips fastened on her breasts, in turn taking each rosy peak into his mouth. He was so good to her, this was so wonderful! But there was more to come, there must be…

Perhaps he sensed her need. There was a chuckle. And then another kiss, but this one so intimate that she cried out again, half in shock and half in delight.

Perhaps some day they could carry on like this for much, much longer. But now she was feeling an urge that was too strong to be denied. She reached down for his shoulders, pulled him to towards her. 'Now, Ross, please, I need you now,' she pleaded. And she knew his need was as great as hers.

So now he was above her. One last glimpse of that wonderful face, in shadow but with all the desire, all the passion showing in it. And some other emotion. Love perhaps? She just didn't know.

He was with her; she gave herself to him, accepting him into her, making them one body that moved to a rhythm that both of them felt. Passion's peak could not be far away. Soon there was a joint cry of joy, a moment that she knew only lasted for seconds but which seemed to go on and on as if there could be no ending. But it had to end, and afterwards was almost as good as before.

'You give so much to me,' she murmured as she lay curled in his arms. She was certain that what they had given to each other had been so wonderful that he would feel just as she did. All would be well. Then she fell asleep.

Next morning she woke early, brought him tea in bed. Then they made love again, gently, almost shyly, as if getting to know each other for the first time. And then, in one another's arms, they slept a little longer.

But it was time to move back into reality.

'That was a night out of time,' he told her, 'and it was magic. But now we have to shift back into the real world. I've got to call into Rosewood for half an hour, then pick up Stephen and take him sailing. Cat, do you know how wonderful—?'

'This doesn't have to end and we can still live in the real world. I've got a proposal for you. It's silly to carry on just as colleagues when we feel like this for each other. And I know you do feel for me, don't try to deny it. But I understand your fear of commitment and you not wanting to go through that pain again. So…'

She took a breath, she had been rehearsing this speech for the last few minutes. 'You told me you had had affairs. Me too, we're both experienced. You're staying here at Benthwaite, I'm going back to London at the end of my year. We'll have to part. But we can be lovers until then. And then we'll say goodbye. A clean break.'

'A clean break? How would saying goodbye make you feel?'

She could be honest about that. 'No worse than I feel now. No worse than if I don't see more of you. What do you think of the idea?'

She could see the feelings warring inside him. Eventually he said, 'Cat, it's so, so tempting. But it just won't work.'

'It will! Lovers till I go and then happy memories and the exchange of Christmas cards.'

Somehow she managed to keep her expression calm. Not so Ross. He looked troubled, his face revealing his thoughts. And then he smiled and she knew she had won.

He kissed her. 'All I know is that I want to make love with you. Nothing would make me happier than to continue to do so. It would be an honour to be your lover.'

'Right!' She kissed him back.

They agreed they had fifteen more minutes before they had to move back into the real world. They lay side by side, holding hands, but in the silence, Cat couldn't completely quieten the small doubting voice in her head.

Could they really part quietly, calmly, with no great regret? Like it or not, her feelings for Ross seemed unlikely to change, but what of his real feelings for her? She knew she'd like nothing more than to have him for ever, she just had to hope that he'd come to feel the same way. Even Ross couldn't deny the reality of their attraction to each other. It had to lead to something deeper. The thought warmed her.

But then he upset her. 'Just one thing I need to say,' he said.

'Mmm? Whatever you want.'

'We'll be lovers but I'll never say I love you. And I don't want you to say it to me. Whatever this is between us, it isn't love.'

CHAPTER EIGHT

SHE had slid into a routine now and she realised that she was happier than she had ever been in her life before. She was enjoying the medicine, found she was developing skills that only came with experience. Medicine was about reading people, as well as understanding symptoms. And if she had a few moments to chat, then that was fine.

Peter Frith's wife came in to see her and she was much happier. 'He has to wear a mask every night in bed.' She giggled. 'Doesn't half make a noise. But he doesn't have to put it on straight away, does he? It's been smashing since he isn't so tired all the time.'

A few days later another older married woman came to see her. She was a friend of Mrs Frith, had been told about the treatment for Mr Frith.

'My husband does the same thing,' she told Cat. 'Seems to go to sleep and then stops breathing and wakes up all suddenly. Could he have this sleep apnoea thing?'

'Get him to come and see me and we'll find out,' said Cat. Was there an epidemic of sleep apnoea in Benthwaite?

She felt she was being accepted into the community.

And she saw a lot of Ross. He called at her cottage whenever he could. It felt vaguely illicit and for the moment rather nice.

'Don't you feel this is all rather hole in the corner?' he asked her one time as they lay happily in bed together. 'Wouldn't you rather we were just ordinary, with all our friends knowing we were a couple?'

'No. For now, I like being in a hole in the corner. All my life I've done things the proper way. This is like a bit of an adventure.'

This was true. But she also thought that perhaps sometimes it would be nice if they were seen as a couple. Occasionally, she went to his house while Stephen was there and the three of them enjoyed themselves together. She liked that too.

One morning a few days later he came into the doctors' room in Rosewood and found her there, drinking coffee. There was no one else in the room and he bent over and kissed her.

'Ross! Anyone could come in! Then it would be all over the hospital.' But she was still pleased.

'I know I shouldn't have done it. But you looked so attractive in that dress that I couldn't resist you.'

Then his face changed and he said, 'But you do remember what we decided, don't you?' He looked uncertain.

'Of course I remember,' she said demurely.

The following week he told her that he was taking Stephen to the fair in Carlisle. Would she like to go with them? Her face clouded as she thought about that, and, ever vigilant, he noticed it. 'Is there any reason you don't want to come to the fair with us? You and Stephen are fine together.'

'We are getting on very well, I love being with

you and him. It's just that, not too long before it…happened I took Kim to a fair and we had a wonderful time. It's the roundabouts that get to me. He loved riding on them.'

He put his arm round her, squeezed her. 'I can feel for you.'

'It's the little things that come back to hurt, even when you think you're over them,' she went on. 'It can be anything—taste, smell, sight, sound. I can't now bear to eat a custard cream biscuit, because Kim loved them.'

Then she said, 'But I'd love to come to the fair with you and Stephen. Then I can take him on the roundabout. Your legs would be too long.'

So they went to the fair and she enjoyed herself hugely. They had ice cream and candy floss. Ross slid down the helter-skelter with Stephen and she took him on two roundabouts. They threw rings at glass bowls and fortunately didn't win a goldfish. The three of them went up on the Ferris wheel, Stephen squashed in the middle. It was a great day.

They were strolling through the park back towards Ross's car when they heard a sudden blast of cheerful sound. They rounded a corner and there was a brass band, on the bandstand, instruments sparkling in the sun.

'This is a march,' Cat said to Stephen. 'You have to swing your arms and keep step to the music. Like this.' She marched forward and Stephen promptly followed her. After a few steps Cat turned and said, 'Come on, Ross, you march too.' Then she stopped, looked at his bleak face. 'Something wrong?' she asked.

'I'm not too fond of brass bands.'

'It's more than whether you like brass bands or not, I can tell.' She walked back a couple of paces to him. 'Come on, Ross, what is it?' And she guessed. 'Something to do with…with when you were married to Judy?'

'I can't hide anything from you, can I?' He smiled, but it was obviously painful.

'Ross, you can tell me. I know that you loved your wife, the fact that you could love her so much makes you…well, it make you more lovable. And it's one reason why I…' She let her voice trail away.

Ross was alert. 'You stopped yourself saying something then?'

She shook her head. 'No, I didn't. Anyway, we have an agreement and I'll stick to it. We have a relationship and it only lasts till I go back to London. Now, tell me what you have against brass bands.'

She could see he was thinking about it. Then he started, 'I asked Judy to marry me in a park like this and there was a brass band playing in the distance. A march by Sousa. Then we had it played at our wedding. And this is that very march. It's called the "Liberty Bell". It brought back memories.'

Stephen wasn't listening. She took his hand and squeezed it. 'I'm glad you told me,' she said. 'It means we can talk.'

But she felt something—jealousy? She had had boyfriends, had happy memories of them. But nothing like this. How would she feel if her dreams didn't come true, if she and Ross had to part?

She closed her eyes a moment, remembered her life in the city. Her friends, the frantic but happy lifestyle she had had, the ever-changing London scene. She could go back to it, and she now knew that she was largely over the depression caused by Kim's death. There was a good life waiting for her there.

Now she knew she had options, choices. And Ross wasn't the only one.

Soon it was autumn. There was the first chill and the lakes and mountains were more beautiful than ever, the air seemed clearer. Life was good.

It was nearly the middle of the day, both of them had had the morning off. She was lying in bed with Ross, holding his hand, the memory of what they had just done making her happy. 'I'm trying to remember a poem we did at school,' she said drowsily. 'It was something about roses. Called a *carpe diem* poem, it means seize the day.'

He sniffed, 'I know what *carpe diem* means. I'm not uneducated. And I bet I know the poem. "Gather ye rosebuds while ye may, Old time is still a-flying." Why did you suddenly think of that?'

'Because that's what we're doing. Gathering

rosebuds. Which is a bit of a poetic way of describing it, but you know what I mean. And time is flying, but it means that the past is past.'

'I see.' His voice was gentle. 'You came to Benthwaite to get away from things, to escape memories. Memories of Kim. Do you think you've done that?'

'Yes, I have. I still weep on occasions but what happened isn't with me all the time. I can say or hear his name without getting too upset. Now I think there's a future as well as a past. What about you? Are you seizing the day?'

He thought. 'I suppose I'm happy with what I've got. I don't think of the future much, I'm happy going from day to day.'

He leaned over her, his hand trailing across her breasts in a small caress that was so exciting. 'But life has to go on. It's time we got ready for work.' He kissed her quickly.

'Ross! You touch me like that and you kiss me and all you're doing is looking at my bedside clock?'

'Just gathering rosebuds,' he said.

They weren't going to arrive at Rosewood together, he left first. And as he stopped for a final kiss, just inside her front door, she said, 'Now I remember some of the rest of that poem. "While ye may, go marry."'

He looked at her sardonically. 'Just a convenient rhyme for tarry,' he said.

Ross felt troubled as he drove to Rosewood. She didn't realise it, but he knew exactly what Cat was thinking—or feeling. She didn't believe that their affair would end next summer. She had no clear idea of what would happen—but she'd expect them to stay together. He shook his head in dismay. He hadn't intended this to happen.

The apparently careless reference to 'go marry'. It hadn't been planned but it showed the way she was thinking.

And he knew it was largely his fault. He should have stopped this at the beginning, refused to start their affair, saved her from pain in the future. And he knew there would be pain. All her talk about parting calmly was rubbish. She would suffer—and so for that matter would he.

Perhaps the honourable thing to do would be to end the affair now. Cut it from their lives, like a surgeon with a knife. It would hurt—and that was the problem. She now meant so much to him, he just couldn't let her go. Being with her brought him so much pleasure. But if he let himself be drawn in, she would mean so much more.

Could he think the unthinkable—consider starting a relationship that would be permanent? And one great obstacle was out of the way. Cat and Stephen now got on very well together. He smiled grimly. Stephen would be as desolated as he would be when Cat moved on.

But…a permanent relationship? He sighed. It just wasn't an option. The thought of the pain he had suffered before—he just couldn't risk that again. No, the risk was too great. But he still felt sad.

It happened by accident, that afternoon at Rosewood. They were in the coffee-room and

Ross dropped his briefcase, as ever stuffed with papers and magazines. It burst open and the contents spread all over the floor. Cat helped him scrabble them together and cram them back into his briefcase. 'Men talk about women's handbags being full of rubbish,' she told him. 'This is worse than any handbag I've ever seen.'

'I've got every paper I might need in this case. All I have to do is find it.' And he was gone.

She was finishing her coffee when she noticed that there was a sheet of paper that they had missed. It had slid under a chair. She pulled it out and glanced at it, an obvious medical letter. Then she looked more carefully. The patient's name was at the top of the letter—Ross McCain.

Well, they were lovers—what they could, they shared. She was entitled to look. But she felt a bit guilty.

It was a letter from an orthopaedic surgeon in Leeds. She recognised the name, he was one of the top surgeons in the country. The letter said that in principle the surgeon was willing to operate on Ross's leg, but that he must understand that the operation he had in mind was still experimental. Only three had been performed. The result might be a complete restoration of all movement in the foot. The worst-case scenario would be that the foot might have to be amputated. The surgeon would be in touch in two months' time, when he knew if the first three operations had been successful.

He had never said much about it but Cat knew how bad Ross felt about his inability to walk as he had once done. She also knew that on occasion the foot caused him considerable pain—though he went to great lengths to hide it. An operation to put things right would be wonderful.

But why hadn't he told her? They were lovers—lovers shared good news and bad. She felt a little hurt.

Later on she found herself again sitting with him in the coffee-room. She gave him the letter and said, trying to sound casual, 'Why didn't you tell me about this? Didn't you think I'd be interested?'

Equally casually, he replied, 'It's no great deal.

If the operation is successful and if I have it, it won't be for another year or so. You'll be gone by then. We'll have parted.'

She felt hurt by his casual acceptance of that. So far they'd never talked about what would happen when she had to leave. It seemed to be a forbidden subject, they were living just for the present. But she said, 'I'll still…be interested in you. I'll miss you and I hope you'll miss me.'

He shrugged. 'I certainly will miss you. But we have an agreement. When you go, all will be over between us. Being together now is good— but that's partly because we know it's going to end. Cat, you have to accept that what we have either has to develop or die. We can't go on for ever like this. It's wonderful but it has to end.'

He looked at her, his face troubled. 'Cat, this is what we agreed. You're not getting too…fond of me, are you?'

His obvious anxiety, his obvious care for her only made things worse. 'Of course not,' she said. 'I was just interested in this operation.'

Both of them knew she was lying.

* * *

Cat tried not to show it but she felt that after this conversation her relationship with Ross altered slightly. So far she had kept her side of the bargain—though she intended to change it—and he had kept his. But now they knew each other so much better. They worked well together, they were happy in each other's company. Her hope had been that he might change. It didn't seem to be happening.

Things were made worse the following morning. Cat received—and sent—regular letters from her brother and sister-in-law in America. They were enjoying themselves out there but still intended to come back to England in time. There had been a letter from them that morning, she took it unopened to work at Rosewood. She would read it when she had her morning coffee-break with Ross.

It was a bombshell.

They had not wanted to tell her before, not until details had been finalised and they had something certain to offer. They had been offered a partner-ship in a new practice in the suburbs of London, starting in January. And they had decided to accept. If it was possible to arrange, would Cat like to transfer and finish her training with them?

And another bit of good news. Anita was pregnant again. She wanted Cat to be with her throughout the pregnancy and birth. What did Cat think? No need to hurry with a reply.

Cat read the letter, reread it then tried to make sense of her reaction to it. Of course she was happy for Anita and Tom. And she would like to work with them, wanted to help with the pregnancy. But...she wished this had just not happened.

Ross had obviously noted her reaction, his voice was concerned. 'Not bad news, I hope?'

Silently, she held out the letter to him. He read the letter, passed it back to her. 'An interesting offer,' he said without apparent emotion. 'Are you going to accept? Personally I'd be very sorry to see you go so soon—but it's the kind of job you've always wanted, isn't it?'

'Do you want me to go? What about you and me?'

He shrugged. 'Sometimes good things come

to an end. In fact, they come to an end quite often.'

And then Cat lost her temper. It didn't happen very often, she tried to keep her emotions under control. She tried to be cool, logical, all the things a good doctor should be. But now she was tired of it. She had tried to be fair to Ross but now she was going to be fair to herself. Fortunately, they were alone on the doctors' lounge and not likely to be disturbed.

Her voice was taut with rage. 'Good things come to an end, Ross? You're getting rid of me just like that? I've been a good thing, like a few days' fine weather or a book you've enjoyed reading? I know I promised not to say it, but just because you don't say something doesn't mean it isn't true. Ross, I love you! And I love you and Stephen. I want to be a mother to him, bring him up as if he were my own child. And more than all that, I know you love me. That's not a good thing that comes to an end!'

She leapt from her chair, stamped over to where he was sitting and grabbed his arms.

Obviously shocked, he stood, took her hands in his. 'Cat, I can see that you're upset—'

'I'm more than upset! I'm angry! For too long we've been tiptoeing round each other, not saying what needs to be said. Well, that's at an end. I want some honesty. I've just told you I love you. So now, Ross, just look me in the eye and either tell me that you love me or tell me that you don't. And whatever you say, I'll accept it.'

Tears blurred her eyes as she stared at him. But she could still see the agony in his face as he stared back. 'Cat…sweetheart. It's hard. And are you sure you want an answer?'

'I do want an answer! And I don't care how hard it is, for you or me.'

He sighed. 'All right, I'll say it. Cat, I love you. I think I love you the same way as…as I loved Judy.'

Cat couldn't identify the flood of emotions she felt. There was excitement there, satisfaction even. But also apprehension. She had made him commit himself, he had said he loved her—good. So why was he looking so grim?

'It's not so hard to say, is it?' she asked.

'It's easy to say. It's the next bit that's hard. I just said I've been in love before. And when it ended, it hurt so much that I decided that love was something that I'd never risk again. So I do love you, Cat. But because I love you, I can't, I daren't take the risk of losing you. I'm sorry. We have no future. We just can't have.'

Then, as suddenly as it had come, the rage seemed to empty out of her. In fact, all feelings seem to leave her. After a pause she said, 'So we just carry on as we did before?'

'If that's what you want,' he said.

For the rest of the morning Ross had patients to see to. Nothing too important, nothing life-endangering. A deep wound to inspect, a pregnancy that wasn't going quite right, a pensioner who wasn't recovering quickly enough from his prostate operation. But he was stopping people from being alarmed, easing pain, promoting cures. It was work he usually enjoyed. He dealt with his patients carefully, always managing to have a small personal query that made people think that they were more than just a case to him.

And while he was doing that he was thinking of Cat and her sudden unexpected outburst. The letter from her family was a challenge to her. She would love to go down to London to be with them. But even more, he suspected, she would rather stay here. With him. All he had to do was offer her some kind of…some kind of certainty. Of security. Then he decided to stop avoiding what he knew to be the truth. Cat wanted marriage.

For a moment he considered the idea again— he had thought about it a lot. It would bring him much happiness. It would make Stephen happy too. The three of them now got on very well. And he thought he could make her happy.

That word, 'happy'. He knew how easily, how quickly it was possible to move from absolute happiness to absolute misery. It was the way of the world. He'd been through it. So he just couldn't ask her to stay. She'd be better off without him. He'd say nothing to her—but he'd be sad.

* * *

Cat didn't go to the doctors' lounge again that day. She avoided going anywhere where she might run into Ross. She didn't think or feel, went about her medical duties, as always doing the best she could. She was detached from her own life. The Cat Fraser she had been didn't exist any more, she was a creature without emotion. Her life had altered radically. And when her day's work was over, instead of going straight home, she drove up into the hills. She parked in a lonely spot, stared out of the car window, looking for peace. But she found none.

Autumn was now definitely here. The weather was much cooler, there were fewer visitors in the little town. The lake, the hillside, the trees, even the very sky seemed to change in colour. These were the colours that signified the end of something, the dying of the year. And Cat felt that her love affair had died with it.

Eventually she went home, made herself a meal of something—after eating it she couldn't remember what she had cooked. Then she took out a set of photo albums, leafed through pictures of her life in London. There were photographs of hospital parties, picnics on Hampstead Heath, trips with friends to the theatre. She was a city girl, she had enjoyed herself there. She should go back. And the medicine in Tom's new surgery would be cutting edge—not slightly antiquated, as it was up here. Yes, there was nothing for her here any more.

Decision taken, she should act on it at once. But she couldn't bear to see Ross face to face, she'd take the coward's way out and phone him.

When she heard his calm voice she almost gave way. But she had thought about this, decided what she had to do. 'Ross, I've been thinking. You've always been fair to me, I'll be fair to you. I think we should give up seeing each other.'

Was that a sigh she heard over the phone? But his voice was calm when he replied. 'I'm sorry about that Cat, and I'm sorry if I hurt you. But perhaps it's the best thing.'

The best thing? she wondered. Was that all? But she had to carry on now. 'And I'm going to talk to Harry about leaving after Christmas,' she went on. 'When I show him the letter from my brother I'm sure he'll understand.'

'We'll be sorry to see you go,' he said gently.

And that was all. If all he could say was that he'd be sorry to see her go…then the sooner she went, the better.

CHAPTER NINE

SHE had come to Benthwaite in high summer. She had enjoyed the warm weather—even the occasional storm. But now things were going to change. Winter was approaching. 'When it gets bad here, it gets bad quickly,' Alanna told her. 'Time you got yourself some winter clothes.'

So they went shopping together—not for a wedding dress this time but for boots, breeches, thick socks, heavy woollen shirts and sweaters, a waxed jacket. 'Get out into the hills and you're going to need this kind of thing,' Alanna said.

Cat wasn't exactly sure why she bought so much stuff as she was planning on leaving after Christmas. But she couldn't give up the idea of never coming back. The Lake District was in her blood now.

She hadn't told anyone but Ross and Harry that she was thinking of leaving. She'd had a private word with Harry who had said that he wouldn't stand in her way but that he'd be sorry to see her go. He thought she had become one of the team. That upset her.

Her new clothes were needed quicker than she had expected. A week later she was woken up in the middle of the night by the noise of rain against her bedroom window. There was some wind but mostly it was torrential rain. And it didn't stop.

In the morning she drove her little car to Rosewood and worked there all day. The weather didn't let up. And in the middle of the afternoon there was a telephone message. An urgent callout. Well, sort of urgent. It wasn't something that she could deal with on her own so she had to go and find Ross. She knew he was in the building.

She hadn't seen much of him over the past fortnight. It had been difficult, after their parting. They tried to avoid seeing each other without causing any comment from the other members of staff. And what was worse, when they did meet she sometimes forgot that they weren't close any more and spoke to him, looked at him the way she used to. Then there was an instant cruel awakening.

But this was a professional matter, she could deal with it in a professional manner. 'I've just had a phone call from a Mrs Belham, she's a farmer's wife at a farm called High Laithdale. Apparently only she and her husband work the farm.'

Ross nodded. 'I know the place. It's miles from anywhere and it's an awful job to drive there. What's the problem? Joe Belham isn't the man to ask for help.'

'He hasn't asked, his wife has. Apparently Joe's had a fall. He's been knocked about a bit and got assorted cuts and bruises, but the worst thing is a cut on his hand. It means he can't drive himself here—and his wife doesn't know how to drive. I suggested they call out the ambulance, but his wife said it would make Joe angry. So I said I'd see what I could do. I thought I might drive out there.'

Ross laughed. 'In that little car of yours? You wouldn't get halfway. I'll go. You need a four-wheel-drive.'

'I want to go,' Cat said. 'It was my call. I was going to stop off at home and pick up my new heavy-weather clothes.'

He looked at her speculatively. 'Right. Then we'll go together. You grab the emergency supplies box and I'll arrange for Stephen to be picked up by his grandmother. Are you sure you want to come?'

The challenge was there—did she want to go with him? Well, now she had to. It was a matter of self-respect. 'Yes, I want to come,' she said. 'If there's suturing to be done, you might need me.'

Apparently he always kept a set of heavy-weather clothes in his car. When she saw him next he was wearing them, looking very much the competent outdoor man. 'We'll stop at your cottage. You have five minutes to get changed,' he said.

'Five minutes will do.'

They set off together in his big four-wheel-drive, a similar vehicle to the other doctors'. The rain was as heavy as ever. For a long while there was an uncomfortable silence between them and then he asked, 'Don't you want to go back to London after seeing this kind of weather?'

'I quite like this weather. It's sort of…elemental.'

'It certainly is that.' He slowed, and the car drove slowly through water a foot deep in the road.

'I was going to drive along here!' she cried. 'My little car would have been carried away!'

The culvert under the road just can't cope,' he said. 'This happens a couple of times every year. But it'll be back to normal some time tomorrow. You know the river can rise six feet in a day?'

'Six feet!'

'This is a rough country, Cat.'

They drove on a little further and then he said, 'In fact, I like this kind of weather too. Sometimes, that is. You can have too much sun.'

She guessed he was thinking of Africa.

After that they were both silent again, engrossed in their own thoughts. It wasn't an easy journey.

They climbed steadily. Finally they drove along the side of a narrow valley, Laithdale Pass, and seventy feet below them they could see the rushing waters of Laithdale Beck. Water was pouring into the stream from a hundred rivulets running down the side of the valley, making the road surface very slick. Ross drove carefully, slowly.

At the far end of the valley the road climbed steeply and then it was another mile to High Laithdale. The rain was as heavy as ever.

The farmhouse itself looked like just another grey rock huddled among other rocks. Only the lights shining out of the ground-floor windows suggested that this was some kind of home. They drove through the muddy farmyard practically to the front door and still got soaked before they got inside.

'I'm glad you came,' Mrs Belham said. 'I really think he's bad. It's the middle of the afternoon and he's gone to bed!' This was obviously something that didn't happen very often, and caused alarm.

'Well, he's got two doctors now,' Ross said. 'Incidentally, this is Dr Fraser.'

'Right,' said Mrs Belham. 'Well, come and see him. I've had to help him get undressed.'

'Just a cut,' Joe said when they entered the bedroom. 'No need to turn out a doctor. Or two doctors, for that matter.' He looked at Cat with an expression of doubt.

'You pay for us with your taxes,' Ross said. 'So you may as well have what you pay for.'

Joe obviously liked that argument. 'Well, yes,' he said.

'Your anti-tetanus jabs are up to date?'

'Up to date. That Dr Matthews is always onto us farmers about them.'

'Good. Well, let's have a look at you.'

Cat noticed that Ross didn't ask her to take part in the examination of the injuries on Joe's body. She understood why. He wouldn't take easily to being examined by a young woman. But when it came to the most serious thing of all—the gash on Joe's hand—Ross called her over. 'What's your opinion, Dr Fraser?'

Cat looked at the hand—calloused and seamed by years of farm work. It was indeed a nasty injury—but after asking Joe to clench his hand, move his fingers, she decided that no tendons, vital nerves or major blood vessels had been cut. 'This doesn't need a surgeon, I think we can deal with it,' she said. 'But one thing is certain. Joe, you've had a narrow escape this time. There's no way you can use this hand for any kind of work—for at least a month.'

'But there's work to be done!'

'Not by you.' She remembered something Ross had once told her: 'Sometimes it's necessary to get your message across no matter how hard it might seem. It's not what the patient wants. But it's what he needs.'

So she said, 'If you damage that hand much more, you'll never shear another sheep.'

'What?'

'Think of how you use your fingers. Now, think of how you'd manage if there was no strength or feeling in them.'

There was silence for a moment. Then Joe said, 'I'll get my son Alex to come up and run the place. He's been wanting to get his hands on it for years.'

'You'll be as good as new in time,' Cat told

him. 'But you've got to give it time. Now, I want to give that hand a thorough cleaning, and then I'll give you a local anaesthetic. Dr McCain, shall I see to the wound or will you?'

'You do it,' he said. 'Use that new kit you persuaded Harry to buy. The glue.'

'I think it would be best here,' she said.

An hour later they had drunk the two obligatory mugs of tea and were driving back to Benthwaite. 'A good job well done, I think,' Ross said. 'That's the kind of medicine you won't get in London. Not too many desolate farmhouses with sheep-shearing farmers. Think you'll miss it?'

'Yes, I'll miss it,' she said after a while. 'I'll miss it a lot. But there'll be a lot of advantages too.' But that was all she was going to say. She didn't want to talk about leaving.

Anyway, Ross was silent after that, driving taking all his attention. If anything, the weather got worse. The dark clouds overhead seemed to press down on them and night seemed to fall more quickly than usual. She was glad she was not on her own. She would have been terrified.

Slowly, they drove down the hill into Laithdale Pass. Now it was almost completely dark. All she could see was the silver darts of rain splashing off the narrow road ahead. Then, to their amazement, they saw the lights of another vehicle ahead. 'Who's up here on a day like today?' Ross asked. 'This road is a dead end—it leads nowhere.'

They neared the vehicle in front. It was a minibus and across the back was written the name of a college from one of the southern counties of England. 'They're a long way from home,' Ross muttered. 'I hope they know what they're doing.'

'Why are they here anyway? We didn't see them before.'

'There's a couple of old quarries just off the road, they're good for fossils and so on. Probably they were looking for specimens. Not a good day to do it.'

The narrow road was still covered in water and a couple of times they saw the minibus skid slightly on the bends. 'They're mad. They need a four-wheel-drive in these conditions,' Ross fretted. 'I think I'll drop back a bit. I don't want to crowd them.' So he slowed down, leaving a good hundred yards between the two vehicles.

The minibus turned a corner, was lost to sight. A moment later Ross turned the same corner. In front of them the road stretched straight to the end of the valley. But there was no sign of the minibus.

'Where's it gone?' Cat gasped. 'They can't have got to the end of the road, they must have… Look, Ross! There's a bit of the road missing. They've gone over the edge!'

Ross was calmer. Cautiously, he drove a little closer to the crumbled edge then stopped. The car nosed towards the safer side of the road. From the back seat he took his coat, wriggled into it and pulled up the hood. He took a heavy torch from under his seat. 'Cat, you stay here. Don't move out of the car.'

'Ross, I'm a doctor! There's people needing help.'

'I've done this kind of thing before! We do

nothing until we see what can be done. I need to look at the road to see how safe it will be to drive. I need to see where the minibus is. We might be able to drive down to it.'

'Drive to it? Down there?'

But he was gone and she watched him pick his way cautiously to where the road had collapsed, shine his torch into the valley below and even wave to somebody. Then he jogged back towards her. Once back in the car he reached for his mobile phone. 'We need help,' he said, 'I'm ringing the Mountain Rescue team.'

Fortunately there was a signal. 'Mike Thornton? Ross McCain here. I'm in Laithdale Pass. We've got a bad one. A minibus has rolled off the road. The road has caved in, so watch where you drive. We need help fast. Can you alert the police and ambulance? Right. See you soonest.'

'Now, we go and see exactly what the situation is below,' he told her. He gripped the steering-wheel, released the brake, they inched forwards…

'Ross, what are you doing?' she screamed.

The vehicle drove to the edge of the road and

then lurched downwards at what seemed to be an impossible angle. Cat was sure that they would roll over—but they didn't. Not yet. 'I've been on a course learning how to drive these things,' he told her. 'Surprising what they can do.'

'Surprising,' she quavered. She wanted to close her eyes but she dared not.

It was half driving, half skidding, but they slowly made their way downwards and a vague white shape half seen in the distance turned out to be the minibus, on its side. It seemed to be caught on a spur of rock and hung perilously thirty feet over the stream below.

Eventually Ross stopped, the car more or less level, the headlights illuminating the rolled van and the forlorn group of people huddled together to one side of it. 'We'll keep the engine running, turn on the heater. If there's anyone in shock—which there will be—we need to keep them warm. We go and triage that little group, move them up here away from the van and into our car. And you keep well away from the minibus. That's my job.'

This was a new Ross, one she hadn't seen before. He was less casual, less laid-back. He was confident and in command.

He handed her an extra torch from the medical box and then they made their way towards the unmoving group of people. Cat had heard of this but had never actually witnessed it. Sometimes, after an accident, people lost all capacity for thought or action. They just stood and waited for someone to help them.

'Hi, I'm Dr McCain and this is Dr Fraser,' Ross said loudly. 'We're going to sort things out for you, see to anyone who might be hurt. Who's in charge here?'

There was a man sitting down on the grass, clutching a scarf to his bleeding forehead. 'I suppose I am,' he mumbled. 'Name's Perry Matthews. I'm a lecturer at the college. I don't know what happened. I was going slowly, the road was all right and then I—'

'Perry, how many people in your party?'

'What? Oh, I suppose…'

Cat saw that Perry was suffering from shock,

and needed treatment. But who there wasn't? Ross had to get his facts first.

'Perry, I asked you how many in the party?'

Perry seemed to react to the snap in Ross's voice. 'Eleven altogether. There's me, nine students and Lucy. She's my daughter and she's five.'

'Where is she?'

Perry looked round, surprised. 'She must be still inside the bus,' he said.

Cat saw Ross's shoulders heave inside his coat, but his voice remained calm. 'Right, all of you. Those of you who can walk, go over to the side of my vehicle. Stay close together.' He looked at the two sitting on the grass. 'If these two can't walk, then some of you help them. Dr Fraser here will look at your injuries and do what she can. Don't worry, ambulances are on the way.'

To Cat he said, 'Triage them and deal with what you can. Remember, this isn't medicine, this is first aid. We just keep people going until we can give them proper attention.'

'What are you going to do?' She stared at the rain-soaked face under the hood.

'There were eleven people in that bus, there are only eight here. Two students and a little girl are presumably still in the bus.'

'It was dark and we got out fast,' a girl said. 'And when we climbed out it started to roll some more.'

Ross turned towards the bus. Cat said, 'Ross, it's just not safe. The bus might roll.'

'Dr Fraser, you have patients who need your attention! This is the golden hour, let's make the most of it.' Then his voice softened and he added, 'Don't worry, Cat, I'll be careful.'

It was one of the hardest things she had ever done, but she turned her back on him and shepherded her group away from the minibus, back towards Ross's vehicle. Ross was right. She had work to do.

First, a quick check on all of them. DR ABC. Danger? They were now away from the risk of falling with the minibus. Response? All of them spoke to her, more or less sensibly. Airway, Breathing, Circulation? All of them seemed OK that way. This had been a vehicle crash so what about possible neck injuries? Only one girl was complaining of pain there so Cat put a hard collar on her.

Behind her she heard a shout. She turned to see Ross perched on top of the minibus. He threw a box out of it and yelled, 'Minibus first-aid kit. Might be something useful inside it.' The he dropped back inside the bus and Cat shook with horror. The minibus moved. What would happen to him if it rolled further? But she had work to do!

She ran and collected the first-aid box then started on a more detailed examination of her patients. Ross had been right. This was not medicine but first aid. She worked along the line, checking everyone. Apart from Perry, they were all girls.

All of them had assorted cuts and bruises. Mostly it was just a matter of putting on a dressing and holding it in place with sticky plaster. There were four with possibly serious cuts, she put temporary dressings on them. She ran her hands over limbs, asked if there was any discomfort, any unusual swelling. Just one broken arm, which she put a sling on. A hand with four dislocated fingers, which she pulled back into place at once, ignoring the yell of 'ow' from her patient.

'Leave it much longer and it would hurt more,' Cat told her.

Another girl had a couple of suspected broken ribs, not a lot to be done there.

And there was the possibility of shock. Perry appeared to be the worst. He seemed totally unconcerned about the fate of his daughter. Four of the girls seemed to be slightly shocked. Cat seated them all together in the car, wrapped space blankets round them and turned up the heating. Then she told the other girls to cram in the car and comfort them.

One tall girl remained outside. 'I've got two friends still in that minibus,' she said. 'I want to help. I'm not hurt and I'm not in shock. I'm tough and I'm strong. I row for southern counties. What can I do?'

'Will you do as you're told?'

'Absolutely.'

'Name?'

'I'm Mary Gee.'

The girl seemed confident, she had broad shoulders, an athlete's build. 'Right, Mary, I'm Cat. Let's see what the boss wants us to do.'

They approached the minibus. Now there were rucksacks and bags surrounding it. Obviously Ross had been clearing the inside. 'Ross, I've done what I can with the others. Now I want to help you. I've got Mary here, she wants to help too. What can we do?'

Ross's head appeared out of the door. 'I've got a Kelly here. Possible broken ribs but otherwise seems okay. We need to get her out carefully.'

He looked at the two girls below him. 'Mary, climb onto the top of the bus here. If it starts to roll, jump.'

'Right,' said Mary, doing as she was told and they got Kelly safely out of the van.

'Take her over to the car,' Ross said. 'Keep her warm and still.'

'What about the other two?' Cat asked. 'The other student and the little girl—Lucy?'

A flat answer. 'The little girl is trapped. I'm

trying to get her out. The other student…' There was a pause that seemed to go on for ever. 'She had a broken neck. I've pronounced.'

'What does pronounced mean?' Mary asked in a shaking voice.

There was silence for a moment and then Cat said, 'It means she's dead.'

Silence again and then a sob. Mary said, 'That's Jade. She was looking forward to this trip and now she's dead. Half an hour ago we were all singing, looking forward to an evening in the pub.'

Ross's voice came from the van. 'Mary! You've got work to do. Help Dr Fraser get that girl out there to the car. She needs to be kept warm!'

'All right,' Mary said. It was the impetus she needed. She and Cat helped Kelly to the car, where Cat treated her as best as she could. Then she ran a quick check on everyone else. All seemed to be as fine as could be expected. 'Where's Jade?' someone asked. Cat looked at Mary, who was now trying to comfort Kelly, and shook her head slightly. 'The doctor is working on her,' she said.

There was little more Cat could do with the group now crammed into the four-wheel-drive. They all needed further attention, but for the moment they were all reasonably stable. She could go and help Ross. She told Mary that if there was any problem she was to fetch her at once. Then she hurried through the rain to the minibus.

Ross was still inside. As Cat neared the bus she heard a grating noise. The bus shook, slid a little. And Cat was suddenly terrified.

So far she had been a doctor, working to tend her patients. Now she saw the situation as it was—or could be. If the minibus rolled and dropped thirty feet into the stream, Ross would be killed. Ross, the man she loved...his life was in danger! The man she loved might be killed. She gasped at the pain of the thought.

She banged on the side of the minibus. 'Ross, what are you doing?'

'Cat! Stay there. Don't try to come up here.'

'I said, what are you doing? This bus is liable to roll at any minute.'

'Lucy was thrown out of the window when the

bus turned over, her body is trapped. She's still alive—but only just. And if the bus rolls further, she'll be crushed. I've got to get her out but I can't!'

Cat could hear the desperation in his voice. He must have moved because the bus rocked. And she froze. She couldn't let him stay in there! Then she had an idea. 'Ross, shine your torch on Lucy's body.' She crouched and peered under the bus. Yes! Excitedly she called, 'There's a gap between the bus and the ground. It might be possible for me to crawl under and get at Lucy that way. You couldn't do it, you're just too big.'

'Crawl underneath! You must be mad. I won't have it. This thing is going to go any minute. You'd be crushed too.'

'If it's going to go at any minute, then you get out. You can't do anything for Lucy, so why should you be killed?'

'I'm not moving while she's alive. I might not be able to do any good but I'm not leaving a patient.'

'Ross! You can't make up for your wife's death by killing yourself!'

Now there was silence except for the drumming of the rain on the bus. She felt a drip trickle down her neck and shivered—but not through cold.

'What did you say?' he asked. She winced at the bitterness in his voice.

'Your wife is dead. You have a little boy to think of. And there's me.'

'You?'

'Yes, me. I love you. I still do, even though I know you can't love me back. And if you die, I don't know what I will do.'

Somehow he managed to laugh. 'You've picked a strange time to talk about love.'

'I don't care. I wish I'd done it more before. Just once I said I loved you, and that's not enough. Anyway, I'm going to crawl under the bus and see what I can do for Lucy.'

'No, wait! I'm telling you, you're not to crawl under the bus.'

It was her turn to laugh. 'You have to learn that there are some things you can't tell people not to do. You can't tell them not to love you, for a start.'

Now his voice was desperate. 'All right! I'm coming out. Just don't do anything.'

She felt the care with which he eased himself out of the door of the bus and slid down the roof. And even so there was a tremor, as if it wouldn't take much for the bus to slip. He knelt by her side, shone his torch into the little gap between side of the vehicle and the ground. Both of them could see Lucy's legs. They could also see the spike of rock the van was balanced on. Only a couple of inches holding it!

'It's possible,' he muttered. 'I might be able to get in there and—'

She put her hand on his shoulder. 'You're just too big,' she told him. The sheer size of you would push the van off that rock. Only one person here can do it—that's me.'

'Cat, you can't try, it's too dangerous!' Then his voice altered. 'I know why you want to do this. It's to make up for the death of Kim.'

That was a new idea for Cat. But the more she thought about it, the more it made sense. 'I'm afraid you've just persuaded me that it's something that I've got to do,' she said. 'I hadn't thought of it before.'

His voice was tortured. 'Cat, you can't do it. You might die and I couldn't stand it. I've lost one person I loved, I couldn't bear to lose another.'

Somehow she managed to laugh again, even though she was terrified. '"Loved", Ross? I thought that was a word we avoided.'

'Cat, I do love you!'

She wondered if he knew just how much his words thrilled her. Even in this dreadful emergency.

'And I love you, so we've got that sorted,' she said. 'Now, there's a little girl dying in there and I'm going to give her a chance.'

She took off her coat and sweater. Then, torch in hand, she started to ease herself through the tiny gap. It was wet, muddy, cold, dark, but she didn't notice. She couldn't crawl. It was a case of digging her fingers into the mud and dragging her body forward. An inch at a time. And above her there was the sound of metal creaking, tearing.

She got to Lucy's legs, felt under the child's

shirt. Still a heartbeat, although a weak one. She took the legs in her hands, pulled gently—Lucy didn't move. Cat inched forward again, fumbled under the frail little body, gouged out mud and stones. Then she tried to pull the legs again. This time Lucy moved. A little.

There was another groan of metal above her, she felt the van move. Not much time! She heard Ross's anguished voice, 'Cat, come out now! Please!'

'I've nearly got her,' she screamed back. Desperately, she clawed away more of the mud. Then she pulled at the legs again—and Lucy's body moved!

It was hard wriggling backwards, pulling Lucy after her, but the mud was slippery. She felt a bit of protruding metal stick into her leg, but there was no time to worry about it, she and Lucy had to get out. She wriggled even more, felt the metal tear into her leg—but surprisingly there was little pain.

Her legs slid out of the gap, she felt Ross grab them, pull her backwards. All she had to do now was hang onto Lucy. And then they were out!

She rolled onto her back, took a great sobbing gasp of air, thought that the feel of rain on her face had never been so welcome.

Ross stooped, picked up Lucy and then had a hand outstretched for her. 'Cat, come on! Move away from the van.'

She tried to do as he told her—and found out to her dismay that her leg wouldn't take her weight. Ross wrapped his arm round her waist, dragged her with him.

Then behind them came a final screech of metal. Both turned to see the van roll right over—and drop into the stream. 'Just in time,' Cat muttered. Then she collapsed onto the grass.

'Cat, you're bleeding. That's a nasty gash in your leg.'

'Just a superficial cut—a sticky plaster will see to it. Ross, look after Lucy! I'm going to be all right.'

She saw him hesitate. For a moment he laid the little girl down, took a wad of bandages from the open medical box, pressed them against Cat's thigh. 'Just hold this tight against the wound. I'll be right with you.' Then he turned back to Lucy.

There was the constant sound of the rain, of course. But Cat thought she could hear another sound. Engines? She turned her head, there coming along the road were four sets of head-lights. 'The cavalry's here,' she said. Then, for the first time in her life, she fainted.

CHAPTER TEN

CAT didn't like being forced to stay in bed. 'I'm a doctor,' she said irritably. 'I don't want to be a patient in my own hospital, being treated by people I work with as if I was really hurt. Just because of a scratch on my leg!'

Ross smiled, pointed at the giving set at the side of the bed. 'Scratch on the leg? Do you know just how much plasma we had to pump into you?'

'Well, I'm all right now. Ross, I've only the vaguest idea of what happened after…after…'

'After you fainted? Well, I discovered you were losing far more blood than I had realised. But fortunately a couple of paramedics worked wonders with you.'

'I didn't feel too bad.' It seemed odd, to have had a serious injury and not realise it. Then she thought of something else. 'Lucy? How is Lucy?'

'The ambulance took her to Carlisle. But sometimes young people are far more resilient than we give them credit for. Surprisingly, when she was examined, there wasn't too much wrong with her. A vast amount of bruising. A head wound that kept her just unconscious enough to stop her worrying. And exposure, of course. She was slightly hypothermic when you dragged her out.'

'So where have you been all morning? Why haven't you been in to see me?'

'There's been a lot of paperwork to deal with,' he said mildly. 'Harry and I have been at it all morning, filling in forms. You'll have to give a statement to the police soon, but I told them that you were too ill today. Oh, and by the way, you're a hero. Or a heroine if you want. That girl who helped us—Mary Gee—it turns out that she's studying journalism. And she knows a good story when she sees one. She sold it to the newspapers. There's a couple of journalists outside, they want your story and photographs.'

'Tell them to get stuffed,' Cat said inelegantly.

'Right.' He thought for a moment then said, 'You seem to be your normal self. The trouble is, I'm not sure if I am.'

'You look tired. Which I suppose is to be expected.' In fact, he looked more than tired, he looked ill at ease, as if he was not quite sure what to say or do. That was unusual for him.

'I sat by your bedside till four this morning. Till I was absolutely certain that you were going to be all right. I sat just looking at you. But then I got a couple of hours' sleep, as I knew that when morning came there would be work to do.'

'You sat by my bedside? Why?'

He hesitated. 'Because I was...concerned about you.'

'Concerned! Just listen to Mr Passionate.'

'All right, I was worried sick! I'd looked at the wound, I knew it was nasty but not really serious, I knew there was no good reason for me to stay. But no way could I sleep. I kept on thinking that things were all right now, but that they could have been dreadfully wrong...'

He stopped as someone tapped on the door. 'There's a little visitor for Dr Fraser,' a nurse's voice called from outside.

Little visitor? Cat didn't want any kind of visitor, not when the conversation was just getting interesting. But still… 'Send him or her in,' she called.

The door opened and there was Stephen, clutching a piece of paper. 'My teacher said you'd hurt yourself and why didn't I draw you a picture as a present,' he said doubtfully. 'So here it is. It's mountains and people climbing on them and those Zs in the sky are lightning.'

'Well, bring it here so I can see it. Stephen, this is wonderful. I'll take it home and put in on my fridge. Come here. Can I give you a kiss?'

'If you want to,' Stephen said generously. He came over, submitted apparently happily to being kissed and then said, 'Teacher says I'm not to tire you and I'm to go straight back.'

Cat saw his eyes stray to her bedside, where there was a bunch of grapes in a bowl and an ornate box of chocolates. 'Would you like a grape or a chocolate to take with you?' she asked.

Can I have a chocolate, please? Is there one with red stuff inside?'

'You can have just one,' his father said sternly. 'You know we have rules about sweets in the morning. But I suppose today is special.'

Cat still managed to give him two. And Stephen left.

'You were saying?' she asked.

But something had interested him. 'I know you've been getting on with Stephen,' he said. 'It isn't the first time I've seen you hug and kiss him like that, and he likes it. It's as if you were his...his...'

'The word you are looking for is mother,' she told him. Then she added anxiously, 'Do you mind that we've got so close?'

'No. I like it. I like it because I think we're... we're a threesome.'

She thought about that. 'I quite like the idea of being one of a threesome,' she said.

Then, for some reason, both of them fell silent. He reached over, took her hand. She lifted his hand to the side of her face, pressed it against her cheek.

And she looked at him. She could tell he was tired but his blue eyes blazed in his face as he stared back at her. She couldn't make out his expression. It was like nothing she had seen before.

After a while, he said, 'Cat, I think we're both different people from who we were yesterday. That accident changed things, it changed us. It made us realise how we really feel, what is important to us. And it made us be honest with each other.'

'How honest?' she asked.

'We've both been carrying too much...well, guilt, I suppose. You over Kim and me over Judy. That guilt stopped us feeling, stopped us taking the good things that life can offer. Now we know that accidents happen but life must go on. Not only do I know it now—I feel it.'

He leaned over, kissed her on the forehead. 'You risked your life,' he said, 'and because of that I feel free.'

Cat felt a great upsurge of excitement. 'Free from what? Or free to do what?'

'Free to realise what I really want. When you

were under that minibus, do you remember what I said to you?'

In spite of the pain and the terror, she remembered very well. 'I remember you saying that you loved me. And that you couldn't bear to live without me. But then you thought that I might be about to die. Now we both know that I'm not.'

'Before that, you told me that you still loved me. Did you mean it? Even after what I told you before? Or perhaps do you regret—'

'Ross McCain! For an intelligent man sometimes you are magnificently stupid! Regret anything? Of course I love you! I've never stopped loving you. Never stopped hoping that you'd let yourself love me too.'

'Good,' he said. 'In that case, will you marry me?'

Her head was whirling. 'Just like that?' she asked.

'Not just like that. I told you I spent most of last night by your bedside.' He reached over, took her hand. 'And at regular intervals I took your hand and held it, and I kissed one particular finger.'

He kissed one fingertip. The third finger of her left hand. 'That's where a wedding band goes,' he told her. 'I realised yesterday, when we were in the rain, trying to drag Lucy out, that I can love you, and that I want to marry you. I didn't think I could live without you. But it didn't seem a good time to bring it up. And I spent hours last night wondering when I could ask you to marry me, when would be the best time. And now, look, I've done it. No big romantic plan, no candlelit dinner, no champagne, no moonlight. Not even a ring in my pocket. It just sort of happened.'

'Well, I was looking forwards to the romance, the dinner, the champagne, moonlight and ring,' she said judiciously. 'But I can make allowances. Ross, I love you, of course I'll marry you. You'll make me the happiest woman in Benthwaite.'

'And you'll make me the happiest man!'

'You can kiss me now,' she said.

MEDICAL™

— ∿ — *Large Print* — ∿ —

Titles for the next six months…

April

A BABY FOR EVE — Maggie Kingsley
MARRYING THE MILLIONAIRE DOCTOR — Alison Roberts
HIS VERY SPECIAL BRIDE — Joanna Neil
CITY SURGEON, OUTBACK BRIDE — Lucy Clark
A BOSS BEYOND COMPARE — Dianne Drake
THE EMERGENCY DOCTOR'S CHOSEN WIFE — Molly Evans

May

DR DEVEREUX'S PROPOSAL — Margaret McDonagh
CHILDREN'S DOCTOR, MEANT-TO-BE WIFE — Meredith Webber
ITALIAN DOCTOR, SLEIGH-BELL BRIDE — Sarah Morgan
CHRISTMAS AT WILLOWMERE — Abigail Gordon
DR ROMANO'S CHRISTMAS BABY — Amy Andrews
THE DESERT SURGEON'S SECRET SON — Olivia Gates

June

A MUMMY FOR CHRISTMAS — Caroline Anderson
A BRIDE AND CHILD WORTH WAITING FOR — Marion Lennox
ONE MAGICAL CHRISTMAS — Carol Marinelli
THE GP'S MEANT-TO-BE BRIDE — Jennifer Taylor
THE ITALIAN SURGEON'S CHRISTMAS MIRACLE — Alison Roberts
CHILDREN'S DOCTOR, CHRISTMAS BRIDE — Lucy Clark

MILLS & BOON®
Pure reading pleasure™

0309 LP 2P P1 Medic

1	2	3	4	5	6	7	8	9	10
11	12	13	14	15	16	17	18	19	20
21	22	23	24	25	26	27	28	29	30
31	32	33	34	35	36	37	38	39	40
41	42	43	44	45	46	47	48	49	50
51	52	53	54	55	56	57	58	59	60
61	62	63	64	65	66	67	68	69	70
71	72	73	74	75	76	77	78	79	80
81	82	83	84	85	86	87	88	89	90
91	92	93	94	95	96	97	98	99	100
101	102	103	104	105	106	107	108	109	110
111	112	113	114	115	116	117	118	119	120
121	122	123	124	125	126	127	128	129	130
131	132	133	134	135	136	137	138	139	140
141	142	143	144	145	146	147	148	149	150
151	152	153	154	155	156	157	158	159	160
161	162	163	164	165	166	167	168	169	170
171	172	173	174	175	176	177	178	179	180
181	182	183	184	185	186	187	188	189	190
191	192	193	194	195	196	197	198	199	200
201	202	203	204	205	206	207	208	209	210
211	212	213	214	215	216	217	218	219	220
221	222	223	224	225	226	227	228	229	230
231	232	233	234	235	236	237	238	239	240
241	242	243	244	245	246	247	248	249	250
251	252	253	254	255	256	257	258	259	260
261	262	263	264	265	266	267	268	269	270
271	272	273	274	275	276	277	278	279	280
281	282	283	284	285	286	287	288	289	290
291	292	293	294	295	296	297	298	299	300
301	302	303	304	305	306	307	308	309	310
311	312	313	314	315	316	317	318	319	320
321	322	323	324	325	326	327	328	329	330
331	332	333	334	335	336	337	338	339	340
341	342	343	344	345	346	347	348	349	350
351	352	353	354	355	356	357	358	359	360
361	362	363	364	365	366	367	368	369	370
371	372	373	374	375	376	377	378	379	380
381	382	383	384	385	386	387	388	389	390
391	392	393	394	395	396	397	398	399	400